W9-AXK-862

Praise for Michael Doane's
THE SURPRISE OF BURNING

THE
LEGENDS
OF
JESSE
DARK

Michael Doane

BALLANTINE BOOKS • NEW YORK

Grateful acknowledgment is made to the following for permission to
reprint previously published material: Richard Duerden: *Moon Is to
Blood*, excerpt courtesy of the author, Richard Duerden. The Sterling
Lord Agency, Inc.: excerpts from *Tristessa* by Jack Kerouac. Copyright
© 1960 by Jack Kerouac. Reprinted by permission of the Sterling Lord
Agency, Inc.

Library of Congress Catalog Card Number: 84-47809

ISBN 0-345-35898-8

This edition published by arrangement with Alfred A. Knopf, Inc.

Manufactured in the United States of America

First Ballantine Books Edition: May 1990

To my father and to my son,
one hand giving to the other

The Legends of Jesse Dark

The morning after Crippled Horse was charged with murder, they moved him out of my cell and into another at the end of the hallway. During the following night, all of the lonesomeness I'd been avoiding for weeks was with me again and I suffered it like a dull ache in my muscles or an itch that I couldn't locate. Like any outlaw, I'd dreaded going to jail. In jail, I dreaded going to prison. Already I imagined legions of kissy-faced brutes drawing straws to see which one would have my ass first. I pictured myself getting cozy with gas station knock-off artists and men who loved knives. "They count the spoons," Crippled Horse told me. Crippled Horse had been there. "Cause if they don't we break the heads off and file down what's left. Hard to kill a man like that but you can sure make a mess of his face." Another man had told me that what he remembered most about prison was all the sounds of closing doors, clangs and clickings that went on seemingly all night. For years afterward, wherever he slept he kept the door, and the window, opened wide.

Crippled Horse, in for three years for armed assault, had spent his time punching license plates. "Whole lotta jobs there," he'd told me. "Laundry, janitor, shoe repair, you name it. *You'd* probably find your ass in the library." Even from the end of the hall, four cells away, the Oglala Sioux warrior could make himself understood. He often recited his innocence as though it were an old ghost chant he had memorized at the reservation school.

"We was drunk and he took my money. Ten dollars, all I had. I showed him my knife like to scare him. He fell down on it an died."

Lying sleepless on my cot, I could hear bottles breaking in the near distance. I was in my hometown, it was the springtime of 1971, and the jail wasn't far from the Icehouse, advertised as the world's only drive-in bar. In the years before refrigeration, it had been an ice warehouse. Abandoned in the late 1940s, it had been converted ten years later into a saloon that served only bottled beer. Customers could empty the bottles in their cars and then throw them at the brick front. The glass was seldom swept away. It always gathered like a weird summer snow along the base of the wall, scintillating drifts that grew higher and higher, shimmering in the sunlight like unmeltable ice: the Icehouse.

I had thought that without Crippled Horse in the same cell talking to me I'd be able to get some rest but his Lacotah chant of innocence, sung from thirty feet away, was more unsettling than if it had come from the cell next door. We had shared a ten-by-twelve space for nearly three days and he had seldom left me alone. Criminals are like jealous brothers; everything that is not shared is suspect. I was his witness, he had told me, though in fact I had been nowhere in sight when his friend had fallen on his knife. Where I had been is the story of this story and one thing always leads to another, no matter how I try to tell everything all at once.

"Wake up, Jesse, I'm talking to *you*!"

"I'm listening, Crippled Horse. He took your money, right?"

"Right. Ten dollars. All I had in the world."

Another bottle hit the brick wall like a cymbal crash, then a flurry, one two three. The night was warm and through the open window—secured by four bars, one for every day I would spend there—I could smell lilacs in the air. We were less than half a mile from the Missouri River, a fast swim out of South Dakota if I could only get to the shore. Yankton was the town of my childhood and I knew the way by heart.

"We was drunk, you can ask anybody. We'd been drinking all goddamn night. Can you hear me?"

"He had whiskey and you had wine."

"NO! *I* had whiskey and *he* had wine!"

When I'd been young I'd played a Bantam League baseball game at the state penitentiary in Sioux Falls. Seeing kids, our coach had told us, would be good for the prisoners, it would remind them of when they were innocent. The field was entirely without grass, simply an empty dirty lot with too many stones in it. The right field fence was made of chicken wire and left field was simply the Wall, twenty-eight and a half feet high with a barbed-wire crown. The prisoners who'd come to watch the game had to stand behind a rope that separated them from us, but that didn't stop them from chattering through the whole game. One of them, an unshaven old man with dirty teeth, told me he played on the prison baseball team. "Yeah," his friend chimed in, "but we don't play any Away games."

"I tried to help him," Crippled Horse was telling me. "He was lying on his belly and had whiskey all over him. I didn't see no knife . . ."

"Cause he was hiding it in his heart."

"Funny funny white man. How'd you'd like a tommy hawk up your ass?"

In three days my case had unraveled too slowly. There were too many unusual factors, the police sergeant had told me. "I'd release you tomorrow, but the parents of that baby want some assurance that you won't be back."

"But I've already sworn."

"Swearin's not good enough. They knew your old man and they don't trust you more'n they trusted him. What were you planning to do with that kid, anyway?"

"Raise him."

"Raise him? You don't even got a job. Which reminds me, I was supposed to book you for vagrancy, too. You can thank your favorite saint that I didn't."

Matthew, Mark, Luke, or John the Divine. For the moment, my favorite saint was Crippled Horse the Innocent, missionary of the sacred alibi. "Thus I showed him my knife to teach him fear / And upon it did he fall / And thereupon O Lord did he bite the dust."

My own alibi was without detail. The child I stole was my home. That he was as yet unnamed was not surprising. Home always arrives in one disguise or another. His birth was two weeks late, I am told, and I congratulate him. I was born on time and did not have the wisdom to hesitate before knocking on the strange door. Even now he is blinking under the holy water that the priest throws in his face while the adopting parents give him a name I wouldn't have chosen. I might have named him Chance or Accident or Dice or Pinball because according to the incomprehensible laws of family he should never have been born. I have my own ideas about families. I have always stolen one to replace another. Perhaps I would have named that baby Outlaw. Or Escape. Escape Dark, Jesse's nephew. Sitting in my cell, I had time to think of names. Crippled Horse, for example, was a good name for my partner down the hall. He was only twenty-three, a colt as it were, but already he had the weathered face and haunted eyes of most modern American Indians. He was raised on peanut butter and wood alcohol and had become a warrior at fourteen, stealing a chalice from the reservation priest and pawning it for eleven silver dollars. One of the few times he had been able to forget his cries of innocence, he had sat across from me on his cot and faced me directly. "I bet I look real mean to you, don't I?" he asked. "Don't it scare you to death, being in a cage with an Indian?"

I told him I had other things to worry about.

"Like being a baby stealer?"

I smiled. "Worse."

He didn't understand.

"Jail is a lousy hideout."

"Who wants you?"

Why should I have told him? He would have sold me for a hot lunch. And at the time I was hoping for a miracle, praying that the routine notice of my arrest in Yankton would stay buried under other such notices in the Vermillion police station, twenty-three miles away. I was under arrest for kidnap but it had been an unusual kidnap, almost a family affair, and in a day or two I would be set free. I was being held to give me time to think or to be sorry and I sat as still as I could on my thin cot, refusing to pace within my cell, knowing that pacing was for guilty men, the condemned without hope of escape. Nor would I do as Crippled Horse and cry that it was all some big mistake. I had taken the baby in my arms and felt his breath upon my neck; I had tried to carry him away with me, the act of an outlaw, not a criminal. As an outlaw, I would never go to prison, my case wouldn't even go to trial. Not unless a man in Vermillion knew where he could find me. In Vermillion, I had been told, my name was legend.

Crippled Horse told me we'd have to find a way to escape. Calling down the long hallway, he asked me if maybe I had a gun or something under my mattress. Very cool he was, my friend Crippled Horse.

"I got friends on the Pine Ridge Reservation," he added. "You won't see many white men coming round there. You can pretend you're an Oglala. God knows you look dumb enough."

I had a lawyer named Simon Larsen Butt.

"I'll bet people make a lot of jokes," I told him.

"Not when they're counting on me to get them out of jail," he answered. He brought an affidavit for me to sign. "It says you renounce all claim to the child for all time; that you will not come back to Yankton without advance written approval of the adoptive parents; that you will not attempt to communicate with the child to apprise him of his origins or of your existence; that you will not communicate to any person or persons in the state of South Dakota or resident thereof the origins of this child; that you are penitent of the criminal act—"

"Penitent?"

"That's what it says. That you are penitent of the criminal act which you have committed and will, in good faith, not attempt to communicate with the adoptive parents, in any way or form, for the rest of your life."

"Is that all?"

"That's it."

"Can we change 'criminal act' to 'outlaw act'?"

"They told me you had to sign it as it reads. No changes."

"How many times do I have to sign it?"

"Twice. Here—" he produced a carbon—"and here. You are advised to retain a copy so as to remain aware of your agreements."

I signed my Jesse Dark to both copies. "How much do you make a year, Mr. Butt?"

"Eight thousand dollars a year and all I can extort. You're a real wise guy, aren't you, Mr. Dark?"

"When can I leave?"

"I'll have to get this notarized, then the adoptive parents will sign your release. You should be free by two o'clock tomorrow." He rose to leave. "I suppose you're not going to thank me."

"You were only doing your job."

He called to be let out of my cell. Once he was on the other side, he said, "You're the type who spends a lot of time behind bars, Mr. Dark. Take my advice and ease up."

He didn't understand that I was an outlaw and not a criminal. The difference is too simple for a man of the law to distinguish. The criminal takes what never was his. The outlaw takes back what he's lost.

Harper was waiting for me in New York, in an apartment that she'd chosen for the two of us. Already I was three weeks late but I knew better than to call her from a jail cell in Yankton, South Dakota.

Is Jesse Dark your real name?

Since birth. Why?

It sounds like an alias. And Rose Dark was your sister?

She is. *Is*.

No need to be hostile. I just need to get the facts.

It started with my childhood. Where else could it have started? My last night in that jail cell, I listened to the breaking glass down the street and tried to imagine what it would be like to be at long last in Harper's arms. I had been foolish, I knew, to have tried to steal a home and family when all along there was one waiting for me at the end of a thirty-hour bus ride. Outlaws are bewildered by love freely given and it would take me a long time to stop searching Harper's left hand for a jackknife just because the right hand offered a lily. I had come back to Yankton only to say goodbye to my sister and to an anger I thought I'd outlived, but the sight of that newborn child, the nearness of his mother, and the incredibility of his birth—chance, dice, pinball—had overwhelmed me. His birth seemed to pay a lot of debts I felt were owed me. Taking him from that crib into my arms was less a crime than an act of faith.

"Hey, Jesse, are you awake?"

"What is it, Crippled Horse?"

"I been charged with murder."

"I thought he fell on your knife."

"They don't believe me like you. Now I gotta get out of here."

"Good luck."

"You coming with me? I got a plan."

"Thanks anyway. They're letting me out tomorrow."

"It's a damn good plan, Jesse, but it takes two of us."

"Crippled Horse, I'm already free. I'm just staying the night, you know, like it's the Holiday Inn."

"I'll tell you all about it tomorrow, during lunch."

We always had our lunch together.

"Go to sleep, Crippled Horse."

A single bottle broke in the near distance of the Icehouse.

"A *damn* good plan."

Late in the night, a drunk was brought into the jailhouse. For a moment I thought it was my father, but that would have been impossible. He was in his fifties and his shirt sleeve was stained with blackberry brandy. "Sonsabitches," he blessed the boys in blue, "all I need is a pot of coffee."

"Sleep it off," he was told. "We'll let you go in the morning."

"Well what're you looking at?" he said to me. I hadn't realized I was staring.

He fumbled with his shoes, taking a long time to get them off. His breath came in long drumrolls and he leaned his head against the bars from time to time to catch his balance.

I fell asleep to his breathing and the lullaby of breaking glass. In the morning, the telephones were ringing, always a bad sign, according to Crippled Horse.

"Who else calls the cophouse?" he asked. "Peoples who got criminals!"

In my case he was right. The one man in Vermillion, where my name was legend, had found me in Yankton, where my name was locked up.

The police sergeant came into my cell to read me the charges.

"Possession of a controlled substance. Intent to sell said controlled substance. Suspicion of sale of controlled substance to minors. Assaulting an officer of the law. Resistance of arrest. Interstate flight. Damage to private property. How do you plead?"

"I want my lawyer. I want Butt."

"Jesus, Jesse. What on earth have you been up to?"

It started with my childhood, my father and mother and sister and me. We lived on Pearl Street, in a lot surrounded by weeds. The foundation of the house was a mortar mixed with broken brandy bottles.

"Hey, white man."

The drunk was given his breakfast and released. I was alone in my jail cell with Crippled Horse.

"What is it?"

"I got a plan to get us out a here. You listening to me?"

The charges, added up, made twenty years. Nearly no one knew the difference between a criminal and an outlaw. My fate was in the hands of Simon Larsen Butt.

"I'm listening, Crippled Horse. Tell me what you want me to do."

The Rose Legend

1

The night after Bill broke a hairbrush over my sister's head, I stopped being taken for the boy that I was; I became a man overnight. For a long time afterward, I lived like a moth circling a light bulb, my past, probing and crashing blind against the light of it, then, at odd times, counting the bruises in the privacy of darkness. It was years ago. I rented a crumbling farmhouse in the wilderness of South Dakota, paying Ingersoll—the owner—from my savings, then moved myself and my sister Rose into that house in the midst of a January blizzard. It was a widowed farmhouse, meaning there was no farm left to it. Ingersoll had long ago bought the house as well as the land around it and the former tenants had moved on. Ten years of neglect had prepared it for us in just the way Rose would have asked. She had wanted me to find a house that no one would want, a place for derelicts or outlaws, with no markings, no address, no mailbox, and no welcome mat. Though she hadn't said so in plain words, I had known it was anonymity she'd wanted, a place more or less where she could hide herself.

Until the night we moved in she hadn't seen the house. She had trusted in my judgment as a saint trusts in prayer. Circling the light, I found a house that was anonymous. Situated well off Highway 81, down a rutted mud road that led from the north of Yankton to Wagner, no place to no place, it was hidden, as well, behind a grove of dying elms. "I could give you directions," Ingersoll had told me, "but you still might get lost, so I'd best show you the place myself.'' On the strength of that description, I had paid him his first month's rent and inspected the place only out of curiosity.

The night we fled, Rose and I, it was Ingersoll who drove us there and who promised, with a gentle nod, not to mention later where he'd last seen us. It was late evening and since noon a wet January snow had been falling. A stiff wind rushed in from the north, blowing drifts across the roads, and Ingersoll had to leave us several hundred yards from the house for fear of getting stuck away from the main road. We didn't have much to carry: two pillowcases stuffed with clothes, a box of books and plastic dishes, a second box with soap, towels, Rose's few cosmetics, and a last shoe box that Rose once told me contained the sum and total of her nineteen-year-long life. ''Souvenirs and keepsakes,'' she'd said. ''Memories are too imperfect, like lattice baskets meant to carry water.'' I hugged the two large boxes to my chest and she managed with the shoe box and pillowcases. We plowed with our knees through the waist-high drifts and I led her through the whited dark to the door. As I heaved against the snow, a lifelong fear of Bill, my father, urged me forward, but all the time I was thinking to myself that I was only a boy, only a boy, as if that somehow made invalid any of the plans I might have had for the coming night. As we approached the porch, Rose lost her grip on the shoe box, the rubber band snapped that held it closed, and the box fell, topless, in a drift. Newsclippings, letters, photographs, poems vanished in the darkness and the heavier objects—jewelry, statuettes, coins— dropped silently into a white abyss. Turning to Rose, I expected to see her in tears, expected to hear her scream, curse, cry out. But her brown eyes met mine and there was within them a mute resignation.

''God, Jesse.''

''Rose,'' I told her. ''Rose, we can dig it out of the snow.''

She shook her head, a tiny shake, like a nervous tic. A frosting teardrop made her right eye glitter. Tell me you have known another who cries with one eye at a time.

''Rose?''

''God, Jesse.''

''Let me help.''

''No. I don't care. I don't. Let's go in. The cold.''

But at the door, she stopped. She looked across the porch, the loose floorboards, past the drifts, toward the barn. She gazed upward to a gabled bedroom window and the long icicles that hung in jagged columns. A shutter clapped against the broken rainspout, a lonely, dull clang. On the front door was a crayoned sign: KEEP OUT.

"What is it, Rose?"

"Here?" she asked, meaning the word in a way that can't be repeated. Meaning, This is where you bring me? Now? You and I? all in one breath.

"Here," I confirmed. When I scraped the door inward, new snow blew into an old darkness.

Ingersoll had warned me that the generator wasn't working and he'd be around in a day or two to help me start it up. In the meantime, we would have to depend upon the fireplace for our heat and light. And even once the generator was working, only the kitchen would have electricity. We closed the door behind us and the wind, which had been screaming, became a whisper.

"I can't see anything," Rose said.

"Don't move." Putting down my boxes, I shuffled through the dark toward where I knew the fireplace to be. On the mantel overhead was a box of yellowed candles. Lighting one, I crossed the room to Rose. "Hold this." With numbed hands, I built a small fire from kindling and trash. The flue was clogged and black smoke fell into the room, so I reached a stick upward and poked out a chuck of ash, clearing the chimney. My arm was blackened with soot.

Rose asked if she could sit.

"Why not? We're home."

"Are we?"

In the dusty room, by firelight, she looked very small and more frightened than usual. Her winter coat was too large for her shoulders and her mittens like rags upon her hands. Together, we were afraid of the cold and of the dark.

"Come sit by the fire," I told her. "You'll warm up."

I shoved the book and dish box near the hearth. "Sit here," I said. "Take off your mittens and your scarf."

She sat quietly but removed nothing. The quiet of Rose could mean anything: oncoming tantrum or expressionless calm. The house was dirty and frozen from a month of winter. Except for scattered piles of rags and newspapers, the room we were in was empty. The trash in the fireplace burned to embers and Rose shivered in the darkness. She was troubled by something and when I rose to go out, she cried, "Where are you going?"

"Firewood," I told her. "Ingersoll says there's more in the barn."

"Do you have to? I mean, do we need it?"

"We'll freeze without it."

"I'm scared."

"Me too. I'll hurry."

When I returned with an armful of logs, she was still sitting in the same spot, her scarf wrapped high around her chin as though she were still outside. "I saw a mouse," she said.

I didn't answer her. Piling the wood near the fire, I sat on the floor next to her.

"It was gray," she said. "Like a squirrel gets in October."

"Are you warm enough?" I asked her.

"I didn't see its teeth. It came from over there"—she pointed toward the pile of old newspapers—"and ran over to there." She pointed to the door. "Did you hear me screaming?"

I hadn't heard her screaming. Between the barn and the house, I had heard only the blizzard.

"I only screamed once. Mice terrify me."

I made a bed of kindling atop the trash embers and placed a log in the middle of it. The snarls of dead wood burning drowned the haunting wind sounds. A vapor of loneliness descended upon me. *If Rose knew how afraid I am.* The raw sensation of manliness that had come over me when I'd first found the house had long since eroded. I was seventeen and all of me was boy. It was years ago. I had a sister who was also a daughter.

"What about sleep?" Rose asked.

"What about it?"

"Where will we?"

"Here." I wasn't getting her point.

"I *know* here," she said. "Are there beds?"

I shook my head. "Not much furniture at all. A few chairs, a dresser with one drawer, a ratty old sofa. But there's some lumber in the basement and I can use it to make a table. If I can find some nails."

"And a hammer."

"Ingersoll will have one."

"But no beds."

"We'll get by. We can sleep on our clothes and stay near to the fire."

"There's only one blanket, Jesse."

"I'll sleep in my coat."

There is danger in darkness, in unmeasured distance—how far we were from Bill, in miles if not in years—but the fire was like a third person among us, burning higher and warmer, even though Rose still wore her oversized coat and rubbed her nose with mittened hands. I wondered if she was thinking of her shoe box and all she'd lost or if she, too, was measuring our escape and measuring me, her brother and defender and provider. A boy with narrow shoulders and soft hands. When we had still been back at the other house packing things away she'd suddenly said, "Jesse, we don't have *any*thing. How will we live?" She often asked unanswerable questions. "At least," she'd said, "I have my shoe box."

Now no shoe box, no souvenirs. Nothing special to remember. Forget the past before we die.

"We'll be safe here," I said, just to say something.

She didn't seem to be listening.

"Tomorrow I'll show you the house. It's dirty right now, but that's not important. In daylight you can see its possibilities."

More silence. She breathed into her mittens.

"The upstairs isn't much. Just a few run-down bedrooms and a broken toilet. But the downstairs is in good shape. The kitchen is big and there are windows on three sides of it. Real good light and a view of the elm grove. There's a fireplace in there, too, but not as big as this one. When I get the generator going, we'll have light and we can use the stove. You can set up your painting things in here if you want. You'll have lots of time to paint."

Rose had once been fond of painting and I'd meant to cheer her up by mentioning it. It was a bad idea. She shivered.

"Ingersoll let me have the place for forty bucks a month. We can make that if I can get a job. And he'll give it to us for less if we keep up a chicken house. There's one behind the barn and he says there'll only be fifty hens and a few roosters. You can take care of them while I'm—"

"No."

"No, what?"

"I'm afraid to."

"Of the chickens?"

She nodded. "They scare me. They peck at each other's eyes. It's horrible to watch."

"Not these chickens, Rose. They're good hens."

"That's what I mean. *Hens.*"

To change the subject, I reached into one of the boxes and handed Rose the apple that I'd tucked inside. She ate it slowly, turning chunks in her mouth until they were like snow, swallowing contentedly.

"We've only got thirty-some dollars left," I told her. "If the weather clears up tomorrow, I'll go to town and look for a job. We won't need much. I can make enough to feed us and with what's left we can fix this place up. I'll buy you a bed like the one back—" I stopped. Rose noticed. She swallowed the last of her apple and asked, "A four-poster?"

"With creaky springs," I promised.

"And in the spring I'll plant a garden." Bill had once drunkenly trampled her zinnias and geraniums. He'd danced on them with his boots for fun.

"I'll help you start it," I told her, "after the thaw."

"We'll grow vegetables, something we can *eat*. When summer comes."

"Sure. In the summer we'll be all right."

"In the summer."

We no longer could hear the wind and the room was newly naked, cold, silent. We both listened for something, each of us knowing what the other was listening for.

"He won't come," I said.

She shook her head.

"No one knows we're here," I insisted. "Just Ingersoll and he won't tell a soul."

"But *she's* still there."

"I tried to make her come. She was afraid to."

"Now she's alone with him. He'll take it out on her, you know how he is."

"He won't. Not this time. I'll visit her and make sure she's all right."

"Jesse, you can't do a damn thing for her from here. Make her leave him. Make her come live with us."

"She won't come. I tried."

"Keep trying."

I said I would but in my heart I knew it was hopeless. Lady was stupid. I thought that to myself, knowing it was a sin for me to do so. The words repeated themselves: Lady is stupid, stupid. I was now a son who thought of his mother as mindless. This was years ago. I am obsessed with memory.

Rising from the floor, I put a few more logs on the fire and stirred it with a stick. "The blizzard seems to be over," I announced, though I was only guessing. I realized I'd say anything to make Rose feel better. I'd been doing so for years. The fire illumined the patch of floor around us and we prepared a place to sleep. There were enough clothes in our sacks to make a decent mattress for Rose. We refilled her pillowcase with wadded newspaper for a pillow and she slept in her coat. I pulled our lone blanket to her chin. Her head lay near the hearth and she looked up at me through the firelight, her brown eyes more peaceful than I'd seen them in a while.

"It's a good house, Jesse."

"I'm glad to hear you say it."

"But it's dirty as all hell. I'll help you clean it."

"We'll start tomorrow."

I gathered an armful of rags from the dusty corner and matted them on the floor near Rose. Still wearing my coat, I lay down on the pile and folded my hands behind my head. The fire warmed my face but my feet, in frozen boots, were numb with cold. I lay awake, staring at the cobwebbed ceiling and wondering if I'd sleep that night, or even the next. Years of being my sister's sentinel had not prepared me for being a runaway as well. Nor Rose, who couldn't sleep either. Her head was only a foot from my own and I could feel her eyes upon me.

"What kind of job will you get?" she asked.

I said I didn't know.

"I can work, too."

"You don't have to. *I'll* work. You take care of the house and your garden. And the chickens, too."

"No chickens, Jesse. I mean it."

"We'll see."

"I'll clean and tend the garden and I'll cook."

"You can paint if you want."

"No. I won't paint."

We tried to sleep. I turned away from Rose, onto my side, and contemplated the wood floor beneath me. It was warped, I knew from having seen it in daylight, with a high bow toward the center of the room. I couldn't help but wonder if the foundation was bad or if the roof would leak or if the plumbing had rusted and would need repair. I compared it to the other house, Bill's, which always seemed to have been incomplete, unfinished, though what had given me that feeling was unaccountable. There had been walls, doors, ceilings, windows, floors, a porch, plumbing, lights. I had grown up there, from the age of two onward. In the spring I had replaced the storm windows with screens and in the fall reversed the order. Grass had grown between the weeds on the lawn and bees had swarmed among the dandelions. I'd fallen from a tree out back and broken an arm. I'd hidden in the basement, in the attic, in any of seven closets, from Bill. The kitchen had smelled of Ajax and the dining room of wood polish. There had always been fresh or just-dead flowers on a table in the living room. A porcelain tub in the bathroom, a clock in the hallway with a stilled pendulum. My bed had creaked when I'd rolled in the night and the refrigerator had hummed to my summer-night insomnia. I'd pinned my baseball cards to the wall above my desk. I'd enjoyed my first hand-made orgasm in my secret corner of the attic. I'd lived there nearly all of my life and had always felt a draft coming through the walls. I could remember broken windows never repaired, torn screens, warped doors, knobs falling from cabinets like leaves from trees. Plaster fell in yellow flakes from the second-floor ceiling and from time to time the electricity lagged, all the lights fading in and out as in a creep show when a phantom enters the room. It was a place to stay but not to live. Bill had built it with the help of a friend, an out-of-work Lacotah Indian named Bad Hand. They had built it with wood and muddy bricks and had used the broken glass of brandy bottles to strengthen the mortar. The house always had a glimmer around the foundation when the sun was shining just so.

When I rolled over to face my sister, I found her eyes were full upon me.

"Jesse?"

"Rose?"

She closed her eyes; reopened them. "We'll never go back?"

"No."

"We'll promise each other."

"We already have."

She awoke only once during that long first night. Though I wasn't sleeping, she shook me with a mittened hand.

"Never," she said again, then she fell to sleep before I could answer her with a Never of my own.

Her face, in photographs, is lost, hollow, not easily recognizable, as though the shutter can capture only the barest tracing, the rudimentary outline of her features but not the true identity. She defies duplication and even in group photos, such as those taken with her classmates, she appears indefinably remote, solitary, alien. *Rose, Among Other Children.* Her smiles are cosmetic and her large eyes stare outward to a point past the camera, over your shoulder. In the past, I liked to watch her sleep. It was the only time in which she didn't seem to be spiraling round something desperate in herself. There was no innocence in her slumber; there was relief from anxieties known and nameless. A smoke in her eyes, a terror in her waking hours, stole the flush of youth from her face. She lived her life in constant dread of something I have yet to understand. I knew her face, her features which were delicate and exact so that a centimeter's revision might have altered her entirely. Whenever I spoke to her, I was conscious of which of her eyes I was looking at, right or left, and I would sometimes look elsewhere, at her mouth, her nose, or her throat so as not to feel the heat of her gaze in full. She had the body of a dancer and although she was pretty enough to attract both men and boys, her look of worry would inevitably drive them away. I sensed early on that she would never marry. Only a very patient man who could watch her sleep, and be content to gaze upon her as I did that night, could have loved her enough to stay around for a lifetime.

As I knew would happen, I didn't sleep. For a while I smoked a cigarette and watched Rose. Fire shadows illumined our cobwebbed ceiling and in black playgrounds within the old walls mice made scratchy music. I thought again of Lady. I was trying not to worry about her, not to feel responsible for whatever would now happen to her. She had made her own stony bed and I could scarcely make it softer. Lady is stupid. I had known before asking that she would never come with us. I'd asked anyway and her voiceless black mouth had fallen open into a stunned oval of fright and sadness and disbelief.

"We have to go," I'd told her. "It's dangerous here. I'll take care of all of us."

Whenever Lady cried, her eyes told a sound all their own, to make up perhaps for her inability to sob properly. Her pupils would grow large and seem to shiver, a look become sound. "Mhuh," she would say, a leaden word, one of her few. "Mhuh, muh," like a whimper. She'd cried this way when I'd said we were leaving.

With her hands she'd asked where.

"A house. I've found us a house."

When?

"Now. Tonight."

"M-muh, m-m-m." She signaled frantically, her fingers in flight, fashioning a covey of *No*'s.

We were standing in the kitchen where I'd interrupted her baking. While we'd wept together, oatmeal cookies had blackened in the oven. Later she would throw them into a snowdrift. The blizzard had just begun.

"He'll kill us," I'd said. "He's killing you."

My mother's hands, sudden as crazed sparrows, begged: Son, mine. Daughter, mine.

"Rose is terrified. She can't stay another day here. Come with us."

Lady had shifted to cursive signs. I'm not going, said the white hands. He is my husband. Better or worse. God sees.

"God is as blind as you are mute."

Her right hand was silent but her left hand slapped my face.

"I love you, Lady."

Do, not, go.

When Rose came into the kitchen, I was holding my mother in my arms. Rose knew at once that she wasn't coming with us.

Lady cursed us when we went out the door, then she tangled her fingers saying goodbye. Rose kissed her and for a passing moment I sensed that I wouldn't see our mother again. Snow blew inward through the open doorway. I said I would return in a few days and that she could always join us later if she changed her mind.

He is my husband. God watches.

We'd fled, Rose and I, into the gathering blizzard. As we reached the road, I heard the door open and I turned to see if it was Lady coming after us. She was throwing oatmeal cookies, one by one, after us, into the snow.

Lady is stupid. I felt a fresh arrow in the bed of my heart. The fire diminished beyond my rag bed and a familiar cold darkness fell over the room. *Lady is lost.* Somewhere in the litany of the beatings she'd suffered for better or for worse, she'd lost herself to God and to her Church, her litany of saints. All her simplemindedness come down to faith in plastic statuettes and water blessed by aging archbishops. Suffering was her joy, her ticket to salvation. Blessed are the bruised. Since the night Bill had kicked the voice from her body, she'd been preparing herself for heaven. The past. It was years upon years ago. It never ends. I remember how she would pray, Lady, folding her hands into each other, lacing the fingers and playing the child's game, Here is the church (index fingers raised) and here is the steeple, open it up . . .

Her hands silent against each other, wordless, still.

God sees.

2

It is a place which the ignorant call empty.

An American Siberia without the tundra. A place Cézanne would not have painted; too few trees.

Viridian in summer, titanium white in winter, riots of brown upon brown in between.

A place of mud and few hillsides.

Rivers—the Big Sioux, the James, the Missouri—amble through its prairie, bearing the red clay of Canada along their shallow bottoms.

The state's office of tourism has in past years referred to South Dakota as the Land of Infinite Variety, a hopeless, untenable claim, though as there are two Dakotas—North and South— there are two *South* Dakotas, variety enough for the easy to please. Bounded by the Missouri River for the most part, these regions are referred to, logically enough, as East River and West River. East River is primarily flat farmland, prairie, endless green in the summer and interminable white in the winter. West River is rougher terrain, largely arid, and includes the Black Hills and the Badlands. It is to the bleakest, most bankrupt of these West River terrains that the government long since herded the Sioux tribes—Oglala, Sans Arc, Hunkpapa, and Yanktonai, among others—leaving the comparably lush East River plain to the American farmer. Yankton is East River, but just barely. In January, the surrounding countryside is blanketed with snow and resembles some lunar steppe, remote and silent and empty. The sun too seldom burns through the pale sky and in April, in rural South Lost Place, sunless day will follow sunless day and the suicide rate is alarming. Dakota Syndrome, it is called. When there are no neighbors, no distractions, no color to the earth, only a day void and a night void, and dreamless slumber ever after.

A friend once referred to Yankton as Nowhere[2]. The Dakotas, he explained, are as indistinguishable from each other as they are uninteresting. South Dakota, to him, was a pointless precision, as ludicrous as saying, for example, South Nowhere. Yankton, thus lost in such parentheses, was a diminished Nowhere. Therefore, Nowhere, Nowhere; Nowhere[2]. I learned later on that Yankton is a Lacotah Sioux word for End Village, or end of the line, a fitting enough alias for the town that was my home.

I had spent my day looking for work and though the sun was gone and the blizzard had left the streets unnavigable, I knew my way to Bill's house. It was enough simply to follow the past backwards. The house was on the east edge of town, not far from a stretch of railroad tracks, on a street named Pearl. To either side of it were abandoned lots where, years back, had been farm buildings: a barn, a chicken hut, a tractor shed, a silo. They'd been built at the turn of the century, before the town had spilled into the near countryside and overrun the farms that hugged its perimeter. Bill had chosen that spot to build his house because he'd wanted no one else nearby, no neighbors who would peer into his windows or come calling for coffee and the time of day. A muddy bog, where ducks congregated in the fall, was to the back of the lot, and the ruins of the ancient farmyard were to either side. The house, lifted above it all by a high mound on which it was built, was like a sad castle reigning blankfaced over mud and ruin. In years to come, after the fire that burned over everything, leaving leafy ash and cinder in the air, no one would build anything in its place. It would be a perpetual ruin of its own, a memorial more dismal and more distressing than those which had once surrounded it.

When I arrived, all the lights were lit and I felt as though I'd walked into a party without people. Lights in the living room, the kitchen, both upstairs bedrooms, the dining room, the bathroom, and the basement. The front door was ajar when I arrived, neither open nor closed, a family motif. I called out for Lady, knowing Bill would not be there. After work he was always at the Hideaway with Dorell. My father loved Dorell. She was a woman who spoke to his soul and saw through the bottom of a deep bottle all the charm and hurt of his strange life. They had been together for as long as I could remember, usually at the Hideaway or at Dorell's. It was our family secret and the whole town knew about it.

But Lady wasn't there either, so I busied myself collecting things we'd need. Finding a large enough box in the basement, I gathered a blanket, old towels, a bar of brown soap, a pillow, and Rose's broken hairbrush. The handle was gone, from when she'd taken it across the forehead, but the bristles were intact. Though I searched high and low for rat poison, there wasn't anything that would serve. I went to the kitchen meaning to steal some food and I found that the radio was playing, Kenny Somebody singing of young love, first love. It was an old radio, a transistor we'd never used except when our electricity had gone out or for a day at the beach. The tinny sound of radio music made the house seem more deserted than it was and I grew lonesome as I passed from window to window, looking outward. Putting down my box, I raced through the hallways, upstairs and down, shutting off every light but the one in the kitchen. There is dignity in darkness, I was thinking to myself, and I shut off the radio as well.

The kitchen was Lady; it bore her signs and evidences of sorrow: an empty pack of Pall Malls on the counter, a copy of *Redbook* with the imprint of coffee cup stains on its cover, cookbooks, pickling jars, canisters, a wadded Kleenex, and an ashtray piled with lipstick-tipped butts, debris of recent crying where she wept often, Lady, at that kitchen table. Unwilling to wait there for her—fearful that Bill would come home first and then there'd be hell to pay—I left the house through the kitchen door, going south when I needed to go north. I had taken the transistor radio with me, knowing Lady had another one which she could plug into the wall. Thinking of electricity, I remembered that I had not fixed the generator before leaving the farmhouse. Rose would be without light and I doubted she would dare to light a fire by herself. She would be cold and alone in the dark.

I ran through heavy snow toward the highway. In the aftermath of the blizzard, few cars were on the streets and in the moonless night I could not be seen by the side of the road. I walked, stumbled, ran. When headlights appeared I thumbed them. None stopped for me. When I grew tired, I imagined Bill behind me, in his hunting gear. I imagined him chasing me as he held his belt high in the air, eyes white and face black as in an undeveloped photograph, life reversed by life.

I am running from the kitchen toward the garage. There is a car parked inside with the engine running. My mother is at the window from where she gazes dry-eyed toward the garage. The car has been running since past three in the morning and its gray exhaust blows like incense into the garage. My father is asleep at the wheel and the fingers of my mother's left hand are crossed. With her other hand she touches the St. Christopher medal at her throat. One hand saying Die, the other saying Live.

The darkness was hours old by the time I reached the farmhouse. My arms were numb from the weight of the box and my boots had filled with snow. I could not feel my toes. Kicking my boots against the porch steps to knock away the ice, I heard Rose screaming from inside. When I pushed open the door, she leaped from a dark corner into my arms, saying, "Mice, Jesse. All over. *Kill* them." I saw no mice and told her so, but she went on crying, her head resting on my icy shoulder. It wasn't just the mice, I knew. It was the cold, the dark, the emptiness of the house. She had worried that I would not come back.

I told her I would start a fire if she would light some candles.

She sniffed and wiped her eyes with the sleeve of her coat. "Did you see Mother?"

"She wasn't home. All the lights were on but no one was there."

"And him?"

I said I didn't know.

"He's probably looking for us."

"That doesn't mean he'll find us."

She trembled. "You don't know. You only pretend to."

After lighting a fire, I went out to see if I could start the generator but even from the porch I could clearly hear its churning sounds in the still country darkness. It was a lonesome sound and I was the only one on earth to hear it. Back in the house, I tried the light switch in the kitchen. The dusty room was bathed in yellow light.

Rose crept in from the living room. In the light I could see that her brown hair was tangled and littered with debris. The sight of her in the doorway, teary-eyed, grimy, and sniffling, huddled in her oversized coat, depressed me. She had the look of an orphan and it was one of the many times in those days that I would feel too poor, too overwhelmed, to go on taking care of her.

"He came today," Rose said.

"Ingersoll?"

She nodded. "I think it was him. I was hiding, in case it was Bill."

"Rose, for Christ sake, he just came to fix the generator."

She nodded. She was always nodding when she wasn't listening to you at all. It happened often. She turned and went into the living room to light some candles, even though the kitchen light was bright enough for both rooms. Sitting near the fireplace, she wrapped her arms around her shoulders, still nodding. I put more wood on the fire and sat next to her. It was always the same, her strange nodding. It was a prelude to a lengthy silence. She would nod slowly and rhythmically as though in calm affirmation of something being asked of her. The nodding meant silence and the silence meant everything I could never know, despite my worrying, about my sister. I was reverent toward her at times like these. I would mimic her silence with my own.

She was named for the flower, she insisted, and not in memory of Bill's dead sister. The rose, she would sometimes remark, was the most precious of flowers, its color and scent signifying all in life that was rare and fragile and mortal. Though she never mentioned thorns or brambles, she was not unaware of them. She had a way of rearranging her memory to suit her moods.

As a very young girl, she tended a garden all her own. For a time, she was obsessed with sunlight, her water pail, her rake, and her hoe. But by midsummer, the midwestern weeds, nurtured by humidity and uncommon rain, grew overwhelming. Their profusion disheartened her and she grimly raked everything away, zinnias, marigolds, weeds, and pumpkin blossoms, then she burned her disappointing harvest at the edge of the bog. Only her roses, the spindly bushes which never would bloom, were spared.

The following summer, she raised homing pigeons, naming them after characters from books she'd liked. She fed them bread and crushed field corn and daily swept the pen which she'd fashioned from scraps of chicken wire and wooden cartons. One September night, Aladdin returned home with a bent beak. Unable to feed, even from Rose's encouraging hand, he starved to death after a week. Rose fasted and wept. She was eleven and had never seen anything die before. She, too, would die, was her notion. Bill said if she didn't eat, he'd bruise her butt. Two days later, her girl-ass welted and bleeding, she ate.

Until the seventh grade, encouraged by Lady's nightly tutoring, she had nothing but A's in school. From the seventh grade on, she never had better than a B. In their notes to home, instructors wrote that she'd grown lazy and inattentive, that she'd drift too often into reverie, that she was a romantic. Some of this was precise, since for Rose a fantasy or a nightmare was difficult to distinguish from life at home. But it does not explain her grades or the full measure of her growing silences. She would seldom answer to her name, almost never raised her hand in class, and was hardly ever seen with other girls her age. No one noticed at the time how she had empathized with Lady, whose voice was lost in the night, in violence, during the summer before Rose started seventh grade. Our mother could not speak and Rose, in mourning, mimed her.

She had a gift, a derangement; was blessed. Once, I sprained an ankle and for days she limped along beside me. If my sleeplessness woke her, she would lie awake beside me, wide-eyed with an insomnia that surpassed my own. Her coughs echoed my own. I will share your pains and sorrows. I once believed it was *her* blood that ran from my wounds. Her endless heartbreak, all the heartbreak of the family, passed unseen by our neighbors. Rose was weird, a curiosity, and I was the lame-brain's brother, nothing more.

When she was seventeen, she painted oils on canvas until a spill of crimson, dripping downward, reminded her of the slaughtered deer that Bill would bring home every autumn. Crimson was out. Then blue, its stillness, broke her heart: no blue. One by one, the colors were eliminated; green was disease, yellow was decay, purple was sinister. Her last canvas, finished a short year after she'd begun to paint, was a huge, startling canvas, eight feet by five, with only the words *my face* stenciled in steely gray. I kept the painting hidden in the basement, disturbed by it, certain that if anyone saw it they would know about Rose as I knew about her. I needn't have worried. One October afternoon, looking for something to wrap deer meat in, Bill found the rolled-up canvas behind the pile of lumber in our basement. He and his friend, Bad Hand, having skinned the deer while passing a bottle of Scotch back and forth, took no notice of the inscription on the canvas. Cutting it into four equal strips, they wrapped the venison inside and the color of the meat soaked through. The canvas today might make a better painting altogether, its surface fulfilled you might say, if I had any idea where to find it.

Rose spoke only to me and to Lady. To the rest of the world she bowed her head. But in her final year of high school, she tried out for and was given the lead in a school play. She memorized her lines before anyone else in the cast, attended every rehearsal, and would stay late each night to discuss her performance with the director. At home, she read books about acting, stage movement, theater convention and history. In the night, through our common wall, I could hear her rehearsing her part and when I awoke in the morning, I could hear her at it again. She was to play Desdemona in *Othello*. But on opening night, she did not appear. I had come early with her so she could have extra time to prepare her makeup and, as she put it, *find her voice*, then had waited in the third row for the play to begin. The curtain never opened. The embarrassed director announced that due to cast illness, the performance would be canceled. When I went home, I found Rose in her room, still wearing the costume, painting. I knew at once who in the cast had been ill. Rose, putting down her brush, decided she never again would use the color blue.

"Where were you? Why did you leave?"

She shrugged, though her eyes were the gray of a Dakota April. "It was just too much for me," she said.

A bitter year had passed and I had found us a house in the remote country, hidden by dying elms and far from the main road. I poisoned the mice and I kept the generator running even during the coldest of nights. I hammered scrap wood together to make a table and repaired the broken chairs that had been left in the decaying attic. I found work at Hanneman's beer warehouse and with my pay I bought our food and our clothes and the hundred things we needed just to get by. Avoiding the streets where my father might be, I made my way home each night to Rose, who was safe at last if hardly sane. I was a boy, I was a magician: zap, and the world was safe for Rose; poof, and the stars were like lamps above our snowy eaves. Rose slept on a mattress of rags but in a halo of firelight, and the winter, all around us, blew the front door open in the night.

"It's him, Jesse."

"Rose, it's only the wind."

"That's what I mean."

My first day at Hanneman's, I forgot my gloves and the blisters that bloomed by noon became the calluses that I have honed and polished in years since. I was part of a team of three, and the youngest, though not by much. Al was a red-faced man-ox who worked silently and sullenly, his eyes full of hell. When we were introduced, I gave him a short nod which he did not return. The other was named Henry Colter and we needed no introductions. The past, in the form of Elizabeth Bad Hand, had been between us since summer. We were enemies and his blue-eyed glare told me that nothing would soon be reconciled. In a matter of minutes, I hated my first job.

"It's hard work," Hanneman had told me the day I'd been hired. "Tough work."

"I don't mind," I'd told him. Later, I would.

"It ain't anybody who can be a good beer-chucker."

"Just so it's full-time."

I hadn't asked how much. Hanneman had told me.

"Two eighty an hour, six-day week, ten-hour day in the summer, eight-hour day in the winter. No extra overtime pay, no bonuses, no benefits. Friday's payday and union organizers get worse than fired. Start on Monday at eight o'clock and bring your own gloves."

I'd forgotten my gloves and no one was offering me theirs when we went to meet the morning train. We loaded three trucks with beer crates from a boxcar that seemed never to empty. Henry, standing in the boxcar, would hand a crate to me and I would pass it to Al, who would then stack it in the truck. One grunt two grunt three. When one truck was full, we would take five and then fill another. Henry worked easily, with a familiar sour smile on his face, a smile suggesting just what he'd do to me if I tried to wipe it from his lips. He was older, stronger, more used to the work, and he was eager to let me know he had not forgotten me. After two trucks had been loaded and I had already grown weary, he began to drop the crates rather than pass them to my arms.

"Easy, Henry," I cautioned.

"Or what?"

Al told us to cut the shit.

"Still fuckin redskins?" Henry asked.

We each drove a heavy truck back to the warehouse and there we unloaded the crates to flatbeds. Six crates high, four deep, four across, ninety-six to a flatbed, eight flatbeds. The slivers in my hands, if assembled, would have made a handsome cross.

Lunch was from noon to twelve thirty. I had an apple and two wads of dry bologna, then I spent my last free minutes holding my hands in the snow to numb the pain. A whistle from Hanneman's office sounded us back to work.

The local trucks arrived, those owned by bar owners, liquor stores, restaurateurs, and retailers. Hanneman seldom delivered, the luxury of his beer monopoly in a small town. It was up to Al and me to do the afternoon loading. Henry, an up-and-coming type, had bookwork, orders to fill and to check, during the afternoons. It was a relief to see him gone. Al made a fair partner. He worked hard and kept his mouth shut. As each local arrived, we had to check and sign the order, then load whatever he had asked for onto his truck. The trucks arrived, one after another, like clockwork, but we occasionally had ten minutes or so to relax. During one of these breaks, I lit a cigarette and sat on an empty flatbed. Al, sitting nearby, cast an eye toward my pack. When I offered him a cigarette, he accepted it wordlessly. When he searched his pockets with no luck, I leaned to light it for him.

"Hard work," I said.

He blew smoke. "Shit work."

We smoked in silence for a while, then Al said, "Just you keep your end up. I ain't lazy I can promise you."

I told him I'd do my best.

He smoked the cigarette to the end, even past the filter, and dropped the butt to the warehouse floor. Then he stood and went into the locker room, leaving me alone in the warehouse.

My hands were throbbing and my muscles grew stiff with ache. Stretching my legs, I tried to multiply $2.80 by forty-eight, rate by hours, but fatigue clouded my head and I couldn't concentrate. I was tempted to quit, to surrender to poverty, to send Rose back to Bill, to perish. Staring at my torn hands, I was near tears and I couldn't see how an empty-minded clod like Al was going to be able to defend me from Henry Colter. Then he came shuffling back into the warehouse with an extra pair of gloves in his hands. They were worn at the fingers, a used pair. With a jerk, he held them toward me.

I thanked him.

"Dumb ass don't bring no gloves." He was almost smiling.

Another truck came rumbling through the double doors and we rose to our feet to meet it.

* * *

At four thirty, wiping my face with a dirty towel, I returned Al's gloves to him, lent him a dollar, smoked the cigarette he offered me, then headed into the early evening winter darkness toward Bill's house. I'd promised Lady I'd be back and she was waiting for me in the only room that still was home to her, her kitchen. In yellow light, aproned. Baking bread. Listening to the radio. Worried for me.

Her hands warned that Bill might soon be back.

"I can't stay long. I just wanted to see you."

I'm glad. I prayed.

"I had to work today or I'd have come sooner." In the presence of my mother, I was proud of my blisters. I bled of labor and already had forgotten my three o'clock despair. Lady smiled, a wan mute's smile, and took a Coke from the refrigerator. She motioned for me to sit, extending her hand palm upward and turning it over. I noticed that there were two places set at the table and knew that one of them wasn't necessarily set for me. It was a symbol of her lifelong wishfulness, one I'd long since grown accustomed to. For years we had eaten, she, Rose, and I, with an empty plate among us, seldom Bill. Only on certain holidays, during hours when the Hideaway—and Lemmie's and the Catch All and the Sunset Saloon—were closed could we be certain he'd be with us. At such times, he would rest his brandy bottle on the table and drink from it as though it were a pitcher of fresh milk. He would eat his dinner silently, as though his thoughts were somewhere else, then rise, belly filled, and pass out on the living room couch. I remember his reddened face and the shivering of his nostrils, the smell of brandy-sweat that seemed to fill the house, the way his breath came in ghastly flutters and wheezings, the way his belt was never buckled and his torn underwear stuck out. The sight of his skin. Rose once thought of stabbing him with a kitchen knife but was afraid of what she'd find beneath his flesh. I thought of all of these things in an instant, seeing that empty plate.

Lady wanted to know where I was working but I said it might be safer for us all if she didn't know just yet. She wouldn't have to lie to Bill, for one thing.

"Is he looking for us?" I asked.

She shook her head and made a quotes sign: Let them go. They'll be back. They'll be sorry.

I could almost hear him saying the words.

Lady was moving fitfully around her kitchen, touching anything in reach, a coffee cup, the fry pan, cupboard handles, like a blind person, endlessly redefining their location. That little yellow universe, her cuisine, my domesticated mother who before marriage could recite Shakespeare from memory, translate French poetry, explicate Nietzsche, but could not boil water. Times change. I realized that later, after I'd gone, she would sit alone at the table and have her dinner with the radio and an empty plate for company. My sister's mother. She would be worse than alone, having not even a manner with which to talk to herself. Her warden would be Bill, who from time to time might reach into the empty pockets of his soul and dig out the last dirty lint of his tenderness for her. She would never leave him. She had been too long with *someone*, him, and separations terrified her. Rather stay with Bill than be alone, as twenty years before she'd been alone, suddenly, when her foster parents had died, one two, kick shuffle, in the space of two weeks. She believed forever after in following unto death. Her foster parents, having taken her from a bastards' orphanage when she was three years old, had drained their bank account on tutor's fees for their little girl: piano lessons, dance lessons, French instruction, the classics, poise and the social graces. They didn't leave a dime. Their funerals were both short and without elegy. It was springtime and baby was on the street. She'd had no friends, none, in her childhood, and therefore no one reliable to whom she could turn. Her only friend, a piano teacher from years back, had taken her in for a week, letting her sleep on the couch, and then had sent her uptown to a friend who'd promised room and board and the possibility of a job. But Lady had lost the paper with the address and hadn't had the courage to go back to the piano teacher. She'd prayed and she'd fretted. She'd searched her purse a dozen times and still not found the address. And when at last she'd gone back to the piano teacher, there'd been only the landlady saying something about an extended trip to Europe, would you like to have me forward a letter or something, dear? She could read Aristotle in the original but she couldn't type. Though she was pretty, she could never have been a model and her musical skills were neither commercial nor overwhelmingly artistic. Nor was she streetwise. It was 1950 and she had been raised on the East Side of Manhattan, but her learning had been undertaken in various salons, never on the streets. She stood on the corner of Seventy-second Street and Broadway with a suitcase and a brown paper bag. In the suitcase were three summer dresses, stockings, underthings, a hairbrush, cosmetics, gloves, a pinbox filled with dime-store jewelry and a wrinkled love letter on blue paper that she'd received anonymously two years before. In the letter she was addressed as thou. All the rest—her books, Victrola, sewing machine, radio, bicycle, dishes, pots, pans, furnishings, paintings, typewriter—had been sold or seized in lieu of back rent. In the paper bag were two sandwiches, the landlady's parting gift. Square one. My mother walked. She followed Broadway the length of Manhattan to Battery Park. Standing in the wind, she ate the first of the sandwiches and the flat taste of liverwurst mingled with the bite of the salty mist in her nostrils. Turning round, she walked again. To Chinatown. To Herald Square. Pigeons scattered at her feet. A Doberman nipped at her shadow. At Times Square, a rangy hooker all in sequins sized her up and sneered, *White stuff so pretty*. In fright, she veered to the East River, which rippled in the June breeze and bore the garbage of the Bronx toward the shores of Long Island. On Madison Avenue, near Forty-fourth, the strap on her suitcase broke. One or two blue tears hit the pavement. She toted the suitcase with both arms, hugging it to her chest. There was rain and then there was sunlight again. In the space of an afternoon, the world was destroyed and recreated. Wars were fought and lost, children were born in the slums, pigeons were diving and shitting on pedestrians, and a man robbed a man who robbed a man. My mother walked. It was June in 1950 and at Columbus Circle she bought *The New York Times*. Entering Central Park, she came to a bench still beaded with rain. She placed the paper over the rain and sat down to eat her last sandwich. The sun died a humiliating death over New Jersey. My mother sat alone in the darkness. Somewhere in that darkness, Rose and I were conceived. Listen.

A man approached and offered to buy her dinner. He wore the uniform of an army corporal and said it was a lovely night to sit in the park. He said he knew of a restaurant nearby, a Greek place that served a wonderful leg of lamb. His uniform was too small for him and he badly needed a shave. There was, as well, a trace of a midwestern accent in his voice; atonal, indifferent. My mother said yes, a dinner would be nice. The social graces. The night, like a blue scarf, covered her blushing.

But the soldier didn't honestly know of a restaurant nearby. Trying to cover his lie, he led her uptown and down until by chance they came to a tiny café called the Athénée. They chose a table near the door but the red tablecloth was peppered with dead or dying flies. My mother shivered. "And how long have you been in New York?" she asked the soldier.

"All of my life," he answered without hesitation.

During salad, he placed a hand on her knee. It was a heavy hand, with callused fingers. She brushed it away. The soldier smiled for a moment, then grew humble, remarking that he hadn't meant to be rude. He addressed her as *Miss*. When at last the lamb arrived, it was rare, too rare. The blood of it unnerved my mother. When she wept, she kept her head bowed so the soldier couldn't see.

"I lied," he told her, swallowing his food. "I mean, when I said I've lived here all of my life."

My mother nodded and rubbed the tears with her forefinger as though she had an itch.

"I'm a stranger, really. I'm from the midwest." He grinned. "I'm in the army."

"I hadn't noticed."

His laughter was the toneless heh-heh of a man on the make. He ate his lamb quickly and spoke with a full mouth. My mother thought he had the charm of a bowler and his manners were strictly boardinghouse. When he was finished eating, he picked his teeth with the corners of a matchbook. My mother stopped crying. She ate her lamb and drank the wine that was offered her. The soldier was telling a joke about life in the army but she wasn't listening. She was thinking of the strap on her suitcase, of the hole in her stocking, of tomorrow. She smiled for no reason. Seeing her smile, the soldier thought she was amused. He grew bold and slipped his fingers under the hem of her skirt. She caught his hand between her bony knees. Leaning across the table, she looked him squarely in the eye for the first time and offered to scream something, anything, "Something from *Carmen* if you like."

"Who's Carmen?"

"Never mind."

She stood in the kitchen, arranging and rearranging its objects. Potholder, pepper grinder, spoon, towel. I lit a cigarette and watched her fuss. Though she had just finished wiping the counter, she wiped it again and in doing so she touched the towel, the cupboard handles, the faucets, her lips and throat. The perpetual running inventory. The need always to touch what she feared to lose. The result of being born an orphan, a bastard, of being orphaned a second time, of being lovelessly married for two decades, of being too long without vocal cords. Such a women raises troubled children. Her fingers trilled across the radio, as though in touching sound she might possess it. Her distress made her seem lovely, just then, though it grieved me to know how our going, Rose's and mine, would age her.

She left the kitchen for a moment and I could hear her going up the stairs, the familiar creaking of the first and fifth steps. She returned with a bottle of alcohol and a box of cotton and motioned for me to lay my hands palms up on the table. I pretended great pain while she swabbed my blisters and I was able to coax a smile from her fallen face.

She spun the cap onto the bottle and placed it on the counter. My grown-up son, her hands said. Have you eaten?

I told her I hadn't and in minutes she had folded a heaping sandwich. I felt a certain guilt, thinking of Rose, and so I ate quickly. The radio, set to the alarm, blasted on, startling us. As always, it was too loud. My mother never had to talk above the noise, only to listen. She moved to switch it off and just then we heard the front door open, Bill calling out for his wife. I dropped the last crust of my sandwich. Lady's eyes warned me to go. I rose slowly, too slowly, from my chair and she pushed me toward the back door.

Go!

For a moment I hesitated, wanting to confront him, but Lady's desperation prevailed. At the door, she stopped me for a second, touched my hands, my face, my tears. Then she pushed me away. The son from the father, forsaking the mother, I fled.

During our third day in the farmhouse, Rose at last had come to life. I returned home that evening to find that she had cleaned

the kitchen from top to bottom, scouring the sink stains with
sand she'd found in the basement, sweeping and mopping the
floor with the broken broom and some rinsed-out rags, rubbing
three years' dust from the insides of the windows, and even
cleaning the oven so we would be able to cook our food somewhere other than in the fireplace. When I came in the door, she
was sitting near the hearth with a book in her hands and the
peace in her eyes was a relief to see. I'd found a store still open,
so I hadn't arrived empty-handed. At the sight of the bread,
fruit, eggs, canned ham, and milk I'd brought with me, Rose
smiled anew.

"I've been thinking all day," she told me, "and I've decided
that this is a good house after all. Without the mice and the dust,
and with a rug or two—not to mention furniture—it could even
make a home. I mean, I don't mind getting my hands dirty to
make it one."

I told her that was good news.

"Have you seen Mother? She'll be along too, once this place
is livable. She can't stay with him much longer. She'll need us
the way we need her. She always will need us."

I nodded because she was smiling. I would agree with anything to see her smile like that. Not like a crazy, my weirdo
sister. Simply a sister.

"And I found these old dish towels under the sink today. It
looks as though they've never been used, so I figured with a
needle and thread I could make some curtains out of them.
Nothing fancy, of course, but curtains all the same."

Mice and dust and curtains and all I felt was hunger. Hard-
boiling half a dozen eggs, I served them to Rose along with a
slice of cold ham, and when we had finished our supper, we sat
munching apples by the fireplace until the flame burned down
low. I went out to the barn for more firewood and when I returned by way of the kitchen, I stopped to piss into the snow.
My eyes drifted to the kitchen window and I could see Rose
through the newly washed glass. She was standing near the fireplace brushing her hair with the broken brush. She was naked.
I stood quite still and watched her. Her brown hair was long and
straight and fine. The brush glided through it slowly, easily. She
stood with her back to me, her head tilted slightly backward,
eyes toward heaven, the right hand bearing the brush like the

bow of a violin and the left hand poised in midair, the palm
open as though waiting to receive a coin. It had been many years
since I'd seen her naked. We'd been children then, swimming
in the brown Missouri River. She was no longer a child and
neither was I. I felt I had never seen anything quite so lovely as
her long back, her fine legs, the movement of that brush through
her hair. I held my breath and blinked a flake of snow from my
lashes. The wood grew heavy beneath my right arm and though
I had an erection, cold and strong, exposed to the winter night,
I felt no shame. Laying the brush on the mantel, Rose knelt and
lifted a blanket from the floor. Wrapping it round herself, she
sat on the edge of the hearth. Through the window, I could hear
her talking to herself.

I hid my erection inside my jeans and took the wood indoors.
That night I slept troubled at my sister's side.

3

The winter turned wet and in place of snow there was ice. Ice
hanging like broken fingers from the eaves, ice in rippled sheets
covering the porch floor, ice on the highway making the cars
dance and sway. In the night would come a cold rain and the
wind would catch that rain and make it ice. The trees caught it
too and held it in their black boughs so that when the morning
sun shone through them, our house was surrounded by pendant
prisms of color and crystal. Rose wanted to take pictures but we
had no camera. I suggested that she try to paint a picture of our
house, the yard, the trees, and she agreed.

With my first paycheck, I bought a bed, groceries, pen and
paper, needle and thread, two pillows, a flashlight, a box of
watercolors, and a pad of strong painting paper. Rose rediscov-
ered her lost art. In the mornings, when I left for work, she
would go into the yard and stand before the house, studying the

light that caught it full across the front porch, the icy rippled roof, the ragged eaves, the surrounding trees and their weighty, brilliant, silvered boughs. And then she would paint, using heavy blacks and whites, always black and white. With a needle-thin brush that she made from her own hair she would trace in fine black lines and use a wide brush to fill out in white what she had defined with her lines. In her paintbox the black and white wells grew empty while the green, blue, red, yellow, violet, ocher, and orange went untouched. Her Winter Period. The work was delicate, oriental, and restrained. I returned home each night to find a new version of our house pinned to the kitchen wall. My admiration was unbridled and I suggested to her that she try to paint something else, perhaps the barn, the distant fields, or even a self-portrait, but she refused. She would do only one thing, she said, and though she didn't offer a title for her work, I sensed she was painting *Sanctuary*.

Borrowing tools from Ingersoll, I repaired the broken furniture that had been stored in the attic. In the kitchen, we soon had a small table and two chairs that rocked on uneven legs. In the living room was a dusty rug and a single torn armchair which we restuffed with rags before Rose mended the holes. As she'd promised, she made curtains from the dish towels, but they didn't reach the bottoms of the kitchen windows. We could measure the hour by the location of a wide rectangle of light that moved from the sink in the morning to the floor by noon, across that floor through the day and to the far wall at sunset.

"I'm sorry, Jesse."

"They're just fine, Rose."

At work, my blisters broke, bled, and became calluses. In time, I felt I no longer needed the gloves that left a brownish stain on the heels of my hands. Henry Colter did what he could to make life unpleasant for me, but it turned out that Al hated him as much as I did and together we kept him at bay. The work was tiring, repetitive, boring. Through the first few weeks, I returned home exhausted, my muscles burned and aching. Rose rubbed the knots from my neck and tended my hands with her own. As a homecoming ritual, I would display my palms so she could examine whatever new breaks there might be in my flesh. But I grew stronger and the boxes grew lighter. My hands turned from mud to stone. The boredom of the work never lessened but I learned to suffer through it with a certain rhythm, a quiet routine. Such labor required no decision making, no awareness, so I was free to ponder, plan, or daydream. In all of my daydreams, it was springtime and the corn was already as high as my knees. Rose was in the kitchen and my mother on the porch. I would lift a case of beer as though it were filled with feathers. I would barely hear Henry telling me to move my lazy ass.

One overcast Sunday in mid-February, Ingersoll came by in his truck to invite Rose and me to his house for dinner. He had wanted to see about setting up a chicken house—which Rose steadfastly insisted was not her domain—then he made a short inspection of the house, the yard, and the barn. Of the seven rooms in the house, we had continued to use only three, the living room, bathroom, and kitchen. Come spring, I told Ingersoll, we'd see to the upstairs bedrooms.

"No skin off my nose if you don't," he told me. "Till you came, I'd given this place up for dead. You done all right here." He nodded to Rose, who blinked but didn't smile.

The short journey to Ingersoll's farmhouse was a shock for Rose. It was the first time she'd left our hideout in nearly four weeks. In the meantime, she had seen no one but me and on occasion, Ingersoll. She'd tended to the house and her painting, nothing more. Sitting in Ingersoll's truck between the farmer and me, she fixed her gaze upon the dashboard as though she didn't want to acknowledge the surrounding countryside and be reminded that we were, after all, only a few short miles from Yankton. Once she had said to me, "This house is nowhere, Jesse. No state, no county, no continent. You can tell me we're in South Dakota and I'll believe you because of what I see out the kitchen window. But when I pull the curtains shut, I'm here and here is invisible. I guess you've noticed there's no address above the door and we aren't getting any postcards."

Though Ingersoll was by no means a big man, he had the brutish hands of a true dirt farmer, the kind of hands I would never wear at the ends of my skinny arms no matter how many cases of beer I slung from train to truck. He had long, mudstained fingers, fat red heels, and the kind of palms that, when clapped onto your shoulder, seem to have a mystical warmth and an exaggerated weight. But he had the sparkly blue eyes of a young boy and a row of perfect white teeth and was the kind of man who looked uncomfortable in anything but overalls. During the drive he gave us the news.

"Your old man knows you're working at Hanneman's. Henry Colter told him. So don't be too surprised if he shows up at the warehouse someday soon. I seen him last week at the Hideaway, Dorell too. They ain't any different than a month ago."

"What about our mother?" Rose asked.

"Ain't seen her. Don't know who has. Does she know where you're living?"

I told him no.

"Best thing for her. And for you too. Keep a tight lip at work and don't get in Henry Colter's way."

"Don't worry about that."

"I ain't worried, Jesse. Not a damn bit. Here's the house."

He drove the truck up a slush-filled road toward a high grove of trees. The house, which years back I'd helped to build, was hidden beyond the boughs. Past the treeline, to the north, were a series of five small white barns where Ingersoll kept his cattle. He was not a profit farmer. What corn he raised was used as feed for the cattle, of which he had fewer than a hundred head. The rest of his farming was for his own subsistence and he had long since plotted his fields with tomatoes, watermelon, carrots, potatoes, cabbage, lettuce, strawberries, cucumbers, radishes, sugar beets, and celery, one hundred and thirty acres, plus a cluster of treelines for timber and firewood, three pastures, and two enormous chicken houses. It was the most unusual farm I had ever known and each time in my life I had come to visit I had remembered how badly I had wished to be a part of it. Helping Ingersoll build that house had been the most joyful time of my life, though seeing his family move into it without me had been my greatest disappointment.

"But you don't have any sons," I'd told Ingersoll. I was seven at the time and preferred him to my father. "How can you farm without sons?"

He'd known what I was after and hadn't known how to answer. "You can always come and give me a hand, you know."

"Great. I'll move in tomorrow."

"No, Jesse. I don't think that would be a good idea."

Ingersoll's wife was waiting for us at the door. She greeted us as though we were her long-lost children and Rose blossomed red with both embarrassment and fear. The wife's name was Caroline and she was a full-blooded Yanktonai Sioux. Making us remove our muddy shoes at the door, she outfitted us with warm, fur-lined slippers and bade us come inside. A fire was blazing and snapping in their huge stone fireplace and when I stepped into that familiar living room I felt a glow of warmth that I hadn't felt since leaving home. The place where Rose and I lived was never warm enough, no matter how many logs I piled on the fire.

A great loom filled nearly half of the living room and Ingersoll's youngest daughter, Mary, whom he referred to as Third Blossom, was seated before it, her small feet pushing back and forth as her hands held the cross-hook and shuttle. The shick-click-slide sounds mingled with the crackling of the fire. The other two daughters, Marthe, seventeen, and Claire, fifteen, came in from the kitchen to greet us. Mary called Third Blossom stopped her work and turned to look at us. At thirteen, she was already beautiful enough to take my breath away.

We sat in the kitchen, which was paneled with a dark-stained pine, a forest of shutters, cupboards, pots and pans hanging from the high wood beams that framed the entire house. Ingersoll had hired a dozen men for a full weekend when he'd laid those beams in place. To the south side, near a wide twenty-four-pane window, was an enormous oak table covered with cider jugs, a bottle of red wine, plates of cookies, crackers, cornbread, a box of candy, a jar of peanut butter, white and rye bread, and a last loaf of black bread that seemed to have just come from the oven.

"This ain't dinner," Ingersoll told us. "Just something to tide us all over for the time being."

Pinned to the wall near the table was a copy of the original deed to the land that surrounded the house. It was a deep, rotted yellow and the corners were torn and splitting. Caroline poured a glass of cider for each of us and remarked that the deed would be nothing but a dry leaf in a few more years. "You can't even read Peter's name anymore," she said. "The date's been rubbed out for years. Goes to show you what paper means, especially paper with writing on it."

Caroline's eyes were a little off center, one of them being slightly, almost imperceptibly, lower than the other, giving her a look of unnatural wariness. She seemed never to believe what she was hearing. Before marrying Peter Ingersoll, she'd been Caroline Small Feet and had always claimed to be a direct descendant of Chief Struck-the-Ree of the Yanktonais. (Though no one had ever successfully translated his name and it was impossible to tell if he had Struck the Ree or been Struck *by* the Ree. To Caroline, it never mattered one way or another, just so long as her great-great-granddaddy had done something to the Ree, his lower-river rivals.) She'd tried to follow his example and already had a reputation in Yankton as *one of those* Indians, a militant if not yet a member of the fledgling American Indian Movement. Radical if unorthodox. Twice she had been arrested for breaking windows at the town hall; she'd lately settled on writing letters and organizing Indian women's groups. She had a master's degree in political science from the state university in Vermillion and insisted that she never had been nor ever would be a drugstore wooden Indian. If married life had taken the rough edges off her radicalism, it hadn't entirely erased her anger or her determination. Her main preoccupation, outside of the farm and the family, was preparing a legal study aimed at upholding the Treaty of Laramie of 1868, which ceded the Black Hills to the Sioux tribes for all time. "We don't want reparations," she'd once explained to me, "because money is not the object. We want the land, the country, home." She and Ingersoll had been married for twenty years. Ingersoll was now past fifty and Caroline in her late thirties. They told me they were married during the years when white Swede farmers did not marry red Sioux women. Years passed and they grew to be less of a rarity because, except for occasional sparks from Caroline, they lived a quiet life. Theirs had proven to be the happiest marriage I had ever witnessed.

It was four thirty and the sun was already setting below the clouds, shredding the gray on its way down. In winter, the Dakota sunset never lingers. In minutes, the frail and distant sun was gone and a blue prairie darkness settled over the house. From the other room, we could hear the shuffling of the loom and I was wondering what would happen if I fell in love with a thirteen-year-old named Mary called Third Blossom and where we might be twenty years hence.

Ingersoll was telling Rose about how Bill and John Bad Hand had built our house—the house we'd fled.

"It was in 1952, just before you was born, Rose. Your old man was working as a carpenter back then, though he wasn't much good at it. When he came back from the army with your mother in tow, he threw in with John Bad Hand and they took building contracts wherever they could find them. Work wasn't too tough to find in those days, so they did all right, even if neither of them was very handy with a hammer and saw. About the time Lady got pregnant with you, Rose, Bill decided he'd need a house of his own, but materials was in short supply. Brick was damned near impossible to find at a decent price and wood was scarce. Everybody was using that asphalt shingling, you know? Throw up a frame, some insulation, a scrap or two of quarter-inch plywood, then feather it over with them shingles. But your old man wouldn't settle on that. He said the shingling was ugly and he wanted a real house. For once he had the right idea. I had some lumber in my barn and I let him have it cheap. Real cheap when you consider he tried not to pay me at all. He found one a them brick ovens over in Wagner and he used it to make his own squares. He and Bad Hand mixed the mortar themselves. They used that red-gray clay from the river, some gravel they shoveled from god-knows-where, some lime, and brandy too for all I know, and they poured a half-dozen molds at a time. I think it was Bad Hand's idea to use their empty bottles as mortar mix. They were getting low on gravel and all summer long they'd been tossing their empty bottles in the bog behind the lot, so they just had to go and gather them all up. I seen them once, out back, smashing the bottles against a rock and shoveling the pieces into the molds. At first, they didn't break the glass down fine enough and the bricks that come out was split. But they learned. Weirdest way I've ever seen to make brick, but it worked out just fine. That's one foundation that won't get washed away in a spring flood."

"You said he almost didn't pay you for the lumber."

Ingersoll stopped, his eyes measuring me. "The truth is, he probably still doesn't know I got paid." The farmer reached into his shirt pocket and drew out a Winston, which he lit with a stick match. I had never before seen him smoke. "You might not like hearing it," he warned me.

"Tell me anyway."

"Just remember it was a long time ago. Years. I'm hoping you won't be judging me over it."

"Tell me."

He put out the cigarette without smoking it. "One spring night I found your old man out back of the Hideaway. He was laying there with his head against a wall and he'd made a mess of himself. Thrown up and such. I imagine you've seen . . ."

"I've seen."

Ingersoll nodded. "He was out like a light and even when I started slapping his face and pushing him around, he wouldn't come to. I figured I'd carry him back inside and maybe get him to come around with some water in the face. It was getting late and I thought Lady might be worried. This was before he started up with Dorell. Anyway, it was a hot night, turning toward summer, and I was in no mood to hoist him, vomit and all, so I started to take his shirt off him. The buttons was already gone so I just had to peel it off. That's how I found the hundred dollars." He relit his cigarette. "You listening?"

We both were, Rose and I.

"You might've gone hungry because of it, and I admit I didn't think much about that. I was thinking of my lumber and of my own family. It wasn't really much of a decision. I already had the old man stripped and slung over my shoulder when I saw the money. He'd lost a shoe and when I reached down for it, there was his bankroll sitting inside of it. I laid your father down to the ground and took the money from his shoe. He owed me two hundred but there was only a hundred there. I took it all. And I left the old man lying there."

"And he never knew?" Rose asked.

"That it was me who took it?" Ingersoll allowed himself a short laugh. "No, Rose, he couldn't have known. He was too gone to the world. Lights out. Shit-faced, if you'll pardon the expression."

"Like taking candy from a baby," I added, surprising myself with my sudden annoyance. In my own lifetime, I had taken money from his shoes. It was a game of his, to display his empty pockets, and I wasn't very old by the time I learned just where and how to rob him.

"I told you I'm not proud of it."

"You did right," Rose said.

Ingersoll simply nodded.

"It's Lady I worry about," said Caroline. When she spoke, the lines in her face deepened. She was one of those women who carry a certain history in their faces. She was no beauty but her expressions were lovely. "Why in hell does she stay with him?" Her imbalanced eyes were opened wide.

"She'll leave him," Rose said firmly. "Won't she, Jesse?"

I wouldn't lie. "Not right away." For better or worse. God sees.

Just then Mary called Third Blossom shouted for her parents. The loom had jammed and we all moved into the living room to watch Ingersoll fix it. I sat on the edge of the hearth to toast my beer-lugging weary back and Marthe sat next to me.

"Long time, Jess."

"Not long." I shrugged. "A month." I had dropped out of school when I'd run away with Rose.

"That's not what I meant."

I had known well enough what she'd meant. A few summers back, when we'd been fifteen, we'd met secretly along the Missouri River, near a sand-locked inlet, and gone swimming naked together. Marthe had neither her mother's unmatched eyes nor her father's bulk. She was slim, black-haired, high-breasted, and her blue eyes came all the way from Sweden.

"I'm like my mother," she told me. "I remember everything."

So do I, but I imagine our memories of those days are different. Our meetings had been just short of innocent, a few rounds of splashing, underwater tag, a few wet kisses, sandy caresses, and a quiet talk while drying on the beach. I hadn't known just what I'd wanted it to lead to and so it had led nowhere, despite Marthe's reassurances.

Fall, winter, spring, summer, fall, and we sat together by the fire. She touched my hand in a way that no one else could see. "Daddy never found out," she whispered. "You don't gotta worry." Then she rose and leaned over the loom, pretending to be interested in all that her father was doing.

"That arm there. It's *always* catching the yarn."

"Not that one," Claire protested. "The one next to it. See the sliver hanging out?"

Ingersoll straightened. "I have three daughters and two hands," he said. "One of you will have to go."

Mary called Third Blossom left in a huff and her mother followed her into the kitchen. Rose took Marthe's place by the fire.

"This is nice," she said, in a voice so low that I didn't hear her right away.

"We have friends, Rose."

She nodded, and for a moment I was content.

Then she added, as she often did, an ellipsis of melancholy. "Mother should be here too."

While the women were preparing the table for dinner, Ingersoll took me out to the barn, claiming he wanted to show me a new horse of his. Since I had never given a damn about horses, I felt obliged to fake an interest, which wasn't easy because the one he led me to was fat and seemed old. Its gray eyes regarded us sadly over the stall gate.

I summoned a compliment. "He's very big," I said.

"She," Ingersoll corrected me. "And she's on death's doorstep." He led me into the stall and turned the horse to the side. "See these marks?"

Fully half of the horse's right side was raw, red with welts and black with dried blood. Had it been summer, flies would have haloed the many wounds. Ingersoll touched those wounds with a probing finger and the horse shivered. A yellow liquid, like a drunk's spit, ran from its eyes and nose.

"You know what made this?" Ingersoll asked.

I had no idea.

"A broken liquor bottle. See, there are still some chips of glass in her flesh."

He turned his flashlight flush onto the wounds and I could see the jagged remnants of brown glass like a little shining constellation.

"Not that these wounds are enough to kill her. No sir. Scratches like that can hurt but they can't kill."

"Then why is she dying?" Another question for which I truly did not crave an answer.

"Because some animal in a man's clothes gave her water to

drink. Sugared water, except that instead of just sugar there was powdered glass as well.''

"Who?" I don't know why but I half expected him to say Bill.

"Some local boys, I'd guess. We get a lot of little troubles whenever Caroline goes on the warpath.''

"What are you going to do about it?''

"Not a blessed thing except keep a closer eye on things. And I'd advise you to do the same. There's all kind of people on the road, bums and rednecks and just plain kids, and people have a habit of doing in the countryside what they'd never do in the city. In the country, nobody can see them but God and the starlight.'' He put out his lamp and the darkness of the barn leaped back at us.

We closed and locked the barn and trudged back through the snow toward the house.

"One more thing,'' Ingersoll said. "I notice Rose is kind of funny. Real quiet, like always, but different too. She can't stay shut up all alone so much. If you know what I mean.''

I knew and I said so.

"I'll swing by from time to time, maybe bring Caroline or Marthe with me. How'd that be?''

I said that would be fine, I said I'd like that. But I was thinking of that horse and the bottleful of glass in its belly. I was thinking, too, that Rose would never be safe, not alone nor in a crowd. I said I'd like it if they'd visit and I must have said it a few times too many because, just in front of the door, Ingersoll stopped short and looked me in the eye.

"You know, Jesse, I think you're getting funny too.''

Then he took his rifle from the living room wall, trudged back to the barn, and shot the horse between the eyes.

The first of several times I ran away, I was seven years old. Filling a rucksack with what I considered the essentials, an apple, a road map, a camping handbook, I took a shortcut across the back alley of Pearl Street in Yankton, crossed the railroad tracks, and followed a long gulley north toward the open country. It was in early March and in the distance I could hear the gunshots of out-of-season pheasant hunters. Once I saw a bird fall clumsily from the sky and what seemed like a second later

I heard the sound of the gun. I thought it was so funny then to see a bird fall before the pellets reached him.

Still following the gulley, I came to a muddy pond about a mile north of town. It was strewn with garbage, beer cans and food cartons, and in the middle of the water was a dead mallard, a female, that some careless hunter had been too lazy to fetch. Beyond the pond was a stretch of wood into which I wandered while the sun began its descent overhead. When I grew tired, I stopped to eat the apple and when it was gone, I felt afraid for the first time. Before leaving the house, I had been convinced I would find apple trees along the way, or sweet corn or strawberries. I had thought that the countryside was filled with food and I had only to choose for myself. But I didn't see any apple trees about so I dug a small hole and placed the apple core into it, then covered it over with soil. I would come back, I told myself, in a year or two, and there would be something to eat. The apple tree would grow, that was certain.

Continuing my journey, I walked deeper into the trees until I came upon a man building a house. Only the foundations had been laid, the holes dug and the cement poured, and around the foundation were piled various sizes of lumber and junk wood, brick, stone, and a pile of heavy sand. The man was shoveling sand into a wheelbarrow and I stopped in the distance to watch him. Though the day was cool, he wore only a pair of trousers and heavy boots. His chest was bare and the muscles rippled along his back as he lifted a shovelful of sand from the pile and tossed it into the wheelbarrow. I watched him for a long time, fascinated with his work, the way I had sometimes watched my father in the days when he'd still worked on our own house. Sometimes I had asked if I could help but he had always told me to get lost. Once I had taken his hammer and begun to pound nails into an old piece of wood I'd found behind the bog. He'd been searching for his hammer for nearly half an hour when he'd found that I had taken it away. That had been the cause of one of the earlier beatings I can remember and from that time on I stayed far away from him when he worked. But when I approached the man in the woods, he turned and smiled and asked me what in hell was a little kid like me doing out in the country.

I told him I was running away.

He laughed. "Running away from where?"

"Home," I said, thinking to myself, from where else?

"Well, if you're not in any hurry, I could use some help. I'm building a house."

I was suspicious right away. I couldn't believe he would really let me help him. Later on I knew he had only been looking for a way to keep me around until he'd have time to take me home.

I asked him what I could do.

He explained that he was finishing the foundation and had to mix sand with his cement. "That's what makes it stronger, you know. Good grainy sand." He said that if I'd mix the cement in the barrow while he poured the sand, he could save a lot of time.

We worked together the entire afternoon and it was the most glorious day of my childhood. The man, Ingersoll, was a tall sturdy blond who let me poke around in his cement with a piece of two-by-four and when a load of cement was ready, he would pretend that I was helping him while he poured it into his ditch. The day grew warmer as we worked and we could hear the sounds of hunters all around us, as though we were in the middle of a battleground. After the first few hours, we stopped for a while and Ingersoll let me drink from his canteen. I told him afterward that it was really good water and he laughed. "Water's always good when you're thirsty." I was so anxious to please him that I refused to rest any longer than he did. If he needed his shovel, I hurried to fetch it for him. Once, when the wheelbarrow tipped over by accident, I started scooping the fallen cement with my hands. I mixed cement with my little stick and if the pile of sand grew too flat and scattered, I piled it up high so he could get a full shovelful without having to scrape it together. When he told me I was a good worker, I flushed with joy. "You must be a lot of help around the house," he told me. "Your daddy must be proud of you."

I told him I didn't have a daddy.

He just looked at me for a long time, then he took another shovelful of sand and dumped it into the wheelbarrow.

I couldn't believe it when the sun slipped below the treeline and Ingersoll began to gather up his tools and throw them into the back of his pickup truck.

"But we aren't finished," I told him. "We've got a whole side left to do."

He laughed. "We can't hardly do it in the dark, can we? By

the time we mix another barrow of cement we won't even be able to see the ditch it'll be so dark.''

With a heavy heart I helped him gather the last of his things, then we took a last walk around his foundation. He told me that the two sides we had done together were a lot better than the ones he'd done alone, but already I was inconsolable. The last of the hunters' gunshots died away in the sunset. Ingersoll got into his truck while I stood my ground. Leaning out the window to me, he asked if I was coming. I nearly leaped into the truck and we drove away. We were almost inside the city limits of Yankton when I asked him where we were going.

"We're taking you home," he said.

I reminded him very coolly that I had just run away.

"You can run away again next week," he said. "On Saturday, we can fill the last side of the foundation."

"We can?"

He nodded. "But first I've got to get you home to your father."

I realized he knew exactly who I was, Jesse, the son of Bill. He had known all along. "Why don't you be my father?" I asked him.

He drove silently through the streets of Yankton, unanswering. Once I was alone in the kitchen with Bill, I learned how fathers do not always choose their sons. I carry his signature forever on my back.

After a week of endless waiting, I found Ingersoll at the site, his truck loaded with wood, his tools scattered around the yard, and a few beads of sweat having already formed along his chin. I nearly leaped into his arms.

"Ingersoll!"

He accepted my kisses with a shy smile and set me back to the ground.

"I waited the whole goddamn week for you," I told him.

"Don't swear in front of a devout Christian."

"But I'm so fucking happy to see you."

He just shook his head. "I'm gonna have to talk to your mother."

"Never mind my mother. Let's get to work."

In the next five months, meeting Ingersoll on Saturdays and

Sundays, nurtured by the sun, the hard work, the box lunches, and the attention of a man who cared about me, I grew muscles and inches with equal pride. Within a few days, we had finished laying the foundation, then we spent two hard weekends rowing bricks above it. When Ingersoll had enough wood, we nailed together two-by-four frames and raised them side by side until the house was a complete skeleton in which we could see the traces, the true outline, of what it would later become. The day we finished the frame, his family came for a picnic lunch and for the first time I saw Marthe Ingersoll outside of the Yankton grammar school. She watched me over her egg salad sandwich with more than a little suspicion. Later she asked me why I was working so hard. "It's not as though you're going to live in this house, so what's it to you?"

She cut me to the bone. I didn't have an answer.

We nailed insulation strips all around the frame and the furry fiber made me itch for days no matter how many baths I took. With the help of a few other farmers, we poured a cement floor along the ground, then Ingersoll and I alone hammered the pine slats around the frame until the house, from the outside, looked like all it needed was a few coats of paint. One week in July the electricians came and the following week the plumbers. We labored for three weekends laying the brick for the two fireplaces, the first one on the ground floor and the second one in Ingersoll's bedroom, crowning them with a high chimney which later would exhale the smoke of a thousand winter nights. Each brick I laid and each nail I hammered home was a source of immeasurable joy to me, a joy I would not define for many years. I knew that the house I was building was not my own, so I worked even harder, as though with each nail, each brick, each beam and frame that I had a hand in, I would add to my claim to it, however tenuous that claim might be. I think now that I might have been planning again on running away, this time to Ingersoll. In those days my father blew hot and cold. Seasons would pass in which he would at least resemble the father I needed. He would drink less and spend more time with my mother. He scolded me but seldom struck me. Beneath his vulgarity, there were occasional moments of warmth between us. But during the summer in which Ingersoll and I finished the house, he turned away and I turned against him. Time never justifies anything, it only blows leaves over leaves. At the bottom of it all is an ambiguous loam, truth and lie become moldy with age. I built a home for a family not my own, that is the only certainty. And in early September, when the floors had been stained and waxed, the doors fitted to their hinges, the porch laid out as in my winter daydreams, and the furniture moved from the old house to the new, the Ingersolls—Peter, his wife, Caroline, and Marthe, Claire, and Mary called Third Blossom—moved in. In the years that followed, I would visit that house a thousand times and always I would note the frame of it, the walls and the foundation, and would feel in it the warmth of my happiest summer, when a man who was not my father was nevertheless my light simply because he put a hammer in my hand and said drive that nail, simply because there was room enough for a boy beyond the shadow of a man. His shadow, in the years since, has never diminished. With my sons at my side, I measure my own against his. My head arrives at his shoulder, as always. And rests there, content.

During the drive home, while Rose kept her thoughts to herself and her eyes on the green glow of the dash, I watched the headlit muddy road and thought of Ingersoll's hands. I'd been thinking of those hands all day, it seemed, since they'd first rapped on our door to invite us over for dinner. The hands that gripped the wheel of his truck so easily, which held a pot of boiling coffee, which gathered dust and splinters and bruises and scrapes and cuts, as though hands were meant, by nature, to keep souvenirs of whatever passed their way. They were rough hands, but nonetheless I'd seen them cupped so gently around his wife's face and surely they had felt their way hundreds of times around her body. With his hands he wielded hammers, rakes, hoes, scythes, knives, pitchforks, saws, and when he spoke he held those hands, palms up, before him as though to show he was telling the truth, just look at these hands with nothing to hide. Though I know better than to judge men by the look of their hands, I often turn my own palms over and I cannot help but measure what I see within them, comparing them to Ingersoll's. In palmistry, there are love lines and life lines, destinies and disasters. I have yet to find a palmist who will tell me what scars mean and I have yet to take a splinter from my flesh and consider myself blessed, as Ingersoll must have, to have gathered another souvenir of his own human labor.

He had taken me aside once more that night, this time while the table was being cleared and the dishes washed. We stood on the back porch and looked across the clear blue winter night, the cold prairie, the empty trees. Ingersoll had been drinking beer for hours and seemed to sway on his feet.

"I talk too much when I drink," he admitted. "Sometimes, when I'm with an old friend, I can sit with a couple of sixes at my side and tell everything I know, everything I think I know, and everything I pretend to know. And in the morning I have a feeling worse than any hangover, like I've given away something I meant to keep inside. Other times, when I haven't been drinking, I clam up when I should be talking. Words are something I've learned to repeat and I don't do well with them when I need to."

When I shivered, he asked, "You cold?"

I nodded. "But it's all right. I like the fresh air."

He offered a black cigar but I refused. He lit one for himself and tossed the flaming match to the snow.

"Anyhow, when I drink, I talk. That's my nature."

I was still shivering and my teeth were chattering so I held my jaws together and let my lips tremble.

Ingersoll smoked and stared into the night.

I told him I'd changed my mind about a cigar, so he lit one for me and I smoked it as though it might warm me.

"I'm not going to tell you a bunch of stories, but I think you should know your old man wasn't always like he is now. I mean, we were friends once. A long time ago, before you were born. Back then, he just seemed kind of hurt about something. He drank whiskey then, always in a little plastic cup, never from the bottle like he does now. I imagine you must hate him . . ."

"I don't."

Ingersoll stopped. We were both surprised by what I'd said.

"You don't?"

I thought about it, whether or not it was true. "No," I said. "I don't hate him. I just don't want to see him. He makes me tired."

"Tired?"

"Of everything. Not just of him."

Ingersoll nodded. "Well, I just think you should know, that is, if it makes any difference, that he used to be a better man. Back before he got in with Bad Hand and then Dorell. He was a kind man and he loved your mother very much."

Ingersoll stood still on the porch, rocking slightly back and forth as though from a breeze. I no longer felt cold though I could see my breath before me. I waited to see if the farmer had anything else to say. *When I drink I talk.* I was afraid he was going to tell me details of the past, my father's history, and though I would have liked to have heard about what a good man he had been, anything that might have helped me unravel the disappointment I felt in him, Ingersoll had nothing more to tell me. He dropped the last of his cigar into a nearby snowdrift and laid a hand on my shoulder. It was the kind of gesture a father makes to a son. Then, as though embarrassed, he took it back and stuffed it into the pocket of his overalls.

He was a kind man and he loved your mother very much.

In the years after I left Yankton, when Rose was gone from me, I would live in other cities and in each of them I would watch the derelicts and the drunks with more than passing interest. I would seek in them the kind man who had loved a woman, I would seek the father, the brother, the son, the friend. Drunks are as universal as flowers, and as numerous. They spring up anywhere and bloom into view most abundantly in summer. They sleep where no one else could, in subway stations, tunnels, empty doorways, beneath park benches, on stairways and stairway landings. In Paris, I'm told, in the summertime, great numbers sleep stretched across the middle of a sidewalk on unlit streets, like stony corpses of some urban battlefield, unmoving, their ears tuned to the cement, noses running but not from colds. I learned to watch drunks when they awaken. In the subways, they are startled by the lights and the screaming trains. Their faces seem to break open, as though cracked by some inner, dull thunder. Or in the parks, where the birds are diving and shitting on their clothes, the drunks awaken breathless and begin to cough. You approach one and he regards you with suspicion. You ask him if he's had a good sleep but language fails him. Words form too slowly, so he simply reaches out a hand, dirty palm upward, and asks for a quarter, or tenpence, or a franc, or a cigarette. You hand over a coin and he asks for another. You hesitate and he pulls you close by the arm and his breath comes straight from his belly, a thick and ratty breath, and he says, More. And no matter how much more you give, if you give at all, the word will be repeated, one way or the other: More, more.

More what?

More of what can be put into this empty palm.

And why is this palm empty?

Because you haven't filled it.

And when you walk away, a curse follows your turned back, but it is a curse without rancor, a drunk's way of saying goodbye.

Drunks aren't pretty. Drunks aren't poetic.

After a monumental night, Bill is slumped over against the east wall of the Hideaway, one shoe on and one shoe off. The morning sun illuminates his face, the stubble, the yellowed skin. He sleeps on a pillow of his own vomit, a bed of broken glass, and a fly circles, lands, bites the back of his hand.

There he is, Rose.

Oh, Jesse.

Shall we call Mother or should we wake him up first?

He's too heavy to carry. Let's wake him up.

But instead we covered him with newspaper, head to foot with pages of the Yankton *Press and Dakotan*, so he looked more like a pile of trash than a man one might recognize as our father.

Then we quickly ran away.

4

She may have loved him once. Before the deluge of fear. She may have swayed from the wind of him, she may have touched his face and blushed and been his lullaby. He may have been, however briefly, her sunrise and sunset. Her devotion to him may have been her gravity, holding her like a centrifuge to the rocky earth of him. She may have loved him, but if she did it was before my birth because I know that in all my life I never saw her look upon him as so many women look upon their men, with a regard I can only think of as female, calm and inflamed, one part passion and one part wisdom.

She may have loved him in New York, when they lived together in a run-down West Side hotel in the weeks before his discharge from the army. He may have told her lies or taken her to the movies. In cabs, emboldened, he may have kissed her. He may have charmed her or dazzled her or perhaps, in simple gratitude for his protection, she may have felt in herself the outline, the rudiment, of romantic love.

That first night, when he paid the tab and she followed him out of the Greek restaurant to the street, they strolled through the jittery Manhattan darkness until they came to a hotel he said was his. In the morning he was off to Brooklyn and she took with her the suitcase with the broken strap and left the hotel. A downtown bus left her at the Port Authority where she stood before the wide signs—not unlike menus—and read the names of the cities they offered: Boston, Philadelphia, Wilmington, Trenton, Baltimore, Winston-Salem, Raleigh. She liked the name Raleigh; the word came so softly from her tongue when she said it aloud. It was barely noon and she bought a ticket for a four o'clock bus, then sat on a bench and waited, holding the suitcase in her lap. A black man in a torn coat sat next to her and blew cigar smoke across her shoulders. She rose and found another bench that wobbled under her weight. Then she changed her mind. She never said why she changed her mind, if it was because on second thought she didn't know anyone in Raleigh or because New York, after all, was home. Maybe she had no reason; she didn't even bother to get a refund on her ticket. She left it on the bench for the black man with the cigar.

She had lunch at Nedick's and read a newspaper. The man behind the counter agreed to hold her suitcase for the afternoon, so she strode in sunshine to the Metropolitan Museum and spent the remainder of the afternoon strolling among portraits, nineteenth-century faces she knew and recognized and almost felt she could speak to. She may have seemed lost because three times she was approached and offered directions. She shook her head and continued to stalk the portraits, moving backward toward the seventeenth century until the museum closed. Then she went back to Nedick's for her suitcase and had to pay the man two dollars. Night fell. She may have later remembered it to have fallen like a curtain or a shroud. She went with her suitcase back to the hotel and climbed the stairs to the fourth floor.

"Lady, where you been?"

"My name is not Lady."

"You're Lady to me. Where'd you go?"

"Nowhere really. Out."

She spent the next morning at the Port Authority, reading the names of cities on the wall, any one of them might have been home, but at nightfall she was at the hotel where a soldier was waiting for her with flowers and a bottle of red wine.

Her devotion, her blind devotion. She would never defy him, never betray him. The deluge of fear. Or devotion. Or fear.

I have seen this kind of madness between other men and women. No matter how deeply the knives are thrust, no matter how freely the blood flows, in what must suffice as love, however deformed, the devils cannot be separated from the angels.

She may have loved him once. She may have rocked him in her thin arms. Once upon a time before.

"Lady?"

"Bill?"

"I'm getting out next week."

"I know."

"I'll be going home."

"To that place in North Dakota?"

"*South* Dakota, Yankton. You coming with me?"

She may have loved him once. She may have tasted the salt of him and thought it sweet.

"Yes, Bill. I'm coming with you. Yes."

She may have believed in the passing of time, the healing, the unraveling. She may have held her hands above her face like a frail umbrella to stop the rainfall of his fists. She may have asked him, Didn't he love her more than brandy, more than sorrow?

5

Living as I did that long winter ago, in that crumbling farmhouse with Rose, working at Hanneman's, and hiding from my father, I began to cease thinking of myself as *I*. Somewhere along the way, I evolved into a *he*, a third and more impersonal person. What he and I held in common was that we could not escape being Jesse Dark. But somewhere along the line, I made a separation between the two. I have never been certain just how I did it or why. It may have been my way of dissociating myself from my fears, my concerns for Rose. The tragedy of the winter and the spring that followed were thus not happening to me, they were happening to *him*. He took care of the chickens in their hut, he walked the snowy roads to Yankton before sunrise, he caught the crates of beer in his weary arms, and he returned home each night to a sister whose grasp on reality was deteriorating, melting like the icicles that lined the eaves of their devastated home.

This gift, the ability to shift my persona to that of a third person, has provided me with a mobility, a fluidity, that others have lacked. I am able to suffer poverty, loneliness, fear, and various illnesses with a certain detachment. When cornered by life, I become a character, a part of a fiction, the story of he, and as him I am heroic. My suffering is magnified, made important, because while *he* is experiencing it, *I* am his witness.

And I believe in him.

Another result of this habit of mine is that I will occasionally prove to be abnormally generous. When I am giving something of myself, I tend to be unaware of the giving, the sacrifice. The implication is that he, my third person, is the generous one, and thus I can fulfill outrageous promises and, without blinking an eye, quite seriously offer more. In the years that have passed,

60

my sincerity has been questioned more than once. Those around me have taken me for a fool or doubted my sanity. Life, I am advised, is never *that* grandiose. I am too willing to offer more than could ever be offered me in return and am, therefore, suspect.

And at the worst of times, I have to admit that there is no *he*, there is only me, cornered and frightened. I reclaim my identity as Jesse, take it or leave it. At least I have an idea of the man I am.

I first became him for Rose. It was after the summer during which I met Marthe at the river and we swam naked in the muddy water. I was fifteen and it was the driest summer in memory. The leaves burned brown on the trees before July was gone and the lawns of Yankton, except for those along the bluff, were yellow and dry. Bill was never home that summer, but by that time I had grown used to his comings and goings. After work he would go to the Hideaway, which was air-conditioned, and only occasionally would he later come swinging through the screen door, the sweat pouring down his face, his breath shallow and pained. "Hottern shit," he would say. And he would pass out somewhere between the stairway and his bed.

Out of boredom, mingled with a fifteen-year-old's sexual curiosity, I agreed to meet Marthe at the river. The first time she was shy, leaving her clothes in neat little piles along the shore and insisting that I keep my back turned until she was in the water. We swam, we splashed, and we stole caresses camouflaged as accidental. She would slip or fall and I would catch her. She would blush and I would remove my hands. Slowly. I would not get out of the water until my erection died away. We wrapped ourselves in towels and talked about school, families, the heat. We parted without kissing.

We met again a week later and Marthe seemed to have undergone a radical change. Stripping in front of me, she tossed her shirt and jeans toward a rock and dared me to chase her across the beach. I chased and she was too easy to catch. Her tongue explored the architecture of my mouth and throat and her cool hands pulled my jeans from my hips. "Let's swim," I suggested, and when she followed me into the water, there were no more accidents, no falls, no slips. She was deliberate and aggressive. I tried to splash her but she held my wrists and tried to kiss me. I kissed her briefly, then pulled away. When she tried to tighten her grip, her hand slipped away and whacked me between the legs. I howled, bent double, swallowed some of the Missouri. "Jee-zuz!"

"Jesse!" Her hands flew to her mouth. "O God, Jesse! I'm sorry! I didn't mean to . . . O *God*."

I crawled to the shore and lay face down in the sand. The pain rolled in my belly, furled and unfurled, and then diminished. An average goosing. I could feel a nipple touch my arm, Marthe reclining next to me. I lay quite still and let the sun dry my back and ass.

"I'm really sorry, Jesse. I would never do something like that on purpose."

I didn't answer.

"Are you mad at me?"

I wasn't, nor was I any longer in pain. In fact, Marthe's nearness and the warmth of the sun were having their effect. My erection burrowed into the warm sand.

"No," I said. "I'm okay. Really."

"Are you?" The worry in her voice was real.

"Yes," I said. "I'm just fine."

"Then why are you laying like that?"

"Like what?"

"All funny like that. On your belly."

"I'm comfortable like this," I lied.

She touched my back, her fingers making circles along the spine. Then she lifted and lay on top of me and began to kiss my neck. "Roll over, Jesse. Please."

She lifted herself a bit and I rolled and embraced her.

"Ooh!" she said, feeling my erection against her belly.

We began to give each other little kisses and I rested my hands on her back. The sun struck me full in the face, so I closed my eyes and could see red through the lids. We remained like that for some time and I began to think she had fallen asleep, but then, quite abruptly, she lifted and looked me in the eye and said, "Oh, Jesse, let's."

"Mmm," I said.

"Now, please. I'll be on the bottom."

She lifted herself away from me and lay upon the blanket

nearby. She held her knees in the air, together. Her brown girl body, half Lacotah, half Swede, was twitching. I didn't know what to do.

"Come *on*," she said firmly.

I knelt over her, touched one budding breast, then the other. My chemistry was overcoming my fear. My blood raced.

"I want to," she said. "Please."

Moving over her, I bent my neck and kissed her lightly on the lips. I was ready, I was willing. To myself, I was saying goodbye to my virginity, what boys my age called the silver bullet. But just then, at the most wrong moment possible, just as I was about to give in to my instinct and my want, Marthe said, "Be easy, Jesse. I won't have a baby. I promise."

My desire, threatened, fled. My blood stopped cold. A baby? I hadn't thought of such a thing. I was thinking now, and as I was thinking I noticed the look of absolute hunger in Marthe's eyes. Ravenous, fearsome, and—to my young eyes—*unusual*. My lust registered a sudden zero. I rolled away.

"What is it? Why are you stopping?"

"I can't," I said. "I'm not ready."

The pain in her eyes was too terrible. "Not ready? You mean you want one of those things, those propo, prophyl—"

"Not a rubber," I said. "I'm just not ready."

"But I can't get pregnant. I had my time last week. *You* know. I just got over it. It's safe now."

"That's not what I mean," I insisted. "I'm not afraid of babies."

"Then what is it?"

I didn't say because I didn't know.

"Because I'm not pretty?"

"You're beautiful."

"You don't like my tits? You're afraid of me?"

"I love your tits and I'm not afraid of you."

Her voice rose slightly. "Because we're here? Outside? I know a place where we can go, with a bed and all."

"I like it fine here. No problem."

"Then what the hell is it?"

"I'm not in the mood," I told her. "I'm just not."

"Shit, Jesse. I mean, *shit*."

I hadn't yet learned how a woman's ardor can turn to anger

or how a woman will hide her sorrow with rage. Marthe slugged my arm with her little brown fist. I didn't mind. She slapped me across the shoulder. I smiled. It seemed somehow funny at the time, her sudden change in temperature.

"Prick," she said. Then she rose and walked across the beach to where she'd left her clothes. I leaned on my elbows and watched her dress. She stood about ten yards away and I couldn't take my eyes off her. I was amazed to feel myself growing stiff once again. I was confused.

Marthe came back for the blanket and saw that I was, obviously, excited.

"Fuck you, Jesse goddamn Dark." Yanking the blanket from under me, she strode away. Just before reaching the treeline, she turned. "If you change your mind about the priesthood, I'll be here on Monday at noon. Got it?"

I nodded.

She seemed to be on the verge of walking back toward me, then she stopped in mid step. "Fuck *you*. Really." Then she walked quite definitely away.

I remained on the beach until after dark, when the moon rose like a fat white lamp over the south bluffs and made the river ripples jump and glitter. I was smoking cigarettes that summer and had a package of Marlboros that I'd spent the last of my precious change for. I lay naked on the cooling sand and smoked and thought about everything there was to think of. When you're fifteen, the inventory of life seems suddenly overwhelming. I was overwhelmed. The sand scratched my ass a little, which was vaguely pleasant, and because of the drought the summer night was mercifully devoid of mosquitoes. I was content to be alone and naked and in the dark, happy to watch the trail of the moon, the high, sweeping July arc it made over the Sioux Valley. The uppermost branches of the trees across the river seemed white against the horizon and the rich depth of the moonlight cast tree shadows across the rippling water. I crushed the cigarette into the sand and lit another. My habitual mistrust of nature, the world's and my own, was temporarily suspended. I was keenly aware of my anatomy, the warmth of my skin, my lazy energy. The hairs on my forearms were rigid and I was alert in a way I had never been before. I began to wish I had made it with Marthe and realized that all I'd needed was a measure of her patience, a softer come-on, or gestures and words less abrupt than those she'd offered me. She had needed me, or it, too much. I could never bear to be so necessary to someone.

When I went for a swim, I believed myself in flight. The gentle current swept across my hips and when I allowed myself to drift it would carry me a few yards at a time downriver; then I would slide onto one of the innumerable sandbars, where I would rest, briefly, and stare upward toward the stars. Prone Jesse and the constellations of summer. Then I would dig my hands into the sand and pull my way back into the current, and be borne away.

I remained there most of the night and by the time I had dressed and begun the long walk home—to Lady, who sat worried in the kitchen; to Bill, who lay passed out on the couch; to Rose, who paced and fretted in her room—I had decided that I would return at noon on Monday and give my boy virginity, my silver bullet, my first letting, to Marthe, sweet Marthe, who, for all her frightening urgency, whether from lust or love or simple lonesomeness, felt desire for me. Marthe, who deserved me, would be my first.

But she was not my first. We never were. We never did.

Her name was Elizabeth Bad Hand and she received everything I never gave to Marthe. She gave me nothing in return except memory of what it was to fall in love and find that love unreturned. She was seventeen and seemed older. She had a sassiness, a way with words, that I both envied and loathed. She worked that summer as a waitress at the Silver Dollar Cafe. Her Lacotah hands were small, her hair was as black as a dead winter night, and she had a sway, just a sway, that sent me, as I stared at her from the ketchup-stained counter, reeling. On the Monday afternoon, I was at the Silver Dollar, watching Elizabeth. Already I had forgotten Marthe, forgotten the decisions I'd made in the moonlight. Elizabeth was my moonlight just then. "Sugar?" she asked, referring to my coffee.

"Cream would be fine."

Marthe sat naked and alone on the beach.

I had known Elizabeth when we both were babes. Old man Bad Hand had disappeared some years after helping my father

build our house and Elizabeth had been sent to the Pine Ridge
Reservation to live with an aunt. She had come back that summer, she said, to be among friends. She swore she'd never return
to Pine Ridge.

"Crazy goddamn redskins living there. Always talking school
or church or forming groups. Petitions to the BIA and a lot of
chatter. And no movies, no dancing. A real drag."

"You prefer Yankton?"

Her smile was sarcastic. "It's a hole like any other. I won't
stay all that long."

I was alarmed. "Where next?"

"Anywhere. Denver, Minneapolis, Chicago. It's a big
world."

I burned and didn't know what from. It was ninety-five degrees in the shade and electric fans pushed the hot air from one
place to another. The summer burned with me. The world
burned.

I was at the Silver Dollar every day and soon learned which
hours were the best for seeing Elizabeth. There was a morning
rush from eight to ten thirty, a lunch rush from eleven thirty to
two, and a dinner rush from five to seven thirty. After eight, I
could talk to Elizabeth alone. She had a way with words.

"I asked Sammy for a raise so he lifted me off the ground.
'Good enough?' he says and I told him he could kiss my ass."

I should be Sammy.

"Forty-two cents. I serve eleven breakfasts and I make forty-
two goddamn cents in tips. This town is full of assholes."

*I left my heart as a tip for you; you swept it away with the
toast crumbs.*

"You know what I want, Jesse? Money. Nothing but a lot of
long green, enough to wipe my ass with. Money is all there is
worth living for. The rest is just for passing time. Houses, families, sweaty little babies. Give me a million dollars if you want
to put a smile on my face."

If desire were currency . . .

I had nothing she wanted, unless you counted the dime I left
from time to time, the lonely silver disk sitting next to an empty
plate. A dime meaning my name, which she would sweep up
later and drop among the other coins that slid and shifted in the
pockets around her thighs. I wondered what she thought of me.

I was always afraid to ask. I had seen her sitting close with Henry Colter from time to time, but I had seen her left lid close, lightning-fast, in a hot wink, once, for me. Burn, burning, burned.

Once, meaning to show my affection—and knowing her tastes—I robbed Bill of his change and bought a six of beer. When I casually presented it to her, she smiled briefly, then tucked the six under the counter. Later I heard her telling Henry Colter that if he took her to the movies he could have some of her beer. I fled the Silver Dollar and walked dizzily through the empty night town.

Sometimes I studied Henry Colter's hard face and heavy hands, hands which I was certain had already left smudgy fingerprints on the parts of Elizabeth I could only dream about. I wanted to understand his attraction for her, what put the itch in her palms and the heat in her oven. He was seventeen and made a poor Romeo. He told dirty jokes, he ate with his hands, his clothes were always rumpled, and his face needed washing if not rearranging. He had bad teeth. He smelled like spilled beer. But he shot holes all over the heart of the woman I was after. Whenever he came slouching into the Silver Dollar, usually near closing time, she would hurry to his table with ice water, post his order to the kitchen, and cha-cha back to his side with a flutter and a squeal. "I thought you'd *never* get here."

Elizabeth.

One evening, emulating his style, I told her a joke I'd heard about a hooker and a whiskey bottle. "Jesse," she said, backing away from me, "I don't want to hear that shit from you. Not *you*." I was made to be a gentleman, a sign around my neck, "Reserved for Romance, Starlight, Moonlight." The dime, my calling card, was perpetual.

Loving her grew more difficult as August drew to a close. I would lie in bed at night and play with myself while she humped and ah'd in the cinema below my lids. At fifteen I was a master of situations: we were fucking in the starlight atop Sutton Hill, my ass waving to Gemini; we were entwined among lilacs, her legs corralling me. Her eyes were wide, her lips dewed with lust, her hair smelled of cinnamon. Always she loved me with that same sway—a rhythm, a way of moving—but my coming, alone in that moonstruck bed, was vacant, hollow, unsettling.

Lightning bolts that left no mark. I would change my sheets before my mother could. Sheets signed Jesse wants Elizabeth.

The end of August brought no relief. The sunlight was monotonous, blinding, the river was low and muddy as ever, and brush fires were reported everywhere. Farmers, surveying their fields of limp corn, were asking for relief from the government, and the public pool swarmed with Yankton brats with chlorined eyes. I suffered headaches and insomnia. Rose had the flu.

On the first night of September I wandered into the Silver Dollar near closing time. It was empty except for Elizabeth, who leaned against the jukebox and scanned the titles of the tunes. I said hello but she didn't seem to notice. Taking a quarter from her pocket, she dropped it down the slot and pushed buttons on the Rock-ola. D8: "It's a Heartache," then J3: "My Girl." Old stuff. She sat down at the corner of the counter, two stools to my right. "You want something?"

The stars, the wind, the moon. My nose in your crotch. "Gimme a Coke."

She moved around to the other side of the counter. Her eyes were red and a few tears were still falling. She drew the Coke from its fountain and laid the glass in front of me, then came around to the other side and sat down, this time right next to me.

"Where's Henry?"

"He ain't comin. We had a fight."

"What about?"

I lit a Marlboro like a man and smoked it as though it were my last. The Coke was warm, she had forgotten the ice. Neither of us spoke while listening to "It's a Heartache." The overhead fan needed oiling. It creaked and shimmied, ruining the music. Was I the only one on earth who noticed these things? When the song ended, I heard the clicking of the jukebox and the next record slapped into place.

"I'm sorry, Liz." I don't know why I said that. Not that I was sorry, but the name Liz. She had always been Elizabeth.

Elizabeth was still crying.

"You want a cigarette?"

She lifted her head and looked at me for the first time. Her face was a mosaic of tears and sweat and badly combed bangs. "Sure. Gotta match?"

"Not since Valentino."

She wasn't listening. She smoked the cigarette between sobs. I don't care, you know. About Henry, I mean. I ain't cryin cause of him. I just cry sometimes I don't know why."

"That's our song," she told me, listening to the spinning 45. "Least it was."

I was thinking I should leave. Somehow her sorrow was beyond me, something I couldn't take home with me to the sanctity of my bed and resolve with my eyes closed. But she wanted me to stay so I did. We kept smoking cigarettes and I drank another Coke. Now and then she would get up from the counter and put another quarter in the jukebox. Same songs: D8 and J3. She began to sing along. We were alone.

Later, when it was time to close up, she rose and wiped down the counter one more time, locked the pantry cabinets and cash register, switched off the power in the kitchen, and sealed the fountain taps. "Fuck the pearl diving, Sammy can do it in the morning." Taking her purse from behind the counter, she followed me out the door and locked it with a bent key.

"Where you headed?"

I told her nowhere special.

"I'm going home to drink some beer. A little or a lot. You coming?"

She lived on Capitol Street, so named because when Dakota was a territory the capitol had been located there. Her apartment was above an automotive supply shop, not far from the Icehouse. She stopped before going in and gazed toward the parking lot, which was full. She was looking for Henry's black Chevy but it wasn't there. "Let's go," she said.

The apartment was small and crowded with records, ashtrays, scattered laundry, a radio, dying plants. A torn poster of Mick Jagger was pinned to the wall above the bed, which was unmade and seemed to have remained so for some time. A cat, Juno she called him, slept on the window ledge. No peacocks, no flowers, no satin sheets. "Sit down do you want a beer?" She put a can of Old Milwaukee on the floor beside me.

"The stereo's busted," she said. "I gotta get that fixed." Still hungry for music, she turned on the radio and we could hear the broadcast of the Minnesota Twins–Chicago White Sox game. "I hope they both lose." She played radio search, zip

zwoop, and settled on Bleacker Street, Little Rock, fast music
for a slow night. We didn't have much to say to each other and
I drank my beer slowly but Elizabeth tossed down three within
half an hour. When she opened a fourth she took down half of
it with five big swallows. "Hot," she said. "Why am I so hot
all the time?" She unbuttoned her blouse by two buttons and
rubbed her neck with the back of her hand. "I'm always so damn
hot."

I opened another beer for myself, thinking me too.

Bottles were being broken down the street at the Icehouse.
Yee-ha.

We sat close together on the floor and listened to the radio.
The volume faded in and out and for a time she fiddled with the
dial, giving up on Little Rock and now earnestly searching for
Minneapolis. Finally she gave up, leaving us to listen to the easy
sounds of KELO Sioux Falls. "Elevator music," she called it.
"Strictly doctor's office."

She finished a fifth beer, then a sixth. "Hot."

We shared my last cigarette. Taking it from my hands, Elizabeth said, "You know, I really hate this town. Nothing happens
here, nothing at all."

I asked her what she wanted to happen.

"Anything that has anything to it. Lights, sounds, music,
dancing. I like excitement but I haven't had much of it."

I told her I had never been further away than Omaha.

"Me neither," she said, then she laughed. "Shit! Omaha!"

I was laughing too and we kept on laughing even though
nothing was funny except the beer and suddenly the volume on
the radio was too loud and when Elizabeth reached to turn it
down she spilled her beer. I reached to pick it up but before I
could I felt her arms around me, her weight pushing me to the
floor where I lay in the spilled beer and she was kissing me, hot,
touching me, hot, and I kissed her back, hot.

She shrugged and struggled out of her blouse and jeans and
I did the same. I was thinking we would move to the bed but
she was in a hurry. The spilled beer wetted my back and Elizabeth hovered over me, her breasts red and the nipples redder.
Hers was not the body I had imagined beneath the waitress
uniform. Naked, she was coarse, ridged, veined. She took my
erection with both her hands and tried to force it inside of her,

to take it for herself, but I wasn't ready and she began frantically to rub me up and down. Her hands hurt rather than pleased me but I grew sufficiently hard all the same and she pushed herself onto me and began to sway back and forth, her eyes half closed. I bucked to meet her and she moaned but we couldn't find a rhythm, we were both the aggressor, and when I held her by the hips to gain some balance, she leaned forward and lay flat against me. I could smell the beer on her breath, on her shoulders, in her hair, stale hot summer beer. I opened my mouth to catch my breath and she filled it with her tongue, then ground her hips down, down. I was not in love. I was led and I followed. Beer bottles crashed against a distant wall. Elizabeth made a grring sound, then she gasped. I pushed and she pushed back; we made a seesaw of our hips and then Elizabeth was making little cries, urgent and near to my ear. She bit my neck, pulsed, and then began to shudder and laugh at the same time. She closed her eyes tight and reopened them. *Jess-see* as in two words, then she was still.

Her breath was hot and awful and our sweat had formed a pool along my belly. After some minutes she rolled away from me and lay next to me, her eyes on the ceiling. "Hot," she said. "I'm always so damn hot."

I hadn't come and I was wondering to myself if that meant I still was a virgin. What, after all, constituted a silver bullet? I felt that I wanted to do it again, to come in her, but the smell of beer and the heat and sweat of us held me back. I reached for Elizabeth's hand anyway but she rose and went to the refrigerator for another beer. Lifting myself from the floor, I sat in the torn folds of the armchair. Juno awoke, stretched, and leaped from the window to my naked lap, terrifying me, his claws bare centimeters from my balls. When I tossed him to the floor he hissed and arched his back.

"Be nice, Juno," Elizabeth told him, coming back from the kitchen. "There's only one can left," she told me. "We can share it, okay?"

I didn't want any so Elizabeth drank it alone.

"That wasn't bad," she said. "I didn't plan it that way, but I'm glad you were around when I needed you."

"Me too."

"Still and all, I don't think you ought to stay the night. If you know what I mean."

I knew what she meant. Buckling my belt, I pulled my shirt over my shoulders and headed for the door. She stopped me.

"Don't think bad of me, okay?" Her hair was in sweaty strings down her forehead and neck. She resembled not at all the Elizabeth of my imagining. I felt numb, tired, and vaguely ill.

"We'll do this again sometime," she told me. "Come and see me at the Silver Dollar."

I didn't want her to be casual. I wanted her to be wind-strewn but not disheveled, dismayed by my departure, forlorn. Please stay, Jesse. Later, I gotta run. But I simply nodded and went out the door. As I was going down the steps, I decided to myself that my virginity was gone because I felt used, or taken, as I never had before. What's next in life? I was wondering, and when I hit the street I found out. Henry Colter was waiting for me.

"I heard you through the door you prick."

I held my hands in front of me and backed away. I might have asked him what he meant to do or I might have started screaming for mama or God or the police. I might have turned and run into the smoky night or I might have stood my ground and bared my teeth at him, hissing danger. But I did none of those things. When Henry came at me, I bowed my head and reached for the earth as though to hide myself below the concrete, the soil, the roots of Yankton. Henry dug deeper and he lifted me with his hairy fists. I had no more questions for him or the earth or the night. He beat the holy shit out of me for the love of Elizabeth Bad Hand.

My bruises healed and the cuts scarred over quickly enough. If Elizabeth ever knew what had happened to me she didn't have a chance to tell me how sorry she was. But then, I'm not all that certain she was sorry. Maybe she was the type of woman who gets a thrill out of her man beating up on a rival. I know she was again with Henry Colter and that later she was with a variety of men, still in Yankton, always in Yankton, aging gracelessly. Whether from my bruises or my disenchantment with her coarse body, I stopped going to the Silver Dollar altogether and though Yankton is by any measure a small town I did not run into her in the course of the fall or the following winter. I was back in school and had no time to moon over her from behind the Silver Dollar counter; and more to the point, it was during this time that I began to notice a change in Rose and I became, for the first time, not her little brother but her shepherd. Not I, he. It was during the autumn after my escapades with Marthe and Elizabeth Bad Hand that Rose was in *Othello*, when she was at play practice each evening until eight, then walked the halls at home reciting her lines and practicing her moves. The performance she never gave because on opening night it was "all too much." During the same autumn, Rose began to talk to herself, or to me, in a streaming, run-on manner, slithering diverse subjects into one, flitting from sadness to gaiety and back again before growing suddenly, stonily, silent. She lost all interest in school, and the last of her friends, a painfully homely girl named Gloria who shared Rose's interest in music, stopped calling.

I spent a lot of time at the library that winter, trying to study books about psychiatry. I wanted to know who my sister was before I would trust her to somebody else. I labored over words like neurotic, catatonic, schizophrenic, but Rose didn't seem to fit any of the labels. She was *pathetic* but hardly dangerous. Cerebro-diagonal was one man's word: she interpreted sunrise as sundown and sundown was ever sundown. Explain that. How the sun never rises but sets twice a day.

Now and then, sitting in the kitchen with Lady, I would ask her if she hadn't noticed something odd about Rose, something different.

Different? Rose has always been different. She is unique.

"That's not what I mean."

What *do* you mean?

I couldn't find a word that would suffice. Crazy, crazed, wacko, loony. I could use none of these words to describe my sister.

"She's not well," I said. "She does funny things."

My mother wanted examples.

"She talks to herself. She stares into space for long stretches of time. She has no friends."

You shouldn't criticize.

"I'm not. I love Rose."

As do I. You let me worry about my children. Rose is fine.

A few days later, following a scene in which Bill whacked Lady with his belt and floored me with a right cross, Rose began to scream. The scream started out to be weeping, a sob, but it rose dramatically into a wail and then a high-pitched shriek that shook the kitchen windows. Bill moved toward her as though to shut her up but there was something eerie in her scream that stopped him short. He stood a few feet away from her and the scream continued, breathless, unpunctuated. Her eyes were on Bill and they were the angriest eyes I had ever seen. The scream was worse than defiance and Bill backed down. Holding his hands over his ears, he fled the house and it wasn't until the car had left the driveway and disappeared that the screaming stopped. Rose stood in the middle of the kitchen blinking and Lady began to cry.

I asked Rose if she was all right.

She nodded but her eyes were blank.

"Do you want to lie down?"

Again she nodded so I led her into the living room and helped her onto the couch.

"Just lie here and relax, Rose. I'll bring you something to drink in a minute."

"In a minute," she said, "you'll bring me something. To drink." She continued to talk, though not particularly to me. I went into the kitchen to comfort my mother, who was trembling. Bill had found a coffee cup full of bills that she'd kept stashed away. She'd been saving what she could to cover those times when Bill forgot to give her money for groceries. She'd been doing it for years. He'd thought she'd been stealing from him so he had slapped her around. In her defense, I'd received a fist in the neck. Which had all led to Rose's incredible scream.

Rose? my mother signaled.

"Resting."

She scares me.

"I told you."

You told me.

We went into the living room. My sister lay upon the couch, quite still, her eyes turned to the ceiling. She did not see us come in.

Take care of her, Jesse. Take care of us all.

I became my sister's shepherd and my mother's apostle. In the afternoons, once school was out, I would accompany Rose back to the house and we would amuse ourselves indoors. We read books, played cards, arranged furniture, compared paintings, baked, or went for walks along the Missouri. What friends I'd had felt my distance as a rejection and I didn't do much to tell them otherwise. How to explain two sunsets in a day? I didn't know myself and so just let it go. I grew a reputation as a sissy or a bookworm because I no longer played basketball in the lot, no longer went into the countryside to drink beer, no longer pursued the girls in my class either for love or a lay. The last of my youth was like money that fell unnoticed out of an envelope because I was so eager to read the letter. This is a metaphor meaning life got in the way.

For an entire winter, Rose circled Bill, leaving him his space and never saying a word to him. During late winter and early spring, he began to spend more time than usual around the house. He was going through another reformation, drying out as best as he could and trying to pick up the pieces without knowing how he might put them together. In place of brandy he drank beer and he made a great effort to integrate with the family, to be a pal to me, a dear to my mother, and a daddy to Rose.

"Getting damned pretty, Rose. How come the boys ain't knockin down the door to get to you?"

Rose silent; eyes on the table.

"Maybe it's cause you don't drop your drawers so fast, huh? Maybe they think you're cold or something."

Rose staring at the breadcrumbs on the table.

"Well, you do as you like, honey. You don't gotta put out for no damn farm boy from Yankton. You're better than that and don't I know it."

Rose hypnotized by the pattern of the napkin.

"Hey, Jesse, did you see that Twins game?"

That spring Rose graduated from Yankton High School. Her transcript said she was one thirty-seventh in a class of two hundred twenty. Friends signed her yearbook with optimistic phrases and in her graduation photo she looked like any other pretty midwestern girl enjoying the lush bloom of youth. A farm boy named Todd came to visit once and told us he was going to the state university at Brookings to study engineering. He might have stayed for dinner but Bill was home that night and we were all too embarrassed to invite him. It was the night after graduation and the May evening was unusually warm. Rose walked Todd out to the porch and though I wasn't eavesdropping, I could hear them clearly through the screen door.

Todd was saying he'd be in Yankton the entire summer and wanted to know if he could start seeing Rose.

Rose said she didn't think so.

"It isn't because of that dance, is it?"

"What dance?"

"The, uh, the Valentine's Dance." He hadn't invited her. His shame and her insanity.

"That was only a dance, Todd."

"Then what is it? I mean, why don't you want to see me?"

Rose wasn't answering.

"You're a funny girl, Rose."

"Good night, Todd. Have a nice summer."

He was the last of her boyfriends. He never had a chance.

During that summer I relaxed my watch on Rose and by early August she seemed to be recovering. Away from school, the ridicule of her peers and the impatience of her teachers, her anguish diminished. She read, painted, helped Lady around the house, and stayed to herself as much as possible. Sometimes she would walk downtown and wander through the stores, buying little things, purchases which amounted to nothing but the shopping for: ribbons, postcards, buttons, magazines, *notions*. She was a passive woman, sorrowful but serene. Bill laid off for a while, drank less, and stayed away from home. All of us, Lady, Rose, and I, breathed easier. I took up with my old friends, passed from beer to whiskey, smoked pot, and made time with girls in cars parked in the country. In Yankton, in the summertime, there is little else to do. I would wander out after dinnertime while the sunlight still burned through the treetops and cross Highway 50, skirting the construction lines and concrete rubble. Progress for us was widening from two to four lanes, two for the farmers and two for people who knew how to drive. Cruising an empty lot behind Gannon's Nursery, I would end up along the riverside, just below the Icehouse. I spent a few painful weeks trying to get into Jean Miller's pants if not her good graces but when it was over there was nothing to tell, much less at least than about Elizabeth Bad Hand. In the fall I went back to school for my senior year and during the first week I was asked to write five pages on my vision of the future, a hopeless task which I settled by writing nothing, not a single line. All I could think of was getting a job but I didn't know at what. Ants in my pants but no bills in my pocket. Back home, Rose got even quieter and as fall dwindled into winter and the first snows began to blanket the lawns, she was almost silent. She seldom answered my greeting and could not be induced into a game of cards, a walk, or a conversation. The change was sudden and I searched for the reason. One afternoon I came home from school and found Rose in Bill's room. His closet was open and I could hear her behind the door, sobbing. Swinging the door open, I saw her flailing a knife through his clothes, stabbing the empty shirts, the overalls, the worn coats. "Yah," she would say with each swipe, "yah, yah, *yah*." When I took the knife from her hand, she bit my arm, then, recognizing me, burst into tears and fled the room.

Is it Bill? Rose? Is it Bill?

Yes.

What did he do?

He did. He did.

What, Rose? What did he do?

He did, Jesse. He did.

It was then that I began to consider finding a place for us. I had always lived in fear of Bill but by this time I could defend myself, matching his fists with my own. But I could not defend Rose, not always. And then I found the house that Ingersoll rented to us and I took Rose there the night after he went to her room and beat her with her own hairbrush. I knew what he was doing in her room and I had to be sure that he never would find his way to her again. In our own hideaway, she took a while to come around but I was encouraged when she began to improve the place, to repair the furniture and clean and sew the curtains and such. But the improvements were temporary: the furniture fell apart and the spiders spun new webs in the corners, dust and cinders settled to the floor and the dirty dishes went unwashed. Her paintings never varied, nothing but pictures of the house, always in black and white. During our dinner at Ingersoll's she was normal, almost cheery, but a few days later I came home early from work and found her in the broken rocking chair. The room was pitch dark and no fire had been lit. She sat naked, her hands on her breasts, and rocked back and forth with a book in her lap. I called her name, first softly and then loudly but she neither heard me nor acknowledged me. Hands on her breasts as though to still her heartbeat, book open on her lap, naked in darkness, she rocked.

Time as fire, time as ice. In every dying winter, every rotting March, is a dream of the coming spring, one-eyed, and an uneasy memory of the previous autumn, the other eye. The snow turns gray and the roads sink into mud. Trees ache and thaw and you are fatigued from the cold of four months, of numb feet and fingers rubbed together endlessly to keep the circulation going. You dream, one-eyed, of what will be in the spring and when the first warmth comes, cruel day of false spring, you could kill yourself from the sudden desires you can do nothing about, desire for green, desire for sun, desire for something you have forgotten since November.

It is in March that Rose comes back to me, returns in vivid memory, sends her voice across the distances to tell me something, to whisper that she is okay, that the sheets are cool and there is sunlight in the window. Though she never leaves me, though she is always at my elbow, over my shoulder, within easy reach, it is in March, on that first day of false spring, that she is most *there* to me, as close as my own heartbeat. The sunlight is fragile and cannot last the afternoon. I stand on the porch and feel the barest warmth on my arms and a breeze comes along, a short breath, to steal that warmth; or a cloud passes, however quickly, and casts a shadow across my upturned face. Spring flashes me, baring one breast, then is gone and I am standing on the porch in nothing but a T-shirt, full of desire, freezing.

As he had promised, Ingersoll visited from time to time, bringing Caroline and one or two of his daughters. The visits were a strain because Rose seldom had anything to say. We would sit, four or five of us, shyly smiling, talking about the weather, the news in Yankton, the coming spring. When I was alone with Ingersoll, he would always ask if I had run into Bill

and since I hadn't we decided that perhaps there was nothing
more to worry about except for Rose.

"You can't take her to the state hospital. She'd die there and
you know it. You've seen that place."

I had, and I had no desire to return or ever to leave my sister
therein. The hospital was just outside Yankton, little more than
a mile from where we were living. Spread across seven acres
were a dozen of the grimmest buildings ever made of stone,
each of them bearing the name of someone from the Dakota
past, Garner, Overby, Holmgren. It was the kind of place where
you could not tell the employees from the inmates, where terminal cases mingled freely with acute part-timers. Spaced-out
Indians roamed the grounds, kicking or tripping on the numerous overfed squirrels. Wild-haired old ladies approached visi-
tors and plucked at their elbows, their ribs, their legs, as though
trying to pick insects from cornstalks. In the canteen, where
they sold Coke and candy and sandwiches, there were always a
number of distressing souls begging money or conversation or
affection. I had once seen a man stand before the menu on the
wall desperately trying to decide what to order. He shifted his
weight from one leg to the other, scratched his neck, sniffed,
counted and recounted the coins in his hands, and squinted at
the large print. In a panic, the weight of a decision too frightening or too overwhelming, he began to fret and whimper. Then
his sobs filled the canteen and he was inconsolable. No one
came to rescue. No smiling nurse dressed in immaculate white
came to lead him by the arm through the cafeteria line. He was
still there, trembling and drooling, when I left.

I had another idea. It formed slowly, the kind of idea that
comes to you in March, when getting out is high on your list of
daydreams. I sensed that as long as we were in Yankton Rose
would avoid people. Her fear of Bill and of the past would inhibit
her from having friends, going outside the farmhouse, or returning to school. I decided we would have to leave, we would
have to live elsewhere. I was wanting that mythical fresh start
and though in retrospect my idea was futile—where you go you
take yourself with you—at the time I had great hopes.

I did not know much about cities but I felt that south would
be the first direction. I wanted to find a place where Rose could
be perpetually out of doors, in sunlight; a place where she could

have a garden year round and there would be no snow or ice or freezing wind to remind her of that winter, or any winter under Bill's roof.

I was bringing home one hundred and five dollars a week and as the summer came and we went to new hours I would make more. If I was careful, I could save close to one hundred dollars a month and I figured that in the fall we would be able to leave. I said nothing to Rose because it was all too far off and I didn't want to give her expectations of anything that I might not later be able to deliver. On the twelfth of March, picking up my pay from Hanneman, I went to the Sioux Valley Bank and deposited thirty-six dollars into an account that would pay $4\frac{1}{4}$ percent interest. Time as fire, time as ice. The cost of dreams, the price of serenity.

I hid the bankbook behind a loose brick in the fireplace, knowing Rose was not the type to search around the house and that the bankbook, even if she found it, would mean nothing to her but numbers. In March, always on the first day of false spring, she comes back to me and tells me not to worry. She says the sheets are clean and they change the flowers from time to time and the sunlight comes in warm enough through the wide windows. Time as fire, time as ice. With one eye on the future and the other keeping the past at bay.

6

I could forgive my father his drunkenness; it was his sobriety that I found inexcusable. When inebriated, he was without pretense and was thus transparent, almost at times likable. The least emotion, the smallest thought, was obvious and exaggerated on his face. He could hide nothing and even in his violent times, when his rage was horrific and unreal, I could anticipate him and thus learned not to fear him. And when he lay sprawled on the couch or the floor or the stairs, his breath labored and awful, he was something enormous to be stepped over or around, troubling but harmless.

It was when he was sober that I would reach for my aspirin. Though no less transparent than when drunk, he would try, in sober times, to present himself as any number of things he could never have been. Generous, wise, trustworthy, hip, fair, shrewd, experienced. Bill Dark had seen the world and he carried the whole of it in his pockets, in his big warm hands, in the folds of his heart. Had he been less obvious and more imaginative, he might have evolved into something of a character like any number of the men who pass their lives away in the dark parentheses of one bar or another, men who tell stories of amazing— and unbelievable—pasts, who spin webs of illusion which, although tenable, contain some element of interest or humor or wisdom. After knocking out Jack Dempsey in a private bout in the alley I slept with Lana Turner who begged me to stay with her but then along come the war and Ike give me a call, you know what I'm saying?

My father, sadly, was a man without mythology, a man who strove, nonetheless, to remind us of his legend. After failing as a carpenter and then as a shopkeeper, he went to work for Sioux Feed. For fifteen years, he stood at the base of a silo and watched grain fall through a steel chute until a hundred-pound burlap sack was full. Flipping a lever, my father would shift the grainfall to a second chute and while the bag was being filled he would stitch up the first bag and hoist it to a flatbed. He started out as a chute operator and stitcher and he finished as a chute operator and stitcher who for all his sins was the man who clothed me, fed me, housed me, and taught me to skip flat rocks, once twice thrice, along the Missouri's flat waters. The burlap ground his hands into a fine leather and the lifting of the hundred-pound sacks rounded his shoulders and knotted his neck. Only his face, which bore the labor of brandy, stayed soft, sunken, formless.

When I was fifteen, toward the end of the spring before my trysts with Marthe and Elizabeth Bad Hand, I danced with Bill, or the ghost of Bill, on the banks of the Missouri River. Until one night when I drank those seven cans of warm beer in the back seat of Lonnie Perkins's Chevy Malibu, I had considered drunkenness to be a somber experience, as depressing as a low mass on a rainy day. I had seen only the afterward, the head-aches and hangovers, rage and weeping, and had heard my father laugh only in sorrow. I'd had no idea it could be so convivial, getting bombed out of your skull, or that it was something one could easily do with one's worst enemy. The drunk, I learned, is another kind of wise man, his wisdom hollow but jovial, his heart decayed but forever swollen with intent. He doesn't have to spit and follow the flight of his silver gob to know which way the wind is blowing because he never feels the wind. He takes all that in life is thorny or delicate or raveled or insane and he puts it into a glass and he swallows it down. Nothing in alcohol but alcohol? He swallows and he always pours another.

I was out until well past midnight, slugging it down as Lonnie Perkins and Henry Colter took turns with Ginny What's Her Name while Lonnie's little brother, Carl, and I lay back and watched the stars which were sharp and long and silver in a sky that wouldn't sit still. Riding home in Lonnie Perkins's steaming car, I was elated to know at last what it was to be drunk. There was nothing to it, no mystery to be unraveled, no language needing translation. I staggered in the kitchen door and the wisdom of it all, the simplicity, was overwhelming. Bill was waiting up for me and he too stood reeling, brandy glass in hand, and looked at his shit-faced son with a kind of inarticulate pride. Red eyes peered into red eyes. Our breaths struggled for dominance in the kitchen sky. Leaning toward the kitchen table, he set down his glass and I sensed he was about to embrace me. "Daddy," I said, and I fell, and I loved him, a disgusting and helpless love. And I fell, and I loved him, all the way to the kitchen floor.

Now and then when I was young we would call the police in the midst of one of Bill's tantrums. Once when he beat Lady for some long-forgotten reason, Rose sneaked down the stairs and used the kitchen phone to call the emergency number. She was ten years old at the time and Bill caught her just as she was giving the address to the desk sergeant. By the time the patrol car pulled up, the house was hushed and buttoned down. Bill answered the door.

"Got a call from some little girl," the cop said. "She said there was some trouble here."

"You're kidding," Bill said. "You sure about the address?"

"I think so," the cop told him. Then he checked his report book.

Bill invited him in and he stood tall and dark in the lobby, glancing around. Rose and I sat in the living room, our faces pale in the glow of the television. A bowl of potato chips was on the floor next to us and we must have looked for all the world like a content little pair. The cop ducked his head in and said hello. To Rose he said, "You the one who called us, honey?"

She shook her head.

"Sounds to me," Bill said, "like a false alarm. Some prank or something. Kids these days."

The cop agreed. "Yeah, kids. We gotta deal with this sort of thing all the time. But this time I had no idea . . ."

"You can stay for coffee if you like. I'll get Lady to make some."

Lady was locked in the bedroom upstairs.

"Thanks no," the cop told him. "Just answering a call, like I said. Looks like it was for nothing."

He turned to go and I could see the fear in Rose's eyes as she watched, or pretended to watch, some bewildering game show. People were wearing funny costumes and falling into tanks of water. The front door closed and we heard the cop's steps trailing away. His car drove off and then Bill was in the living room, standing between us and the television set, a towering man who was slowly taking off his wide black belt.

The night Lady lost her voice, I was the one who called the police. This time it was the sheriff who came, since he was on duty that night. I met him at the door and breathlessly told him all that had transpired. Bill was trapped and he wriggled.

"Boy says you kicked his mother and she's hurt bad. That true?"

"Lying little shit. He's making it up, trying to get back at me cause I whipped him."

"Mind if I see Lady?"

"Yes I do. She's had a fall, down these steps here, and she's upstairs resting."

The sheriff was a patient man. "I'd like to see her all the same."

Bill folded his arms. "That'll take a warrant."

"I'll be back in the morning."

And in the morning my mother was in the kitchen making breakfast when he came. Though it was mid-autumn and the day was still warm, she wore a heavy turtleneck sweater and sat calmly at the kitchen table while the sheriff asked her questions. Her voice was gone and she could only write her replies.

"What happened to your voice?"

" 'Bad cold. Laryngitis.' "

"Are you badly hurt?"

" 'No.' "

"How did you hurt yourself?"

" 'Fell down the stairs.' "

"Anything broken?"

" 'No.' "

"Your son says your husband beat you. Did he?"

" 'No.' "

Not that our sheriff was a complete fool. When my mother failed to regain her voice, it was obvious she had more than laryngitis. The sheriff dropped by from time to time and he always asked the same questions. But Lady refused to accuse Bill, refused to point a finger at him and say that it was he who took her voice from her, that the last shadows of her speech were like stains on his brown boots.

The law within a family, the domain of a father, is strangely sacrosanct, no matter how miserable that family may be. There was no protection for my mother, my sister, or myself outside of the protection we afforded each other. We learned how useless it was to call the police. Lady began to call God and Rose called for something distant and deep and unknowable within herself. I do not know who or what I was calling, as I have never known, but I was calling all the same.

We spent the winter learning to listen to my mother's gestures, the language of her hands. Hooked index fingers meaning *sit down*. A fist emerging from the heart: *to want*. Fingertips to the forehead: *reflection*. We learned to look at her when she spoke to us, her hands held upward to her face, touching her eyes, her lips, her chin. She found a friend on the other side of town with whom she could converse, a deaf-mute who took in sewing and would have to set the thread and needle to her lap to get a word in, a sign, then pick it all up again without missing a stitch. In the space of a winter, Lady was just as fluent but Bill took many more months to understand her. It troubled him to look at her and he would often ask me to translate for him, being too drunk or guilty himself to cast his eyes upon the everlasting, *speaking* evidence of what he'd done to her. The house was more quiet than ever. There was Lady's radio, the sound of Bill's boots on the stair, Rose in the next room turning and turning in her bed. Sometimes in the night I could hear my mother moan, a desolate and unknowable verb, and by the time the spring sun dried the mud on the porch steps and the first weeds were climbing that glittering foundation, I had given up all hope that her voice would ever heal itself, that she would ever say my name, or her own, aloud.

There are times when I wish to remember a father of other dimensions and I mine my memory for the thin ore of his kindness. There were moments, fleeting, when he seemed large and warm to me, but all of these moments seemed to belong to my earliest youth, a time that defied memory. The world of men is three parts brute and one part poet and I have a vague and shifting memory of my father walking with me along the banks of the Missouri as the sun slipped like a warm yolk over the summer horizon. In my memory, there is very little imagery, only that of a tall masculine presence leading me over the rocks and puddles and high weeds. He may have taken me by the hand or he may have lifted me now and then over those obstacles I could not manage alone but I have no memory of his touch or his aid, only of his presence, his pervading nearness. I follow this presence away from the town, toward the east, away from the dying summer sun, and we walk in the same direction as the river's flow, that presence and I, that presence to which I bestow the name Father, and I follow him like a helpless shadow toward night.

7

A dry spring, my mother's hands told me, means fewer mosquitoes in the summer.

"Do you think so?"

She nodded, signaling: It never fails. The mosquito eggs won't hatch without rain and the sun burns them. No rain, no bugs.

She cleared the lunch dishes from the table and began to run water in the sink. Lifting her wet hands, she asked me if I wanted more coffee.

Don't go just yet. I have to talk with you.

I rose and took a dish towel from the rack and began to dry the dishes she left on the counter. Lady was humming. The sound at least approximated humming, a high, throatless kind of moan, drawn out into notes. Finishing the last of the dishes, she shook her hands over the sink and signaled to me how happy she was to see the springtime. Winter was long. Drying her hands, she lit a cigarette and sat again at the kitchen table.

"I thought you'd quit smoking."

Does it bother you?

"No."

I needed something. For my hands. Something to do.

It was hard for her to smoke and hand-signal at the same time. She would light a cigarette, hold it to her lips, take a drag, then put it in the ashtray so she could use both hands for speaking, signaling. She blinked when the smoke hung near her eyes. For my hands. Something to do. It occurred to me for the first time that my mother had no way of talking to herself.

I've been thinking, she said.

"Yes?"

She lifted her cigarette, puffed it, and put it down. I've been thinking, she repeated.

86

I said I was listening, which meant I was watching. Her hands were at rest in the vicinity of her forehead, still making the sign for thinking. It was her way of emphasizing something that she was sincere about, by holding a gesture or a signal. Manual italics.

Thinking about what to do.

"What to do?"

About my life.

She held the signal for life, which also meant "all of me." I have been thinking thinking thinking about what to do about all of me all of me.

"And?" I was growing impatient. I caught myself drying dishes that were already dry.

I've decided to move out.

I dropped the plate and it shattered on the floor. Lady hurried to help me sweep up the bits of porcelain and she patted my face to tell me I was forgiven.

Are you happy? she asked me. Happy that I'll be with you?

"No more than Rose will be."

But I can't come right away. I'm not ready, I need time.

"When?"

The week after this. Or the week after. I have to do something.

"Like what?"

That's my business—thumbs to her chest—*mine*.

"I just meant . . ."

I know. One more thing.

"Name it."

Not a word to Rose. She mustn't know.

"That won't be easy. She asks about you all the time."

Promise me.

I promised. Already I was imagining all that I would have to do to be ready for her. We would need another bed, a dresser, sheets, and I would have to renovate one of the dilapidated upstairs rooms. To do all that without telling Rose would be next to impossible.

My mother poured coffee and we drank it in silence. The back door was open wide and the soft spring breeze filled the kitchen. It was the driest May on record, the twenty-fourth already, and not a hint of rain. The winter had seemed to die so slowly, lingering right into April, and the thaw had been sudden, leaving patches of mud everywhere, Dakota clay goo, winter's coda, that went bone dry in the space of a warm week and already the cornfields were weakened with dust. In time there would be grasshoppers and the usual talk of drought.

Putting down my cup, I rose to go and Lady stood at the door with me.

You'll be here next week?

"Wednesday, same time."

She nodded and seemed suddenly unhappy. She sighed, hands lifted: He's never here. He's always with her.

Hands resting on *her*.

Sometimes they come here together. I can hear them from my room.

"Mother, stop."

Next week, Jesse. Wednesday. Come on Wednesday. I'll be ready to go with you.

I said I would be there. She said she would be waiting. I didn't know. I had no way of knowing. Her hands held me like a word. I kissed her goodbye without knowing.

Delirious with spring and filled with new optimism, I made my way home along Highway 81, but my delirium died when I saw Dorell's Pontiac swing off an adjacent road and roar toward me. I instinctively leaped into the ditch to avoid being hit but Bill wheeled to a stop and rolled down the window. "I should have known you'd be hiding behind Ingersoll," he said. His eyes were full of hell. "It always was just the two of you." I rose from the ditch to answer him, a rock in my hand, but he sped off and when I threw the stone in his direction it fell short and clattered down the country road. I ate my father's dust.

At home I found Rose in her rocker, weeping.

"Jesse?" Her voice was diminished, a violin. "Jesse?"

"Rose." I stood before her, clenching and unclenching my fists.

Tears rolled down her face. "He found us."

"What did he do? Did he hurt you?"

"He found us."

"Did he touch you, Rose? Did he do that?"

"He found us."

I shook her. "What did he *do*, Rose?"

"He . . . found . . ."

I slapped her and the blow was too hard. In fright, she rose from the rocker and fled to the kitchen. I followed her. She circled the room, avoiding my touch. I lunged to catch her but twice she slipped away. She was weeping hysterically and then settled in a sad half-laughter, a giggle and a sobbing all at once.

"Damnit, Rose! What *happened*?"

Stopping in a corner, she turned to face me. Her eyes were full of the hatred of fear, of love, one or the other. "He found us," she said evenly. "Isn't that enough? He found us. Where in hell do we go to now?"

We shared an unhappy, silent dinner. Rose cried a little but then would angrily wipe the tears away with the back of her hand. I didn't feel hungry, I ate to avoid talking.

Afterward, Rose washed the dishes and despite the warmth of the night I lit a fire. Taking the bankbook from its hiding place, I scanned the columns and saw that I had nearly two hundred dollars put away, something more than nothing but not nearly enough. I decided that Rose would have to know.

She sat in her rocker and stared into the fire.

"He found us," I began. "But we didn't go far enough away."

"We couldn't. We never can."

I showed her the bankbook. "It's not much, maybe just enough for a good long bus ride, I don't know. I'll take a second job. We can leave in June."

She took the book from my hands and scanned the pages idly, as though it were a magazine.

"We can go just about anywhere," I said. "South, maybe. Or west. Even to California."

"Far," she said.

"West?"

She sighed. "Far. I don't care."

"We'll go in June."

She returned the book to me. "We can't go anywhere, Jesse. Not without Lady."

"She'll come too."

"Words, Jesse. You can't even get her to come out to the farm."

I shook my head. "She'll come. I'm certain of it. She's like us, she needs to get far enough away."

Rose was adamant. "Never. God sees, that's all she ever says. God sees."

I was desperate to convince her, to have her know what I knew, anything to solve her sorrow, the same mistake I'd made a hundred times. "Believe me, Rose," I said, and before the words could be retrieved, though for years I would be wishing to retrieve them, to reel in the time lost, to rearrange the past, I told her, "believe me because she said so."

The rocker stopped and Rose looked me in the eye. "Today?"

I nodded. "I visited her at the house. She says she's coming. She's leaving him."

Rose was breathless. "When?"

"Next week."

"When next week?"

"Wednesday."

"When on Wednesday?"

"Does it matter?"

"It matters," Rose said. "It matters to me."

"I'm going to pick her up after work. I'll borrow Ingersoll's truck so we won't have to hitchhike."

"What *time*, Jesse? I have to know what time!"

I should have read the smoke in her eyes or, as in reading my mother's hands, recognized the quivering of fingers. Hunted rabbits, Ingersoll taught me, leave illegible tracks in the dust, erasing even their own footfalls, hiding from death in life. "I don't know," I said. "About six thirty, maybe. Seven."

"God. Imagine." Again she wept but this time the tears were those of joy. "We'll leave together," she said. "We'll go wherever *you* want, wherever you think you can work."

"West," I said. "Or south."

"Far," she said, a smoke in her eyes that I would only remember later, late, and never again forget.

"Yes, Rose," I told her, anxious about something I couldn't name. "Far."

8

Rose found the matches in a drawer near the kitchen sink. They were under some forks and a cookbook she had once stolen from the library. Jesse had brought them home with the groceries but she hadn't noticed them when he'd unpacked everything. She didn't remember. She'd been peeling potatoes or stacking soup cans in the cupboard, or sweeping, or daydreaming. They were wooden matches, the old-fashioned kind made by the Ohio Match Company, and the box said there were 500 inside. The cover of the box was a pastoral of some midwestern valley, Indiana or Iowa or Illinois. They were all the same to Rose, midwestern valleys. On the back there was a recipe for Chattanooga Chili. The Ohio Match Company put recipes on the backs of that series of match boxes and Chattanooga Chili was Recipe No. 11. Each match was one and a half inches long, made of white wood with a red-tipped sulphur ball at the end. The flints on either side of the box were new and unscratched. Virgin. Then Jesse took the box of matches and used two of them to light a fire in the fireplace. Rose didn't know why he'd lit a fire, it was already hot in the living room. She had to open a window so as not to roast. But she noticed that he put the matches back in the drawer when he was finished with them. They were still in that drawer, 498 of them, and the flint had two yellow scratchmarks on its gray-black surface.

It was hard for her to sleep. The fire was hot on her face and she had a headache from so much crying. Jesse was watching her. Her eyes were closed but she knew he was watching her. He was restless and couldn't sleep and he was burning himself up again, as he did when he grew anxious about something. He would light a fire and he would be his own fire and he would burn himself up with worry.

She couldn't sleep. She was thinking of her mother, counting the days until they would go away together. She measured the days, the number of hours, then tried to multiply by sixty to know how many minutes but she couldn't do it without paper in front of her. Whenever she began to count or to divide or to multiply, she went blank inside. She didn't believe in numbers, not even those on clocks and calendars. Numbers told her, for instance, that Jesse was younger than she but she felt sometimes like his true child, conceived by his fretfulness. Turning her back to the fire, she thought of the places they might go together but not a single city came to mind, nor any particular location. She couldn't remember the numbers of the highways or the names of mountains and rivers. Far, that was all she could think of. She dreamed of distance but was unable to imagine another house, another home, bedrooms, a kitchen, a porch, a fireplace. She could not picture her mother anywhere other than where she'd always been. But she could see endless miles of space without roads, horizon upon horizon of distance, a paradise of travel between here and there, wherever there turned out to be.

Where she was was not home; it was a house, and nothing was familiar to her. It was like one of those paintings or engravings so full of intermingled detail that they were never what they seemed to be. One could look upon them forever and find that what looked at first like a tree was really a hand, the branches were veins in the hand and they led to fingers which had fingernails which really were infants' heads or moons or exotic fruit and between the branches were spaces in the shapes of children. She had seen a painting like that in a book somewhere and the farmhouse, to her, was that painting, hide and seek, that's why she wept every day, waiting for Jesse to come home to her.

She swept the kitchen floor every day and in the morning there was new dust. Jesse left poison out for the mice and many died, but there were more, hundreds maybe, hiding and waiting. Rain trickled downward from a faulty roof and the plumbing backed up from time to time, filling the tub with sludge. Flies hatched by the millions in the front yard.

She'd known he'd find them some day. Sooner or later. When she'd heard the car pull up outside, she'd known it was him. Ingersoll's truck made a different music and anyway when Bill drove a car he seemed to punish it. You could hear the wheels tearing at the road and the engine thundered when it should have purred. He'd parked in the middle of her new garden and that morning she'd had to smooth over the soil and replant the new seeds. It wasn't the first garden of hers he'd destroyed with his carelessness. She'd gone out of the house after Jesse'd left and the cold had reminded her she was naked. She'd meant to put on jeans, a shirt, a sweater, but had forgotten. She'd felt compelled to speak to the seeds, to the soil, to tell them who had come and to console them with water which she'd warmed in her palms. But the earth already knew Bill and there'd been no consolation.

She hadn't known what he'd wanted. It might have been enough that he'd found her but he'd been in a mood to inspect everything. He'd opened drawers, pulled down bedsheets, rummaged through cupboards, and had even taken a peek up the chimney. As though Jesse was hiding some treasure in a little fireproof box. Maybe that was all he'd come for, some treasure he'd assumed had long been hidden from him. The drunken had a way of robbing the poor before the rich, family before strangers.

Dorell had come along. She'd been wearing a slutty summer dress she must have found at Woolworth's and Bill's fingerprints had been like glass jewelry all over her, as his fingerprints had been on Rose like bruises since the day she'd been born. Whom had he touched more? When he touched Dorell, did the moon hide its face? Did dogs howl? Did birds throw themselves to the ground and flap broken-winged on the empty roads? When Rose had been fourteen he'd touched her and she'd heard a chorus of dying angels; glass had shattered in her heart. He'd put his hand up her shirt and felt her breasts. When she'd pulled away, his fingernail had cut her and left a half moon along her rib cage. It had been the first time he'd touched her like that and later he'd touched her between the legs. "Daddy loves you," he'd said. She'd whimpered and pulled away. "Be nice, Rosie. We won't tell Lady, will we? Just you and Daddy."

He'd opened the door with his boot and Dorell had followed him in. Rose had been drinking tea when they'd come, jasmine tea that Jesse had brought home for her. There had been no sugar so she'd sweetened it with a little honey. When Bill had come in the door, she'd thrown the spoon at him, then the cup, then

the saucer. Nothing had touched him and he'd only laughed.
Dorell had laughed too. She'd thought he'd come to hurt her but
he'd only wanted to tease her and to look for money. There'd
been three dollars on the kitchen table and some change on the
fireplace mantel. Bill had been drunk but only lightly so, not
like he could be at other times. Rose had followed him wherever
he'd gone, even when he'd gone upstairs to where she'd never
been before. Tripping over some old boards, he'd fallen and
cursed God and Dorell at the same time. Rose had liked seeing
him on his knees. The only time his face had character was when
he was bewildered and in need of help. He'd reached his arm to
lift himself up but Rose had backed away. His touch was painful.
"Daddy likes your soft skin, Rose. Daddy wants to hug you."
When she'd been fourteen, he had made her naked and she
remembered shivering despite the summer heat. When he'd
kissed her and held her by the knees and come into her, she'd
died; she'd bled and she'd died.

But he'd led her to the matches. Getting up from the floor,
he'd gone back downstairs and searched the kitchen. Nothing
under the sink, nothing on the windowsill but a dying geranium.
Too much water, too little water, sunlight, shadows, mites, dust,
death; Rose had never known how to care for, to make live, to
preserve. Seeing Bill again, she'd hurt from her breasts to her
sex, scars that never heal, and Bill had only rummaged through
her house, digging for whatever was left to steal.

She had long since cut pictures from old magazines that Jesse
had brought home and she had hung them on the walls. Portraits
of old men, their faces bleached in sunlight. They'd stared va-
cantly into the kitchen while Bill had shuffled through the drawers. He'd found her cookbook, pens, clothespins. He'd taken the
drawer out altogether and had pawed through its contents. The
match box had fallen to the floor. She'd picked up the box and
rattled through it. The flints had been clean and unused. Ohio
Match Company, 500 Matches. When Bill had gone into the
living room, she'd followed him, clutching the match box in her
hands.

9

The anatomical chart of a broken heart. Here is the disappointment which leads to disillusionment and an irreversible sense of loss. Here is the brief reaffirmation of love and devotion which follows. Note how delicately it trails away into grief and is enveloped by cruelty. This artery of hope is swollen shut; love is a withering ventricle bleeding into itself and hemorrhaging. Here is despair and here is surrender.

Though I was far away at the time, I have often imagined the scene between Bill and Lady on the morning she told him she was leaving him. Her palms sweating, she signals across the kitchen table to him that she has lived under the shadow of his infidelity long enough, that she can no longer wait and pray for him to change, that because of Dorell he has no further need of a wife.

I am telling you now because you are sober and will understand me. My bags are packed and I am leaving tonight. I won't be back.

Bill is already wearing his work clothes, the blue jump suit with the Sioux Feed insignia. One elbow is patched and the other is worn bare. He puts down his coffee cup and stubs a cigarette into a crowded ashtray. He almost smiles. She can see his teeth between his curved lips. "Going? Going where?"

Away, she signals, her right hand coming from between her breasts and reaching outward. To Rose and Jesse.

"Don't make me laugh."

I'm serious. When you come home tonight, I won't be here.

He is slowly grasping the truth of it and his eyes widen slightly, then narrow. "You ain't going anywhere, Lady."

I am. You cannot stop me.

He rises from the table and strikes her, a half-hearted blow with none of the thunder she has learned to withstand. She takes it in stride, wiping her cheek as though to remove excess makeup. Her eyes are dry and clear. She looks up at him and it is as though she is already gone.

Goodbye, her hands tell him and she leaves him alone in the sunlit kitchen, climbs the stairs where she once lost her voice, and goes to her bedroom to finish the last of her packing. There is a box of books and another box filled with keepsakes and female paraphernalia: cheap jewelry, a plaster Madonna, scarves, photographs, prayer books, sewing bag, and alarm clock. Under her bed is the ancient suitcase with the broken strap. She has filled it with clothes that she has mended for what now seems like years, a yellow skirt, stretch slacks from Woolworth's, sweaters, brassieres, stockings, blouses, underthings. She feels she has less than she had twenty years before when she packed the same suitcase and left the home of her parents—the day the strap broke and her things were strewn on the Madison Avenue sidewalk. There was a love letter lost, the anonymous love letter. What else? There is no more room in her heart.

Then Bill is standing in the doorway and his eyes are strangely clear, as though the brandy fog has miraculously lifted, the cataracts gone. Beneath the fog is hatred. "You ain't going nowhere, Lady."

She is taking the bus to Raleigh. She snaps the suitcase shut and sets it next to the boxes.

I am.

He steps into the room and something like a cloud passes over the sun. She sees the chain in his hand and fears that he will strike her with it. It is a chain with a combination lock, taken from Rose's old bike with the two flat tires.

What do you want from me? her hands ask him. What more?

The combination to the lock was three four five. I knew that and Rose knew that but Lady did not.

"You ain't going, Lady. You can't."

Put down that chain.

He lays the chain on her bed and towers over her. His right hand is trembling. "Stay," he says.

She signals that she is afraid of him. As I have always been. But I am going. I can't—

His right hand slaps her face and with his left hand he forces her to the bed. She strikes him in self-defense but her blows are like gravel, almost painless against the stone of his. He continues to slap her and then with a curled fist, he silences her. When she awakens, she is chained to the bed. Her hands, bound together, are muted.

Bill is standing over her, his breath labored, leaving a vapor which trails downward to her face. She opens and closes her hands to him as if to say please.

His rage has subsided and the fog returned to his eyes. "See how far you get," he tells her and he leaves the room. She can hear the screen door slam, the car pull away. The day will last forever. Late in the afternoon, he is back and Dorell is with him. Doors opening and closing, the noise of their bed, laughter from down the hall. Rose coming in the back door, match box in hand. Ingersoll, in the last minutes of his life, buys me a beer before we leave to get my mother.

If she smells the smoke, she cannot scream. Her hands, chained to the bed, open and close like the beating of a large bird's wings or the pulse of a heart; my mother's hands open and close.

The Legend of Veronica

*Since beginningless time and into the never-
ending future, men have loved women without
telling them, and the Lord has loved them
without telling, and the void is not the void
because there's nothing to be empty of.*
                                    —JACK KEROUAC

*"They think they're having fun, smoking dope
and messing with the young girls of our town.
These drug dealers, they don't know what fun
is. I catch me one, just one, I'll show him
all the fun I can have with the butt of my
gun. You can count on that."*
          —LIEUT. J. E. BOLT, VERMILLION P.D.,
           in an interview reprinted in the
           Pioneer Shepherd Weekly

1

For what seemed like a long time but was in fact the normal
succession of spring through summer months, Harper went to
Billy for her grass, but now Billy is gone. Since August he'd
been talking about Chicago as home—the place where his space
was—and now, just past Thanksgiving, he is two months
gone, leaving Harper without a connection and, less easily con-
cluded, without a lover.

He who is alone, wrote Rilke, will be long alone. Will waken,
read, and write long letters. But Harper has eyes for the summer,
the past one, and winter is only a wasteland of time, threatening
to undo even the summer.

And through the barren pathways, up and down, restlessly
wander where dead leaves blow.

When she speaks to herself, her voice is familiar. Harper, twenty
years old and frightened by her youth, addresses herself as She.
"Back to work, She. It's getting late." "She, there is nothing to
smoke, not so much as a roach." "She, you are aging."

Her Vermillion apartment which she shares with Lisbeth is

dark this night and though twice she has leaned to light a lamp, each time she has changed her mind. Darkness, its neutrality, suits her. Having begun the evening intent upon her work, her photography, she has suddenly shuffled her prints into a box and kicked it into a corner. Better to stare uselessly out the window. She stares for an hour and although there is nothing new to her— a gray frame of black and leafless trees, a parked station wagon, still shadows, ribbon of cracked sidewalk, sagging wooden porch—she sees past seeing. Her eye, sharpened by her art, sees things outside in, as though her face reflected in the window is the true one. She is mourning but tells herself it has nothing to do with Billy. Billy can go where he likes and mournfulness, like rain, simply happens. They had slept well together despite his restlessness, had listened endlessly to music, gotten high, read books, and traded bitter biographies. He had found her too serious and she'd felt he was irresponsible. Worse, he was careless. He had a way of bestowing on her little distances, solitudes, like offhand gifts, trinkets of time to herself that she never asked for. He had given her marijuana which she thanked him for but had also given her speed—Dexedrine—for which she'd despised him. She returned this last favor by offering him mescaline, to which he reacted badly. "Down to the ground, Harper. I don't think I'm gonna get back up." She'd been sorry. No more pills for She. She only smokes. Mournfulness on winter nights a time for finding grass.

Nights without Billy go uncounted and some pass better than others.

She goes to the kitchen, lifts a pan from the sink, rinses it, and puts water on to boil. Reaching for the coffee, she sees a photo long ago taped to the cupboard. Herself at the river's muddy edge, jeans rolled up, testing the current with an outstretched foot. Billy took that picture. It was the hottest day of summer and she'd burned innocently under a white sun. That night, her skin aflame, she had slept uneasily on her belly and in succeeding nights her skin had come away in flakes that left her itching. In the middle of the night Billy slapped her ass and lit a stick of Colombian.

"It's four in the morning. Don't you ever stop smoking?"

"Why should I?"

She kicked the sheet to the floor and took the joint he offered between thumb and forefinger. "I'll never sleep again."

"You'll sleep tomorrow."

She inhaled, held, gasped. "I want you to hold me but my skin hurts."

When he slept and she could not, she burned anew.

She measures the coffee with a teaspoon and pours boiling water over it and through a filter. The cup warms her hands. She considers loading her camera with night film and infra-red lens and going into the hardening darkness to record or capture or gather or invoke, whatever one does with the memory eye. She knows she is no artist and has no firm idea of what she's after, but her camera, what she does with it, fills her time. She is unsure about the word *snapshot*, knowing how other photographers she knows, intellectuals all, claim to loathe the word, photography to them being so much more than a forefinger exercise, a mindless blink and print. She only knows that she wants a live and indelible art for a live and erasable world, nothing less. She takes the coffee back to her room and is face to face with a black and white blowup of herself and Lisbeth. She is everywhere; she inhabits the walls she walks among. She is young and yet aware of each day of her recent past, each one a pebble marking the way backward. She sips and the coffee burns her tongue. When she lights a cigarette the tobacco has no taste.

It is Friday night in a college town in South Dakota. Students outnumber the locals and the streets belong, from September to June, to them. In Vermillion, there are four policemen, six campus guards, five stoplights, five motels, seven cafés, and endless elm trees dying slowly of a Dutch disease. On Friday night, in winter, the streets are as empty as a junkie's eyes, except for Main Street, which is strung with beer bars and concert joints, each lined with pinball, *foosball*, nickel-debt machines, the little strip is called Downtown, har de har. There are two cinemas and two nightclubs, the Red Rock Lounge and the Grande Finale, where the bands come and go amid pools of red beer and a haze of marijuana. Lambda Chis get laid in Prentiss Park by Phi Delts and now and then someone gets married. The dancing crowd, smaller in number as time goes by, goes to the Wonder

Club on Highway 50 where the staring and humiliation last until 2 A.M. Sioux City is thirty miles south, Sioux Falls sixty miles north, and Yankton twenty miles west, or twenty-three, depending upon where you start from. Harper, a Lambda Chi two years ago, lives on the second floor of a wood-frame house at the north end of High Street, a popular place in name alone, and on this first night in December she is feeling far from Main Street, far from Friday night, far from Billy, far.

It's not his fault, she reasons. He wanted to go home. Home is where he is, not here.

Taking the box of photos from the corner where she's kicked it, Harper lifts a sheaf of prints from a brown envelope and scatters them across the bed. A dozen Billys smile, wave, glare, laugh upward to her. Billy in faded jeans, bare-chested, by the river. Billy asleep beneath a walnut tree. Billy in the kitchen, hung over, a piece of toast between his fingers. Billy's long face doubled by the mirror before him.

"You've had other boyfriends," her father said. "You'll have more."

Billy said: "I'm not the lasting type. I don't stay anywhere. I belong to myself, look elsewhere."

She believes in endurance, or wants to believe in it. You get used to someone and the world takes on a focus, a rhythm, you think you've searched for. He's gone and she wonders whether she wants him back or not.

Before he left she asked him how he'd remember her.

"You're the only thing I'll miss in this shitty little town."

"Is missing me remembering me?"

"Life goes on for years," Billy told her. "Years and years, Harper."

He took me for a girl. He repeated the obvious.

"I don't write letters," he said.

Nor does she.

Hell is other people, Sartre told her in a play.

Wadding newspaper, she lights a fire in Lisbeth's room, the fireplace being there instead of her room. She has the better windows. Harper wants light and Lisbeth fire, a fair exchange, but on this night Lisbeth isn't home, at the Grande Finale no doubt, and Harper can do as she wants.

The firewood, stolen from an alley near Marshall Street, is wet, rain-soaked. It burns slowly and the flame is a dull blue. Harper adds a dry log to the damp kindling and waits for it to catch. The apartment is dark and only the fireplace gives it light. The floor is chill and her feet are numb. Waiting for the fire to blaze, she puts on her boots and goes to the bathroom to examine her face. In the darkness, she presents to herself a familiar shadow; she knows her profile, her long chin, her high cheekbones and compact nose. Beauty, her own, accuses her. Pretty girls have no right to be unhappy. She smooths her makeup with gentle fingers, pats her chin, runs a forefinger like a pencil across each eyebrow. She's had other boyfriends, men as well. Before Billy there was Adam, a linguistics professor; before Adam, Paul. And so on.

Billy telling her, "I never talked about staying."

She never asked.

In Lisbeth's room the fire blazes, throwing shadows like running men over the oriental rug. Harper gathers the photos from her bed and flings them like old leaves into the flames. Seventeen Billys roast as one. So there.

The telephone rings like cathedral bells.

Lisbeth: "Come party with me."

"Where are you?"

"The Finale. And I'm lonesome. Let's get high."

Harper admits she is without. "Maybe we can find Willie."

"If he's anywhere tonight he'll be here. Are you coming?"

Harper hesitates. "I don't know. I have some reading to do. I have a headache." Her mind is on ashes. She adds that she's tired of the Grande Finale.

"Who isn't?" Lisbeth argues. "We'll buy some stuff and smoke it elsewhere."

Harper chews a nail, considers. No decision seems easy anymore.

"And bring some money," Lisbeth tells her.

"How much?"

"Whatever you've got. I'm busted." She sounds tired; there is beer in her speech.

"Give me an hour," Harper tells her.

"Twenty minutes. I'm fading all alone here."

"I'm on my way."

Harper, walking, forgets. Without noticing, she passes the house where Billy lived.

Lisbeth is waiting outside the Finale, her long hair blowing in the cold wind. "It's stuffy inside," she explains. "A lot of people but no Willie." She is taller than Harper, a Norwegian from Minnesota, a descendant of farmers. She searches for men who are taller than she.

"Who's there?" Harper asks without caring who.

"Everyone we already know. Give me a cigarette." Lisbeth is drunk, or halfway there. Having gone to the Finale at four in the afternoon, just after her last class, she has that bar-worn look. It is past nine. "I waited for Dusken," she says. "I guess he had a gig tonight."

A car passes with six people inside. Empty beer cans float from the window and rattle along the gutter. The wind rises and Harper shivers. "Are we going in or not?"

The Grande Finale is worn and without color. It is a place to drink beer, play pool or pinballs, buy grass, see who sees who. Wobbly tables are circled by wobbly chairs and a glass of beer costs a quarter. On the wall over the bar is a cracked mirror and a poster of Nixon seated on a toilet and glaring outward, shitting bombs. Tonight there are four long-haired cowboys playing doubles pool. Their faces reflect the sobriety of the game, the deathly seriousness, as they pass the cue back and forth, their eyes never leaving the table. The ceiling is painted black and the red-tiled floor is grimy. Cigarette butts gather in piles in the corners. When the bands come, they play in the basement, but tonight there is no band. The jukebox is loud. Marvin, the owner, has it specially wired and Harper's headache deepens as she steps inside. It is a place where she feels she has lived her whole life. She met Billy there, probably Lisbeth too, though she doesn't remember. Coming to Vermillion three years ago, she'd been a Lambda Chi for a while; then, itching in her brain, her soul, her panties, she'd dropped out. She had come upon the Grande Finale as though led there. Despite or because of its shabbiness, it had been a place where magnificent things had occurred; her first true taste of grass, nights of rock and roll to bands she'd never heard and would never hear again, conversation, argument, promises and lies. The night she'd lost Adam, or he her, she'd cried brokenly in the basement with a pitcher of red beer in front of her while Willie had sat nearby, whispering occasionally how all she had to do was go home with him and he'd read to her from Henry Miller. The Finale had, in short, history, at least as far as Harper was concerned. But three years is three years and she senses now that she only goes there from habit. She knows the faces, the music, the Saturday afternoon sound of pool balls clicking together, the scraping of chairs. Hangovers, heartache. Sitting in a booth with Billy, watching him roll a number with slick fingers, she has faced herself from an angle, wondering what he has seen when he's looked her way. Tonight she sits in the same booth with Lisbeth and waits for Willie to appear. Willie wears a cowboy hat, dirty jeans with a belt buckle shaped like a steer's head, and any of three T-shirts. Willie seldom shaves and his blond beard is soft and uneven. He has been in Vermillion for six years and every summer he goes away for two months. Willie sells.

"Did you bring any money?" Lisbeth asks.

Harper says she has twelve dollars.

"Willie wants fifteen these days."

"Flutter your eyelashes when you pay him."

"Maybe we can share an ounce with somebody."

Harper says why should they. "I could smoke an ounce myself, that's my mood."

Marvin wanders by, his face weary. "I don't serve tables," he tells them. "You still gotta order at the bar."

"You look tired," Lisbeth tells him.

"Capitalism," he says. "Free enterprise wears me out." Marvin, years back, was a political science major.

Harper orders two taps. "That leaves us eleven fifty."

Lisbeth needs to buy cigarettes. "Why don't I ever have any money?"

A sober-faced student, hair tied back in a long braid, approaches their table, an upturned hat in his palm. "I'm collecting for the Vietnam vets," he tells them.

Lisbeth, for some reason, laughs.

"These aren't funny times," he replies, moving on.

Harper and Lisbeth drink their beer in silence. Harper goes to the cigarette machine and gives two quarters for a package of Old Golds for Lisbeth. She returns to find Willie in her spot. He is wearing the T-shirt that says "Triumph" across the front, referring to the bike, and his smile seems to hide a leer beneath it.

"No deal," he tells her right away.

Lisbeth says, "I told him we've only got eleven dollars."

"My price is always fifteen," Willie says. His eyes are more red than blue. Harper can see he is speeding.

"I'll pay you the rest tomorrow. I'll go to the bank."

"Tomorrow's Saturday, bank's closed."

"Monday, then. Why are you being such a hard ass?"

"I've been burned before," he says dryly. He begins to recount stories of people in Denver taking his two pounds of Panamanian and splitting out the back window while he counted a pile of blank pages sandwiched between Grants. The friends who had called him in the night, dropped by to test his new shipment and drink his wine, then wandered off without buying. Paperless IOUs papering his memory. "I got expenses," he adds.

"Willie, this is Harper, not some creep from Denver."

"Harper who never slept with me."

"Fucking would make us friends?"

"Billy thought so."

"Take off. We'll buy elsewhere."

Willie smiles. "These days there is no elsewhere, babe."

Lisbeth offers, "We can split an ounce, can't we?" but Willie has already moved off. She glares at Harper. "Nice work."

Harper yawns. "I miss Billy."

They order more beer and wait. They are not waiting with anything in mind. Woman waits and time arrives. Harper still wants to get high. Being in the Finale reminds her of being stoned and she hasn't been there in a week. She tells herself she doesn't need it like she used to. Days go by when she enjoys the sharpness of living, the full impact of bruises, human contact, the clear smell of the wind. Not Lisbeth, who weaves from past to future and back again, I was or I will be. Harper lives nearer to the present, telling herself that one step at a time is more than enough. "You don't come loose," Billy told her. "You don't fly very high." She hates landings; she finds rock where she seeks grass. Lisbeth, in contrast, soars and she gives herself too easily. She often comes to Harper for comfort.

Within an hour they know what they are waiting for: Lisbeth for Dusken, Harper to get high. Marvin passes their table and collects the empty glasses, dumps butts from their ashtray onto his tray, and pockets the small change they have left for him. "Go home," he tells them.

Harper asks if he knows where they might buy something.

"Willie's downstairs."

"We know. Do you have any other names?"

"No." Marvin goes back to the bar, returns a minute later. "Thirty-one Canberry Street, second floor door on the left. A new guy who sells real cheap, but quality like Willie's. Try there and don't tell Willie I told you."

Thirty-one Canberry Street looms white in the blue winter darkness, an enormous mock-Victorian house built in the twenties, gone seedy with student tenants. A second-story window shines yellow light and Harper hesitates before entering the wide front door.

"Marvin told us everything but this guy's name," she says.

"Does it matter? His name is upstairs door on the left. Let's see what he has for sale."

They climb the carpeted stairs and stand before the door. Piano music from a cheap stereo drifts outward to the hallway. Arpeggios and trills. Harper shivers, whispers to Lisbeth, "Dealers always want to get laid. Let's buy some stuff and take off. I'm in no mood for parties."

Lisbeth nods and they knock. Footsteps, gentle as a child's, sound from the other side of the door and the music abruptly stops.

"Who?" says a voice.

"You don't know us," Lisbeth answers.

"Good enough." He opens and stands before them, an average-sized man, slightly thin, with long unbrushed hair, pleasantly wary eyes, a joint in one hand and a glass of red wine in the other.

"I'm Lisbeth. Marvin sent us."

"Harper."

He offers a nod and the mosaic of a smile. As so often happens in Vermillion, Harper feels she has seen him before. It's a small town and no one is entirely anonymous. They enter and remove their coats. Except for the window, the apartment is unremarkable, a floor with scattered pillows, books, open magazines, a stereo mounted on a low stack of bricks, various bottles, a lamp, stacked ashtrays. There is only one chair and it is covered with clean laundry. But the window. Even in the dark, with no illumined view, it is magnificent. Extending from the floor to the ceiling, wall to wall, facing west, it dominates the room, making, with the darkness as cover, a vague mirror of the interior. Beyond, Harper knows, is a view of the west Sioux Valley, a flat reach of fields outlined with treelines, extending fifty miles westward, toward Yankton and beyond. In the winter, it is lunar, suggesting a remoteness, a distance immeasurable but not endless.

''Wine?'' the dealer asks. Lisbeth nods and Harper says no. He pours from a half-empty bottle and Harper notices, with slight surprise, that the glasses are clean. The dealers she has known have been notoriously unkempt. Billy was. Is. God, where is he when I need him? Harper moves toward the window, thinking, *I* should live here. What I would give for this window . . .

Her eye sharpens and she photographs without camera. Her sense of place is disturbed. The apartment is wrong, somehow. It is not, she thinks to herself, the home of a dealer, and she wonders why she feels so. Despite the scatter of things, there is no sense of clutter; the window promises space and, the shutter of her gaze clicking constantly, Harper sees there is space fulfilled. For each of the three walls is a single poster, impressionist (she shrugs inwardly), and there is no bookcase, no dresser, no desk. Two small plants on the floor before the window. The dealer sits cross-legged beside them and gestures to a pair of pillows in front of him. He is neither inviting nor enduring their presence. Lisbeth sits but Harper remains standing. The present tense fails her and she wishes she could photograph the room. Billy accused her of ruining things that way. Let go, he had said, and he had misunderstood. He had assumed that with her pictures she had been trying to distill life, to cage it, to seize it and play it onto paper to be huddled against during the bad times;

when all she really meant was to embrace, and to have that embrace last for as long as is humanly possible.

The dealer puts a record on the turntable, an album of classical guitar studies that Harper doesn't recognize. Then, producing a plastic bag as if from nowhere, he opens it, takes a pinch of green-brown leaves between his thumb and forefinger, and sprinkles them onto a folded white paper.

At last.

He seals the joint with his tongue, blows lightly across the seam to dry it, then hands it to Lisbeth.

"You a student?" she asks, then lights the joint and pulls hard on it.

"Sometimes," he tells her. "Not lately."

Lisbeth nods, exhales a thin cloud, and smiles. "Sweet," she says, meaning the grass. "We're students. Harper's a photographer and I read poetry."

"You don't write it, too?"

"Never. I can't. You?"

"I only read." He smiles the way others shrug: up, down. Not really a smile at all.

Lisbeth passes the joint to Harper and she tastes it, her lips making the smallest of o's, drawing inward. She closes her eyes, opens them, and leans to pass to the dealer but he already has rolled another and is lighting it himself. They continue to pass and smoke, smoke and pass, now two joints at once, and the guitars, southern European, play among each other's arpeggios like vines in crossing winds. It is quality grass, Colombian. Harper decides she likes the dealer; he has neither Willie's rank sexual insistence nor Billy's sophisto cool. She asks him if he is a regular dealer.

"I usually have a little something around the house," he says. "But I'm not a big mover, just your corner grocer." And then, as if compelled, he adds, "But I don't deal any pills. I don't run a Rexall."

Lisbeth tells him no one is asking for more. "We just smoke."

"Usually." This from Harper.

"I drink," says the dealer, and for proof he downs his wine and pours glasses all around.

Harper decides to sit. Choosing a spot from which she can look at the window, she relaxes. The pot is really *very* good and she has that pleasant sense of falling inside of herself, swaying and in perfect balance. She remembers having been afraid the first time she smoked, before coming to Vermillion, therefore before Billy. In Chamberlain, upriver, in a parked car during the summer after her graduation from Chamberlain High School. "We should have done this in *high* school," her friend had joked and no one had laughed somehow. She'd been afraid, she'd known so little about such things. Life on the farm with her father and no one else had made her grow her branches inward. No boys, no drugs, straight A's. Lisbeth smokes and talks with the dealer about whatever cosmic subjects come to mind and Harper remembers that first feeling of giddiness in the extreme, of a height which caused her no dizziness, of the sudden excitement of music on the radio, a song she'd heard a hundred times before but never heard quite like that. And the longing, the sense of having come into a dream and slid beyond it and wanting to burrow backward toward it.

When Lisbeth smokes, she talks. As if in free association, she tumbles out stories, confessions, opinions, insights. Though she has just met the dealer, she already is opening up to him and the conversation is three parts Lisbeth and one part Harper and the dealer. Harper envies her this ease but knows that it is fear which leads Lisbeth into her innumerable blind alleys. Lisbeth can never enter a room normally; she either explodes through a door or creeps in timidly. And she talks because she fears what others might be thinking of her during moments of silence. Even now, talking with the dealer, she is not as at ease as Harper would like to imagine. The dealer listens, nods, and smiles as though amused. Just two more silly buyers, he might be thinking. While Lisbeth has that look in her eyes which tells Harper she may be going home alone tonight. Lisbeth asks him where he's from and he tells her the Wild West.

"Wyoming? Colorado?"

"Just west."

"What do you study? When you're in school, I mean."

He shrugs and lights the third joint. "History, art, linguistics. Anything to help me figure it all out."

"You're not enrolled?" Harper asks him.

"Yes and no. I've got a kind of, ah, scholarship. If I don't stay in school, I lose it. I live mostly by dealing these days, but maybe later I'll finish up and get a degree.''

''What kind of scholarship?''

''Just aid, really.'' He seems uncomfortable. To change the subject he changes records. Pink Floyd replaces the guitars.

''The Dark Side of the Moon.''

They smoke another joint and fall silent. The window, to Harper, is as compelling as a fireplace. She can see the shadow of her own reflection, the single lamp burning, the dealer's arm reaching across to Lisbeth with the joint, Lisbeth touching his hand first and then taking the joint, puffing it, making it glow red. The night deepens and the dealer produces food from the adjoining kitchen: black bread, apples, cheese, peanuts. ''I never cook,'' he says.

''Why not?'' Harper asks him, thinking he will answer with some religious explanation or a macrobiotic analysis, the body rejects burned things, my physiognomy lacks vitamins, fire kills.

''No oven,'' he says.

It is suddenly an intimate dinner party. Lisbeth slices cheese and passes it round while the dealer cracks peanut shells and leaves the meat in a small bowl. Harper has the impression that he has long been on his own. He has a domestic touch she has seldom seen in men her age. The cheese is on a cutting board, alongside a small loaf of bread. The apples are in a porcelain bowl. The wine is poured into clean glasses. He has lived alone, she thinks. Not many of us can do that.

The phone rings while they are eating and the dealer reaches across the floor to answer it.

''Howdy . . . right . . . okay. Sure it's good, it always is. Right. Twelve dollars. I'll be here.'' He hangs up. ''Money,'' he explains. ''Buyers are on the way.''

Harper says, ''I should have told you. We can't buy a whole bag. We've only got about ten dollars.''

He dismisses the notion. ''First time is cool. This bag is short anyway; we've already smoked three.''

''We can pay you the difference later,'' Harper answers.

His gaze is suddenly level. ''No need.''

''I just don't want you to feel burned.''

He tosses a handful of peanuts into his mouth and shrugs. ''I paid eight,'' he says. ''I'll be all right.''

It is the first time a dealer has ever admitted his buying price to her. Not even Billy had ever said what he paid. And Billy charged fifteen like almost everyone else.

They share the last of the bread and cheese and leave the apples untouched. The third joint has gone to Harper's head and she is feeling distracted and uneasy. Something, she feels, is happening and she doesn't know which it will prove to be, pleasant or painful. Her mouth is dry and just as she is about to ask, the dealer returns from his kitchen with an armful of bottles: mineral water, orange juice, 7-Up, rosé. Again he changes the music, this time to the Doors, ''people are strange when you're a stranger,'' and begins to roll another joint. ''Do you ever stop?'' Harper asks him, and just then they hear footsteps on the stair outside, heavy boots, *men*. They knock as if with stones in their hands.

Of the three who enter, Harper already knows two, Mac and Lenny, old customers of Billy's. Mac is twenty-four, bearded, a graduate student who will never finish, one of those lifelong college types unable to leave the university. Lenny is from Chamberlain, a year older than Harper. Once a basketball player and straight as an arrow, he has changed considerably in recent months, growing his hair long, sprouting a dirty little goatee, and looking high and low for the best drugs he can beg from strangers. Lisbeth counts him among her many one-night mistakes. They have come to buy and the third man, a Lacotah Sioux in a ragged blue coat, is unnerved.

The peace of the night seems broken. There are loud greetings all around and the three remove their coats, tossing them to the floor. Mac kicks over a glass of orange juice, mumbles a vague apology, and changes the music on the stereo. The Rolling Stones. ''Shit it's cold,'' he says to no one in particular, then installs himself on the patch of floor nearest to Harper. Gesturing to his Indian companion, he says, ''This is Harold Two Tongues. Say hello, Harry.''

''H-h-howdy,'' says the Indian, looking thoroughly miserable.

Lenny has taken the new joint from the dealer and is lighting it with a fancy gas lighter, specially made for Eastern water pipes. ''His real name is Two Trees but he talks with two tongues. Right, Harry?''

Harry nods and shakes his head all in one motion.

"We found him in Sioux City," Mac explains. "He was getting whaled on by a couple of rednecks down there. We saved his life, Lenny and I."

Harry has just taken a deep hit from the grass and is coughing uncontrollably.

Mac turns his attention to Harper. "So what are you up to, little sister? Buying yourself a bag? Must be tough to pay for it again, huh?"

Harper doesn't answer. With a sickly smile, she removes Mac's hand from her knee then lights a cigarette and blows the smoke unmistakably toward his face. She notices that the dealer has removed the bottles from the room and realizes that he does not consider his customers as welcome.

"You g-got some w-water?" Harry Two Trees asks.

The dealer returns from the kitchen with a tall glass and the Indian drinks gratefully.

"Not bad shit," Lenny remarks, speaking of the grass. "What do you say, Mac?"

"Everyone else is dry. Where's your supply come from anyhow? Even Willie is running low."

The dealer shrugs. "I grow it in the attic, under sunlamps. We harvest every seventh day."

Harry Two Trees's eyes widen.

The dealer, for once, smiles a true smile. "Minneapolis," he answers. "Everything comes from Minneapolis."

"That means Tucson, really," Lenny remarks. "This stuff is Mexican. You can tell by the little dots on the seeds. They fly it in from Tucson after Mexicans pass it over from Nogales."

Again Lenny is misinformed. Billy has taught Harper how to know where her grass comes from and she knows she is smoking Colombian, which has come not from Tucson but from Miami through a Minneapolis connection. Neither she nor the dealer bothers to correct Lenny and she has a new appreciation of the dealer. She remembers how she meant to come, taste, buy, and leave, no more. I misjudged him without knowing him. An old bad habit.

Mac is passing money to the dealer who has offered two bags at cut rate, eleven fifty each. Knowing Mac, Harper figures he'll sell the second bag at a healthy profit, cutting his costs. The same man, in a term paper or during one of his teaching assistanceship lectures, would rail against big business, the profit ethic, the power of the dollar in sub-Vietnamerica. He is a political science major, a confused Marxist who once organized a sit-in at one of the women's dormitories. After the speeches they passed a water pipe. After the water pipe there was a panty raid. "If we give back the panties," Billy had said to Harper, "maybe Nixon won't bomb Cambodia?"

Mac wants to know the time but the dealer says his clock is broken and no one is wearing a watch. "Hey, 3DB is playing in Sioux City. Anybody want to go?"

Lisbeth suddenly looks up; 3DB is Dusken's band. "I thought they were in Kansas or something."

Mac shakes his head. "Sioux City, at the Burning Barn. If we hustle we can get there for the last set."

Lisbeth considers for a moment, as if measuring her courage or her bankbook or her willpower. "I don't think so," she says. "I've already heard the last set."

"What about you, Harper?" Mac again touches her leg.

"GET YOUR HAND OFF ME!"

Lenny snickers. "Guess she means no."

"I'll g-go," says Two Trees.

Lenny says, "You forget, Mac. We're out of gas."

"We've got a quarter tank."

"That gets us there but it doesn't get us back. And I don't have dime one."

"Friend dealer'll lend us a few bucks. Right, Jesse?"

There is a moment in which the dealer's eyes go empty; there is no color, none at all. It is a fleeting moment but it does not escape Harper's notice. Her shutter flickers and it is a look she will not soon forget.

"Fly," the dealer says.

"No all around," Lenny says flatly.

"Right." Mac stands, pulls on his winter coat. "We'll see you around, Harper."

Two Trees rises. "Th-thanks," he says to the dealer. He seems as though he would like to stay.

"Let's move, Two Tongues." The three of them go out the door and their feet rumble down the stairway, gone.

The dealer's place is again peaceful. He removes the Rolling

Stones and plays classical guitar. "I'm not high," he says matter-of-factly. "I was but now I'm not."

"I know what you mean," Lisbeth says. "Something about Lenny . . ."

"Two Trees was all right," the dealer answers. "He could have stayed."

"You don't mind that we're still here, do you?" Lisbeth is not so coy.

The dealer pours more wine. Turning to Harper he says, "Mac called you 'little sister.' You're not, I hope."

"If I were I'd change my name."

To Lisbeth he says, "Then you're *both* welcome."

It is again night and no one knows the time. The window shimmers and they see that there is snow, the first of the winter. They watch while Harper rolls a joint to get them all high again, after the dampening visit of the buyers. The window attracts them and the music is compelling, incessant. Harper shivers but not from the cold. Something is happening to me. She lights the joint and passes it. Something, thank you.

The dealer leans forward to pour a glass of wine and she, all eyes now, measures the blue veins in his hand, the mosaic of them. She sees. He hands her the wine and when she looks into his eyes she sees stones; stones and no fire. When she looks closer he turns away.

Something dear God.

Lisbeth, eyes closed, rocks from feet to toes, listening to yet another record, the blues. She is thinking of Dusken. Harper *knows*; this mood is a photo of Lisbeth, swaying on the hammock of lonesomeness. Dusken, who never really was there, is beckoned back. Eyes closed, rocking to music, Lisbeth waits and the photograph is Lisbeth Waiting. And all he did was take her home one night, after the last set.

Burning longed-for angel, he is coming down but no halo of flame encircles him.

The white cross has left a long cerebral skid mark but not a single sound. "Speed," someone has advised Dusken, "burns your voice right down to a snarl. Not exactly the Caruso sound, know what I mean? Hone it with whiskey and you're a singer."

The singer drinks a beer with one crippled hand and smokes

a Marlboro with the other. Burn with speed, hone with whis-key, sand with tobacco, moisten with love, and get off my back. Harlan, the sound man, tells him, "Five minutes." The band, drummer guitar bass keyboards and Dusken the choir, wanders among strewn bodies inside the Burning Barn with one set left to be played. The morning set, the finale, is due and Dusken is in no way ready for it. The speed has left him and he is lurching inside, grounded, abandoned. There was a time when, drugless, he could sing his way through Paris, Cairo, the Andes, and the back door of his own heart, when the sweat flowed freely like a water and the words were something more than stick-on slogans for another planet. "You got anything left for tonight? I mean, are you going anywhere later?" He turns to answer the voice behind him. She is, he sees instantly, too young, a local, and her boyfriend, glaring from a dark corner, steams in his cowboy boots.

"I like your band. I'm Gena."

He hands her a beer as though in greeting but she can't open it. "I've got a place," she tells him. "I mean, I like your band."

He would not, if asked, describe her as faceless. In everyone, he knows, is a universe; people are as eternally varied as plan-ets. Give her a chance. He is familiar with her terrain simply because he has preceded her there. Headbands and hash pipes and apartments full of music and garbage, like his own. In Ver-million, when he looks out he sees snow and when he looks in he sees books records a broken water pipe empty bottles dirty laundry and a floor full of marijuana seeds, god would they ever take root in the oriental rug?

It's the speed, he is telling himself. I'm a cynic because of all the speed. Remember other images. Conjuring kindness, he looks at the girl in a way he hasn't before. She wears a tan leather jacket with fringe along the sleeve and her blond hair—without headband—is clean. She has one of those jeans-packed tight little butts, a handful happily, and with the stage lights glowing behind her she has a red aura, a kind of visual heat. She tells him she is on the pill.

He says so what.

With five minutes to the last set, he is coming down, the strings are pulling backward in his right hand. His hands, as they often do in winter, hurt like hell. All those broken bones.

How is he supposed to *sing*? Even when he was high he had nothing, no kick, no slur, no pout, no pain, just a nervous kind of murmur that was sleazy enough for rock and roll but it didn't light a fire in his heart and groin. The morning set, the set you can't not play because there are juiced-up eyes watching you, speedy hearts beating something flaming through swollen veins. He feels he's never had less in his voice, less in his soul. He considers the girl at his side and wonders how she would like to crawl blond and naked into the ice of him, pill or no. The singer dies of no song.

"I mean, if you've got a girl around already, that's cool. I don't want to, you know, bug you or anything."

"Walk away," he thinks he says, then realizes he has not said it aloud. "Walk away," he says in a whisper.

"I asked the bass player and he says you ain't married."

The cowboy is watching the rock singer from his dark corner. I know he is not faceless, Dusken reminds himself, but I've seen those cowboy boots here and there. The cowboy is leaning against a broken cigarette machine, both hands like six-guns in his pockets. There is certainly a pickup truck parked outside. It could very well be red. Styrofoam dice hanging from the rear-view mirror. Bang, bang, Dusken is thinking. If eyes were bullets I'd be on the floor, a dying angel. Gena would weep and no one would play Veronica ever again.

He says to Gena, "Your boyfriend is waiting."

Gena shrugs. "He does that a lot. Waits, I mean. I can find my own way home."

Radio Veronica. Dusken nods but not for Gena. He is listening for Radio Veronica, come in, the pirate station from the English Channel, *his* channel. Interference is everywhere, the skies filled with parasites, and the station eludes his needle. Three years with the same band is too long anyway. Three years, four gigs a week, five sets per gig, and he hasn't written anything new in six months. Three four five six. Radio Veronica has gone silent, the speed has failed him, and Gena is too young, seventeen at the most, for twenty-three-year-old Dusken Dark Angel Rock Star Lowe with a whiskey-honed voice.

He rolls the litany of the last set through his mind. It opens with a solo piano, Aaron, an arpeggio that reaches from a romancy sweetness into enraged urgency, a drunky drum kick, then a guitar jam, flash, and off they go with "Trial by Fire," followed by "Crawling Through Midnight," which dissolves into a smoky "Rock Me Baby," lifts again toward daylight with "Third Last Song" and then the finale, "Veronica," the lid-lifter. Trip-hammer rock through and through, the one meant to leave them on the floor gasping or to blow them out the smoky doorway into the black night.

"You gonna play 'Veronica' tonight?" Gena asks. "Play 'Veronica' for me."

Just for you, he is thinking.

She says she has a bag. "Panama Red, no shit. My brother bought it in Omaha. We can take a bath. Get high."

The words are senseless but they always want to hear it; the blade in his voice sends them where they want to go. Veronica made me, Veronica slayed me.

"Sing," she tells him. She lights a cigarette that isn't tobacco and hands it to him. "Go on."

Aaron is fiddling with his keyboard, Diamond is tuned and waiting.

"Be here after the set," Dusken tells the girl. "I'll know how to find you."

Words and music by Dusken Dark Angel.

Harper Adams, at the window, smokes a cigarette à la Dietrich. Lisbeth, stretched across the floor, sleeps and is watched over by the dealer, their guardian this night. Dawn, Harper considers, cannot be far off, but she is wildly awake, sensitive to the least sound, the subtlest movement. Saturday. Today will be Saturday and if the sun comes the snow will melt, leaving mud, black pools, a dampness in the air. Watching the window, she waits for dawn as though waiting for the postman who may or may not bear with him a letter in her name.

The dealer changes the music and Lisbeth stirs. "We should go home," she says sleepily.

Harper turns away from the window and the dealer looks into her eyes. She meets his gaze and for a moment it is as though they are holding hands across a table, fingers entwined over oak. "Soon," she says to Lisbeth. "You should wake up a bit first."

The dealer offers to make coffee. "It's only instant but I have a hotplate so we can boil water."

"I'll help," Harper tells him.

His kitchen is small and crowded. The oven, broken and disconnected, is used as a cupboard, spare storage. The dealer has sacrificed kitchen space to keep his living room simple and organized. Leaning over the sink, Harper fills a pan with water and turns on the hotplate while the dealer rummages for coffee, sugar, spoons, cups. They bump asses in the cramped darkness and then, shoulder to shoulder, watch the water begin to boil.

If he touches me I'll scream.

No I won't.

He lifts the hissing pan and fills the cups with water. She stirs with a bent spoon and they take their cups into the living room where Lisbeth is waiting for them. A bluish dawn light stains the window.

"I dreamed," Lisbeth announces, stretching her arms. "It was a long dream, but all I remember is being hungry."

They drink their coffee slowly, letting it cool. Having waited for dawn, Harper now misses the darkness. Light means I'm leaving. Something was happening and now she is tired, ready for sleep. She too will dream of hunger. Dreaming *is* hunger or made of hunger. The three of them rise from the floor and the dealer distributes coats, scarves, purses. "Is it far?" he asks. "I could drive you."

Lisbeth says she needs the walk. "Nowhere in Vermillion is far. Is it cold out?"

They walk through the new snow to High Street, home, their warm beds. Harper realizes she has gone several hours without thinking of Billy.

"We don't know his name," she says to Lisbeth.

"Whose name? The dealer's?"

"Who else?"

"Mac called him Jesse."

"Like the outlaw?"

"Right. Which reminds me, we forgot to buy the grass."

Harper, arriving first at their door, pushes it open, yawns. "I'll go back," she tells Lisbeth. "Tomorrow. Maybe tomorrow night. Don't let me sleep too late."

And then she is naked and in her own familiar bed. The sheets are cool and the window, framed with frost, is blue. Something has happened. Lisbeth, wrapped in a bathrobe, stands in the doorway. "You didn't tell me you had a fire last night."

"I didn't. I just burned a few things."

"Like what?"

"Billy."

"The ashes blew all over my floor." Lisbeth is too tired to be angry.

Harper tells her, "I'll vacuum in the morning. I mean tonight. Forgive me."

Tired or hungry, she doesn't know which she is. When she closes her eyes, a blanket of warmth descends on her. Hungry, she decides, and hungrily she dreams of her night with the outlaw.

2

Dusken Lowe, musician and reluctant myth, has never fully understood how his music can inspire such diverse and extreme reactions. When he sings there is wrath or mourning, delirium or rage in his wake. His hands betray his voice. He is known to sing with his fists curled against his chest, his fingers tight against each other as if for protection, but this gesture only lends legend to the legend.

"He sings from pain."—*Rock Gazette*

"He represses his rage and his voice seems to ache from the withholding. He seldom explodes but gives the everlasting impression of the imminence of that explosion. His voice is all tension and threat, like a live wire thrashing electricity in the open air."—*Rolling Stone*

"He holds his hands close to his chest as though his lungs are aching. His voice smokes forth as from between those hands."— *NY Times Review of Music, Winter Rock Supplement*

"What does Mr. Lowe hide in his hands when he sings?

Some say a copy of the lyrics, though it might be to our advantage if he would forget them altogether.''—*Regents Quarterly*

He remembers having read that Liszt was forced to perform because no one else could play his compositions to his satisfaction. What he gave, he got back deformed. Dusken holds his deformation in his hands. What he gave he sure as hell got back and those fingers, once long and thin, no longer extend so much as an octave on the keyboard. He would give anything to have those hands hide lyrics rather than scars.

''They only take pictures of my face.''

Once, under hot lights, bathed in red and blue and gold, on a wooden Los Angeles outdoor stage, he had not been able to recognize his hands at all. This was in the days when his right hand could stretch a full tenth and the left was as active with a melody as the right. Under strobe lights, his fingers on the keyboard were thinner and longer than he'd ever seen them and though he was drugless that night he'd had the sensation of having become elongated, an El Greco rock star. His legs reached an eternity to the soft/loud pedals and his cowboy boots glittered. He'd played his finest concert and the sea of the audience, shivering at first in the horizon, had seemed to gather and rise and swarm above and around him while he'd played parts of his unfinished Veronica Quintet, those movements that could be adapted to a piano, bass, guitar, and synthetic violin. It was his one great concert, his first and his last to be recorded, *Dusken Lowe in LA*, the critics should have been there. And in the middle of the concert he had thought he'd heard a hissing from the orchestra pit, a wind whistling some aria in the distance. He'd imagined it was Radio Veronica, tuning, searching him. He'd been suddenly afraid and at the end of the concert his fingers were their normal length, his boots were heavy on the loud pedal, and he even shanked a closing chord. Fame was caught in his throat like a drug that couldn't be swallowed. ''You're on your way now,'' someone told him and he'd wondered if he was talking about the flight back home. Backstage, everyone was looking through him, seeing gate receipts, album covers, posters, three-night stands at the Fillmore East.

''Fame is like a bullet fired by a madman with bad eyesight. How is it then that this same madman fired so cleanly and so true at Dusken Lowe?''

After the concert he had gone to a house somewhere in Laurel Canyon, a producer's home where everyone was snorting cocaine in the back garden or swimming naked in the glowing blue swimming pool. Quaaludes were passed like popcorn from jeweled hand to jeweled hand. Stock in Dusken Lowe had just peaked and he found his agent in one of the many bedrooms playing snakes with three girls. "There's room in our bed, Dusken. Lay yourself down."

When he did, Radio Veronica had whistled like a Dakota blizzard in his ear.

He had difficulty remembering the titles of even the most famous of works. The numbers confused him. Concerto No. 11 in E Minor or E-flat Minor? Opus 6 or 7? But he remembered perfectly the poetic names given to various works, the "Moonlight," the "Tragic," the "Pathetic." Allegro molto vivace, Adagio lamentoso. When he was twelve, his piano teacher had quit on him, telling him he had all the tools, the ear, the dexterity, the fingers, and the timing, but he had the musical sense of a savage. "In thirty years, I've never seen a child who can play like you, but your instincts are all you know or care about. You're like some wild animal. I only teach those who can listen."

Dusken had listened and had heard Radio Veronica. He had found the name when he'd read of the pirate radio stations in the English Channel, stations with few sponsors and little financial backing, broadcasting new sounds, original music across foreign shores from ships always ready to pull up anchor and flee the coast guard. His piano teacher, to his twelve-year-old mind, had been that coast guard and his sound, Dusken's, was Radio Veronica. "We'll find you another teacher," his father had told him, but there had never been another. He had taught himself, or Radio Veronica had taught him, and the boy-savage had moved from keyboards to strings to woodwinds and back again, shaking the trees and the stones and the sands of his sound, discovering in the meantime his own voice, the rise and fall of it, the growl, the slur, the stutter and gasp, the wail and the whimper. The sounds he made surprised him, at those times when he just let himself go. He learned to sing along with his piano, therein discovering the voice that later would be but another instrument in his Veronica Quintet, sound upon sound upon voice, his music. For his father he played Brahms, for himself, Veronica, and after a while it seemed to him that one had nothing to do with the other.

Whatever his father heard, atonal gibberish or incessant bass narrative, he struggled to put a name to, a reference, as though to identify Dusken within a web of musical tradition. "That phrasing," he would say, "reminds me of a passage of Stravinsky's. *Le Sacre du printemps*. Do you know it?" Or: "I've listened to Cage and he could learn from you. Why don't you send him a tape recording?" He brought home books that Dusken never read, discussed magazine articles, the avant-garde, middle thirds, modalities, dissonance, and anechoic chambers, while Dusken nodded at his keyboard. "I'll keep that in mind, Dad." Distracted advice, distractedly filed away.

They seldom looked at each other, a habit dating back to the death of Dusken's mother, ten years before. Each reminded the other of her and the early going had been painful. Though the years had passed, the habit of looking away, avoiding the heat of each other's eyes, had persisted. Dusken's father spoke to hands at a keyboard while Dusken answered to the wall.

He had always played alone, having refused to join ensembles, local symphonies, and the occasional chamber orchestras being formed at the university. But when he started playing rock music, it was a music from the other side of the world, his side. He was uncomfortable in the beginning, playing weekends with a band called Danger. He'd hooked his electric piano into the background shadows and while hidden beyond the lights he had followed guitar leads with flash floods from his keyboard, prompting the drummer to tell him to cool it. Lifting his head, he would see that drummer go into a phony lather and the bass player shake his groin at the high school girls who came to watch. He was sixteen and all he liked about the band was the guitar player, Diamond, who played with feeling and not just to get laid. Diamond had lightning fingers and he always gave Dusken something to play to, a touch of Veronica, the pull of gravity, the release, then freedom, all of it mingling with the smells of sweat and lust and electricity. They discovered that Dusken could sing and so they turned over a few of the background numbers to him, but that didn't satisfy him at all so he and

Diamond formed Third Degree Burn with a new bass player and a new drummer and the music began to flow as never before. The late sixties were like a wildly growing vine in which one blossom had to lead inevitably to another and another and all that mattered was the continuation, there was so little time and therefore no time at all to rest. Dusken had his first taste of marijuana, his first speed, and one very bad line of cocaine. The drugs were pointless but they were entertaining. Getting high with Diamond, he could play a note or two and the guitarist would follow him and although he would lose his discipline when stoned, shanking keys and tossing trills into the wrong octaves, there were certain magic moments of flight or inspiration as recompense. Clapping headphones over his ears, he would gobble a palmful of white cross and play to himself all night long, then go to school red-eyed and drained and full of wonder. Even then, he considered it temporary, the rock scene. He saw how there were limits to what one could do with it, how his ideas were often rejected as too difficult to play or too vague or too weird. All they really wanted was the crash of electric sound, the fast guitar ride downhill, the bass banging on the heart's stone floor, and a voice come wailing from the heavens. Song after song, number after number, the same thing. Even then, in the beginning, he had plans for other things, even if they included playing cocktail piano in a Holiday Inn lounge.

Apart from the band he had his own music. At home, alone with his piano, he left rock music in the distance and went his own way, though inevitably the rock crept back and had a last word on the keyboard he had come to know so well. Using the money he had made on his numerous gigs, he bought an electric piano with headphones and a variety of controls for sharpening or dulling his sounds. He could augment the volume with a series of foot pedals, and record his spontaneous ramblings for study at a later time. In a very short while, he grew bored with the electric piano and bought a cheap synthesizer which he learned to wire himself so he could produce, for example, a hundred violins instead of ten, or add a low bass hum, indistinct to the naked ear but pushing forward a wall of sound against which all other sounds reverberated. For the first time, he felt ready to compose. Taking segments from his spontaneous runs, he pieced together a half-hour tape which he called Sonata Zero, but within the space of a month he had outgrown it and had erased it so that he'd have enough tape time left over for his next work, all piano, in which he played up to twelve simultaneous parts, an orchestra of nothing but piano, and he labeled the tape, Mine Excess, or simply XS. He had for a long time avoided playing rock music on his own but he began to discover that music, like the world, is a sphere. The farther east he would go the closer he would be to the west. Taping a session one night, he could not hear his own voice over the music and the earphones. Later, listening to the tape, he heard what he at first took to be a violin. Only later did he realize it was his own voice, screaming.

At a point where boredom with the band might have set in and thus freed him, Laura came along, biting him like an asp and consoling him with her body. She was twenty-one, two years older than he, and seemed to like everything about him but his innocence. "This, sweetheart, is speed. It pumps your blood and keeps you racing till dawn. You can play as if you had five hands. Take it." He played with five hands and sang like a demon. "I like you, Dusken. I won't say I love you. Come on, let's do some mushrooms and go to bed." In bed she said she loved him and in a cloud of psilocybin he came inside a woman for the first time. She was his and he loved and bled and played for her. He wrote a song called "You, I See You" which the band wouldn't play because it was too slow, so he wrote another, a lid-lifter called "Raise My Heart," which became their first recording, a 45 that sold about a thousand copies and brought Laura's old man down on Dusken for the first time.

"You write another song like that about my daughter and I'll have your ass," Bolt had told him.

"I don't know what you mean."

"Them sex lyrics and all that druggy stuff. Everybody in town knows what you're talking about and I won't have it."

Like nearly everyone his age, he had grown his hair long, then longer. Even farm boys from Viborg had hair down to their shoulders but it was the rock and rollers like Dusken who took the heat in a town like Vermillion. Laura was delighted.

"Your hair is a statement. It sets you apart. When you wear jeans to church, you are saying no to a three-piece suit."

"I don't go to church and I don't have a three-piece suit."

She nodded. "*They* do, though. The lawyers and tax specialists."

She believed in conspiracies and structures of tyranny. "Surprise is a crime and imagination is a sin according to men like my father. They see evolution in terms of inventing things like washing machines and curiosity is only for those who are on unemployment."

When he was away from her, free of the hypnosis of her eyes and the allure of her hips, he could see that her ideas were only half-formed, knee-jerk repetitions, and were not particularly original. Vermillion was suddenly crowded with second-rate poets and boys with beards who were fond of quoting men whose books they hadn't read. Dusken felt surrounded by the oldest of children, self-proclaimed vagabonds of the twentieth century who in their own words had been there and back. But he went along with Laura because she never failed to surprise him and thus was never boring. She gave him books to read, Rimbaud and Thoreau and Hesse and Lao Tzu. She rewrote his lyrics from time to time to give them a bite of anarchy or sting of rage. "I feel so gentle inside of me," she would tell him, "but there are scorpions in whatever I write or say." She bewildered him with her passions, which overlapped and supplanted one another. They were vegetarians, they were antiwar activists, they were Buddhists, they were astrologers. Each role required a costume, a face to meet the moment, a music to fill the space of whatever room they shared. One week she would not go to bed with him because her bio signs were counter and she needed her sexual energy to survive. Another week they fasted, permitting themselves only water or white wine and when they made love he felt himself to be ghostlike, moving the shapeless weight of his body in and out of her without feeling. Borrowing a friend's apartment for a three-day weekend, they sat naked in the lotus position for hours on end, eyes boring into each other's, in search of something Dusken could never satisfactorily define for himself. First man and woman. The animal of you & I.

"I'm not up to this, Laura. I follow you as far as I can go. Let me be a musician. Let that be enough for you."

"I can't help myself. I'm in a spiral and I need you with me. This has to end somewhere. Stay with me."

They drove to Minneapolis for a concert and found themselves in the midst of an antiwar demonstration. The tear gas was more than they'd planned on and they drove back to Vermillion congested and red-eyed, certain the apocalypse was at hand.

Dusken finally moved out of his father's house and into a studio apartment off Main Street. For a time, he and Laura could see each other freely, away from her father's shadow, and they avoided the crowds and the parties and the antiwar rallies that had become such a part of their routine. Dusken would later remember the time as peaceful and he would wonder if memory had transposed it in his mind. They had done masses of drugs, primarily pills, mescaline or acid or speed. They had shared biographies to the most intimate of details, they had painted each other's body and then writhed together on the bare floor, *Domestic Love Landscape No. 1*, they wrote long and pointless poetry, and when the acid wound down they slept like stones on a bare mattress and awoke at midnight to a hunger neither had ever felt before. Then the band began to take off and Dusken was getting week-long stands in faraway cities from Denver to Nashville. He wondered later whether he'd had to leave Laura behind or whether he'd chosen to. Diamond had brought his girl friend on tour with him, as had Aaron. Laura, without Dusken, suffered in the gloom of her father's anger.

"When you're out of town, I go crazy, really I do. I hole up in my room as though it were some mountaintop in Nepal and I smoke grass until that nice blur takes over. When I open my window I pretend you're in the trees across the way. My father thinks I'm studying so he leaves me alone. Why don't you take me on the road with you? No, don't say it. I can't go anyway. Have a good tour and call me when you can, okay?"

Once, when Billy was out of town, Dusken went to Willie for his acid. The dealer pocketed his money and passed a thin strip of paper to the singer.

"What's this?"

"It's a blotter. The acid is in the paper. They use an eyedrop and the paper soaks it in. It's not much to swallow. Just cut a piece off around the circle about the size of this." He held his fingers very closely together. "Just a sliver. Don't take a full circle of it. About half should do, a quarter at a time. It comes on real slow, so give it time."

There were six circles on the blotter, enough for Laura and himself for six different trips. Holing up in Dusken's studio, they sliced a circle with a razor and dropped the halves onto each other's tongue like a micro-host. Hoc est acid, corpus meam. Laura had made a little dinner of chicken and potato salad and they ate happily, drinking wine and listening to Dusken's newest tapes while waiting for the blotter to take effect. After about an hour, Laura became impatient. "It's never taken this long before. Are you sure we didn't just eat paper?"

"Willie said the come-on would be slow."

"Who can trust Willie? One time he sold a bag of dead leaves to high school kids. Told them it was Acapulco Gold."

When another half hour had passed and the acid still hadn't taken hold, Laura asked Dusken where the blotter was.

"On the table."

With the razor blade, she sliced another circle into two parts and offered one of them to Dusken.

He shook his head. "Willie said just one half."

"Willie's full of shit." Before he could stop her, she had swallowed half the circle.

Where she goes, he thought, I follow. And he swallowed the other half.

Some time later, when he reached for the wine bottle, he was surprised to find it was already empty. Laura went to the cupboard to look for another.

"Take it easy," he told her. "The alcohol won't mix."

She didn't seem to hear him. Bending over the cupboard, she knocked bottles and cans aside, searching for the wine. Not finding any, she angrily pushed over a row of empty bottles.

"It's here, Laura." Dusken pointed to the windowsill where he'd left a second bottle.

She spent another eternity searching for the corkscrew, then split the cork trying to remove it, leaving half of it still in the bottle. Watching her poke at the remnant of cork with a kitchen knife, Dusken felt a tingling heat around his lips and knew that he was at last coming on. Laura, having opened the bottle, was laughing. Her face was bright red and she held the bottle to her chest like a baby as she laughed. Then he saw tears running down her cheeks.

"I think we're coming on," he said.

She fought to stop laughing. Finally she said, "Like a freight train."

Usually when they took acid together, the experience was both electric and relaxing. Taking a gallon of orange juice for vitamins, an ashtray, and a carton of cigarettes, they would install themselves in bed. It was best to make love during the first hour or so of the high; later, they would be too nervous, too physically disjointed. After making love, they would talk and the conversation would wander high and low, each and every subject being wondrous or profound or hilarious or terrifying. In the fifth or sixth hour they would have passed their peak and though they would have begun to twitch a bit from the exertion of the drug, they would simply lie back and listen to music, smoke a little pot to cool their hot nerves, and caress each other like lazy cats. Sounds and vision were distorted but not unpleasantly so. Colors had a feel to them. Dusken imagined he could smell his own music. Toward the end, the ninth or tenth hour, Dusken always felt as though he had not slept for days. His lips burned from a weird heat, his neck ached, and the muscles in his hands would tremor and twitch. Only once had he tried to compose music during an acid trip and the recorded results were confused and empty. Acid trashed his sense of sound and although he could listen with an ear for nuance and isolate sounds, he could not play because on the keyboard all keys were equal, black or white, true or false. He couldn't distinguish one note from another. Toward morning, he and Laura would settle back under the sheets, their bodies heated and sweating and the ashtray piled high with cigarette butts and garbage. Looking around his studio, Dusken would have the feeling that the garbage was multiplying by itself, another version of the miracle of loaves & fishes. He could see dust and lint all around him and the dawn sunlight seemed only to illumine the chaos of his little home. He would like alongside Laura and wait for sleep but the acid kept slumber at bay for far too long, and only when the sun had climbed midway up the sky, in the eleventh or twelfth hour, would sleep, both shaky and indifferent, overcome him.

Tonight, something was different. The air around Dusken seemed to vibrate and sizzle, as if his room had transposed itself into the interior of an old radio, smelling of burned tubes and melted wire. Laura, pacing the studio, was on edge and her movements were jerky and abrupt. She was making fast work on the wine, which she drank straight from the bottle, and the stereo, usually loud, was deafening. Dusken rose to turn it down but she shouted above the sound, "NO. LEAVE IT." Then a moment later she crossed the room to shut it off altogether. Moving to the table, she took the blotter in her hands and gazed at it.

"Confetti," she said. "It's just confetti." She turned the blotter in her hands. "Four little circles of confetti. Four *little* circles of confetti." Then she turned her eyes to Dusken and the look she gave him was almost sinister. "This is really it, then?"

"It, what?"

"This . . . confetti. These four circles. I'm holding the end in my hands."

Dusken was confused. He was now feeling the acid in his blood but instead of the amusement and wonder that the come-on usually brought with it, he was feeling cramped and unhappy. Laura frightened him. "What do you mean, the end?"

"What would happen," she asked, "if I were to swallow these four circles?"

Dusken shook his head. "Don't."

"I mean, I've taken acid before, so I know what it's like. But what if I took all this?"

"You'd die. You'd go insane. I don't know in which order."

"The end." He saw it in her eyes, what she would do, a moment before she lifted the blotter toward her mouth. Leaping from the bed, he caught her hand but already she had placed the paper to her tongue. The force of his jump pushed her backward and before she could swallow he had reached into her mouth and snatched the blotter away.

"Let me have it!" she screamed at him, clawing at his face. With one arm he held her to the floor and with his free hand he crushed the blotter into a tiny ball. "You bastard! Give it to me! I want it I want!" And then she began to howl no language at all except one of pain and, stretching out on the floor, she went into spasms of rage unlike anything Dusken had ever seen. Her face went scarlet and her eyes were those of an animal. For a moment, trapped as well in the drug, he saw her as an animal, her teeth yellow and sharp and her hair swinging in tangles like a great mane. Then he slapped her. Once. A second time. She

HUNGRY MIND

1648 Grand Avenue   (612) 699-0587

37801   7:24 pm 08/14/90

S LEGENDS OF JESSE   1 @   4.95   4.95
SUBTOTAL   4.95
TAX   .30
TOTAL   5.25
CASH PAYMENT   10.00
CHANGE   4.75

No fish ever caught with mouth shut.

continued to writhe and scream and he slapped her continually. Later he would wonder why he was slapping her: to calm her or to hurt her? When she stopped screaming he thought she would be all right, but she lay gasping on the floor and staring at him as though at her murderer. Then she said, "Kill me."

"What?"

"Kill me, Dusken. I'll never come back again. Please I HATE THIS I'M UGLY just kill me."

He saw in her eyes a sincerity such as he had never seen, a pleading and a panic, and he knew that she meant it, she wanted him to kill her. It was the drug, it was not Laura. The monster in his blood was momentarily caged and he leaned over her and bent to kiss her but just as suddenly her hands leaped to his face and she clawed him, drawing blood. He was stunned just long enough to give her room to get up and she hurried toward the window. Just as she was about to leap through the glass he caught her by the arm and dragged her backward into his arms. She struggled against him, hurting him with her arms and legs, but he held onto her, knotting his hands together to hold her in a chain of his arms. She fought him until they were both exhausted and lay panting on the carpet. Then, renewed, she fought him again, catching his eye with a closed fist. Long minutes later, when he felt as though he had too little strength left to hold her, she grew calm. He relaxed his grip and she lay gasping on the floor. "The circle," she said with the voice of a very young girl. "I ate the whole circle."

When he felt certain that she wouldn't make another break for the window, he reached across the carpet for the remainder of the blotter. With his lighter he turned it to ash.

Though she no longer wanted him to kill her, Laura was still on a roller coaster of sickness. Dusken debated whether or not to give her a Valium to counteract the Dexedrine that was surely mixed with the acid, but he didn't know what the combination might lead to. They were barely into their third hour and he knew that the night would last forever. Keeping one eye on Laura, he toured the studio, taking knives, razor blades, pills, any sharp objects, then he threw everything out the window. Laura sat on the floor and watched him as though he were committing a terrible crime, as though he were preparing to rape her or to tear the wings from her body. She was talking to him now, telling him how low he was, a serpent, a snail, a slug, but he tried not to listen. Setting a chair between Laura and the window, he sat down and began his wait. The acid was in his veins as well and he fought to control in himself the same reactions Laura was having. One of them, he knew, had to be there, one of them had to cling to the last rock in the sea, or they might be swept into the tides before the speed could let up.

It was the longest night of winter. Laura spent one hour telling him how she hated him, how she had given herself to anyone whenever he was on the road, then for another hour she walked in tight circles around the carpet, each turn tighter than the previous one until she had come to a full stop in the middle. "I won't move," she said. "I'll die here. Try to stop me. Try."

She lit cigarettes and put them out in her own palm. When he dared to put music on the stereo, she held her hands to her ears and began to tremble so he switched the volume down to the minimum and although there was no sound at all she continued to hear it until he had unplugged the speakers and the amplifier and shown her the disconnected ends.

Toward dawn, she began to wind down. She sat silent on the floor for a very long time, saying nothing, looking nowhere. Dusken didn't stray from his chair and his neck and back began to ache. Only when she asked him if there was any orange juice did he know that the night would end.

It was nearly noon when they undressed and got into bed. Laura was as she had been before, and the idea of *before* had a new significance to both of them.

"You hate me," she said, but it was a question instead of an accusation.

"I love you."

"Tell me," she said, "tell me that we're going to sleep soon."

"We will," he told her. "In another hour or so."

"And when we wake up, can we make love? Like before?"

He assured her that they could.

The sky, through his window, was a magnificent shade of blue and the sunlight was warm upon their tired faces. When Laura fell asleep, he could not take his eyes off her. The madness of the night had left them bruised and he knew that his face was a chart of cuts and welts and dried blood. Laura, sleeping under his shoulder, seemed to tremble and the acid had receded in his blood so that all he could feel was a tremor and an ache in his weary veins. He knew beyond a shadow of a doubt that never again would he do what he had done that night, that his fling with acid was finished forever, that he would live his life quite happily without another look into that awful mirror, and that his music would be none the poorer without it. But when at last he closed his eyes and was able to keep them closed, and the blue daylight darkness began to envelop and calm him, he also knew that for Laura it wasn't finished. She would elude him, she would place the unholy circles, one after the other, onto her tongue, and all the love he might feel for her would do nothing to stop her from swallowing them whole.

3

I have these two sad-looking plants whose lives I saved, one after the other, and now the three of us have ideas. We are not so ambitious as to want to become a jungle, or even a garden. The peperomia (variegated), which I stuck under my coat and saved from a drunken hipster, will soon be strong enough to propagate. Where it was before, it was doomed. People in that old house were always spilling beer on everything from cats to oriental rugs to this variegated peperomia. I had no choice in the matter. Had I left the plant where it was, it would have died. I would have saved one or two of the cats as well but they might have been missed. People don't notice the coming and going of plants. I found the heart-shaped philodendron a week later, in a garbage can behind the student union. Someone had tossed it there apparently because two of the leaves had gone brown; not yellow as from too much water but brown as from none at all. The world spins on a delicate thread and sometimes I feel myself wading through mists of carelessness. I never even liked plants. I was afraid they would die in my care but they haven't. The three of us are alive and well and living inside the window on Canberry Street. The window gives us what we need and when I can get the peperomia to offer a branch or two I will make it into two plants. The multiplication will mean absolutely nothing outside of this home but what do I care? It pleases me to see things growing.

That's about as far as I allow myself to inventory. I still have trouble shaving; all that gazing and peering at my own face is bothersome. Dusken says I should be more vain, that my face is pleasant and could be handsome if I would pay it more attention. Easy for him to say; he *likes* to look at himself; he composes himself every day like one of his songs. Here, honey, sing this for me will you? I know my name better than I know my face and unlike other outlaws I know where I come from. Ever since the fire, the state keeps sending me money without knowing who I am. I have a newfound talent for growing things—or reclaiming them from death—and I am a trustworthy dealer, no doubt about it. Willie can complain all he wants about my low prices, but I just can't see myself getting all trenchcoat-and-underground-board-of-directorlike over it. I buy it, clean it, bag it, hide it, then stay loose and low and calm. I am the still point of the turning world and they come to me to get high. The plants look on. I never know whether or not they are sleeping. We are alert, my plants and I, for all manner of threat: a sunshine too bright, red spiders, cold drafts, and the law. Bolt is the law, J. E. Jack Bolt, a man who almost certainly has no knowledge of my name but who knows without a doubt that I exist. From time to time, mimicking any of his matinee idols, Bolt gets a professional itch to shake down Willie or Tom Keefe, the serious dealers. "Open your pockets," he tells them. "Turn them inside out." When they do, everything falls to the floor, dollar bills, dimes, roach clips, rubbers, but not a gram of pot. Who carries it around like that? I've seen freshmen hide the barest slivers of cheap Mexican yellow inside hollowed-out copies of *Catch-22* and lay them behind secret loose bricks in trick fireplaces. Users keep their eyes open and dealers believe in Nixon the way nutty old ladies believe in crucifixions, resurrections, and immaculate conceptions. One hand stealing from the other. Bolt is a tiring old man. He amuses himself with his clichés, right on down to his dog-eared copy of *What Every Parent Should Know About the Demon Weed*. Dusken tells me that years ago Bolt was just a normal patrol cop but after his daughter OD'd he decided to diversify. Special Section, he calls himself and considering the fact that there are only four cops in the whole town, not including Chief Henderson, being a special section is not very impressive. In Bolt's behalf it must be said that he orchestrated the big spring bust. Nine freshmen and a sociology professor were caught red-handed in the professor's apartment passing one bowl. One. Detective (Mr.? Officer?) Bolt took them away at gun point. Ten arrests and one conviction, the professor. In an interview published in the *Pioneer Shepherd Weekly*—the kind of rag one finds in Sunshine Supermarkets and on Presbyterian pews—Bolt mentioned his one regret: "I didn't get the dealer and for all I know he's still around, poisoning our kids." I took offense at that because I was the dealer and I don't sell poison. Willie sells pills, mushrooms, herbs, and cannabis; he fancies himself a travel agent—"takes you where you want to go, babe"—and despite his rhetoric, or because of it, he could probably sell the Original Apple, once bitten, to Lucifer. I pretend to be a criminal and to Bolt I am invisible. It's Willie he wants, and Tom Keefe as well. And for some reason he thinks Dusken is at the center of things but I know Dusken pretty well and although he may be among the select circle of heavyweight users, he never sells. Bolt needs a playbill to distinguish rock stars from outlaws. Maybe he's confused by all the hair.

When I first enrolled at the university, nothing was clear to me. Time was out of order and I confused historical dates with chemical equations. DNA was in 1922 and Napoleon was born in H_2O. One answer was as right as another to my way of thinking and I felt a certain surprise when my carefully crafted term papers were returned to me embroidered in red ink and crowned with an F. This was some time after the fire and I was numbed beyond failure. My student adviser suggested I try a vocational school. "Academia isn't for everyone. It all depends upon what you want to become." Pupa, larva, butterfly? I spun in a cocoon of pain, bright and white and without sound, after the fire. After the fire there were months named May and June and July and August at the end of which I found myself in a classroom wondering if the square root of two-seventy-six might not be Attila the Hun and why not and no explanation was sufficient. After the fire, I turned eighteen and was no longer a ward of the state but I qualified for state aid provided I was a student at a local university. This is what I became, this is what I am, more or less. These days I am signed up for the minimum load, ten credits: three in astronomy, four in French, and three in art history. Only astronomy absorbs me. French is the Babel experience and I fake it on a temporary basis just to keep up my monthly allowance. Art history is one of those classes for the masses. Twice a week two hundred of us pile into the auditorium for an hour's worth of slides and commentary. No weekly tests, no term papers, one final—pass or fail. Though I regularly miss my French class, I haven't skipped art history once. In the murky film-projector glow, I average three bags sold per hour. Hands across the aisle passing Hamiltons. Giotto painting childish landscapes behind monumental figures and Rembrandt inventing the color of shadows while football players roll sample joints.

School was Caroline Ingersoll's idea. The day of the funerals she told me hers was my home, but I couldn't go there. Some weeks later she came to the boardinghouse where I was living and told me she wasn't going to let me rot like my father and, through her intervention, I found myself in this playground where nothing is too strenuous or too complicated and days go by in which I am content to read, water my plants, and answer phone calls from customers. Classes take care of themselves, the trick is not to say very much. Pot and government checks pay the rent. I am living on a life raft and although there are no islands on the horizon there are no storm clouds either. The first year wasn't so easy and, looking back, I suppose I was one of those weird-eyed hippies, aimless and sad, like Two Trees, unable to string a coherent sentence. Autumn was difficult and winter unbearable. White days followed black nights and I remember being unable to read for weeks on end. I could hold a book in front of me as I lay in bed in a pool of lamplight and the words would simply slide off the page. I lost weight, I smoked too much, I didn't have any friends. Hard times. There was a girl, Shay, for whom I seemed to hold some special attraction. She dug the melancholia that she found so rampant in me, that seemed to curl around me like a vine, a sadness that for her was as warming as summer sunlight. She said she loved me and she took me to bed from time to time as if to prove it. In the halo of her passion, I felt neither ecstasy nor lust. There was only a certain kind of relief, a sigh not unlike the sound a paralytic makes when he is wheeled from a dark corner to the sunlight of a window. Shay was kind but she was also cinematic. "I look into your eyes and I don't see the bottom," she would say. "Hold me," she would plead, or, "Touch me, I'm frightened." Further poetry, worse poetry, would ensue but I was cold and so I rubbed myself against her, stone and flint, to conjure sparks in a blue darkness. I sensed, during our month or two together, that she didn't have the least idea who I was, that Jesse Dark was for her some specter in her own misty personal legend, that she wrote flowers in her diary, starlight moonlight, that she suffered from my silence—"You never say you love me"—that she might have been more at home in a Thomas Hardy novel than in my bed. When she was gone I barely noticed. I lived the spring and the summer alone in Vermillion. She sent me a postcard from St. Louis and she disappeared.

I reappear as I was and I like to sleep alone. I like to sleep on the floor with books and ashtrays and bottles all around me. I like to watch the window and listen to music. I like to smoke my own stock late into the night and then awaken, clear-eyed, to the shick-shick of my record player and the album I forgot to turn off before falling to sleep. I am not alone in this world, I live with a crowd of objects and two growing plants, customers come and go, Dusken drops by from time to time, and in a garage behind the Grande Finale I have a 1964 Ford Galaxy, blue and rust, for which I paid two hundred dollars. The tank is always full, the oil is clean, and although there is no radio, no spare tire, no dice hanging from the rearview mirror, no mags, and no seat covers, it is my own, my machine. Now and then, when the spirit moves me, I walk downtown, get the garage key from Marvin the bartender, and go for a drive. I drive west on Highway 50, in the exact direction where the sun should set, cornfields over either shoulder, hypnotizing rows of winter-blank landscapes. In half an hour or less, I cross the James River north of where it flows into the Missouri, glide into Yankton and turn a sharp right toward the hospital, the Angel Ward, the catatonia hotel. Parking my car, I check my coat with the head nurse, turn my pockets inside out to show I have no sharp objects in my possession, no literature, and no valuables. I am led down a dismal gray hallway where I can hear voices from vague distances, cries, murmurs, someone coughing and spitting up soup. I arrive at room 232 which has two grate-framed windows, a bed, a steel-blue dresser, and a rainbow-colored rug. Near the larger of the two windows is a rocker, wooden, with armrests carved in the shape of upturned palms. Sitting in this rocker and grasping those hands is a woman who never says anything, my sister, Rose, unmoving, placid, where she has been sitting every day for some time now, a time distressingly measurable. When I look into *her* eyes I truly do not see the bottom and she never looks back at me. I sit on the window ledge and she sees through me or beyond me or I am merely a shadow filtering the sunlight. I converse with her as though it matters and my words fall like leaves to the cold pavement. I am speaking to myself for myself, for the sake of sound. I lift her hand from the armrest and hold it to my face. I take her chin into my palms and turn her face from side to side; she nods, she shakes her head, she looks upward, she looks away, and I miss her terribly. And when in frustration I pinch her or strike her or shake her or embrace her with my hot hands and the rocker dips backward and forward, backward and forward, she doesn't even blink. By the time I leave, the rocker has ceased rocking and there is no sound, no gesture, and I have never been there except as one ghost visiting another.

4

Dusken awakens at noon in the arms of the cowgirl, Gena, and remembers her boyfriend, he of the red pickup truck and the hurtin eyes. He senses that revenge will be his breakfast, a fist in the teeth.

I took his girl and he won't forgive me.

Gena sleeps like a cat, her body humming. Unlacing his limbs from hers, Dusken begins the bedroom ballet of dressing himself as silently as possible. His shirt unbuttoned and belt dangling, he squeezes the doorknob, praying she won't awaken and ask him where he's off to. To Jesse, he would say, and I'm going alone.

Dusken believes in Jesse because Jesse believes in Dusken as Dusken. The outlaw cares little for the image of Dusken as Angel of Rock, so when the singer comes to visit he leaves his guitar and his makeup at home. His arrivals are usually sudden, he has no use for telephones, and his departures are marked by swift farewells. *"Later,"* he says, meaning, as in a novel, dot dot dot. When Dusken describes Radio Veronica, the source of his sound, Jesse knows he is not referring to the pirate radio station but to the sound inside his head. If Dusken, meaning to shake the leaves on Jesse's lonesome tree, offers to bring along a groupie—any of a number of baby-blue-eyed camp followers—Jesse shudders. When Dusken smokes grass from Jesse's personal stash, he always leaves money on the bookcase. Jesse shrugs. When the Dexedrine of the all-night gigs in small towns burns Dusken around the edges of his heart, he comes to Jesse to get himself together. Dusken can sing, Jesse can't. But Dusken will never cheapen their friendship by writing a song about it. Songs are for memory, or for love, or for revenge.

Their breakfast is a bottle of flinty California white wine and a basket of communion hosts that Dusken has lifted from St. Agnes Catholic Church. Rummaging in the cramped kitchen, Jesse finds the salt and they munch their way into the snowy Saturday afternoon. Clouds blow east then west and a ragged sunlight fills the great window.

Jesse remembers how afraid he was the first time he had communion. "I took the host on my tongue and I was obsessed with the thought that it was really a body; limbs, blood vessels, the whole works. I was afraid to chew and I couldn't get up enough saliva to swallow it whole. I held that host on the tip of my tongue until we got home and then I drank a glass of water to wash it down. I remember saying Hail Marys in case I'd drowned him."

Passing the salt, Dusken says, "It always stuck to the roof of my mouth and I figured if I broke it up with my tongue I'd be tearing the body to bits and be sent directly to hell."

"Do not pass Go."

"Do not wear a rosary round your neck like some crusader's dog tags. Finally, I learned to just let it melt in my mouth like some sacred M & M."

"And you were saved?"

"Pass the salt, I'm working on it."

The snow has stopped falling and the sun is bright, exaggerated, like floodlighting. Postcard weather. Dusken finishes the basket of hosts and pours the last of the wine. They share a joint in silence. It is a Saturday in which there is little to be said. Their laziness is profound and Jesse enjoys the cloud that comes over him leaving him free to think of the women who came the night before, especially her, Harper. He says to Dusken, "I like the feeling of not being in one place at the same time. To get far away, with the barest thread, like a lifeline, between me and the present. I like to drift and when I smoke I have no idea at all what time it is."

Dusken tells him again that he is going to leave the band. "The music isn't mine anymore. I sing it but I don't feel it. Half of what I write is deformed when we play it. Diamond changes things around. He's into arranging, he says."

Jesse yawns. His yawning has nothing to do with Dusken. "I didn't get much sleep," he explains.

" 'Lowe no longer plays what one can call music. Convinced that his tribe of followers has gone stone deaf, he is content to hunker down with them and like an annoyed little boy he bangs a tin drum with one hand while with the other he searches the architecture of his nose.' "

"Who wrote that?"

"I did. I'm thinking of sending it to *Rolling Stone*."

Jesse smokes while Dusken rambles. "I took home this cowgirl last night. Not a cowgirl exactly. It was the western look, fringe and cowboy boots and a heavy ass. Her boyfriend followed us to her place and he parked outside. It wasn't very cool, if you know what I mean. She was making all kinds of noises and I got the impression it was for his benefit, like he was right outside the door. And you know what I did? I just kept whaling away, trying to get more sound out of her, like she was a goddamned Moog synthesizer."

"Heavy on the trumpets," Jesse adds.

"And light on the violins."

"Did he stay all night?"

"I don't know. He wasn't there when I left."

"You broke his heart."

Dusken nods. "I think I meant to. I don't know. I didn't care all that much about the girl."

Jesse rummages in the kitchen for more wine. There is none. "You need a vacation," he tells Dusken. "Go to Palm Springs. Wear white pants and play golf. Drink gin and tonics and hustle the cocktail waitress."

"Write me a script."

"I just did." He can't help adding, "Or else finish the quintet."

In response, Dusken holds his fists to his chest, then he opens his hands and extends them in the sunlight. "What shall I use for hands? Yours?"

"You can still play," Jesse tells him. "I've heard you."

Dusken shakes his head. "Playing isn't composing. I can't play what I hear. One finger holds the note while the others strangle it."

His hands are still extended and Jesse dares to look at them. The right hand is worse than the left. The right thumb knuckle had been crushed and a surgeon had tried to rebuild it with plastic. Impossible, Dusken had shown him, to bend it toward the palm. The index and ring fingers are intact but have become shortened where the breaks have healed badly. The middle finger is bent round like a half moon and where the lower knuckle should be there is only a chalky-looking scar. The little finger is missing its furthest half. The left hand tells another story: twisted fingers lying at the end of a collapsed palm, the bones that fan out from the wrist in splinters. Dusken has never said what happened and Jesse never asks. He is ready to ask when he hears footsteps on the stairway. Someone is outside the door and they listen. Seconds pass. Whoever it is goes down the stairs, then climbs them again.

"Come on in!" Jesse calls.

There is a moment's hesitation, then a female voice answers: "I didn't even knock yet."

Jesse recognizes her and rises to open the door.

Harper wears snow like glitter in her hair and she offers him

a bottle of red wine. "I came to get the pot I forgot last night."
Her eyes tell him she came for something else, but she is slow
to enter his apartment, as though by putting her feet inside the
door she will forever be unable to leave. He remembers how
he meant to touch her in the kitchen, while they made coffee in
the dark. In daylight, he doesn't dare.

Entering the room, she looks immediately toward the great
window. "Gorgeous," she says, then she sees Dusken in the
corner, a bowl containing a last host at his feet. He holds his
hands together as if in prayer. "Howdy," he says.

"This is Dusken," Jesse tells her.

"We've met," Dusken says. "Harper took my picture."

"I haven't forgotten. You were throwing me your best profile
when I was looking for something else."

"Those infamous hands?"

She shakes her head. "Your unseen soul."

"If you've kept any prints I'd like to see them."

Harper shrugs. "They're probably in a drawer somewhere. I
keep anything." She is still wearing her coat and the snow has
melted in her hair. Pulling a few stray strands from her eyes,
she turns to Jesse. "I was walking under a tree and a boughful
dropped. I keep having these accidents," she adds, looking
sideways toward Dusken.

Jesse no longer feels at home. He feels, instead, like a sliver
of light between opposing darknesses. This isn't my movie, he
tells himself. I should go to the bathroom. Or something. He
tells Harper to take off her coat and when she does he sees her
in jeans and a blue T-shirt, her nipples stiff.

From me or from Dusken or from the cold?

"I can't stay," she says flatly.

"Then don't," he tells her, but he is smiling and when she
doesn't smile in return he thinks, This is *definitely* not my movie.
He goes to the bathroom, smiles at the sink, the toilet, the show-
erhead. He rearranges the bottles and brushes and soaps, unzips
and zips his fly. Holding his hands in front of him, he compares
them to what he's seen of Dusken's. Five whole fingers that can't
play a note. And for all that he feels for the man, his anger and
his loss, he would never give him his hands, his fingers, his
octave span, because these are the hands which soon may touch
Harper's and Harper, and hold her, if they can. He wastes long

minutes in the bathroom, uncertain what to do. Harper has come for him but so has Dusken. I can't wait here forever. All the same, he lights a cigarette and smokes it while staring at his own face in the mirror. What he sees seems of no importance whatsoever.

Stepping out of the bathroom, he finds Harper alone, searching through his record collection. "Where's Dusken?"

She shrugs. "Gone. He said something about a two-fingered search for a five-fingered quintet. Whatever that means."

5

Priests read from testaments and lovers from their diaries. Technicians read from cathode ray screens and Dusken, spreading his tragic fingers across the wastes of a silent keyboard, reads from his hands. A week after the terrifying acid trip, during which he and Laura had remained close to each other, vigilant against a return of those horrible hours, the band went to New York for their first major engagement. Their reputation, particularly that of their demonic composer, had preceded them and the concert hall, a converted warehouse on the upper edge of Greenwich Village, was filled to capacity. Three thousand hyped fans stood clapping whistling pleading for a full half hour before the lights went down and Aaron, taking Dusken's place at the keyboards for the first time, opened the show with a rising spiral of progressions that avalanched back into a sonic boom of "Trial by Fire." Dusken wasn't wasting any time, he went straight for the heart with his first number. Tasting blood, he drove the blade deep, and twisted. It was the first time he had ever sung before such an audience and the fear he felt added something immense to his voice, something even worse than rage. He was almost able to step outside of himself, to astral project as Laura would say, and to see himself only vaguely recognizable on that stage lit with blue and silver, his face swollen with speed, the veins on his forehead popping, sweat running down his chin. Terror laid a patch to the lyrics and Diamond shook the rafters with his ax while the eyes of the crowd seemed to glow in the hazy darkness beyond the footlights. He could smell something burning as he had smelled the burning of what he had taken to be himself during the acid high, a sizzling of fused wires. This was fame, New York City, and the band responded as it never had before, the sound coming as if from canyons, from the marrow of bone, a broadside of bass and strings and a voice telling a story with every word in italics. Dusken felt the fingers at his throat.

At other times, a 3DB concert would include a set devoted to Dusken, during which he would depart from the iron-bound rock to play various short compositions with a background assist from the rest of the band. He would reconstruct melodies from memory, threading them with breathtaking piano stairways or chord progressions summoned from his thousand solitary sessions. It was the one part of the concert that was lacking in gut force and the thrum-a-thrum of blitz rock, and although Aaron had learned to collaborate on a second keyboard, following Dusken's leads with alternate energy and discretion, Diamond invariably bitched that the music was too weird, too sophisto, and had nothing to do with the band. In New York, he had his way. The crowd hadn't come for Dusken the composer, they had come to see that mythical dark angel from a midwestern nowhere and at the close of "Crawling Through Midnight," the usual signal to lead into the compositions was dropped—by Dusken—who signaled instead for "Take Me to the Highway," a knock-em-on-their-asses number usually reserved for the finale. Diamond, nodding his satisfaction, swung his ax, and down came the delirium of the crowd like a curtain of electrified snow. The show was on the road, dig it, and Veronica had quit the scene. No, maybe in the third row was some pony-tailed girl from Julliard, wailing and keening in disappointment, *Dusken's sold out, given in, he's part of the tribe now, another naked animal*. . . . No, there must have been a bemused professor of music, or a critic back in the shadows behind a pillar, smiling, nodding, knowing Dusken at last in his true colors, black on black and blue.

They didn't want Veronica and so Dusken gave them what they wanted, and they plugged into him, into his every socket, fuse, and outlet, and the concert came to a crashing, dying finish of feedback, smoking amps, and floodlights bursting one by one till the whole world had gone dark and silent, time for the kids to go home.

Later that night, Diamond and Aaron and the others went on to Max's Kansas City with a flock of women in tow to catch the last act, but Dusken simply wandered out the stage door and went the opposite way, traversing the alley and disappearing into the depth of the city's sleeves. The Lone Fucking Ranger, Diamond called him, but Dusken had never felt more peaceful, less burdened. Telling three thousand people how you loathe them is a tonic for the soul; shouting is bliss, squared. The concert already was distant, not a single echo could reach him where he walked, not a single refrain. He thought he felt rain-drops on his neck then found he had passed under an air conditioner dripping condensed air. He felt careless but he did not feel free. If anything, he was more chained than ever to his odd music and he felt fresh guilt, regret over the fact that he'd wandered so far away from where he'd started. He came to a blind alley and instinctively turned around. Adjusting his eye to the glare of a streetlight, he found his way to the open street. He walked the length of Manhattan, to the southern boundary of Harlem, then turned and walked back downtown. As he approached Times Square, the noise began to pierce his calm. Taxis, lined up at the red lights, raced their engines at the crossing pedestrians. Hookers screeched across the streets to one another. Two old drunks fought over a dollar bill found in the gutter. Steam rose from the subway grilles and seemed to crackle in the neon light and there was, everywhere, the hum and rattle of electricity coursing through the atmosphere. A small boy, walking with his tourist parents, blew a whistle over and over until a cop told him to knock it off. Having no idea where his hotel was, no sense of address or direction, he checked into another hotel near Times Square where the only room available was on the first floor facing Broadway. Stepping over a troupe of sleeping derelicts, he punched the key into the lock and stepped into his hired darkness. Peeling off his clothes, he got into the bed and fell immediately into a deep and untroubled sleep. He was awakened by Veronica.

The curtains were drawn tight together and although his eyes were wide open he could see nothing, not even his white hands outstretched before him. A bus, an oboe, lurched in the street, the brakes as clarinets screeched and sighed. Two operatic Puerto Ricans screamed Latin at each other from across the street and there was the uneven drumroll of a man with a bad leg running past the window on shoes clipped with steel. Klaxons and French horns, the Madonna wail of a mother pulling her children away from the onrushing cymbals of taxis. The satin static of falling rain, the plucked strings of puddles under footsteps. Dissociate sounds, random and chaotic, but in the black of his room each sound was distinct and tuned and *on time*, even the vibrato of the alarm clock sounding in the room next door and the odd moments of silence were measured and he knew the measure before it happened, he and Veronica, he made the sound in the hearing of it, the cacophony and the symphony. The sound that comes from nowhere, from the tapping of a ring finger on an empty wine glass, the rush of a pulse, the shifting of coins in a loose pocket, all the listening comes down to hearing it all, even the sound of sunlight, or the anatomy's restless symphony of blood coursing through veins. Blind in the darkness, he had only the sounds to guide him and he felt the tremor of his own music in his belly and chest, the turning of the earth as one great groan from a bass cello lifted him at last from his bed and all he could do was stand naked in that darkness, day or night he had no sense of which, he stood in darkness and listened and remembered and in a sweat of beatitude unbecoming to a demon, he held his thumbs to his throat, and crossed them, and sang.

When the band returned to Vermillion, he started working on the Veronica Quintet, first in his studio and then in a second room he rented only to work in. He worked on his music drugless and clean, and though Laura felt that he was withdrawing into himself he knew the truth to be the opposite, he was coming back. All of him, his nerves, blood, sight, skin, heart, and ear were engaged and he worked joyfully, unaware of the time, telling Diamond he would not go on the road until later and fending off his partner's complaints with a vague smile.

Diamond persisted. "You can at least let me listen to this project of yours."

"Not until it's finished."

"We're getting restless, Dusken. If we don't follow up on that New York date, we're gonna be old news fast."

"This quintet will get us back there. Relax. Take some time off."

"You're the one who needs some time off. You look like hell."

"I never felt better."

"Just don't forget there's a band waiting on you. We're not a one-man show."

Not yet, Dusken was thinking. Then he went home to Veronica.

Growing more and more lonesome, Laura would sometimes drop by to listen to him while he worked. She was the only one allowed in and she would sit on the other side of the room and smoke pot, waiting for him to finish and be with her again. But whenever he was finished, he wanted only to lie still in the bed, saying nothing. It was enough, he told her, to have her body humming next to his. It was all in the same sound, he said. These days he could hear little else.

She admitted that what she'd heard was powerful and alluring. "I'd forgotten how you can play when you're not with the band. It's different, more lasting somehow, though I'd never be able to reconstruct a phrase of it on my own later on. How far along are you?"

"Two or three more segments and I'll be finished with the third movement. I need a bridge piece from the wail to that series of rolling octaves."

"You know," Laura told him, "the band will never play that quintet. When they hear it, it will be all over between you and Diamond."

Dusken knew and he didn't care. In writing the Veronica Quintet, he was writing his way out of the maze he'd played and drugged his way into. He had even changed his style at the keyboard. During one torturous week, he abandoned the soft/ loud pedal on his piano and taught himself the keyboard all over again, using the different weights and strengths of his fingers to mute or detonate or sculpt the notes. He played the anchor notes with his thumb, heavy-hearting them, using his index finger for the notes that reached from one place to another, his middle finger for the bridge notes, his little finger for the notes which were short-lived, little cries in the dark, and with his ring finger he played the repetitions, for obsession, for notes that held in themselves an echo, a memory that would last even after the other fingers had again come forward with their musics. He mingled piano with the synthesizer, layering his sound with a variety of tracks, and inevitably he took himself apart, changing finger progressions, weights and depths, until his fingers had become a motion far beyond his consciousness, beyond his will, simply moving as though animate of themselves, until the third movement had completed itself. With a sigh, he slid another cassette into its place and submerged into the fourth. He did not even notice that for over two weeks Laura had not been by to see him.

6

Harper awakens in her High Street apartment thinking of the film she has recently seen. In the film, a woman asks the mad-man, "Who are you, Jack?" The madman, having come to his senses, answers, "I am myself." As if to say, "Who else might I be?"

Harper can't remember all of it. Lying in her bed, she pulls the covers close to her chin. The apartment is cold and filled with white light, the sun reflected in the new snow. The madman had thought he was Jesus Christ and then knew he was only Jack. He had said to the woman, "I stand outside myself. And I watch myself, and I watch myself." His eyes had widened. "And I smile and I smile and I smile."

In the bathroom: Harper, unsmiling. Hung over not from wine but from no sleep. Her face in the mirror, at twenty, showing the first signs of age. None of the intricate character lines of, say, Katharine Hepburn, but no longer entirely unadorned by time. Her eyebrows, a professor once told her, belie her pretense of innocence, something in the way they arch when she is suspicious. He should know, he had slept with her. "Your eyebrows imitate curtains, or the veils of an Arab demoiselle. Sometimes your whole face plays hide and seek."

Blinking, she washes the slumber like sin from her reddened eyes and then scrubs the nicotine from her teeth. The outlaw named Jesse hadn't seen the film. She had asked him. He never went to the movies, he said, he made his own.

That's what they all say.

In the room with the fireplace, Lisbeth sleeps like wood, hollow and fallen over, as if tipped into bed. Though it is past noon, Harper knows better than to waken her. The room smells of spent burning, the ashes of Billy which have lifted white and gray like winged phantoms from the fireplace and scattered like dirty snow across the oriental rug. In the kitchen, she brews coffee, strong and black, the way she's told they drink it in Mexicali or in Buenos Aires. Lisbeth, like nearly everyone else these days, drinks tea, mixing her own from various pouches of leaves she can buy at the Whole Earth shop, along with whatever she thinks will do her up right: ginseng and thyme and bitter roots, even marijuana if the water isn't run to a boil. Potions, charms, elixirs, she wears her wants on her sleeve and her dreams in a steaming cup. Today I drink love, tomorrow desire. Harper drinks Mexican black coffee, one great cup has the same effect as speed, making the heart race and the lips burn. Nothing in life is better than the day's first cigarette, when the tobacco is laced with caffeine, her clock is winding up, breasts warmed from the insides. It would be nice to have someone touch them, it's been a long time. Maybe the outlaw, whose hands she should have photographed, she must remember to take her camera with her when she goes to get her pot.

Finishing her coffee, she dresses with care, choosing silk panties instead of the dull cotton, the same silk numbers that Billy once bought for her—he'd wanted her in something black and crotchless but she'd settled on black silk, crotch intact thank you—her most faded jeans, cloud blue and too tight, suggesting every known line of her ass, her best feature, and a simple white blouse, long-sleeved, which she had once saved painfully to buy and was later disappointed with. Looking in the mirror, she is disappointed all over again. Going back to the bedroom, she exchanges the blouse for a blue sweater that doesn't quite set off her brown eyes. She is taking her time, thinking *A man knows*. What does he know and who said that? Lisbeth, speaking of Dusken long ago: "He knows he can have me whenever he wants." How does he know? Did you tell him?

A man knows.

Bullshit. Clothes, jewelry, makeup, and scents do the telling. Whisper, Harper. With a lisp.

She changes the sweater for a blue T-shirt.

Being Harper.

Pulling on a coat, she remembers to pack her camera and at the last moment she takes a bottle of wine from the kitchen table, thinking of the cheap wine, sugar sweet, that the dealer had offered her the night before. But when she arrives at 31 Canberry Street, Dusken is there. She didn't know they knew each other, he and the dealer, and she cannot mask her disappointment. She thought they'd be alone. Dusken looks as ever Dusken, bored if not bitter, and is looking at her nipples which are stiff from the cold, pushing forth from the T-shirt like young tubers, she should have worn a bra.

"This is Dusken," Jesse tells her.

Dusken says they've met. "Harper took my picture."

She hasn't forgotten. "You kept showing me your face when I was looking for something else."

"Those famous hands."

She shakes her head, wondering what Jesse is thinking. "Your unseen soul." She might have said unknown.

The outlaw takes her coat and for a moment his hands brush her shoulders, making her nipples flare. When he goes off to the bathroom, she is sorry she came.

"What's new with Harper?" Dusken asks. He has a face worth photographing, the eyes and mouth, like sun and moon, in opposition; mouth smiling, eyes wounded.

"Nothing much," she answers. She gestures to her camera. "School."

"You still living with Lisbeth?"

She nods. "On High Street. We moved."

The outlaw takes forever and she wonders if he is waiting for her to leave. Maybe these two would rather be alone and she, not Dusken, is intruding. Though she had brothers, she has no idea what goes on between men, what they talk about or why. Even Billy, ridiculously blunt, was foreign territory. At times like this, she would like to be a man, moving forward rather than between invisible lines, saying what she likes. Her nipples deflate. The room is warm and Dusken is putting on his coat.

"Tell Jesse I had to get moving," he says.

He has understood. A man knows.

"Don't leave on account of me," she tells him.

"Got to," he answers. "I'm on a two-fingered search for a five-fingered quintet." Stopping at the door he adds, "Jesse's my friend," saying it in a way she can't immediately decipher, like a warning maybe, or a poem, or a salutation. There is weight to the word *friend*. When he's gone she feels naked, waiting for Jesse to come out of the bathroom, an odd hideout, maybe he's waiting for the whole world to leave, her included.

Sifting through his records, anxious to hear music, noise, anything but the silence of that room, she notices the basket with a single host remaining. Grains of salt are spilled across the rug and she wonders, Where did *this* come from? Like finding a rubber in a convent, inverted morality. She holds it in her fingers and is about to put it on her tongue when the outlaw steps out of the bathroom.

"Where's Dusken?"

She shrugs. "Gone. He said something about a two-fingered search for a five-fingered quintet. Whatever that means."

They are alone for the first time on earth. Her nipples, barometers beyond her control, stiffen anew. Jesse sees the host in her hand and smiles.

"Communion," he says. "Ever had it before?"

"No," she answers. "I've always wondered . . ."

"Superstition says that the host is a man."

Which man? she asks herself, swallowing it whole.

The wine that she has brought for him is French, a château something. Though he has been smoking pot all afternoon, he still can notice the difference in the taste. He is used to bargain brands, thick and fruit-laden. Harper holds her glass near to her face and when she drinks she closes her eyes, as though there is more than wine in that glass. With Dusken gone, she is more relaxed and they pick up where they left off the night before. Jesse feels himself endlessly on the verge of touching her, he is perpetually leaning in her direction, a tropism, the way his plants lean toward the sunlight so that he has to turn them from time to time.

After she has been there for an hour she remembers why she came. "The pot," she tells him. "I forgot to take it with me last night."

Jesse digs a bag from his cache and hands it to her. "It's the same as last night. You can try it first if you want."

She hands him his money. "No need. I trust you. You're not Willie."

"You've noticed?"

"Willie's a big mover. He takes it so seriously, like every deal he makes will get him closer to the big time. He'd really like to be a distributor instead of a bag man. You know, one of those fat guys in a tan suit who always seem to be waiting for a phone call."

"I don't have a tan suit but I do take a lot of calls."

She shakes her head. "Not the same thing. You're not ambitious. There was another dealer I knew."

"Billy."

She blinks. "You knew him?"

"We're in the same . . . domain. We shared a few favors when things got tight. If my stock was low, he covered for me and vice versa. We didn't think of ourselves as competitors."

She pours more wine and Jesse asks, "Do you miss him?"

"Billy? Does it matter?" Her eyes jitterbug ever so slightly.

Jesse will be the last to admit that it matters. His eyes move from the window to Harper to the window. "No," he says, the word meaning, clearly, yes.

Harper, who will forever be a millisecond ahead of him, who will forever anticipate him as though she feels what he feels at the same instant, leans forward to kiss him. The kiss lasts for a second, then they part, then they move together again and this time she closes her eyes. When she opens them she sees his eyes shining. "Does this mean I'm invited for dinner?"

* * *

She watches him in his tiny, cramped kitchen, filling a bowl with fruit, putting bread and knife on a cutting board, arranging crackers, boiling eggs. For every cup there is a saucer and his napkins are made of cloth, not paper. He is a man who has been alone. This is all she knows. A man who has been alone, who sells grass, who is a friend of a rock star.

She removes her camera, the mini, from its case and attaches the electronic flash. The shutter opens three times before he turns and sees her. His gaze freezes her for a moment and she wonders if he is angry but he doesn't say a word. Turning his back to her, he goes on with the business of making their dinner. The perfect model, she is thinking; incapable of a pose. The winter sun has already gone pale and blue shadows crisscross the room. Encouraged, Harper goes into the kitchen and photographs his hands over the sink, his fingers stripping the shell from a hardboiled egg. Though she is young, a beginner, she has already learned not to ask permission before snapping the shutter, not to warn, not to prepare. She focuses on his face, his unshaven chin. Leaning against the crowded counter, she overturns a bowl of fruit and catches the flight of his eyes to a fallen orange. She knows better how to shoot from the hip; she reacts. A frame of light is momentarily hers. He lights a cigarette and lays it in the ashtray. Satisfy yourself and not the camera. She catches him smiling at his hands and then he lifts the shorn egg in his fingers and when he puts it into her mouth she swallows it all at once.

Later, when the bowl of fruit is empty and the floor is littered with orange peels, cracker crumbs, bits of crust on otherwise empty plates, and the night has come, they sit in lamplight, neither of them really wanting to get much more stoned. Jesse knows it is time for him to make a move, this is the moment. But the world of moves is beyond him, beyond his experience or his want. He is both timid and lazy and is incapable of even touching her hand, caressing the back of her neck, saying something about starlight or moonlight. He cannot smile like a lighthouse and gather her to the island of his bed. To undress and to worship, yes. But he holds his own hands, like Dusken, one inside the other, while Harper, reclining, smokes a cigarette ever so slowly and seems to be waiting. Suddenly she asks him, "Are you really good friends with Dusken?"

"As friend as I have, he is." Jesse, when stoned, is given to changing his speech.

"I wouldn't have guessed it. You're not at all alike."

"I can't sing and he can't roll a decent joint."

She catches the drift. "It's terrible about his hands. That's a part of what's between us, why he's so hostile with me."

"He wasn't."

"You don't know all of it. About a year and a half ago, after his accident, I saw him at the Grande Finale. I had my camera with me because I'd been shooting the interior of the place for a composition class. When I wandered over toward him and started taking pictures, he thought I just wanted a few shots of his face. It may have been morbid, I know, but I've been taught not to think twice about getting anything on a negative."

"What's morbid about taking his picture?"

"Nothing at all, except that I was trying to position the lens in such a way as to give the impression that I was taking his profile while I was really trying to get a close-up of his hands. I could already see the title of the slide, *The Deformed Pianist*. You're right to look at me like that. I was wrong and I've paid for it. Dusken reminds me of that every time I see him and I think of it plenty of times on my own."

"Did you get any pictures of his hands?"

She shakes her head. "Not one. He caught on to what I was doing and hid them under the table. Asked me if I thought I'd like him to come touch my tits with those hands."

"Pure Dusken."

"It might have ended there and except for my imagination maybe it did. Dusken started acting like a rock star later on, when the band was re-formed and started getting top billing again."

"When was that?" Jesse asks. "Dusken doesn't talk much about the past."

"A year ago. Maybe a little longer. Dusken and Diamond went out to LA for a few weeks and when they came back they had a recording contract like it was the easiest thing in the world. That's when we all saw how Dusken had changed. Maybe it was that accident he had, his hands. I don't know. Before the accident, he was kind of quiet and afraid of something we never knew about. Afterward, when he and Diamond started up the band again, he grew nasty and loud and he was doing drugs twenty-four hours a day.''

"Speed," Jesse corrects her. "He only does speed."

"Speed, then. About that time he picked up with Lisbeth. She was in love with him, still is, and would have done anything for him. It only lasted a month or so, then Dusken just told her not to come around anymore. He was living out at the farmhouse with the band and since there was so much going on out there, she still saw him quite a bit. To get close to him or to stay in his line of sight, she started sleeping with anyone else who knew him, who was close to him. She just passed herself around to get his attention and even though he'd sleep with just about anyone, he wouldn't let Lisbeth get within ten feet of him.''

"Why not?"

"Because of me. Because of what I'd tried to do. That's what he told me once, when he was pretty drunk and hanging around the Grande Finale. I was really hurting for Lisbeth, seeing the way she was carrying on, so I just asked him what the score was. He admitted he had nothing against Lisbeth, but when he was with her he felt like she was another me, wanting nothing more than to brood and salivate on his hands. Those were the words he used.''

"He has a way with words."

Jesse is thinking in particular of a Dusken song that he plays often when alone. He never lets on to Dusken that he is a fan as well as a friend but he has all three of the recorded LP's and one bootlegged tape of the concert in LA.

> Burn down the signposts
> Throw away the welcome mat
> Take down your goddamn home sweet home
> I'll have no more of that
>
> Turn down the gaslight
> Bolt and lock the door
> Rattle the rusted chains of freedom
> Sing mom and dad no more
>
> Burn down the signposts
> Shut up the noisy night

Lay down your head upon the spinning bed
You have no home in sight . . .

"Dusken isn't a rock star to me," Jesse tells her. "I'm a fan,
sure, but when he's around me I forget about all that. He doesn't
play that game with me. He says sometimes he feels the way a
priest must feel at those times when he'd like to give it all up
and rub himself against some sixteen-year-old. Dusken lives just
the opposite of that priest and gives in to what's believed of
him."

"Why?"

Jesse shrugs. "I just got here. I missed most of the movie."

"And I never got my picture."

Words form like a vapor in Jesse's mouth and then disperse.
Her quiet, her waiting for him, makes him uneasy. "Take my
picture," he tells her.

She sits up. "Your picture?"

"Yeah, like the others." He reaches across the floor for her
camera but her hand reaches his first.

"No more pictures," she says. "Not tonight."

The moment is gone. All the talk of Dusken has shifted the
current, bearing Harper away from him. She is sitting up and
searching for a record to play. He considers reaching for her
from behind, folding his hands around her waist, something
desperate and ridiculous, some movie gesture, but the phone is
ringing and there are customers on the way. In half an hour they
have come and gone, it is Saturday night, but the phone is still
ringing and more are due to arrive.

"Don't you ever go out?" Harper asks him.

"Out?"

"Out of this apartment. Or do they always come to you?"

"A little of both. They find me wherever I am."

"And you like being found?"

He smiles. "I'm not bothered. I get by." Now he wants to
get freshly stoned but he doesn't want to do it alone. He waits
for Harper to ask him. Do women ever ask? Will you dance with
me? Take me in your arms?

"I'd rather be alone with you," Harper tells him.

He should have left the phone off the hook.

The buyers arrive to taste and appraise the grass. They pay

for it with wrinkled ten-dollar bills which have seen the bottoms of deep and mysterious pockets. Jesse smooths them against his thigh and folds them into his jeans. The routine is so familiar to Harper after her experience with Billy that she barely notices the gestures. She recognizes the buyers and they recognize her. Billy's girl, what's her name. One of them, a long-haired loser from Des Moines, smiles to her, but it is a nasty smile, a smile saying *I know what you're after*. She wonders if, as with Billy, she is another in an unbroken chain of women who have come to the dealer and not gone home. The dealer owns the candy store and there is a line of babes just outside, noses pressed to the window, breath fogging the glass. Waiting for a taste. The image troubles her and her night is ended. When they are alone again, she lifts her camera and takes a final picture: *Jesse Counts His Bread*. And then, burning and uncertain, she rises, wraps her coat around her shoulders like a cape, says good night into his ear, and leaves.

He sits alone in lamplight and waits for yet another buyer. We never close. If he knew how to follow her, he would. If he were not a guardian of orphan plants, if he knew the language of moves, if he were careless, he would follow. The phone is ringing and he answers, "Five and ten," the price going suddenly up, and they know where to find him, just knock twice. But then she is knocking on his door, he wonders how it is he recognizes the sound of her hand on wood, and when he answers she says, "You didn't follow me home."

He admits that he meant to.

She says she wants to take his picture, "Just one more, maybe two, of you standing over there, by the window." She is out of breath as though she has been running. Behind the lens, she stoops and clicks, firing blanks from a filmless camera, though Jesse doesn't know the difference. Framed against his great window, he looks in her direction, toward her neck, her forehead, her hands. She leans forward, clicks again, and sways as though to find him in another angle, and he watches although his watching has nothing to do with the lens or the shutter, he is watching her breasts rise and fall, and then he is moving across the carpet and grows big in the lens so she clicks again, she shoots him naked, shoots him through and through, and then he is beside her and she isn't taking pictures anymore.

7

Radio Veronica, like some long-suffering lover, has packed her bags for good, leaving Dusken on his own and with no music whatsoever. The only lyrics that make sense to him are laundry lists, sports scores, slogans, and graffiti. A song is written on the wall of the men's room but it isn't his. He is writing his own song one drink at a time and in the Grande Finale he shoots pool and smokes Marlboros like one of the boys. "Your shot, Two Trees. Move your ass." Radio Veronica has stolen away, leaving no farewell note, no forwarding address. Turning the dial, Dusken hears whistling, a baby-cry sound of send and no receive. But she has never been reliable, his Veronica, and like moonlight she could come slinking back to him in the night, any night, through the window, whispering forgiveness.

Harry Two Trees drops the seven ball into a side pocket and cruises slowly around the table, cueing and recueing. He loves to fidget, to savor, to appraise, and Dusken watches him with a certain envy. Two Trees can't count, can't write, can't sing, and is painfully ugly, but he can shoot pool with anyone in Clay County. They play Cutthroat, three ways, Dusken and Two Trees and Lenny, two of them sore losers. Jesse sits at a table in the back, his office, where he watches like an owl for buyers. Gena sits opposite him, balancing her apple ass on a broken chair. She watches Dusken with an obvious, pouting hunger and the ants in her pants are fierce.

Lenny, fresh with Dexedrine and wet with beer—an up and a down—is going on about the weather, how the winter is coming sooner and ending later. "Like we're moving away from the sun, man. Like every year we move a little further away and in a hundred years or so there won't be no more summer anywhere."

Marvin answers from behind the bar. "That's bullshit, Lenny."

"Yeah, well, that's what I read, man." Lenny stretches a skinny forearm and braces his cue.

"In what comic book?"

"*Time* magazine." He fires and balls scatter, clash, bump, but none fall.

Marvin laughs aloud and Two Trees risks a giggle.

Lenny turns on the Indian. "What the fuck are *you* laughing at, Crazy Horse?"

The Sioux continues to titter. "*T-time* magazine. That's c-crap."

Willie gives Two Trees a beer. "Crap is right."

Now Lenny is offended. His eyes are red and his veins, shot with Dex, bulge along his forehead. "It's the goddamn truth. We're moving away from the sun. It's in the stats, man. We're headed for another Ice Age."

In the distance, Jesse measures time and hastens the night, night meaning Harper.

Gena shakes her tail.

"No way," Marvin argues. "If anything, it's just the opposite. The sun is dying, it's on its last legs, the final act. Resulting explosions are heating the atmosphere, burning it away. It'll take ten thousand years to die and in the meantime we're headed for an Age of Tropics, perpetual sunburn, a new equator, not the fucking Ice Age."

"Sing me another song," Lenny tells him.

"The lakes will evaporate into salty marshes. The oceans will boil and form rain clouds the size of Texas, and when the rain falls it will be like acid, all sulphur and carbons."

"And your subscription to *Time* will be canceled." This from Dusken, who is lining up to sink one of Lenny's balls. Cutthroat.

"You gotta have faith," Lenny says to no one in particular. "You gotta believe in the moon."

The moon? Dusken eyes the ivory ball before his cue. What does Lenny know about the moon?

Lenny says the moon is his personal symbol. "That's what they called me in high school: Moon Man. Cause me and the moon have this special relationship, you know?"

Dusken fires his cue and the white ball cracks a red one, bumping it into oblivion.

"You forgot to call it," Lenny reminds him. "You've got to call your shots, man."

"Shut up, Lenny."

Dusken chalks his cue and lines up a bank shot, Lenny's two ball. The cue ball lies nestled against a bumper, a blue-pocked moon at rest, and Dusken gives it a squint. Who began these myths about the moon? he wonders. Aztecs, Eskimos, Neanderthals, aborigines, and song writers. Moon madness, moonstruck, by the light of the silvery moon, it rhymes with almost anything, cheap lyrics. "Two ball," he whispers to the green felt, his lawn, his earth. The moon is no mystery at all, a man stepped on it just a few years ago, there is nothing left to moon over. Here is a moonscape Dusken might believe in: cigarette butts on the floor and stale beer sitting in dirty glasses on cracked tables. Dimes rust between the floorboards, ancient medallions with which we might have made that phone call. Hello, fame? The line is busy. If Marvin would change a light bulb from time to time there wouldn't be such a sick yellow glow to the place. The pool table, like a garden lawn overrun with dogs, has grown worn, too many hippies with bad tempers have missed their bank shots and taken it out on the felt, and if a chair doesn't rock on uneven legs, its cushion is torn. No. The moon is no mystery at all, nothing but a cold rock floating helplessly around a warm one and Dusken prefers the left-handed world of the Grande Finale, a world where everyone walks with a limp— something unholy or unhealthy in his pants—or talks like Two Trees. Diamond wants LA, he wants picture windows and swimming pools, dime-store blondes he can autograph between the legs, a highway lined with coke that he can snort a yard at a time, that's what fame is for. Resting his palm against the felt, Dusken takes great care in lining up his shot and Lenny grows annoyed. Time is speed. "*Play*, Dusken." The singer ignores him. Slipping the cue across the edge of his left thumb, he considers that since the operations only his pool game has improved. His crippled thumb offers a groove that is ideal for a pool cue and his gnarled right hand, though less sensitive to the wood, is somehow steadier. The surgeon has filled his hands with all manner of elements. His right metacarpal is a network of plastic and Fiberglas thread and in place of muscle is a kind of sponge which keeps the remaining bones from rubbing against one another. Instead of a knuckle on his right middle finger there is a glass disk which holds the two halves of the finger together. There were nine separate operations over a period of two months and when it was over he had worn casts in the shape of boxing gloves for another six months. When the casts were removed and his hands hung like empty torn gloves at the ends of his wrists, he had not even been able to hold a cigarette to his lips. Two years later, he can strum a guitar, play pool with the best of them, squeeze the ass that's offered him, and even play a bit of piano, on his own, alone. He pulls the pool cue like the bow of a violin and he can hear the wail of a high and urgent E.

"The moon," Lenny says, "should still be considered a god."

He waited all night for Radio Veronica. Drugless and innocent, he banished Gena, telling her to sleep in the bathtub, on the stairway, *away*. Then, clapping the earphones over his head, he sat in moonlight and practiced a new way of fingering the keyboard, one which would require less of a finger span. His limit for the moment is six notes, two impossible steps away from a longed-for octave, but he has learned to cheat the chord by an eighth-count, brushing the low note with his thumb and flashing his right pinkie at the octave; his chords therefore seem to tremble and drip and are unfulfilled. He has devised a method of recording which makes slow work of his compositions but allows him at least to carry on. Playing single notes with the few fingers he can summon, he overdubs himself in six tracks instead of two, creating chords in three recordings that he could previously play in one. But nothing he plays has Veronica in it. The music is an approximation of Dusken Lowe, "Chopsticks," and "Twinkle, Twinkle, Little Star."

"*Play,* Dusken."

He regards the cue with a reddened eye and he coughs. Diamond in LA. He can have the band if he wants it that bad. He'd be the leader, he's as pretty as I am.

At last he shoots and the two ball, licking a bumper, falls soundlessly into a leather pocket.

"You didn't call *that* shot, either," Lenny scolds.

Gena, rising from her chair like smoke from a gun, wanders

to the pool table and leans her crotch against the pocket of Dusken's next target. The singer backs off, lights a Marlboro, and lays it on the edge of the table. "You're in my way," he says to the wall.

"I'm bored, Dusken." She drawls the name, Dus-*ken*.

"Go home."

"I don't got a car and there's snow out there."

Dusken takes the keys to his MG and tosses them to her. "Don't wait up for me," he tells her.

"I never do," she replies, and with a nasty snap of her hips she heads for the door. At the same moment, the cowboy, her lonesome ex, stomps in. He is wearing black, a tough guy in mourning. Black leather jacket, black gloves, torn jeans, and his black boots are wet with snow. He makes a grab at Gena, his gloves thrashing air as she steps away from him.

"I been looking for you!"

"Keep looking," she says, and with a last glare at Dusken she pushes past him and out the door.

In the wake of her going, the cowboy is undecided. His eyes follow her until the door swings closed, then he turns his gaze toward Dusken as though to confront him, to say something dangerous, to draw a six-gun from beneath his jacket. There would be a moment of tense silence but Lenny can't shut up. "Who the fuck is this?" he asks no one in particular. But the cowboy has neither a six-gun nor, for the moment, his tongue. He takes two menacing steps toward Dusken and then stops, as though he's reached some invisible canyon between them. Dusken is thinking he has never seen such pathetic eyes, like dog's eyes, incurably lonesome. If the cowboy were angry, he would feel himself in danger. Rage is terrifying but sadness is reassuring. Sorrowful men never win their fistfights.

"She used to dig me," the cowboy informs Dusken, as though in three words, Shoosta dig me. "She used to be with me, you know."

Dusken is tempted to say it doesn't matter, nothing matters all that much. He doesn't want Gena anyway, Gena wants him. There are no star-crossed lovers. Romeo was out of his mind and Gena is hardly Juliet. When he goes home tonight, if he goes home at all, Gena will be there waiting for him, stoned, weepy, plaintive, and hot to trot, just as she has been for two weeks now. He feels nothing for her. She is an annoying stray cat, feeding on his fame, and he blames her for keeping Radio Veronica away. "Yeah." Dusken nods. "Yeah, well, take her home then."

The cowboy is confused. "I can't," he says. "She ain't here." His eyes brighten with hope. "You mean she don't want to stay with you?"

"Cut the shit," Lenny warns him. "Dusken's got a pool game going."

"Right," Two Trees tells him. "We're sh-shooting pool."

"Gena? She's just hanging out. She likes the rock and roll scene, I guess. She'll be home soon."

"After Dusken knocks her up."

The cowboy visibly whitens.

Marvin tells Lenny to shut up.

"Or else he'll just turn her over to the boys in the band like he did with Lisbeth. Diamond says he likes sloppy seconds."

The cowboy is trembling with rage and his eyes bulge.

"He's only kidding," Marvin reassures him. "Here—" He draws a beer from the tap and places it on the bar for the cowboy. "Drink this and go home. Forget all this opera. Get drunk and watch TV or something. It can't be that bad."

The cowboy downs his beer in one pass, as if to show them all something, and the gesture reinforces him. He swiftly turns on Dusken. "I know you're giving her drugs, man. Doping her up and suchlike. I seen you at the Burning Barn doing speed and stuff and I know all about you."

Dusken watches and listens. He has put his cue away, the pool game is over, and he is sitting on another broken chair. He is fatigued, smoked out, yearning for something that will put him on the ceiling, the roof, away.

"Yeah." The cowboy is warming up. "I seen creeps like you around before. Long hair, dope, electric music, all that shit. I seen it before and I *ain't impressed*."

Dusken imagines a pack of big brothers, all older than the cowboy in front of him. One of them named Eugene or Jim Bob would have fists like hammers and would drive a Trans Am. I seen creeps like you around before. "So we've seen each other before," he tells the cowboy. "I've seen you and you've seen me, every day of our lives. Cowboys and Indians, hippies and straights, and we're all of us best friends, right? You come to my bar and I go to yours. Draw him another beer, Marvin. This man's got a thirst that won't quit.''

But the cowboy is past humor and Dusken's little poem is over his head. ''Fuck that, you goddamn hippie. We ain't friends and you ain't staying with Gena no more.''

''That's cool. Very, very cool.''

The cowboy, for a final effect, kicks the door open and slams it behind him.

''Asshole!'' Marvin calls after him.

There is a silence in his wake and the game is ended. Marvin wipes beer glasses, Lenny fidgets and smokes, Two Trees drinks, and Dusken scratches but can't find the itch.

Jesse, smelling The Law, steals out the back door.

''Get your life together,'' Marvin tells Dusken.

Dusken, searching for a cigarette, finds holes in his pockets. ''Write it on a postcard,'' he tells the bartender. ''From far away.''

Laura, back from nowhere, told him, ''You're so far away. I come to find you and you're not here, you're never here.''

''I was here all night.''

''Playing,'' she said. ''You ride that synthesizer like a horse into your own private sunset, forgetting the rest of us are barefoot and trying to follow.''

Her eyes were red but not from tears. Since he had started writing the Veronica Quintet, she had gotten in with some heavy dealers, the boys from Denver who had come to Vermillion to cultivate the college market. They would offer her what she thought she wanted, acid or mescaline or speed, and she had a way of saying yes, a quick and nervous nod, that left them no doubt where she was headed. Bolt came down hard on her and she wept to Dusken that she'd been sleeping with one of the dealers because she didn't have the money to pay for her pills.

''You could have gotten the money from me,'' he answered hotly.

''No I couldn't. You're off it now. You've let me go it alone and it's lonesome.'' She said she missed his sound, his music. Not the listening but the crawling into. She had followed him once to Chicago and seen them all there, his followers come to hear the word, or the Word, eleven thousand of them under a finite dome and hundreds more outside in the rain, trying to crash the police lines. Sitting on the floor behind the stage, among wires, cords, fuse boxes, switches, all the paraphernalia that would grasp and couple and shake the sound into electric life, she could see through the mike stands and the floor lights a haze of faces turned toward Dusken, waiting. Diamond tuned and Aaron plugged and unplugged while the singer, hung over, stood by idly picking imaginary lint from his leather pants. They started off slowly, lazily, while Dusken teased the crowd nearly to death, holding tight the reins on Diamond and Aaron and the others, denying the audience what they had come for, that vibrant circle of sound—the blade, the crash, the acid rainfall—and the crowd grew uneasy with the waiting, some clapping and others whistling. Diamond went renegade, reviving his guitar upward, but Dusken stepped back and let the moment pass, the music die downward. There was a long moment of silence as the band wound like a dying clock, the last piano chords trailing into oblivion. Laura could hear Diamond saying something to Dusken, the singer answering, "Whatever they want, I don't have it." A girl in the front, crushed forward by the crowd, cried helplessly as though in a death throe, her hair swinging back and forth like curtains in the wind. At last Dusken shook himself from his stupor. Raising his arms high, he looked backward toward Laura but could not see her behind the speakers. Dropping his arms like heavy wings, he lifted the mike to his face and the band threw a 20,000-amp bolt of sound into the night, caving it in once and for all.

Laura never hears it anymore, she says. Dusken is like that night, denying, holding back. "We don't get high anymore. We don't make love anymore."

"Because you can't. Even when we feel like it you're too strung out."

"I'm too strung out because you're never here for me. You're playing that goddamned Veronica and I'm just in the way."

"It won't last forever. Nothing does. I'll be finished in another month, maybe two. Hang on."

"What do you think I'm doing? Hanging on, hanging out. There's not much else left for me to do." Her eyes, for a moment, had shone through the fog. ''Why don't you take me to bed or something?''

Her body was wilted and weightless and when he entered her her arms hung limp around his shoulders as though she were asleep. Neither of them came and when it was over it was as though it had never begun. When he was certain she was asleep, he rose from the bed and went to his synthesizer. Slipping on his headphones, he played the tape of the third movement, all but complete, and in a few moments the music had him, and he began to compose, to alter the movement here and there, to discover a missing bridge or a new resonance. Sometimes while working on the quintet, he was inside of her, Radio Veronica, among the tubes and coils, the receptor, the amp, his composing was never easier and the music was alarming and fantastic, an applause of notes like doves scattered from the eaves, first in disarray and then re-forming in a blue void, then circling to land in tranquil chords, one after the other, giving way to last isolate single notes. During a furious weekend, he wrote a series of lyrics and added the vocals, sometimes in chorus, his own voice harmonizing, other times in solo, and with a voice modulator he added a female voice derived from his own, the tones more vivid, cloudless and serene.

Late one evening, Diamond came to visit. Kicking open the door with a cowboy boot, he demanded to hear the quintet, saying that if Dusken couldn't get his act together, he'd take the band elsewhere with a new singer/writer.

''I suppose,'' Dusken answered, ''that you've already got a drawerful of new material.''

''Let's say I've put a few things together.''

''Trip-hammer rock, heavy on the ax.''

''I play what I play.''

''I haven't forgotten. Go to it.'' His wave was his resignation. He was already working for Veronica.

Late that same night Laura told him she was pregnant. The father was either Willie or Dusken or one of the Denver dealers. ''The Tarot says it's you.''

''What are you going to do?''

She shrugged. ''Have it, I guess. What else can I do?''

He wouldn't say. ''Does your old man know?''

When she shuddered, he felt a chill, an untouchable sadness.

"Too late," she murmured. "Everything is too fucking late."

He hadn't known what she had meant and he hadn't had the courage to follow her down her dark hallway. She had said so many things, filled his ears with words and dreams and nightmares which had become crowded and indistinguishable. She had taught him the power of drugs and when he was away from her he would allow himself to take speed in order to stay awake, the headphones like wings over his ears and the keyboard glowing in the moonlight before his outstretched fingers. There were times when there was no Laura, no Diamond, no band, just Dusken playing hide & seek with Veronica, putting the third movement, the best of them, to bed. Then late one night, Bolt came to visit, kicking down the door and flashing his badge. He pretended to search for drugs but Dusken knew all along he was looking for Laura. A farmer found her the next day, in the backseat of a borrowed Volkswagen she'd parked at the edge of the river. Her eyes were open and her face and arms were bruised as if from a beating she had not resisted. She had left the windows open and the mosquitoes of June had found the sweetness of her neck, her shoulders, her breast.

It had been the first overdose in Vermillion and the authorities were determined it would be the last. Dusken was questioned and had little to say except that he knew Laura as if from long ago, that she was unhappy, both at home and elsewhere, that she had lost her way.

"Did you know that she was pregnant?"

He nodded.

"Then you might know who the father was."

"Me," he told them. "Or you, or anyone. There were a lot of fathers."

During the inquest, Bolt tried to pin the blame on Dusken. He brought forth witnesses to Dusken's drug-filled past and tried to illustrate a scenario in which Dusken, the demonic rock star, had lured an innocent girl into the circle of his tribe and poisoned her deliberately. One witness, considered by most to have been paid by Bolt, insisted that he had seen Dusken Lowe insert a needle into a sleeping Laura's arm. But the coroner admitted to having found no needle marks on the corpse.

"Where is the *law*?" Bolt had shrieked but Dusken had not

even been charged. In the hall of the courthouse the cop tried to strangle the singer and was restrained by two patrolmen.

The echo of her death was noisome and everlasting. Dusken returned to the Veronica Quintet but within the space of a week it was a jangle of tragic and mismatched chords, notes more dissonant than he meant them to be, broken arpeggios, unfulfilled gestures. It had all the subtlety of two cymbals dropped down a flight of stairs and his despair overwhelmed his ear. Veronica had said her first goodbye.

Bolt was given a job as a special investigator into South Dakota drug traffic and he focused his research on Dusken Lowe. Wherever the musician went, he was followed by any of a half-dozen paid informants, college narcs who would turn over information to avoid prosecution, old enemies, old friends. The finality of death which might have been so sobering had the opposite effect. The tribe sought the myth to be its priest and Dusken, in sorrow, wore the robes, returning to the band to sing Laura's requiems. But he remembered her without detail of the girl as she had been. Her eyes and arms soon became blurred in the arms and eyes of others. He was the oldest of children when he thought of her and he felt better when he thought of no one in particular, when the headphones were tight against his ears and the keyboard was before him and a tab of white cross, like a host upon his tongue, would melt.

One late summer evening, while he strolled restlessly among the first fallen leaves at the edge of the Missouri River, he sensed that he was being followed. It was an acquired instinct. Searching the treeline along the shore, he saw two men in brown deputy shirts watching him. Finding themselves discovered, they stepped away from their hiding place, training their guns on Dusken. Behind them trailed Bolt, his eyes already narrowed, as though he were holding Dusken within the sights of a twelve-gauge shotgun. There was no place for the musician to hide. The shoreline was empty and the river was to his back.

"Search him," Bolt told the deputies and their hands were upon him at once. But instead of searching him they clubbed him to the ground then lifted him to his feet.

"You know what they do with drug dealers in some countries?" Bolt asked him.

"I'm not a drug dealer."

"They hang them," Bolt told him.

"Listen, Bolt. What happened to Laura was . . ."

The cop struck him with something metallic and when Dusken wiped the blood from his eyes he saw it was a pair of handcuffs.

"I'm an officer of the law," Bolt continued. "And as much as I'd like to see you swing, I'm not a killer." He seemed to consider for a moment where he was, out in the open country, so he told his deputies it might be a good idea if they went back into the woods. Dusken was dragged from the shoreline into the trees and handcuffed.

"I can't kill you," Bolt was saying. "That's the law. But there's another law that says I can damn well revenge my daughter."

Dusken began to tremble. He was on his knees, his hands spread before him, those long fingers that could span ten full notes on the keyboard, that could move like trip-hammers or butterflies or anything in between. He could no longer hear even a whisper of Veronica and he didn't know later if he'd begun screaming right then or when the deputy had bent low to hold his hands against a rock. He knew he was screaming when Bolt took the hammer from his belt, he was screaming as the man measured the distance downward, and when by force of his own terror he was able to tear his hands from the deputy's grasp so that the other deputy leaped to hold him still, he was still screaming. His hands lay flat and trembling on the rock, white and thin, helpless as wounded birds. His screaming never ended. It became his only music. Bolt held his gavel high above his head and the hammer, sweeping downward, shrieked Veronica.

> *"To do is to be"*—ARISTOTLE
> *"To be is to do"*—SARTRE
> *"Do be do be do"*—SINATRA
> —*written on the wall of the men's room at the Grande Finale Bar, Vermillion, So. Dakota*

8

Jesse, in a dream, pursues Jesse. The two of them are equally fast and one cannot gain on the other. He runs himself ragged, along the shore of the muddy Missouri, and when he awakens there is a mysterious ache in his legs.

"Growing pains," Harper tells him.

"Premonitions," he answers.

He is a careful outlaw and he covers his tracks. If they were to be traced in the new snow, they would lead to Harper's place on High Street, where he goes whenever he senses the law, or Bolt—one and the same—whose presence is preceded by Jesse's unnameable ache, a drumroll in the heart, hornets circling overhead, the sound of sabers rattling in the distance. It is his proximity to Dusken Lowe, their strange friendship, which threatens his anonymity. The singer and the cop have it in for each other and they circle each other with drawn switchblades, aiming for the heart. The circle is getting constantly smaller and Jesse reasons that inevitably he will be caught between the two of them, one blade for his hit side and the other for his flip side. Dusken has him thinking in jukebox terms. With bags of marijuana tucked inside his coat, he moves from bar to bar, a nocturnal milkman, appearing and disappearing according to his weather and his want. He reappears in Harper's bed, the best of all possible hideouts. She tells him she loves him and when he doesn't answer her she tells him again. He wavers.

"This is where you say, 'Harper, I love you too.' "

He lights a joint and smiles.

In a dream, Jesse pursues Jesse. One of them has been left

behind. Since the fire, one of them has been long steps behind the other, uncertain where he will follow next.

"Just look at all the Jesses," Harper tells him.

She is wearing only a faded red University of South Dakota T-shirt and she pads around the room in bare feet, pulling photos from drawers, from notebooks, and from the wall. She brings them to the bed like a pile of leaves and lays them on his lap, asking him what he thinks. The photos are all of him, there are dozens of them, some enlarged, others just on contact sheets, waves of Jesse, he has never seen so much of himself, he has never known he had such a face.

"I've seen this man before," he says.

"Where?"

"Here and there. Mostly in the mirror."

"Mirrors don't show anything."

"In windows, too. I've seen him reflected off the glass."

"What was he looking at?"

"Toys, when he was little. Watches, diamonds, the weather."

"You're sure it's the same man?"

"I'd recognize him anywhere."

"Me too." She removes the T-shirt and joins him under the blanket. Her lips seek his neck. "I like to shoot you," she tells him. "You don't change yourself for the camera."

"That's good?"

"That's what I'm after."

They examine the photos, one after another. Jesse Lights a Joint, Jesse Reaches to Catch a Falling Orange, Jesse at the Great Window Watching the Snowfall, Jesse the Shadow, Jesse the Silhouette, Sleeping Jesse, Yawning Jesse. Jesse with Eyes like Clouds.

There is too much of him, he is thinking. One photo crowds another. Individually, they are recognizable, but the collection startles him. He has never seen true photographs of the man he is, only badly focused snapshots taken by his mother or by Rose. Jesse at the beach, swimshorts slung low under his boy belly; his face sunburned, he squints at the camera. This way, Jesse. Jesse, look this way.

"You see things I've never seen before."

"Like the back of your head."

Jesse ponders. "Captured life. Like catching butterflies."

"And tearing off their wings. I sometimes feel cruel when I'm taking pictures of you."

"Cruel?"

"You're like an Indian. They felt that if you took their picture you were taking their soul away from them."

"With a difference. I gave mine away."

"Not yet, you haven't."

He shrugs. It's the words she wants, as much as the man. He looks at the photos of himself spread across the blanket but he would rather look at Harper. This is his comfort, the looking for, the wanting which he hesitates to call love. And when the word rises in his throat, he stills it with a drink, a joint, a cigarette.

They pass a joint back and forth in the lamplight and she tells him who she is, who she has been.

"I slept around a bit, just after high school. Nothing like Lisbeth, but I had my moments. When I was a freshman, I got involved with my psychology professor. We spent a lot of time talking about me and that was nice, caressing my ego like that. You know how it is with psychologists. He used words like id and ego and catharsis and libido. He made me feel like my whole personality, my experience, made up some great forest of meaning and motive. Each action or thought or dream seemed to fascinate him and I fell for that, I fell fast and hard."

"What happened?"

"We went to bed and it was okay at first. He was an explorer and I was the explored. We'd thrash around for an hour or so and then smoke a pack of cigarettes while analyzing what we'd done. He'd say, 'You bit me when you came. The animal in you emerged, did you feel it?' Or he'd have me describe in detail everything that happens when I'm coming. Is it like falling or like flying? Are there levels or degrees of joy? Is pain a thrill? Do I feel violent or tender? It was exhausting and after a few months I was analyzing myself at every turn. I couldn't eat without asking myself why I had the fork in my left hand or why I put butter on my peas. If I chain-smoked, it was because I was orally fixated. If I was afraid of the dark, I was womb-shocked. Everything had a why and a because."

"So you broke it off?"

"I had to. One day he told me that his wife knew about us

and she didn't mind. She was in favor of our seeing each other, he said, and he wanted me to let her join us in bed. 'Making it with another woman might liberate you,' he said. 'This could be a purgative experience.' He was right. I purged him from my life. I suppose he decided I was anal retentive.''

Jesse is curious. He is aware of a stir of jealousy and knows it is pointless. To everyone there is a past, sad or imperfect. His thoughts wander to Elizabeth Bad Hand and back again. ''Is he still around? I mean, do you ever run into him?''

She stubs out the joint. ''No, he's gone. I heard he got a fellowship or something from New York University. He disappeared.''

''And you've stopped analyzing yourself?''

''Completely. I get along with myself better as terra incognita. I make important decisions with coin flips or a roll of dice.''

''Destiny's darling.''

''Something like that.'' She rises from the bed and he watches her as she goes to the kitchen, her long smooth back, thin legs, valentine ass. The sight of her thrills him and saddens him all at once and when she returns, wine in hand, he gazes at the rest of her, Harper in lamplight, her breasts and lips and tangled hair. The word rises in his throat like a moan and he stills it by kissing her.

''I'm stoned,'' she tells him. ''And I'd rather be drunk.''

They drain the bottle and continue confessing, each in turn recounting how it was, what it was, when it was, before. Mostly it is Harper who does the telling. Jesse offers too little detail to his stories and is less generous with his past than she would like him to be. She complains that he is secretive. ''I have to ask a question to get an answer. You give yourself away in spoonfuls.''

''My autobiography bores me,'' he lies. ''If it were a book, it would be out of print.''

''I can write on a match book what I know about you,'' she answers.

''What do you want to know?''

''To start with, what gets you out of bed in the morning? What are you after? What do you like?''

''These days, you.''

She shakes her head. "That's not what I mean. I *know* it's a dumb question, I *know* it sounds stupid. I just wonder if you have any ambition."

"Very little."

"No plans? No dreams?"

"Get back what I've lost. See my peperomia flourish. Swim in the Missouri River and get a good tan. Put my hand between your legs to see if we catch on fire."

"You're being elusive."

"I'm being honest. I like hiding."

"Where do you come from?"

"Yankton."

"That much I know. I mean, what about your family?"

Fire and ice. Time and the sun. "There's no family to tell you about."

"You've split with them?" She persists. "They kicked you out?"

Ice and fire. Clouds gather and disperse in Rose's eyes. "They're all dead."

"Oh, God." Her breasts quiver. "Oh, damn."

"Never mind," he tells her. "It's been more than a year. There's nothing to say."

"I'm sorry."

"Don't be. It was a sad family."

She wants to know more, how it happened, but all he tells her is that his sister is alive if not well, living on the Angel Ward. Any more, he doesn't know or can't say. When she persists he tells her that there are some things that don't photograph so well. "Leave it in the dark room," he tells her. "Just let it be."

After an awkward silence, she tells him she has another bottle. She is offering to change the subject. "I think we should drink it, don't you? Tomorrow is Monday and I've only got one class. We can sleep till noon. Jesse?"

They drink and they explore each other. When they kiss they can taste the alcohol on each other's tongue. Night has long since blackened the window and Harper spills the last of her wine on the pillow.

In the middle of the night, Jesse wakens and he reaches his hand between her legs, twining his fingers in her hair, her swamp. When she stirs he falls back to sleep, but later he again awakens, strangely sober, and when he reaches he awakens her with his fingers and the sparks, as it happens, fly.

She is the most familiar stranger he has ever known. She is a far cry from Elizabeth Bad Hand.

Once, while making love to her, he sees that she is blinking and he imagines that within her there is a lens and a shutter, that she is exposing him somewhere hidden and deep, in her womb perhaps. Her images of him, her picture taking, give her an advantage over him which leaves him self-conscious. She sees in splendid detail the parts of him he can never truly see: the back of his head, his shoulder blades, his nostrils, and, in the dark, his terror. "Something is happening," she tells him, meaning in her heart and soul. "Something amazing is happening." Preferring his great window and the simplicity of his home, she comes to his apartment more often than he to hers. Anyway, *she* has a roommate. Still new to each other, they sleep entwined, then, awakened by ambition or hunger, she rises early, bathes and dresses in the winter morning darkness. He stays in bed until noon and awakens to her evidence. At times he is overwhelmed by her debris, her female presence in the room. Late one morning, awakening to an overcast sky, he feels an inexplicable sadness, like the legacy of some stupid dream. His window is a white glare and his sleep has left him troubled. There is a scent of Harper in the bed and this too is troubling though he does not know why. Kicking the blanket to the floor, he goes to the bathroom and there the sight of her underwear draped over the tub reduces him to tears.

"Be easy with her," Lisbeth advises. "She has bruises that don't show. She pretends to be invincible but she burns easily."

Jesse pretends ignorance. "Nothing to worry about. I'm just passing through."

Dusken is playing at the Grande Finale and he has gathered his band around him for the next to the last set. Jesse sits in the back with Lisbeth while Harper, sulking, makes the rounds. Her annoyance with him is obvious. "We only talk about me," she tells him. "Jesse Dark likes to play the mystery man. Jesse Dark can go to Hollywood and make a movie for all I care."

"I don't know what you're after."

"Who you are. Your history."

"Is loving me loving my autobiography?"

"I just wish you'd trust me."

"Who says I don't?"

She wanders among friends and acquaintances while he broods and boozes. The Grande Finale is a place to nurture bad humor. Bring your unhappiness and admission is free. Dusken, in blue light, wears his victim face, hollow-eyed and slack-jawed, and he sings without luster. Songs begin as hopeless murmurs and evolve into grunts and howls. He can barely remember the lyrics and the band disintegrates in his wake. All the same, there is the usual noisy crowd. It is three nights before Christmas and everyone is going home. There is just enough time for a last blowout. Tomorrow, Vermillion will look like Deadwood, all wind and cockroaches and untrampled snow. Lisbeth, drinking from a tall pitcher of red beer, is sweetly and seriously drunk.

"I'm having this problem with time," she tells him. "I'm too full of it. You know, dates, hours, deadlines, anniversaries."

"Burn your calendar," Jesse advises. "Give your watch to a man with a life sentence."

"That's not what I mean. I don't need to measure. I just know how many days have passed *since* or how many days *until*."

"Since or until what?"

"Anything, anytime. And I'm always taking inventory, like how many guys have I slept with, how many of them loved me, how many were complete strangers, how many had blue eyes, and on and on."

Jesse remembers an old customer who measured time in haircuts. Since his hair was usually long, time had a kind of breathless duration. "Two haircuts ago," he would say, or, "That was after the haircut of last fall."

Lisbeth is fascinated. "Like an Indian," she says, "measuring the seasons by the fur on a dog's back."

Jesse shrugs. He is watching Harper, who pretends to flirt with a law student. Seeing him watching, she smiles and moves on to a football player.

"In Minneapolis," Lisbeth continues, "I knew this guy who tried to live without numbers. He said they were a straitjacket, an aberration in the evolution of man, so he worked things out another way, with images or events. His calendar was unique. Long Ago Day, Fall in Love Day, Get a Job Day, the Cold Month

When I Was Stone Broke. A lot of days were just Day Days, no need to record them at all.''

"Like tomorrow?"

"It was really a trip talking with this guy. You'd ask his age and he'd have no way to tell you. Or else, how far was it from place to place and he'd say something like 'In that direction smoking a filter cigarette and singing a short song once you get past the hill.' He turned a lot of people off. I think he had trouble keeping a job.''

Harper wanders by to hand a joint to Jesse. "I'm screwing around as best I can," she tells him. "Are you jealous?"

"Burning."

"I'm a little out of practice. Fidelity takes the edge off my act. Maybe I should show a little more tit." She adjusts her sweater as if to bare a breast.

Lisbeth tells her she's a tramp.

"Jeepers," Harper mimics a sugar baby. "I sure hope someone notices." Winking at Jesse, and then giving him the finger, she merges with the crowd.

The band is on break and Dusken is holding court at the end of the bar. Seeing Jesse with Lisbeth, he waves and his eyes, briefly, flash with amusement.

"I hear he's a friend of yours," Lisbeth says to Jesse.

"We get high together."

"Sounds cozy. I used to sleep with him."

"I know."

Lisbeth lights a Winston and blows smoke rings. "I suppose"—she wafts a halo toward the ceiling—"he told you all about it."

"He didn't need to. I just heard."

Lisbeth shrugs. "It's a small town. Word gets around. Anyway, it didn't last very long." She gazes across the bar toward Gena, who is hanging on Dusken's arm like a heavy bracelet. "Nothing does with Dusken."

"He's not what you think he is," Jesse tells her. "He's more or he's less than he's given credit for. Everyone looks at him through filters. Women throw their bodies in his path and he doesn't know how to step over them."

"So he steps *on* them."

"He says goodbye after saying hello."

"In words and music."

"Isn't that what you came for?"

Lisbeth, growing drunker by the minute, natters on about how alike they are, she and Jesse, because they have nothing in particular to do with their lives, they are drifting, bobbing along the surface, headed out to sea. "Everyone we know has a gig of some sort, something they love to do, something of value. Dusken's music, Harper's photography. Marvin has the Grande Finale. Even Two Trees lives and dies over his two-bumper bank shots."

"I sell grass."

"That's free enterprise. I give my body away. That's madness. Neither of us has much to show for what we do."

"I'm working on it."

And he is. He is at times absorbed with what he does, the circles he walks among, the various moods of his customers, their appetites, their wants, their timing. He wonders where they go at night, where they smoke, and with whom. Grass exaggerates half of the world and deadens the other half and when he sells he imagines the ripple effect, buyers giving to friends, smoke rings growing wider as they grow closer to the ceiling. Dispersal, sleep. They don't know what they want, his customers, but he gives them what they ask for. They smoke for reasons as varied as they are unoriginal: boredom, lonesomeness, a need to giggle or just to kill time. They smoke alone, while reading, and watch the words blur and jiggle on the page, a pressure coming from deep inside their eyes to know what it means, whatever it is on that printed page; or they smoke along the hillsides, or the banks of the Missouri River, imitating poets or astrologers, watching a star move red across the sky, blinking, hey Bobby it ain't a star it's a airplane. Or they smoke in bed, boy and girl, and in the beginning it is a thrill to feel skin on skin but then the grass fatigue comes down like a heavy cape and a stoned sleep follows. They don't know what they want. He gives them what they ask for. And though it may truly be free enterprise, there are times when he suddenly feels himself *at work*. The feeling evolves slowly and he becomes aware of it in slow degrees, even when he's carrying nothing with him. His nerves tighten and he finds himself listening intently for certain sounds, sighs, any voice saying anything about smoke. He doesn't advertise, they come to him, knowing either his face or the look on his face, never once knowing entirely his name. He is Jesse the grocer and he is comfortable among his heads of lettuce, his oranges, and his Campbell soup cans.

"Three fingers of Colombian, please."

"An ounce of red."

"Do you split down to nickel bags or do I have to buy a whole lid?"

Dusken is back on stage, singing a slow, slow number having to do with getting lost and staying there and Jesse is aware of a change in his act, a certain fire that wasn't there before. He is singing as though he believes the song, he simmers and cries, and then Jesse notices that Bolt has appeared. He stands off to the side in his civilian clothes, gray slacks and brown corduroy coat, his black hair slicked back like some old rock and roller out on the town. His gaze sweeps the floor as though he expects to find some treasure of evidence among the cigarette butts, paper cups, and spilled beer. With one hand he snaps his fingers to approximate the beat and he leans against the wall as though into a shadow, mingling, under cover. Were it not for the three bags of Colombian grass he is carrying with him, Jesse would laugh aloud.

"He can sing," Lisbeth says. "Sometimes I forget how he can sing."

"He misses Radio Veronica."

"Who?"

"A woman he stepped over."

It is one of those moments, more frequent as time goes by, when Jesse knows he should feel fear but doesn't. Law students, English majors, football players, and assorted hipsters around the bar are busy swallowing joints, crushing out butts, or dumping precious ounces down the toilet. He should be afraid. The three bags he is carrying could cost him a year each between four walls north of Sioux Falls. But he is amused and suppresses the urge to giggle. Dusken sings, slurs, rants. He is singing to Bolt now as though there were no one else around and the cop, in response, stares into the singer's speed-red eyes. Hate fills the room like heavy breathing. Getting lost and staying there, Dusken sings, makes outlaws of us all. Bolt is alone, a wolf among tigers, and seems to see no one but Dusken Lowe. Jesse is safe and he titters in the shadows. There is no escape. There may be deputies at the front and back doors who have come for Dusken and anyone who wants to come along for the ride.

"This is weird," Lisbeth says and Jesse can only nod. Dusken has moved to the near edge of the platform and sings down to the shadows that surround the cop. The cop is uneasy now, aware of his mistake. He meant to remain in the darkness, to observe and to intimidate the way the book advised. Wear your enemy's clothes. His broken hands curled toward his chest, Dusken sings "Razor Heart" and from a distance Jesse can see that he's shaken. The crowd no longer sways to the music; the Grande Finale is a roomful of statues and Harper, in fright, threads her way through them to Jesse's side. "Let's go," she tells him but he says he is staying. Dusken is no longer singing rock and the band behind him has gone silent except for a touch of bass and an occasional piano run. Bolt is unnerved but he holds his ground, still leaning against the wall, an unlit cigarette dangling from his lip. Gears and flywheels and a rusty chain.

"That was an ungodly performance," Jesse tells Dusken. "How are you feeling?"

"Like I've reached the end," Dusken rasps. "Hey, my throat is killing me."

"Have another gin and tonic."

"I won't say no."

They have fled the closing-time shambles of the Grande Finale for quieter confines, the Red Rock Lounge at the west edge of town. They are out of their bounds and they know it. The lounge is for locals, the over-forty set. Cowboys might be welcome but rock singers and the like are regarded with loathing and suspicion. Their waitress—Howdy! I'm Arlette, her name pin tells them—grudgingly serves them at their corner table where the dim light soothes Dusken's ravaged eyes. A pianist opposite the bar tickles and twinkles the keys, smiling like a moron all the while, as if to say "Isn't this fun?" though among the twenty patrons only three or four are paying any attention. The decor of the lounge is Midwest Deluxe: the high-backed chairs are covered with blood-red vinyl and the walls are adorned with silk paintings of clowns and crying children and bullfighters, various mirrors, and a neon waterfall which flashes DRINK HAMMS DRINK with maddening regularity.

"Hey, Arlette, a gin and tonic for my friend."

"Ain't he had enough? That's his third already." She empties the ashtray onto her tray. "These don't look like no cigarette butts to me."

"We roll our own," Jesse tells her and as proof he displays his tobacco pouch.

"Like fun."

"Please," Dusken tells her. "Gin. And tonic."

"Be a sweetheart," Jesse adds.

She gives them her Mother Superior glare. "One more won't hurt, I suppose. A drop in the ocean is all." She sniffs. "You two oughta take a bath."

"Not without you," Dusken says.

"Fat chance."

She moves toward the bar and a man calls out to her, "Hey, Arlette. How're you doing?"

"I serve drinks, not autobiography!"

She returns with Dusken's drink and he downs it before her eyes. "One more?" he asks.

"And a beer for me," Jesse adds.

"You two are too cute for words."

"My throat hurts," Dusken says. "I've been singing all night."

She makes the round trip from table to bar to table. "Here you are, Mario Lanza. And a brew for your sidekick. Drink up and get lost."

The pianist, wrapping up a *West Side Story* medley, launches into "Moon River," which he burdens with fruity arpeggios and annoying trills. Six notes to do the work of one. "Watch this," his grin suggests as he smothers the song in sugar and sassafras.

"My head hurts," Dusken complains. "My head and my throat."

"You blew us all away," Jesse tells him. "I've never heard you sing like that. It was awesome."

Dusken shakes his head. "It was a tantrum, that's all. I got mad. I had to keep singing or I would have thrown up all over myself."

"He'll never leave you alone, you know. You're his reason for living."

Dusken drains his gin and tonic. "I killed his kid. That's the way he sees it. I killed Laura and he's going to get me for it."

"It seems to me," Jesse says, gesturing to the singer's hands, "he's already done his job."

Dusken looks at his palms as though at the pages of a book. "I suppose he doesn't know," the singer says, "how much he's taken away from me. He sees me singing and thinks it's all the same. Dusken Lowe is back in town. Dusken Lowe didn't crawl away and die."

"What I don't understand," Jesse tells him, "is why you never reported him after what he did to you."

"Report to whom? The sheriff? Half of Vermillion was already convinced I was the one who killed Laura. I was convinced myself. Losing my hands almost struck me as the logical result of things. I played with fire and I got burned."

"And now?"

"Now I'll have to deal with Bolt one way or another. But not with six-guns or with music. I'll have to come up with a new kind of violence, one that won't leave any marks."

"Maybe you should lay off the speed for a while. Especially after tonight. He really lost his mind in there."

"We both did. I felt like a whole galaxy of exploding stars. I went blind. It was like before, when I knew I could kill with that sound, when the crowds were all around me just waiting for me to light the fuse."

"Any requests out there?" queries the pianist into his microphone.

"Hey, right!" Dusken calls out. "Beethoven's Ninth!"

"Any serious requests will be respected."

"How about the sound of one hand clapping?"

"Hey, shut up, faggot!" It is a balding man at the table next to theirs. He wears a Westway Bowlers shirt and sledgehammers at the ends of his arms. Turning to the pianist, he asks for "My Way."

Grinning neon, the pianist bows his head and begins.

Dusken moans.

They beg another round from Arlette and watch the clock. It is nearly two and the bar will close in a quarter of an hour.

Serving their drinks, Arlette asks Dusken what happened to his hands.

"Got em stuck between an old virgin's legs."

"What the—"

"They grow teeth, you know, if they carry the cherry too long."

"Stupid punk."

Jesse wants to know where they're going next.

"Mexico?" Dusken answers. "South America? I worship sunlight, you know."

"So did Icarus."

"What are you suggesting?"

"Stay cool. Slow down."

"Easy for you to say. You don't have a half-dozen tabs of speed like Harley Davidsons in your blood."

"Last round," Arlette calls to them. "We're closing up in ten minutes."

Jesse signals for one more.

"I thought so."

The pianist, his smile wet at the corners, has wrapped up "My Way" and slithered into a fast-paced version of "Exodus." Where the progression should be slow and intense, a music filled with longing, he plays it fast and spritely, in the meantime in the lean time ain't we got fun, boop. Dusken holds his hands to his ears, gasps, groans aloud. Arriving at the refrain, the pianist tosses trills hither and yon, like a madman dealing cards to sparrows in the park.

"WHAT ARE YOU DOING?" Dusken leaps from the chair. The pianist half turns but continues to dribble and tinkle and flutter.

"SILENCE!" Dusken shrieks. Then he reaches for his own throat, panting. "Turn it off. Stop."

The balding man, the Westway Bowler, rises and grabs at Dusken's arm. "Siddown!"

The pianist persists. "Exodus" trips and patters. "Mary Had a Little Lamb." "Twinkle, Twinkle, Little Star."

Dusken crosses the lounge toward the pianist and Jesse is too late to stop him.

"You cretin. You moron."

"Hey, what the hell?" Arlette races from behind the bar to

intercept him but Dusken is already at the keyboard. Shoving the bewildered pianist aside, he fingers the keys angrily, then softly. Then he launches into "Exodus" from memory, a simple song that anyone, even a cripple, can play. "Listen," he says between phrases. "It's a story of lost people getting found. Hear it?"

But before he can get very far, they are upon him, the balding man, Arlette, and the house bouncer. There is a tug-of-war and his shirt is torn. Jesse leaps into the tangle but is pushed to the floor and pinned by the bartender. Dusken has gone down under the weight of the Westway Bowler and his rasp-throated howl is muffled by a slap to the throat. Someone is shouting for the cops but Arlette says, "Not in my place. No cops."

"You filthy hippies," the bartender says to Jesse's nose. "Lousy communists."

"Toss em outta here," Arlette orders.

Jesse is lifted by the legs and shoulders by the bartender and another man.

"Music," Dusken rasps. "Veronica. Not your fucking noises."

Chairs are knocked over and tables upset. Jesse hears a lone glass roll from a table and crash to the floor and the door is pushed open. He feels the cold of the night on his face. The bartender punches him once again in the throat and once across the forehead.

"Once more, with feeling," Dusken rasps.

As he and Jesse are tossed like bit actors in a B-western into the mud and the snow.

Deaf and dumb night. Starless, moonless, blind winter night. On the edge of nowhere, in Jesse's car, they count their bruises and giggle into the dashboard. Across town, Harper helps Lisbeth up the stairs. Everyone in the world is drunk. Two Trees, alone in his dormitory room, digs under his bunk for the tit & ass magazines he keeps stashed among empty bottles of Southern Comfort. Bolt consoles himself with a bottle of Jack Daniel's and repeats to his wife the litany of youth's sins. Gena, waiting for Dusken in his chaotic studio, examines his books, his papers, the kitchen cupboards, searching for a trace of his love for her.

Jesse drags from a fat joint and coughs into the windshield.

"Scintillate, scintillate, tiny asteroid. How I speculate as to your existence," Dusken quotes.

"Wha?"

"Twinkle, Twinkle, Little Star."

"I get it."

"For what reason did the bird of poultry plumage traverse the ribboned highway?"

Jesse rolls with it. "To arrive at her desired end."

"We need beer," Dusken tells him. "My throat is like steel wool."

The middle of the night, the uneasy night. Jesse fumbles in the glove compartment and finds a bent can of old beer. "That's all there is," he says. "You can chill it in the snow."

"Take me to the Twenty Four," Dusken tells him. The Twenty Four is the only place open in Vermillion at this hour.

Jesse admits that he doesn't have a dime. "Your gin and tonics wiped me out."

Dusken digs into his jeans and extracts a wad of tens, fives, twenties. "Rock stars have it made," he mumbles.

Jesse guns the engine. Two Trees, safely under the sheets, curls his palm and goes to work. Gena empties the wastebasket and paws over Dusken's rejected lyrics, smoothing the wadded paper across her thighs.

Jesse wheels the '64 Ford Galaxy into the Twenty Four parking lot and they stagger inside to the sickly yellow lights of the tiny grocery store. An old bird glares at them from behind the cash register as they wander up and down the packed aisles. There are mirrors in every possible corner of the place and they see their refracted images, the bird in the background, advertising; nearly everything is overpriced and on sale at the same time. The old lady watches them in the mirrors as they wander toward the junk food, rack after rack of Twinkies, cupcakes, fruit pies, Fritos, Doritos, Ripples, jalapeño bean dip, peanuts, crazy corn, popcorn, cheese puffs, and half a wall of sunflower seeds. The old lady eats sunflower seeds, cracking them between her teeth, spitting the shells into a brown paper bag, and swallowing the meat.

"What'd we come for?" Jesse asks. "I forgot."

"Beer," Dusken reminds him. "Over this way."

They cruise past the canned goods, the dog food, the kitty litter, toward the cooler. Jesse accidentally knocks a bottle of Napa Valley wine to the floor, breaking the bottle open, and the bird leaps from her perch. "You'll pay for that," she informs him. "Peoples gotta pay for what they break here."

"This ain't our night," Dusken remarks. Yanking open the cooler, he extracts a six of beer and slams the door shut.

"Not so hard!" the old lady warns him. "Break that door and it'll cost you!"

They cannot stop giggling. The pot is doing its damnedest. As they straggle toward the cast register, Dusken kicks over a neat little pyramid of canned peaches and one of the cans splits open, spilling yellow across the floor. "Shit."

"You'll have to pay for that, too," the lady tells them.

Jesse leans over the spilled peaches which resemble tiny sunsets on the dirty linoleum. "Sweet chaos."

"How much?" Dusken asks the woman.

"Seventy-nine cents," she tells him. Jesse notes that the price on the can is 47¢. "The wine is two fifty and the beer is three dolla."

The singer lays a ten on her withered palm. She spits sunflower seeds into the brown paper bag. "I ain't got no change," she tells them.

Exasperated, Dusken hurries back to the cooler for another six of beer. "We're even," he tells her as they dance out the door, cans tumbling in their wake.

Lisbeth sleeps dreamlessly and Harper dreams without sleep. Bolt, remembering his Laura when she was six years old, his little princess, weeps into his wife's clavicle. Night shudders and stumbles toward dawn. Jesse drives toward the Blue Max, where he can have a cheeseburger for forty-five cents, chili, french fries, anything to fill the void in his belly. But when he steps out of the car, his throat opens wide and he bends and vomits on his shoes. "New plan," Dusken tells him, pushing him back behind the wheel. They tour their sleepy little town, crisscrossing from street to avenue, passing beer back and forth, raising and lowering the volume of the radio depending upon the music. Gena, hearing a car approach, hurries to the window as Jesse glides by. "Dusken!" she calls. "Dusken, I gotta talk to you!" The singer slides down in his seat. "Get me to the

border,'' he tells Jesse. ''Mexico, South America. Anywhere.''
Jesse imitates Mario Andretti and the tires sing against the icy
road. ''Dusken,'' Gena whispers to the snow. ''Dusken, I'm
pregnant.''

Two Trees, out of Kleenex, sleeps with his seed. Bolt, passed
out in the arms of his wife, dreams black & white dreams.

The light of dawn appears in the rearview mirror, or it is only
the headlights of another car.

''Get us lost,'' Dusken advises and Jesse, knowing the way
by heart, obliges.

9

Harper has long believed that South Dakota summers should be
consecrated to sleeping or to reading bad novels or simply to
idle drunkenness. The July sun seldom rises without bursting,
frogs gasp and shimmy on dry riverbanks, and the corn, swaying
and bowing in the night breezes, thrives. Dakota weather, in
any case, is exaggerated, nine months of winter and three months
of hard times. Winters too cold and summers too hot. Spring
and fall are blinks in time and Harper remembers a bad poem
a distant aunt of hers wrote which compares Dakota weather to
a sticky window shade. All the way up or all the way down. One
way or the other. She strips naked, showers, and lays the cooling
peach of her body on the bed. It is the deadest hour of the day,
somewhere between three and four in the afternoon, and even
the flies, motoring from wall to wall, are lazy. She has awakened
from a brief nap which she'd hoped would refresh her and open
her eyes. She yearns to see Jesse but isn't sure where to find him
just now. He appears and disappears, and anyway she has work
to do. Work before pleasure. What if they are the same thing?
Her camera is loaded and pictures need taking. If only she knew
where to find them.

She brushes her damp hair with her fingers and reaches again for the letter. "These photos are not up to your standard," it reads. "Unlike those of the 'Jesse' series, they do not tell an endless story." Disappointment arrives folded among flyers for occupant and hers is a letter full of the bad, not quite awful, news that she is not yet as good as they thought she was.

And I thought I'd arrived. I should have known better.

In the spring she had been, to her secret self and assorted others, a success. A collection of the pictures she'd taken of Jesse, seventeen in all, had been accepted by a gallery in Chicago on a commission basis. This alone had thrilled her but later, when all of the photos had sold, most for two hundred dollars and a few for as much as five hundred, she'd been delirious with joy. One lucky domino had tipped another and a magazine had reprinted six of the photos with a short article describing the photographer "Harper Adams, exhibiting a special gift for theme and texture, debuts here with the 'Jesse Series' . . ." and paid her another five hundred. She'd then received a letter from a known New York photographer offering her a scholarship to study in his class at Columbia.

"He says I have a unique sense of depth, Jesse. He says my shadows are inspired."

"They are."

"He thinks the influence of New York will do me good. I'm an interior artist, not rural. I can't stay in South Dakota much longer."

Jesse had agreed that she should go. He had smiled and was sincere. You should go, you really should. They had laughed and gotten high and shared champagne. Lying together in bed, they had looked again through the Jesse series, the seventeen photos she had chosen from among fifty for the collection. She had felt a sweet kind of certainty, the world had for a moment ceased to spin, and she felt herself to be more alive, more aware of being alive, than ever before. She studied in the day, worked on her pictures in the evening, and slept with Jesse at night and all was well except that Jesse wasn't saying much whenever she mentioned his coming to New York.

"New York is another planet," is all he said. "New York is somewhere else."

"It's what we need; somewhere else. This isn't home, not for either one of us."

"Home is another planet."

Swords are drawn and neither gives ground. Jesse seems to want nothing more than what he has and Harper has uneasy visions of their future being spent in Vermillion or on a farm somewhere like so many of Jesse's buyers: country hipsters going back to nature, wearing simple cotton, listening to simple music, whose children are always badly dressed and who wander, late at night, through the farmhouse, stepping over stoned guests, empty bottles, broken toys.

In the giddy wake of her success with the Jesse series, Harper had put together another collection she'd called "Peopled Rooms," a too hastily accomplished series of "shots" of the Grande Finale, a women's toilet, a bus terminal, her own bedroom. She'd sent this collection to the New York photographer and awaited his word.

Lying in bed, she rereads the letter half a dozen times, laboring through the faint praise and agonizing each time over the same phrase: *they do not tell an endless story*. She regrets her hate, her laziness, and admits to herself that the pictures she rushed off in April were badly conceived. She'd been so filled with a sense of accomplishment, the magnificence of her name in print, that she'd been aware of herself behind the lens. This is me taking this picture, I am the photographer. Such awareness would forever destroy a picture.

My eyes deceived me because I was looking the wrong way.

She insists, in the heat of the bedroom, that she will go to Columbia in the autumn and her star will rise in the east. The Jesse photos, if anything, are more famous than ever. Some of those which originally sold for two hundred dollars are said to have since been resold for as much as a thousand. Reprints of "Jesse Through the Window" have been included in four different reviews of photography.

If I did it once, I can do it again. I can do it forever.

She folds the offending letter in half and tears it down the middle. She will believe in herself, she will not doubt what she has come to know. Life is a living tree and the fruit is for those who shake the branches. Harper shakes, Harper shivers. And in the worried depths of her heart, she wonders if perhaps the art in her photos is really Jesse's, the art of the enigma, and not entirely, not truly, her own.

Somewhere in my unknown past, my forbidding European origins, there may have been farmers, or, better, botanists. There is, in my Dark blood, an appreciation for that which self-multiplies, whether it is flesh or plant or spirit, and the sight of my window, haloed with vines of my own growing, my own propagation, is both a joy and a comfort. From the weary branches of a single peperomia, I have raised three more. Cuttings from my heart-shaped philodendron, though slow to take root, have given me two distinct plants, both of which hang and sway in the breeze of my great west window. The newcomer, a devil's ivy I found rotting on the steps of the student union, has recovered, and I count three new waxen leaves in the past ten days. In my garden I have ideas, inspirations which seem to bud and flower and burst and disappear. I have a plan for every morning and a wish for every evening star and when I lay myself down next to Harper at night I forget everything but the smell of her hair and her neck and I have to force myself not to start whining, not to ask her to stay with me instead of taking a long bus ride to a crowded city to become famous. I keep playing the same song over and over on the stereo because there's a short saxophone piece, a ten-second moan and wail, that gets to me. Saxophones save me from my own stupid melancholy and Vermillion summers leave me with too much time on my hands. I can lie for hours in the sand alongside the river or waste an afternoon on the porch of some farmhouse smoking grass and drinking beer. I can read books without understanding them and I can watch my plants grow. Then I am sitting with a handful of useless ideas and a mattress full of unsold marijuana, looking through that window and wondering what's keeping her. Harper. She searches high and low for my ambitions or my aspirations. "You can't sell grass forever," she tells me, and the summer has proven her right. In the summertime the students go home and my market disappears. Picture the corner grocery store overflowing with rotting oranges, wilted lettuce, browned apples. Unable to advertise, I smoke up my stock and my lethargy adds hours to the summery-long days. I mark time, sleeping till noon and then waiting impatiently for night so I can hide myself in starlight and in the vines of Harper's arms. I pray to my dead mother though I have never visited her grave. There is nothing there, nothing in her casket I can believe in or speak to. Someone, I don't know who, had to go around that burned-out house and gather up their remains. Something to put into the casket, bones or teeth or even a charred shoe. How they distinguished Bill from Dorell is a mystery to me. Or did they get the ashes mixed up and bury a little of each with the other? I never knew what they buried. I just saw the holes in the ground and the boxes lowered into them and for all I know there are ashes of pillow and bedpost, wallpaper and floorboard, in those graves, though there was evidence enough of the bicycle chain around the bones of my mother so I assume she was buried with their rust. The day of the funeral was incredibly sunny, bad fishing weather, the sky a shallow and touchable void. Ingersoll, more than ash but just as forever dead, was buried elsewhere and I never understood why no one blamed me the way I blamed myself. He had gone into the house and just like that it had fallen down around him. From time to time I go to the Angel Ward to ask silent Rose for advice, for her opinion, for guidance, but her eyes look somewhere past the window and her lips never move except to disengage a tear of spittle or to suck the proffered orange juice from a straw. The body goes on living by itself, divorced from the rest. I watch her as I watch a sunset and I wonder, at times, if her insanity, her catatonia, could be the reason she grows more beautiful. She is lovelier each day or I am crazy. Her complexion is clearer, her breasts have grown full and heavy, her fingers longer and smoother, and her hair shines in the sunlight. It may be my love that makes me see her this way. In place of lifelessness, I see beauty, the stillness of marble. I see oceans in her irises, storms and countless histories, but no Rose, nothing of spark or recognition I can identify as my sister. There are those who place their faith in plastic St. Christophers with metallic bases. They drive full speed ahead, toward the setting sun, and are comforted by the little statue of a saint who never lived, a myth, a legend. I place my faith in Rose, in her stillness, and when I drive west out of Vermillion toward Yankton, I count the cornfields on either side of me, the sun is full upon my face and my path is only occasionally blocked by farmers on their tractors or in pickup trucks, or lost tourists wondering which way the Black Hills might be, their windows rolled up tight to ward off the arrows of hidden Indians. She will never recover, they tell me, and I believe them because Rose, in her still and awesome beauty, concurs. To recover she would have to remember. To remember is to relive. Rose, miming mother, plays dead.

A few weeks ago, I went with Harper to visit her father, who lives alone on what's left of his once sprawling farm north of Mitchell, nowhere country south of Fort Pierre where the Indians, even in defeat, refused to go. Without sons and suspicious of hired labor, Harper's father had already sold away most of the land in fifty-acre parcels. All that remained was a scatter of chickens, half a dozen skinny cattle, three acres of cornfield, and an enormous vegetable garden which he tended by hand. Old farm machinery was rusting in the yard and apples fell unpicked in a grove by the front road. We arrived on a Saturday evening and he came out to the porch to greet us. He was a tall man with broad shoulders and enormous hands, the kind of man who had probably won all his fistfights when he was younger. Leaning over the porch steps, he reached a hand to me. "Calvin Adams."

The hand engulfed my own and my knuckles whitened. "Jesse Dark."

To Harper he said, "You might have called ahead."

"This isn't a hotel, Dad. It's my home. Besides, we wanted to surprise you."

"You did a good job of it. There's nothing for dinner."

Harper blushed, avoiding my glance. "We'll manage."

Like so many Dakota farmhouses, Calvin Adams's was something of a family museum. The furnishings were mostly of wood, the kind of imitation Louis XV that optimistic pioneers had brought from the east, sanded and restained to a dark grain, preserved from one decade to the next in a region where time is measured in seasons rather than days. The living room was deep and warm, littered with wool rugs and cast-iron lamps and dominated by a fireplace with a marble mantel upon which were dozens of photographs, nearly all of them dating from 1950 or long before; pictures of bearded, staring men or high-coiffed unsmiling women, farm families in sepia lined up in front of old Packards, and in the center were portraits of Calvin's two dead sons, Gregg and Donny, like honored guests in the past's hall of memory.

The kitchen was painted yellow and white, with red-checked curtains over the windows and the unsurprising "Lord Bless This House and All Within" in tapestry hanging near the oven. Calvin offered me a wooden chair at the big white table and poured a beer from a blue porcelain pitcher for each of us.

"Homemade beer," he said. "Get it from a friend in town."

Harper rummaged through cupboards and shelves, searched the refrigerator, and scoured the pantry. "We've got rice, green beans, and lemon pie, but nothing for a main course."

"I was telling you," Calvin said. "And it's getting a bit late for a trip into town."

"It's no wonder you're getting so skinny." Harper smiled.

He didn't take the bait. "Do just fine," he answered. "Got my garden, too, but I don't suppose you thoughta that."

"Can we butcher a chicken? I could make chicken and rice in a white wine sauce."

"Why the hell not?" her father answered. "Why the hell not butcher another chicken? Chickens is a pain in the ass anyhow." Taking his glass of beer with him, he went out the back door, leaving Harper and me alone.

"He scares you, doesn't he?" Harper asked.

"A little."

"He's not what you'd call warm."

"I get the feeling he'd rather be alone."

"He would, but that doesn't mean I'm not going to visit my own father when I want to."

Dinner, thanks to two good bottles of white wine, was easier. Calvin asked me the usual questions. Why didn't I get a haircut, what did I do for a living, did I plan on marrying his daughter, what did I think of the stinking war, and I answered him with the same calm as if he'd asked me less poisonous things. If he was giving me some kind of paternal test, I knew I had failed when I admitted I didn't like baseball. Calvin was a Chicago Cubs fan, which apparently meant he was a believer in faith and not in manifest victory.

"That's where I come from, if Harper didn't tell you. North Side Chicago. I been a Cubs fan since 1930 even if they ain't won shit since '45. You fall in love with a team, you stay in love, no matter where they are in the standings. Around here all we got are Twins fans. You know, that team up in the Twin Cities. But I can't get interested in them. Too many Cubans and such. I get the Cubs games on my radio and it takes a hell of a good radio to get Chicago tuned in. You ever play the game?''

"Only a little. I was kind of small when I was—"

"No excuse. Little guys got their role, too. Shortstops, for example. Ever hear of Rabbit Maranville?''

I was ashamed to admit I hadn't.

"He wasn't half your size. And the White Sox, they had this Venezuelan kid, Aparicio, he was about your height.''

"I didn't—"

"I used to play with my boys out past the apple grove. Gregg couldn't hit a lick but he had an arm to beat the band. He used to pick rotten apples and throw 'em at birds on the wire. Course Donny was the hitter of the two. Made All-State Bantam League three years straight.''

Thinking of his sons, Calvin Adams grew quiet. The wine had been Harper's idea and he hadn't had the liver for it. Calvin was a beer drinker, a Protestant who thought wine was for funny business over altars.

Harper rose from the table. "I'll do the dishes,'' she said. "Jesse, you can dry.''

Calvin went into the living room and began to fiddle with his radio and I was alone at the sink with Harper.

"Rabbit Maranville?'' I said, taking a towel.

"You're just lucky he didn't start talking about Ernie Banks. We'd have been here all night.''

She had told me about her brothers, but until coming to the farm her stories had been abstractions to me. Now I felt the loam of them all around me, their memories stitched into the carpets, the curtains, along the mantel. Harper had been six when her mother died and a year later her oldest brother, Gregg, had rolled his tractor and been crushed beneath it. The other brother, Donny, had gone from high school to Vietnam, where he'd stepped off a path to take a leak and found himself at the bottom of a spiked pit. "I was never really here for him,'' Harper had said, "just as there are no pictures of me on that mantel of his. I didn't know my mother and I barely knew Gregg. I didn't even cry when I heard about Donny because for one thing he was always such a brute to me and for another he was five years older than me. I sometimes felt like I lived alone here. I used to pick eggs and tend the garden, feed the chickens, do the laundry, and keep up the house. I lived in the periphery, I was like furniture. And ever since Donny died in Vietnam, I have the impression that my father never really looks at me, that he's never noticed there's another biography going on around here. He was always obsessed with sons, like that's what it means to be a farmer, to have bumper crops and hordes of sons, all kinds of elbows leaning on the supper table. Daughters just come with the landscape like chickens or cattle.''

While Calvin listened to a Cubs game on the radio, we went for a short walk to smoke some grass. The night was moonless and the sky was unending, cloudless, and the stars seemed smaller than usual, though it may have been the wine or the grass that made it so. Harper led me across the yard toward the apple orchard and she held my hand tight in hers as though otherwise I might drift away into the darkness. It was a warm night and I'd thought she'd just wanted to stroll, but I realized soon enough that she was leading me along, intent upon taking me into the trees. ''Thank God there are no mosquitoes,'' she said as we sat beneath one of the apple trees. ''Bugs can ruin everything.''

I lit a fat joint for the two of us and we smoked it in silence for a while, then Harper said, ''I like having you here, away from Vermillion and all that goes on there. You seem more real to me tonight.''

I didn't know how to answer that, if an answer was required. I said nothing.

''When I was younger, in high school, I used to come here and think about boys. No boys in particular, just boys, men, whoever was on their way. Once I masturbated out here, under the stars. It wasn't very good. I mean, it was lonesome. Boring. I came but I didn't sing.''

I finished the joint and dropped the butt into my shirt pocket. Breakfast.

''You know we can't sleep together tonight.''

I nodded.

"My father is pretty strict about these things. I'm not even sure he's very pleased I brought you home."

"We can wait," I told her, meaning we could wait to make love.

"*I* can't, Jesse." She turned and looked into my eyes. "I can't wait." Unbuttoning the top buttons of her blouse, she pulled it over her head. "Let's do it here."

"What?"

"It's okay. There are no mosquitoes."

Though the night was warm, the open air was cool on my bare ass. I laid my jeans and shirt across the thin grass as though to make a bed and Harper pulled me down, pressing her lips to my neck. "Fuck me, Jesse," she said. "Let me know you've been here. Make me sing."

She had never been a screamer in bed. She had moaned, oohed, crooned, and sighed, but that night, in the sight of God and of apple boughs swaying in a moonless sky, she scratched and cried and, coming in long waves, screamed so loud I was certain Calvin would think that someone, somewhere, had hit a home run. I did what I could to keep up with her, pushing and pulling and leaping within her, and she urged me to come too, which I did with surprising force, and I held myself up on my arms to watch her eyes which were filled now with tears of joy and regret as she was saying how she loved me there, stoned, like that, that was good, tonight, and she shook her head from side to side, I love you Jesse don't worry I love you and it's all right.

Then we lay unmoving for a while, belly to belly, as I took inventory of words spoken in unbroken trails. Had I said I loved her too? I could not have, would not. I had matched her sigh for sigh, gasp for shriek, but loving words, as always, had died in my throat like birds before their first flight. Harper, beneath me, stroked my back and thighs with her long fingers. She kissed my neck and said again how nice it was like this, outside and all, we should have done it long before. "I never knew. Love. I thought I knew." And then, as though to convince me, as though to assure me of her sincerity, she said again how she loved me and not to worry about New York, we'd work it out. A breeze stirred ripples along my spine and when I shivered she said I had grown heavy. I came out of her, diminished and

bathed in glory, and we sat naked for a time, enjoying the nov-
elty of outdoor nudism, and smoked another fat joint. She was
looking away from me, off into the grove of trees, as we moved
from one high to another, and then we heard Calvin calling for
us from the porch so we dressed and brushed the leaves from
each other's hair and tucked in our shirts and kissed again. Heading back to the farmhouse, I did what I could to wipe the I-just-
fucked-your-daughter look from my face.

In the middle of the night she crept down the hall to my room
and awoke me with kisses, whispering "Let me be on top this
time" and in the darkness she rode me to a silent orgasm, collapsed, dozed at my side for a while, then left. When I awoke
again there was sunlight and Harper came with coffee, saying,
"It's okay. He's gone to church. We've got at least two hours to
ourselves." I smoked the day's first joint and drank my coffee
before Harper dropped her robe to the floor and took me in her
arms. "Do you mind, Jesse? I don't know what's happening to
me." But instead of using the bed, we went downstairs to the
kitchen and in the white morning light we made it standing up,
briefly, then on the cool linoleum floor and then, giggling, on
the wide kitchen table. "What if he found us like this?" Harper
was saying but I knew that was the thrill of it for her, to be
plowed and furrowed in the midst of whatever was home, that
yellow kitchen, the oven, sink, toaster, Lord Bless This House
and All Within. As if to prove something nameless, we even
tried to continue on the front porch but she got splinters in her
ass from the wooden rail so we released each other and lay
exhausted on the steps.

I felt peaceful, spent, in a way I hadn't in some time. The
yard and garden and porch were awash with summer sunlight
and although we'd already made love a half-dozen times, the
sight of Harper, naked in sunlight, stirred me and the warmth
of the sun on my erection was pleasing. Turning her leg, Harper
reached to remove the splinter but she couldn't get it all so I
turned her over, laying her on her stomach, and took it out for
her, and kissed the spot once, twice, again. Then she said,
"He'll be home soon," so we climbed the steps and dressed
and hurried back downstairs. Her father's car pulled in just as
she was pouring orange juice for me and the old farmer came
bounding in the door, saying what a beautiful Sunday it was,

just a lovely day for prayer, don't you think? We agreed with
him, self-consciously and probably with too much fervor, because he stopped and looked first at Harper and then at me, and
his eyes seemed to reflect his understanding. He knew and we
knew he knew.

"Daughters," was all he said. And he shook his head vaguely,
as if in disapproval, camouflage for a father's secret pride or
sorrow.

Driving back to Vermillion, we took Highway 81 south from
Mitchell and I was aware that we would be driving directly past
the hospital. Harper knew it as well and we were silent for a
time, each pretending to listen to the radio, the news of the
world, casualties light in Vietnam, the Paris peace talks stalled
anew, drought in Texas, floods in Malaysia, two hundred dead
and thousands homeless, and in the news closer to home . . .

Harper shut the radio off. We were a few miles north of Yankton and the hospital was coming up on our right. "Jesse, can
we see her?"

There were hours of daylight left to us and the wide prairie
horizon seemed empty of everything but that hospital, the car,
the road. Geometry as cruel as a switchblade. I had never told
Harper the whole story, had never told her about the fire. I had
only said I'd had a rotten father and a mute mother, both now
dead, and a sister in an asylum. I drove more slowly. "Jesse,
can we see her?" I had told her about Rose in her rocker, lifeless. I had always gone alone to see her, it had never occurred
to me to take anyone along for the ride.

I said why not.

Parking the car along the side of the road instead of in the
parking lot, I led Harper across the grounds, where crazies were
strolling or being pushed around in wheelchairs or playing ragged games of softball, running the bases the wrong way, holler-
ing at each other, enjoying the Sunday sunlight. Rose's ward
was on the northern edge, bordering a wide huddle of trees
where a man-made lake had been left in neglect and was now
only a pool of silt and cigarette butts and gum wrappers.

The afternoon sun was shining into her room and she sat in
her usual place before the window, in the rocker that she never
rocked. The nurse had tied a blue bow in her hair and because

it was a Sunday there was a radio playing gospel music up and down the hallway. Nothing was changed. The bed was made up and the dresser top was arranged as always, with cold creams and baby oils, a few old magazines, a steel ashtray. Rose wore a brown skirt and one of the half-dozen white blouses the hospital provided her every year. I leaned against the windowsill and took her hands in mine but as always she didn't look at me or acknowledge my presence in any way. Harper stood off to the side and I motioned for her to approach. "This is Rose," I said needlessly, and I imagined what it would be like to introduce them, Harper and Rose, but I didn't say anything at all and the silence was less painful than unanswered questions might have been.

"Does she see things, Jesse? Anything at all?"

"I don't know."

"She's beautiful."

"She is."

"I hadn't expected . . . I thought . . . I thought she'd be sort of unhappy-looking. Neglected, I suppose."

I nodded. "She gets more beautiful every day. I don't understand it." I pressed Rose's hands with my own, wishing again she could feel what I was feeling. This is Harper, Rose. Harper loves me.

"How does she live?" Harper asked. "I mean, they must have to take care of her for everything."

"The nurse feeds her twice a day and sometimes they give her injections, for vitamins and things. And they dress her up in a kind of a, you know, a diaper, so she won't mess herself." I refused the tears that were heating up in the corners of my eyes. "She does okay," I said. Change the subject.

But there were things Harper wanted to know, questions she'd never known to ask, having never known of my past, only of my present. I found myself telling her about how I'd run away with Rose and how we'd lived in the farmhouse, how I'd planned to get my mother and to take all of us far away, and her hands went to her mouth when I told her about the fire, and finding Rose in flames in the backyard. I told her about the days after the fire, while Rose was in a hospital, buried under an oxygen tent while being treated for burns and shock while they dug through the ashes of the house and found the bones of a woman chained to the frame of a bed and I knew it was my mother long before the coroner told me. How the day of the funeral some doctor told me Rose was catatonic and should be sent somewhere for treatment. I told Harper everything she'd thought she wanted to know and she just shook her head and wept and hugged herself. And when there was nothing more to tell we said goodbye to Rose and crossed the hospital grounds to the road and I started the car, driving east, toward Vermillion. We slept that night without having made love, in each other's arms, and Harper held me as though I were newly fragile, as though her touch might bruise me. Now you know and nothing is changed.

The next time I went to see Rose I went alone.

July is nearly ended and the summer has been too listless, too tranquil. The dogs may howl but none have come to gnaw upon me in the night. Dusken just returned from a three-month stay in Denver, but he's moodier than ever, like a reptile unable to shake his old skin. He rubs himself furiously and yet the old self hangs on him like a shadow, a ghost. He left town in a hurry and we said goodbye on the run. When Gena got pregnant it was as though the sand in her hourglass had run out and Dusken will never be remembered for the softness of his rock-and-roll heart. Gena took her reserved place in a dustbin of disappointed valentines but unlike the others she went down in spectacular flames. Breaking into Dusken's studio, she smashed his guitars, his electric piano, his stereo and all his records, burned his tapes, broke his windows, and burned every sheet of paper—book, magazine, lyric sheet, or letter—that she could lay her hands on. It was Bolt who pried the singer's hands from her throat and then took her away in his squad car and he'd sworn he'd be back for Dusken. The singer, unshaken, took refuge in my apartment and waited for the whole affair to blow over. "I've got a set of Veronica tapes stashed at my old man's." And Gena? "She'll go back to the cowboy, get a D & C, and forget all this in a week or two." He said this in early February but after a month of living in the thin shadows of a small town, hunted by Bolt, by Gena's brother, the cowboy & co., et al., he'd had enough so he'd taken a Greyhound west, to Denver, where he'd organized a summer session with a little-known jazz band. He sent a single postcard in the space of three months, writing

simply, "I'll be back when I'm forgotten," but his homecoming
was far too soon. The cowboy held a solid-gold grudge and had
spent a good part of May and June skulking Main Street, playing
pool with other rednecks and describing, in living color, how
he would rearrange Dusken's anatomy if ever he showed his face
in the county. Being incapable of violence, I have an exaggerated respect for thundering fists and grunted insults. I've seen
too many Indians bleed red from broken bottles across their
skulls and Lady with her hands at her own throat, scratching
away the boot marks. Closing my eyes, I can clearly remember
the feel of Henry Colter's knuckles across my face the night I
went home with Elizabeth Bad Hand, or the sting of my father's
belt across my baby ass and thighs. A blindness like loyalty
makes me shiver for Dusken Lowe. The cowboy won't do anything on his own, but we live in a world of clans and tribes and
those of us who walk the earth alone are forever at the mercy of
families with common causes. Like Stepin Fetchit, we can only
say "Feets, don't fail me now," run, and see what the next dice
roll offers.

With the money he made in Denver, Dusken bought a new
synthesizer and he spends most of his time alone with it. I drop
by every now and then and we get high together on the rooftop
of his new hideout, from which we can see across a littered
parking lot to Chandler Feed & Seed, the Texaco station, a
sparse grove of trees, and the inevitable cornfields. We smoke
cigarettes, drink from 16-oz. cans of beer, and talk a lot about
things we meant to do, as though we are already growing old
and time is growing measurably short. When the sun goes down,
the crickets come out and their racket is strangely comforting.
We are alone and have the feeling that we will remain forever
so, that autumn will never come, or winter, or Bolt, or the cowboy. They'll never find us here. Late in the evening we climb
down the fire escape to Dusken's new studio and he seats himself
before his keyboard, slaps a tape into place, pulls on his earphones, lights a cigarette, and goes away. Without headphones,
I hear nothing except the plastic clicking of the keys and Dusken's soft humming as he moves his fingers like crippled spiders
across the board. I slip away and walk a few miles to Harper's,
where she waits for me with lemonade and music. We sleep
naked and without covers but I sleep very badly and awaken a

dozen times each night. There is the heat of the summer and the heat of her body and when I lie awake alone and watch her sleeping I am pointlessly angry with her, as though if I cannot sleep then neither should she. Sometimes I awaken her to escape my lonesomeness and she thinks I just want to make love. She doesn't say no and the sex, sharpened by our thoughts of separation, is always urgent, energetic, and exhausting. She falls back to sleep and I am still awake. In my mind I go for a long walk, to the river and back, crossing cornfields, dirt roads, stepping over cowpie, swatting at flies. I bathe in starlight and the river and arrive again where I started, waist-deep in Harper's bed where I am kissing her neck like some little boy, pebble kisses, and she stirs and says Again? and that's not what I meant, I meant something else but I can't say it, so I just say please and she circles my neck with her arms and pulls me down, blinking, to her open mouth.

10

For a long time, Dusken thought he would have preferred to have died among those swaying trees at the edge of the Missouri River. He had awakened long hours after Bolt had left him there and night had fallen starless over the Sioux Valley. The blood of murdered Indians dissolved along the river bottom and a wind meaning rain parted the leaves of the trees. His face was in the dirt and his shattered hands lay splayed across a flat rock, a few blue flies circling the open wounds. His agony was worsened by the sight of the scattered fingers, one tangled among another, resembling kindling for a small fire.

A farmer had found him along the side of the road where he'd later fallen and had taken him to the hospital in Vermillion. A surgeon had driven down from Sioux Falls but on seeing those hands he had admitted that the damage was beyond his skill to

repair. Emergency surgery saved the ring finger on the right
hand, but Dusken had to be flown to Minneapolis for the rest.
His hands had been opened wide and altogether twenty-two
bones had been removed or repaired or replaced with sponge or
plastic. There was nothing to do for the muscle or the synapse
or the hundred ruptured blood vessels. You will always feel a
numbness in your fingers and thumb. The right little finger is
entirely without nerve endings. The left wrist has been grafted
back into place but can't be bent forward or backward. Learn
to hold a spoon between thumb and forefinger. Write your name
and see what hieroglyph spells You.

Whenever anyone had asked him what had happened he had
replied in vague terms about having caught his hands in the fan
belt of an old tractor.

What kind of tractor?

A red one. The old-fashioned kind.

Where is the tractor? Were you alone?

I was alone. I don't remember where.

No one believed him but no one pressed the point. He had
remained in that hospital for more than three months and had
gone home to Vermillion with his hands in enormous, weighty
casts. He wore those casts for over six months, during which
his father fed him and took him out for walks and filled his ears
with stories of doctors in New York and San Francisco who were
said to have done wonders with the new plastics. He hadn't
believed a word of it, particularly when anything he lifted fell
out of his grasp and in the night he couldn't even scratch himself
where he itched. Women held joints like turkey legs to his lips
and he inhaled and held the smoke in the deepest reaches of his
lungs, aching to be high and stay there forever. As long as he
was high he heard no music, he heard only the sound of his
breathing, in and out, or the ticking of a clock, or the wind in
the trees. Without him, the band had gone nowhere and when
his hands were strong enough to hold a microphone he felt like
a priest putting on his chasuble, head bowed, breathing deeply,
hands rolled together like dry leaves for the funeral pyre. "We
need you," Diamond told him. "The tribe is getting restless."

Down from the mountain, up from the dead sea bottoms.
Helpless without a keyboard, he used Aaron as his fingers and
in the space of a weekend he had written "Crawling Through

Midnight,'' ''Razor Heart,'' and ''Fool's Weather,'' all of which were in time the most successful numbers that 3dB ever recorded. They played in Chicago, in St. Louis, in Los Angeles, and in New York. Their first album since the comeback went platinum and Diamond thought they should move out of South Dakota and settle into one of the bigger cities but Dusken would have none of it.

''Just what the hell is so important about Vermillion?'' Diamond demanded. ''In LA we'd be playing the big halls every week. Coke, broads, deals we never even imagined before. I can hear us on the radio.''

''Did you listen to Bleacker Street? They got hold of an old tape and ran it in mono. I sound like I'm singing in the shower.''

''What I'm saying,'' Diamond pushed the words through his teeth, ''is we are big time. There. Arrived. But every time I look around, I see Vermillion. I want to look out my window and see the ocean, Dusken. The Atlantic or the Pacific, take your pick.''

But Dusken chose the Grande Finale. Veronica lives here, or she did. He still had the tapes of the Veronica Quintet and he would play them from time to time, marveling at the talent he had once had. Diamond, hearing the unfinished fourth movement, stole a copy and on his own he rearranged it into a rock piece, playing time 22:14, Joybuzzer LP, side 1, track 2. ''It was easy,'' he later told Dusken. ''All I had to do was blow the dust off the needle. You may think you were better off composing but all I have to do is listen to that quintet to know your ear is tuned to rock.'' An unintentional pun but all the same Dusken felt slandered.

The first time he went to bed with a woman after losing his hands, he was afraid to touch her, to grasp her or to caress her. She had climbed on top of him and rolled her flesh over his own and only when he'd realized that she didn't give a damn about him, that she was only one of those women who liked to be fucked by fame, had he forgotten all about the scars and scales on his palms and he had savaged her with his nails, gripping her back, her thighs, her ass, pinching her and pulling this way and that until they had both collapsed from the exhaustion and violence. Word soon spread that Dusken Lowe was a demon in bed and from that time on he seldom had to sleep alone.

Once again he moved out of his father's house. The old man had grown older tending his son's broken hands. He was only sixty but cataracts had formed over his eyes, blurring his vision. While Dusken was packing his things, he leaned against the doorway and reminded Dusken not to overdo the painkillers. "I know you used to, uh, do things. With drugs, I mean. I wish I could help."

"You've already helped. You've been good to me."

"Love can't heal anything, Dusken. It just helps pass the time."

Dusken said he knew that.

"Don't be a stranger, son."

"I'll call you next week."

Six months after the casts had been removed, he tried, for the first time, to play the piano. His fingers were stiff and wooden and refused to curl so that instead of falling like rain to the keys they seemed to push at them. He found he could play single notes but any chords that required a finger span of more than three keys were beyond him. He exercised his fingers daily, squeezing a rubber ball for strength and pressing his fingers together to bring back their muscle tone. At night he slept with rubber wedges between all of his fingers to help stretch out the damaged muscle and when the pain of playing was too much for him, he turned to Willie, who supplied him with Novocaine and a syringe. Pushing a needle into the middle of his palm, he would take just enough Novocaine to deaden the pain but not so much as to smother the feel of the keys. He always played alone so that when he shanked a chord or missed a note or had to stop in the middle of a progression to yank a finger back into place, no one would see or hear. Veronica had fifty notes for every one he could reproduce on the keyboard and single notes often replaced whole chords so that his compositions were hollow and isolate and lacking in resonance.

Once, crossing a snow-filled street in downtown Vermillion, the singer had run into his tormentor.

"I thought I'd seen the last of you," Bolt had told him.

"You'll never see the last of me. I'll be singing at your funeral."

"I wouldn't count on that. More than hands can be broken, you know."

A year later, when the cowgirl, Gena, had said she was pregnant by him, he had known better. Since their first time together, their opening night, he had not had the will to enter her. She had tried him with her hands, ass, mouth, between her breasts, but had not coaxed him between her legs. Danger there, darkness beyond belief, loneliness, desolation. The seed of the singer hardened on the bed sheet where nothing blooms but blood stains. He runs to Jesse. Jesse knows. Dusken will never again be a father to anyone.

11

In a baseball world of getting high, I was already on second base, dusting my pants and hitching up my belt in anticipation of making it to third. Dakota cornfields shuffled and unshuffled to either side of me as I drove Dusken's battered MG through the new night's darkness toward the farm. The singer passed a joint and cursed when I dropped it. Bending forward, he retrieved a burning ash from the car floor, held it to his lips, inhaled as though just emerged from the depths of the ocean, then passed again, and Jesse, the nightdriver idling on second base, made the catch.

It was the first night of the homecoming, back to school daze, professors at home digging through yellowed notes for lecture material, mommies loading up on pens and notebooks and new black shoes for their kids, and Vermillion reacquainting itself with its tribe. Jungle drums and the throb of familiarity. The farm, belonging to Dusken's band, was twelve miles south, on the Dakota side of where the Missouri River bordered Nebraska, hidden amidst a maze of rutted-out dirt roads and dusty groves of riverside trees. In decades past, before the light-years' evolution of John Deere and International Harvester, a Dakota farm was more or less a patch of anywhere from forty to two hundred acres. Then the big farms replaced the little ones, leaving un-inhabited farmhouses hither and yon along the midwestern prairie. The two dozen or so surrounding Vermillion became the homey hideaways of the young and poor, hippie havens where the stereo could be turned to the max, little plots of marijuana could be raised in secrecy, and the night could last all night, no questions asked. All that needed to be done was to raise the hundred dollars monthly for farmer John and find some way to heat the place in the winter. Dusken and Diamond had rented their house three years previously, intending to convert the two largest rooms into a sound studio, but drugs, insanity, and sloth had sabotaged their efforts and the place had evolved into a sloppy home for three musicians, occasional girl friends, two dogs, six cats, three junked cars, and Rachel, who played earth mother to practically all of them. Rachel was an enormous young girl who had early on taken to wearing loose-fitting long dresses like some impoverished pioneer. She was a natural, meaning she didn't shave her legs or armpits, didn't wear makeup, and practiced a severe kind of vegetarianism in which even the vegetables she ate had to be raw because cooked things were "dead." Rachel made beds, washed dishes, fed the cats and dogs, and nursed overdose cases back to health. During the summer I had visited the farm to make a sale or two and while unspeakable acts were occurring indoors, Rachel would be sitting on the warped porch, seeming to smile eternally—though she may merely have been squinting into the sun. She allowed herself to smoke unfiltered Pall Malls and from time to time would lean forward to scratch a cat with her hardened fingers or to shift her weight from one massive haunch to the other. "They're all inside," she would say, "but I've got what you came for." And she would hand me a nest of dollar bills and a fistful of change for two baggies full of green. "I like you, Jesse, and you want to know why? Cause you don't sell no pills. Pills can make you crazy, Jesse." She would drag deep on her Pall Mall and cats would rub against her great thighs. She was the goddess of the Dakota hipster farm life and pills had made her crazy too. "Don't never sell no pills, Jesse. Specially to little girls, okay?" She had a good heart, as they say, but there were great windy spaces in her mind; as thoughts are like foliage, hers were leafless. All the same, I felt a tenderness toward her and once had considered taking her to bed to soothe her lone-someness, an act of arrogant charity if ever there was one. What stopped me is what always stops me from doing things which may or may not be termed good works: I lived my life as a spectator, an outsider, and was more comfortable watching than doing. My intentions were invitations unanswered. Rachel smoked brown cigarettes, patted her cats, scratched her thighs and the wind blew gently inside of her eyes. I would take the money she had for me and head home, the easy way out.

It was Rachel who greeted us at the farm as we drove into the yard. Lights were lit in every window of the two-story turn-of-the-century wood-frame house and electric music shook the floorboards of the porch, wailed across the abandoned farm-yard, and dispersed among the dark trees that bordered the nearby river.

"Hey, Jesse. Hey, Dusken." She wore a blue cotton dress that fell loose as a bathrobe around her calves but strained the material where her ass heaved outward. The dress had been patched and mended and washed to the point of having faded to a pale blue. "They's all inside and Diamond's been asking for you, Dusken." She asked me if I had a joint for her. "Not really for me but for Thaddeus." Thaddeus was one of her cats. "He been acting weird, scratching and biting people all night." I fished a joint from my shirt pocket and handed it to her. She kissed my cheek and hurried back to the porch. Dusken went inside but I stayed on the porch to watch Rachel care for Thaddeus. Lighting the joint with a wooden match, she puffed vigorously until it was burning a steady orange ember. Lifting a large brown bag, she dragged on the joint and blew the smoke into the bag, holding the end semiclosed so as not to let the smoke escape. When the joint had burned down to the roach end, she put it out and called to Thaddeus, who hurried across the porch to her side. The cat mewed once and she lifted him by the torso, leaning his head into the top of the bag. Thaddeus was still for a brief moment and then began to kick his hind paws against her thigh. She released him, closing the bag with her other hand. The cat sneezed, shaking his head in short, abrupt snaps. He licked his lips. Rachel opened the bag and put him back in. This time he kicked immediately but she held him for a long ten seconds before releasing him. Thaddeus sneezed again and lifted a leg to scratch behind his ears. Rachel bent and kissed his forehead, murmuring, ''One more time, baby.'' The cat was docile as she opened the bag and this time he did not struggle at all. When ten seconds had elapsed, she opened the bag and the cat wandered away from it, padding slowly across the porch as though sleepwalking. He stopped once to turn and gaze toward Rachel, then continued across the porch. When he reached the other end, he staggered and fell, landing very uncatlike on his rump. Rachel rose, crossed the porch, and lifted him from the ground. ''Nice Thaddeus, sweet Thaddeus.'' She stroked his back and neck. The cat was dead asleep and she laid him in a safe corner, under a wooden chair.

I went inside where the screen door led to the kitchen. Half a dozen people were standing around talking and drinking wine from big green bottles or paper cups. The only one of them I knew very well was Two Trees, who sat alone at the kitchen table, trying desperately to roll a joint. The paper kept tearing and he had forgotten to separate the stems, so that when he did manage to get one rolled there were stems and seeds making it unsmokable. I offered to give him a hand but he waved me away, not taking his eyes from his tangled fingers. '' 'S okay,'' he said. ''Sh-she's in there.'' Sh-she being Harper, whom I'd come to see, but I told myself bravely that she could wait. Her bags were packed and in the morning she'd be off. I'd said goodbye a hundred times already and each time was more unsettling than the last. When it came to Harper, I would forever be wanting one more of everything, one more night, one more roll in the hay, one more walk along the river, and she had already postponed her going on two occasions, leaving it to the last possible minute. And all during the month of August she had been reaching for some male thing in me, a denial of tenderness, as though she truly wanted me to act unfeeling toward her. She had kept her distance so that in leaving she could say to herself that I never cared that much anyway.

The enormous living room was a jungle of strangers, near-familiars, and a few friends. When Dusken had moved off the farm over a year before, Diamond had moved the recording equipment to the basement and put a pool table in its place. The stereo system, including two turnables, a reel-to-reel tape set, cassettes, and four mammoth speakers, filled the house with a cathedral sound and joints and bottles were being passed like babies from hand to hand. I saw Harper from across the room and she saw me as well but we both pretended otherwise. The plan was to spend the night together once the party was over and I would drive her to the bus station at dawn.

"You'll write to me?"

I had never written a letter in my life.

"I might be back at Christmas. You could come with me and stay at my father's house. I'll send you prints from time to time. Say something."

"What time does the bus leave?"

Her face flushed red. "Listen, Jesse, I'm going to miss you terribly but I'm not going to cry."

Wandering from friend to stranger, I sold four of the six bags I'd brought with me, knowing that everyone in town would be looking for the smoke. The trouble was that I was smoking it myself in ever increasing quantities and by the time I'd reached the party I was already in a lost mood, misjudging distances, hearing voices that didn't say anything at all, and being less discreet than usual. I bumped into a dozen people, drank whatever wine was passed my way, and, suddenly, like Two Trees, I could barely roll a joint. Dusken came over to ask me if I was all right. "Never better," I replied from the floor where I'd fallen. He offered to help me up but I felt like staying where I was, so he wandered off. I leaned my head against the wall and felt the music rumbling through it like a high tide in a gigantic seashell. I had taken a few pills, cheap Dexedrine, and was feeling them kick in to the right points in my brain. I knew what I was doing, I was getting lost, and all kinds of late late shows were playing in my mind and heart as, from the vantage point of the floor, I could see all that was going on in the room, the laughter and seduction and joy and terror of a night at the farm. Though I didn't want to, I couldn't help but keep an eye on Harper and I was aware of myself growing hotly jealous of her least movement, her easy laughter, anyone who happened to brush her in passing. And then as quickly my jealousy would pass, evolving into a pointless, sticky tenderness for her that would make me choke and flush and sigh. Sentiment would overwhelm me and transform joy to giddiness and back to jealousy. I stayed where I was, anchored to the floor, and let the moods wash over me for what seemed like a very long time. Then, feeling an urge to pee, I climbed upward, stumbled over one of Diamond's dirty hounds, apologized to the mutt, and headed for the stairway.

The steps were littered with people but I lurched forward, stepping over legs, landing on outstretched hands, dodging slaps and curses, until I was free on the upper flight. A bag of new Colombian green slipped from my pocket and slithered down the steps where a young blonde intercepted it. Turning her baby-blue eyes upward to me as though I were Raphael on high, she gasped, ''Hey, thanks, man.'' I didn't object. With a certain stoned rapidity, I calculated the effort involved in redescending the stairs, finding the words to say no, it was only an accident, the bag was for sale after all, and on and on. Anyway, she had already pulled it open and was measuring out the grain for a big party-sized cigar. ''Anytime,'' I told her and, fumbling in my mind for a road map of the second floor, went searching for the john. In even the worst of conditions, I have always had a way of going straight to the men's room, the commode, the toilet. In crowded cafés, bus terminals, train stations, or hotel lobbies, I seem to know the direction, as if my bladder has a kind of radar. So of course there I was, in the only bathroom the farm possessed besides the open air and I locked the door behind me. No crazed hippies searching frantically for the lost roachclip or the spilled cocaine would come busting in on me in the midst of my personal hosanna. I was alone with the mementos of my predecessors: a fur-lined toilet, discarded rubbers, stacks of mildewed magazines and three-year-old yellowed issues of *Rolling Stone*. Holding myself erect as much as possible, I pissed downward, splashing the wall, the floor, and the rim before finding my aim. Someone was banging on the door but I paid them no mind. My business was my own. ''Hey, this is serious! Open up!'' It was a man's voice, vaguely familiar. Finishing, I closed my eyes and felt myself spinning. This was a way of measuring myself to see how stoned I might be, closing my eyes and seeing how long I could remain on my own two feet. The answer was, not long. Kicking the toilet with my right foot, I flushed it with a certain violence and turned to the mirror. In the yellow bathroom light, my face seemed small and red, as though my head had shrunk, and the vision reminded me of an antidrug film I'd seen at Yankton High in which the typical American teenager, crazed on acid, looks into the mirror and sees a hideous monster. Half of the class had been horrified by the film and fully convinced that drugs were no damn good; the other half was hotter than ever to get hold of something flashy, mescaline or psilocybin or acid, anything to make your own home movies with.

The pounding on the door was furious so I zipped up and left, catching a few parting insults from the beered-up crowd waiting outside. Moving down the hall, I opened the first door on my right and saw half a dozen people hovering over a bed, a small lamp lighting their vision. "Close the door," someone whispered and I saw it was Willie, my competitor, the mucho-serious dealer. He was lining cocaine in little rows along a mirror and those around him held their breath, cautious not to sneeze or to jiggle the mirror lest the least grain be spilled. A sneeze could cost a hundred dollars. Willie rolled a twenty-dollar bill into a tight straw and handed it to the redhead at his side. She lifted the straw to her nostril and bent to the mirror. I closed the door with a malicious whoosh and heard swearing from within.

The next doorway held more tranquil passage, a man and a woman in blue lamplight. The room smelled of the summer and their bodies as the man lifted himself away from the heaving woman. I recognized Diamond. Seeing me, he reached for his jeans, saying, "She's yours, man. I'm all done." Stoned as I was, I forgot myself for a moment, thinking myself a part of some rite, and my hand even reached for my belt buckle. Diamond pulled on his boots and a shirt and wandered out but I stood silently in the doorway, neither coming nor going, when I head the girl say, "Jesse, hey, come on over here." Lisbeth sat up and reached out a hand, wanting not me but the joint I was carrying. I had forgotten about it and it had gone out, so I approached the bed, relit the remainder of the fat joint, and offered it to Lisbeth. She lay her head back on the pillow and I held it to her lips; she opened wide and took it between her teeth with a contented smile.

Back downstairs the music was thrumming and crashing and imaginary chandeliers were swaying and shaking. Two Trees, still rooted to the kitchen table, had begun to talk to anything and everything, particularly inanimate objects. He cursed the table, his broken chair, the water pipe in front of him. When Two Trees was this stoned, he didn't stutter quite so much. He had an amazing way of drifting in and out of coherence and, in comparison with his usual verbal meandering, he took on aspects of a Dakota Olivier. Go thou to Hades, toaster. Get thee fucked, spoon. An impassioned drama major, in from New England, was trying to convince Dusken to be in her play, a rock musical she had written herself. "I've already got six hundred dollars for production and all we need is the right lead. You're it, no questions asked. I'll give you complete control over the music, backdrops, and sound play."

"Why don't you ask Diamond?"

"Because he's never sober and this is a serious project. We're headed for Off Broadway if you get what I'm talking about."

"Off or Off-off?"

"Off."

"Woof woof." When Dusken suggested that they discuss it somewhere privately, she said fine as long as she could bring her girl friend along. "I'm not into men all that much, do you mind?"

Since going upstairs, I hadn't seen Harper anywhere and I began to search for her, punctuating my stops with hits of grass which I watered with red wine. She wasn't in the kitchen and she wasn't in the living room. Rachel was alone on the porch with her sleeping cat and the same stoned cast was scattered along the stairway. I ran into Dusken and the drama major in the den, but still no Harper. In a rising panic, I opened and closed drawers, closets, peeked into bookcases, and scanned the ceiling the way castaways scan horizons. I began to have the impression that I was lost in some haunted house, I was surrounded by spooks, tangled in silvery cobwebs. I was sorry I'd avoided Harper, aware that I'd been avoiding the end of it all, whatever it had been, home or harbor, in the spaces within her arms. Suddenly I had the idea that if I told her I loved her, if I said the words, something between us might be changed, might be retrieved. I knew it was probably too late, too late for words I'd never trusted, it had been strange enough to feel those words inside of me.

I searched the house anew, forcing myself to concentrate, to focus. Speed forces the mind to react to a different clock, from a waltz to a frenetic cha-cha, and I had searched too rapidly the first time around. She was not on the porch, she was not in the kitchen, she was not in the living room, she was not in the den. Someone said Lisbeth was pulling a train upstairs, that she had already had her eleventh man tonight. The downstairs was filled with strangers and I was the strangest of them all. To myself, I said the words, Harper I love you, I love you Harper, like some bit player rehearsing his only line in a tedious play, I love you I do. Struggling up the stairs, I yanked open the bathroom door and shouted "I love you!" to a girl I'd never seen before. Sitting on the toilet, she smiled to me, saying simply, "Kinky and original, but not very convincing. Now close the door."

An old customer met me in the hall, asking me what I had for him.

"I'm cleaned out," I told him. "Ask Willie."

"Willie's a rip-off artist. That's why I'm asking you."

"Call me tomorrow."

"Tomorrow won't do tonight any good."

I found her in the bedroom, in dim light, seated on the edge of the bed from where she comforted Lisbeth. Since leaving the joint behind, I'd missed something: the sad passage of men with numbers, and so I wasn't sure what I was seeing. Lisbeth, still naked, covered her face with her hands and wept, saying over and over again, "No more no more no more. . . ." I felt I was intruding and so stood immobile in the doorway; my line now memorized, now ripe upon my tongue, I waited. Hearing perhaps my breathing or the beating of my heart, Harper turned to me, her eyes lost in the shadows of the room. Bracing myself against the doorway, I opened my mouth to say, to confess, to declare. My tongue shook at its root. "Ilvyou," I said and holding a finger to her lips, she angrily answered, "Shhh."

You can sit on any hilltop and watch the sky at sunset and although you are watching carefully, noting the streaks of gold and red, the wild blue, and although you watch it to the last and final twitches of light, you cannot say at exactly which moment the sun actually set, when the dark dominated the light, when day, like some cheap light bulb, caved in.

I sat on the porch and smoked a cigarette. Two Trees was in

the yard, telling the cars to go to hell. Thaddeus slept his way toward the twenty-first century while flies circled his ears. Feeling a rising breeze, Rachel unbuttoned the top of her dress and held her breasts to the open air.

"So nice," she said. "Like I'm sailing in a boat, you know? Like I'm the one who's moving and not the wind." She reminded me of Rose just then and I was about to answer her when Dusken came out and tapped me on the shoulder.

"Let's roll," he said simply and I rose to join him. He was in some kind of hurry and I had to run to keep up. Reaching the car, I turned and said good night to the upper-story window where Harper would be. I said good night to Rachel and, mimicking Two Trees, I said good night to the porch, the screen door, the bushes, every star I could find, then Dusken yanked me into the car, saying, "Drive," so I put my foot to the floor and we leapt through the darkness, good night.

If I had not been thinking of Harper, if I had been less stoned and mournful, if I had not had illusions of little children running across the road or of birds dive-bombing at the windshield, if fleets of grasshoppers had not been leaping at the headlights and the radio not filling my ears with thrum and noise, I might have noticed the cowboy following us and thus taken a different route.

As it was, I never noticed the headlights—or he drove in darkness, stalking only the taillights of the rumbling MG—and I drove the way drunks drive, with a kind of lazy sway. The cowboy must have followed us very easily. We were bathed in moonlight and headed nowhere special. I took the dirt roads that bordered the river, stopping once to throw up and once to pee. Dusken cracked open a can of beer and I washed down the taste of vomit and dust. Cruising in the general direction of Vermillion, I downed a second can and began to feel the drugs recede. The Dexedrine was wearing itself out and the open air revived me.

We drove in circles for an hour or so, smoking and talking and listening to the radio. At one point a local deejay played a tape from Dusken's LA concert. We listened as though we'd never heard it before, his voice, in the open air of the Hollywood Bowl, seeming to come from a great distance. Turning up the sound, he sang along, matching note for note what he had sung three and a half years before; then, in the midst of a song called "Resurrection," he snapped off the radio with a laugh.

"I give up," he said.

"What do you give up?"

"Rock and roll."

"You're always saying that."

"There's too much death involved, too much insanity."

"You sing it so well."

He laughed again. "Yeah. 'You damned me to hell/but you sang it so well,' " he quoted himself.

Arriving on the outskirts of Vermillion, we stopped at a gas station for cigarettes. Had I not been obsessed with Harper and had the cannabis not been floating like sediment in my veins, I might have noticed the pickup truck parked behind us, on the other side of the trees. But Dusken wasn't watching either. Coming out of the gas station, he bumped into a drunken farmer, knocking him to the ground. The old man was unhurt but by the way he went on about his knee, his shoulder, his ribs, it was as though he'd been flattened by a bus instead of a 140-lb. hippie singer. Dusken lifted him up, dusted him off, and asked him where it hurt. "You long-haired pissant," the man said. "Where's the fuckin sheriff?"

"Are you hurt or what?" Dusken asked him.

In reply, the farmer took a swing at him, a roundhouse right that caught Dusken across the forehead. He staggered to the car, throwing the cigarettes on the floor. "Get me outta here," he snarled and I laid a patch from one end of the lot to the other.

"Death," Dusken was muttering. "Death and insanity. Let's go to your place."

Harper wasn't there. Only the plants, the window. Night like the stocking over a burglar's face. While I rolled a few bedtime joints, Dusken went through my record collection. "I've got a few ideas," he told me. "I don't want to sing anymore, not with 3dB."

"What have you got in mind?" I rolled a Zigzag with renewed skill.

"Nothing specific. Not jazz, not rock. If I hear Veronica anymore, all I get are long piano runs, windy stuff, high notes. Last week I got lost in it but I was having trouble with my right pinkie, the one with no nerves in it. Ever since the surgery, it's been curved inward toward the ring finger, costing me one step toward an octave. I lost my cool and just yanked it over the other way, see''—he showed me how the finger now bent outward—''and I didn't even feel it. That extra half-inch reach adds all kinds of possibilities. Maybe I'm coming back.'' He found some albums that interested him. ''Mind if I take these?'' He displayed them.

''Go ahead.'' I offered him a joint which he accepted with his free hand and dropped into his shirt pocket.

''I'll smoke it at home,'' he told me as he went out the door. The man who never said hello or goodbye. I figured he was going home to play. That was usually what he did in the middle of the night, injecting his hands with Novocaine. But all the drugs in the world would never still his ache for long enough and that's what I was thinking when I switched off the light and folded myself into bed. Who knows where the hurt is? Later I would wonder how it was that they came for me on that particular night, how they knew which door was mine, how they knew that I would be alone. But in bed I hung up all my outlaw instincts and burrowed into thoughts of Harper, waiting for her to come and wondering how to get through the last night of her.

Where is he, Dusken?

Who?

The man. The dealer.

I don't know what you're talking about.

The great window was like a blue and silver screen, curtainless and clear with moony light. For a moment I thought I heard footsteps on the stair and I said aloud, ''Harper?'' but no one answered.

How many bones in a hand, how many tendons, muscles, blood vessels, can be broken, ruptured, or torn before the hand is no longer a hand but a limp and useless glove of skin? How did they threaten him, how did they put fear into him all over again? Did they hold a hammer in the air or did they simply grip his fingers and promise to pull them away from their scarred joints like so many blades of grass?

The room, the door. Which one?

Second floor, first door on the left. Don't.

Is there a number?

No. It's a white door.

Does he have a gun?

A gun? Fuck no. Now let go of my hands, you bastard.

Lighting a joint, I eased my head into the pillow and let myself wander moodily from sadness to joy to the wonder of what it would be to sleep alone again. Without Harper, life threatened to slip back into black and white, long nights of doing nothing more than losing myself in detail or, in imitation of Rose, going blank for days at a time, feeling no mood and no weather, time on my clasped hands. I had dreams of earning great sums of money, enough to get Rose out of Yankton and into more pleasant surroundings. Though I had never been there, North Carolina sounded like a good idea. She could sit year round on a porch or something, smelling magnolia blossoms instead of cowshit, and those sweet southern voices, "Heah's your lemonade, honey," might have soothed her. I finished the first joint and lit the second, wondering briefly if Harper would leave the party and come looking for me one last time. In the fog of my high, any pain I was feeling was dull, like an old bruise. In the morning, if morning came, I would feel the hurt anew. I remembered how, as a child, I had said my bedtime prayers with my mother at my side. "If I should die before I wake . . ." I would say, not realizing how I was covering my bets, placing unbearable conditions on the night ahead, "If I should die before I wake, I pray the Lord my soul to take." I was intoning this prayer aloud when the door crashed open, falling from its hinges, and Bolt stood silhouetted in the hallway with his pistol drawn. "GET UP AGAINST THE WALL!" he shrieked and when he burst into the room I leaped upward, trying to get out of the sights of that awful black gun. Bolt found the light switch and the flash of the overheads blinded me. I held a hand to my forehead to shield my eyes from the light.

"KEEP YOUR HANDS WHERE I CAN SEE EM!" Bolt bellowed and I reached for the angels on the ceiling. The cowboy shuffled in behind Bolt and smiled as though he'd just won the big hand at the last poker game. Searching around, Bolt seemed suddenly ill at ease. "You see anything?" he asked the cowboy.

"See what?"

"Drugs. Grass. You know what it looks like?"

I was standing in the middle of the room, wearing nothing

but a pair of cut-offs, and Bolt gave me a look meant to wither me. My knees were shaking. All I had to do was look at that black gun to feel the vomit rising in my throat.

"I told you," the cowboy said. "I don't smoke that weed. How'm I supposed to know what it looks like?"

There were half a dozen bags lying around the apartment like so many pairs of socks but Bolt seemed to be looking for droppers, spoons, white powder, and a syringe or two among the silverware. Then he noticed the kitchen door beyond his shoulder. Keeping the .38 trained on me, he backed up slightly, reaching into the kitchen for the light switch. I was about to tell him where it was, the light switch, when I thought I saw something flickering in the window. It was a flash, as from a falling star, and when it vanished it left the same blue light in the window. For a long moment, I kept my eyes upon that window, searching the frame and the depth of it, measuring what I had looked clean through a hundred times.

Dusken's out there somewhere.

"Don't let him move," Bolt told the cowboy and he turned, cop-style, shoulder-first into the kitchen.

I glanced again at the window, trying to remember the distance down the short cliff to the ravine below. It was thirty feet, or a hundred, or ten. I had no way of knowing which. The cowboy stood to my right, blocking the doorway. To my left was the window. It was the only way out.

"Nothing in there," Bolt said, but as he emerged from the kitchen I leaped forward, shoving the door against his forearm. He dropped the gun and with a bare foot I kicked it out of his reach. The cowboy lunged for me but in two quick bounds I had reached the window. Screaming instinctively, I crossed my arms over my face and lifted my knees and as I crashed through the glass I heard the symphony, sounds like Dusken's Radio Veronica, the bells and cymbals of shattering glass and the sudden thunder of Bolt's .38, my arms and legs were alive with stinging and I was for the barest moment naked in the low sky over Vermillion. Then I fell, I was falling, and the falling might have lasted forever, toward an abyss, toward light, but for all of my wishes the earth was forever there with its arms so blessed and goddamn wide. I fell through the trees and through incredible starred darkness until the earth took me outlaw, dead or alive, into its heavy hands.

   And then I laid me down to sleep.

The Legend of
the Burning Rainbow

1

The last Twin Cities station to sign off in the early morning hours was nearly always KMSP. After the late late movie, there was a local minister who delivered a short homily. For the longest time, Elaine had believed that he stayed up until 2 or 3 A.M. to tell his story, but then she read that it was prerecorded. She was listening to a man who had spoken the previous afternoon and was by now long asleep, or did he lie abed and watch himself and listen carefully to his own smooth words? He always dressed casually and smiled as though he were mildly uncomfortable but was bearing up just fine. His homilies were meant to be simple, like stepping-stones on the stream to glory, but Elaine seldom understood them because she was preoccupied with the man's clothes, his face, his frozen smile. After he closed his talk with a blessing, there was a black moment while the late-night technicians changed reels or whatever they did, followed by a film of U.S. Marines storming up a hillside with an American flag. Elaine would listen to ''The Star-Spangled Banner'' and listen to the drumrolls and count the cymbal crashes and had never entirely understood the words, nor had ever cared to. She would be thinking of the minister and what he had been wearing, the color of his sweater and the curl of his lapel. He often wore blue, her favorite color, the color of baby boy things, booties and jumpers and bluebirds on the wallpaper. Then, in a jet of electric vacuum, there would be only the static buzz, a video blizzard, on her screen. She would fall asleep to that buzz as though it were a lullaby, but later in the night, transformed into a horde of flies, it would awaken her. A glow from the cathodes made the room vibrate and she would move naked from the bed to shut it off. A part of her seemed to follow the light that retracted on the screen, held for a moment in the last center of the matrix, and then extinguished itself. Wait, wait, gone.

Before going back to bed, she would often turn on a lamp and sit at her vanity. Taking out pen and paper, she would prepare herself for her writing. It bothered her to write while her own face, lined with sleeplessness, looked on, so she would press a sheet of paper against the center of the mirror, closing the curtains on herself, the voyeur. She sometimes felt foolish with a pen in her hand and a blank sheet of paper in front of her. "Should it be a diary?" she'd asked her counselor and he had answered that it should be whatever she wanted it to be. For the first week or so it had gone very badly for her. Her words looked clumsy on the page, more like drawings of insects or stick men than words. She'd said so to her counselor and he'd said it didn't matter. Words are pictures. At the worst, you're killing time.

But I don't write so good. I mean with grammar and all.

It doesn't matter. There's no such thing as grammatical error except in a recipe. Your teachers lied.

But how do I start?

Write a letter to yourself and sign it Love.

Making a letter out of it made everything easier because she said it aloud to herself before putting it to paper. As a joke for the counselor, she added a postscript with a recipe she'd copied from a magazine but he didn't remember and when he read it and didn't laugh, she'd had to remind him. *Then* he laughed but not for very long. Later she wrote other things, sometimes stories, sometimes lists of things to do. Once she rewrote a late late movie she'd watched but in her four-page version she changed the ending and no one died.

Her counselor took a new job in a different state and a woman took his place. Elaine could not write letters for a woman and so she stopped. Then she quit going to the center altogether. In the winter, when the hum of the television awakened her, she would turn it off, then sit quietly in the darkness, writing her thoughts as though on paper and reading, or reciting, back to herself just to pass the time.

Dear Elaine, today she was thirty-one years old and despite her solitude she didn't feel exceptionally alone. Once she had been a prostitute but now she worked as a secretary in a grain supply warehouse. Her boss was twice her age and though she had been married and divorced he called her Miss. She typed invoices, delivery slips, and stock lists. There was a telephone on her desk but it seldom rang and almost never for her. She shared the office with her boss, who despite his age kept a nudie calendar pinned to the wall behind his desk. The grain foreman always flipped through the months while waiting for Elaine to finish the delivery slips. He cheated on his wife and had sometimes asked Elaine if she'd like to see his cabin in the north woods.

"I hate the woods. They're full of mosquitoes."

"No mosquitoes in the bedroom, babe."

She worked from eight to five and had one hour for lunch but never took more than forty minutes. Work gave her something to do. Time was not of much use to her except as a way of turning today into yesterday. Tomorrow she would still be an ex-prostitute, an ex-wife, and an ex-mother, but the void of it, her past, would blur. Like the foreman, she looked ahead to other months. In the meantime there were forms to be typed, one carton for the files and another for the customer.

She lived alone in a suburb north of St. Paul, in Minnesota. A highway separated her little tract house from the city limits. She had neighbors she'd seldom seen, no stereo, and no pets. She read the same magazines that housewives read, wanting to learn what she felt they already knew. Home is an efficient kitchen, home is a new bedroom set; lemon restores the beauty of wood and flowers wilt in sunlight. She watched television from eight to sign-off and was not alone. She knew what she was waiting for and she would wait forever, she told herself, long enough for a criminal record, denying her her son, to grow yellow and forgotten in whatever damned file it was in.

Sometimes, bored with the television and feeling a familiar weight of ache in her chest, she would take a bus into St. Paul. Getting off at the north end of downtown, she would walk past Shanty's bar and Mickey's Diner, places she once knew inside and out but which had become strangely unfamiliar, rearranged in her memory as though they were not on the same street anymore. Crossing Wabasha Avenue, she would come to an aging apartment house. There were two doors, front and side, and she always went in the side door. Climbing the steps to the fourth floor, she would stand in front of a door for which she no longer had a key. Alone there, she would listen through the wood for any sound, but she seldom heard a thing. She would only stay a minute or two, too terrified to knock, then when she was certain she could stay no longer, she would steal back down the stairway and out the side door. Crossing Ninth Street, she would wait on the corner for the 12E bus to take her home.

"You will have to prove your worthiness," her counselor had told her. "You will have to be able to demonstrate your rehabilitation. After that, it's up to the father and whether or not we can show proof of his alcoholism."

On the other side of the highway, she would turn on the television. The reverend would be wearing a white V-neck sweater and he would be telling a story—the man carried baby Jesus across the river, he bore him up on his broad shoulders, and he carried our Infant Savior to glory—and then the marines would charge up the same hillside to plant the flag, cymbals would crash like breaking glass, and the home of the brave, then a blackness, then snow.

2

Dear goddamn Jesse, I'm giving this letter to Marvin, who doesn't have any better idea than I do where you might be, and I'm not sure if he'll hang onto it until he finds you or just throw it out. I should already be on a bus to New York but this morning Bolt came down to pick me up for questioning and I spent the morning in his office. It was a real circus with Willie and about half a dozen other dealers, Marvin, Lenny, the bottom of a deep Vermillion barrel, and no one knew anything worth telling. Afterward, Marvin—who was about as hung over as a man can get—told me you'd come to him for money and clothes and you'd taken your car somewhere, so I'm not as worried as I was. Everyone is talking about your magnificent escape. Marvin drove me past the house and when we saw the broken window and how far you must have fallen, I got the shudders. We were pretty sloppy about saying goodbye and all day long I've been regretting it. What if you don't come back? What if you don't call? I've always blamed you for the way you come and go and I wouldn't be surprised if you just disappeared completely. But I wouldn't be happy, Jesse. Imagine me elsewhere and imagine how much I already miss you. One good thing is that you won't be dealing anymore. I know I never said so but sometimes it made me nervous to sleep in your apartment. I never knew who was calling or who was knocking on the door and I resented how the phone would ring when we'd be asleep or making love. You never minded, or if you did you never showed it. I got the feeling you were most comfortable when you could think of yourself as some kind of antihero living on the fringes. Like you were warm out there. Like being with me weakened you somehow. And now you're just another dealer in exile. You can go back to Vermillion but not for a long time, so where are you now? My bags are packed and I'm taking tomorrow's bus like I should have taken today's. When I have an address, I'll be sending it to Marvin and I'll be hoping, even if I shouldn't be, that you'll be in touch with Dusken or Marvin or anybody who can be a bridge for us. I couldn't stop myself from going to New York any more than you could stop yourself from jumping out that window. What would I have been to you in Vermillion? Your female hideout? I need so much to know where you are and I feel so stupid writing a letter that I'm not even certain will get to you. I'm sitting in a room I've already said goodbye to, drinking warm wine, and writing this letter and I just noticed that I haven't even made my bed. It depresses me to look at it and I'm sure that if I wanted to get good and nostalgic I could go and dig around the sheets and find a stray hair or two, some souvenir of the now infamous Jesse Dark, who loved me but never said so. But I'm not that drunk yet. Maybe later I'll take a picture of that bed. I'll turn on the bedside lamp and pull the shade down just a bit to leave a symbolic shadow over *your* pillow and maybe I'll mess up the covers just a little bit more. I'll call it *Jesse Slept Here* and maybe the magazines will buy it. I can get even more famous off you and maybe I'll miss you a little less and not feel like some kind of elephant is kneeling on my chest. Anyway, the bottle is empty and I've got a bus to catch at dawn. Don't stay away forever, my heart breaks easily and I don't have a broom, can you even read my handwriting I can't love Harper.

3

I awoke, as from a short nap, at the black bottom of the ravine. My arms and forehead were laced with little cuts and when I lifted my head from the wet ground, I felt a throbbing and was overcome with dizziness. Then I heard voices, Bolt and the cowboy peering out the broken window and screaming at each other. I had fallen thirty feet, through intertwined trees, but I might have fallen a hundred had I jumped farther out. I was lying on a narrow ledge, a few feet from death or the life of a cripple, and Bolt, leaving the window, was on his way down for me.

I rose as if on roller skates, dipping and swaying with hurt and vertigo. Bracing myself against a tree, I took a few deep breaths and then, shot with renewed panic, I tore off through the trees, away from the broken window and the sounds of Bolt as he staggered down the hillside. He was shouting and cursing and calling into his walkie-talkie for help and my only direction was away from him and the pandemonium he carried with him.

I had run perhaps a mile when I noticed for the first time that I was barefoot. I had torn my tender feet on the brambles of early autumn and, stopping to catch my breath, I noted the hundred tiny cuts, scratches, and bruises along my arms and torso. I was wearing only cut-off jeans and they were unzipped and somewhere along the line I had peed my pants, most probably from fright.

I stood unmoving in the woods and listened for Bolt but he had long since ceased to shout. I was at the base of a hill that led from the old settlement—Lowertown—to downtown Vermillion. Not far from where I stood was a hover of aluminum sheds, abandoned garages, scattered junk. I wasted long minutes trying to decide what Bolt would do. Would he search for me in Lowertown or would he wait for help and make a sweep of the woods beyond me? The night was like day, the sky was such a milky white, and I was tempted, for a time, simply to dig a hole somewhere and bury myself in it. The night was cold on my naked chest and finally, whether from terror or the chill of the wind, I began to climb the hill toward Main Street. Like some amateur Indian, I flickered from tree to tree, Jesse Running Scared, and the rising wind made sounds in the leaves, whispers and cries, all of which I took to be someone calling my name.

Struggling to the top, I found myself in the alley behind Main Street. Parked cars were scattered along the way and in one of them were two grinning boys taking turns on a girl whose feet hung out the back window. One sat in the front seat drinking while the other banged his way home. The drinking one saw me emerge from the woods. "You want any of this?" he asked, gesturing to the backseat.

I shook my head and struggled to catch my breath.

"Your loss," he said, tipping his can of beer. Then he noticed my condition for the first time. "Hey, what the fuck happened to you?"

But I had already turned away and was heading for the Grande Finale. The alley was littered with broken glass and sharp gravel and I had to walk carefully, picking my way through it like a minefield. Arriving at the back of the Grande Finale, I banged on the door, praying to every angel whose name I'd forgotten that Marvin would still be there cleaning up, that this would not be one of those nights he left the place looking like some cosmic swamp.

It was his helper, Todd, who, after long pounding on my part, came to the door.

"Closed," he said.

"Where's Marvin?"

"Upstairs."

I pushed past him, into the 3 A.M. mess of the Grande Finale. Wading through garbage, broken chairs, and splintered glass, I climbed the stairs and knocked on Marvin's door.

"He's drunk," Todd called to me. "Leave him alone."

"You haven't seen me," I told him. "I didn't come tonight."

"Yah, right." He went back to cleaning up the Friday night carnage.

It took a while to get Marvin to come to the door and another fifteen minutes to sober him up enough to make it clear I wanted the keys to the garage and the spare key for my car.

"Nowa get it," he declared at last. "You've made some kind dzzzn." Decision.

"Marvin, where's the garage key?"

" 'Bout time you made a dzzzn. Been floatin like a bufly too long."

"Marvin."

He took the keys from his dresser top. "Graj. Car."

"I need money, Marvin. I'm on the run."

His bloodshot eyes fought to focus.

"I'll pay you back," I added. "You know me."

Returning to the dresser, he took a worn leather bag from the top drawer. It was fat with bills, mostly ones, his take for the night.

Not bothering to count it, I took the lot.

"Spose you want my girl friend too."

I was out the door and down the stairs before I remembered that I needed clothes. Climbing back up the stairs, I knocked again on Marvin's door.

"The shirt off my back?"

I didn't say no.

I had driven a hundred miles, in zigzag as if to imitate a mob of cars all weaving through one another's paths, first north, then east, then southeast, when at last I had to stop, noting that the fuel needle was down to its nub and my bladder was as full as the moon.

It was the last half hour before dawn and I found a shelled-out gas station near Spencer, Iowa, that had already opened for business. There were two pumps, pyramids of oil cans, tangled air hoses, and, next door, C & W Parts and Repair, a peeling aluminum shelter with two sliding doors. I went into the station to buy food, potato chips and candy bars and whatever caught my eye, and the attendant, seated in front of a sunglasses display that doubled as a pinup—each pair of sunglasses sold left a little more of the girl in view—stretched and rose to fill my chariot with gasoline.

I went into the men's room and peeled the zipper on Marvin's oversized jeans, leaving a stream that echoed my sigh of relief. And then, for the first time, my fear returned to me in waves. My knees trembled and I had to grip the sink to hold myself upright. When I vomited, it was as though iron hands had gripped my gut and forced the gagging. I threw up until there was nothing left to give and then, strung out from the dry heaves, I held my hands against my belly as though to hold it inside of me.

The panic, like a high tide, receded and I was oddly aware of everything around me, the yellow toilet and gold-rusted sink, no mirror, faucet trickling cold water, a machine selling Sultan Sheaths 25¢ each, and a worn-out towel dangling from its roll machine, unchanged since World War II and bearing the imprint of the hands and faces of humanity like some twentieth-century Shroud of Turin. The images, in the yellow light, have never left me and although it is sometimes pointless to measure life in stages, I have often thought that that particular moment was, for me, a closing of the curtains. I stood in that midwestern gas station men's room, the fly capital of northwest Iowa, and it might as well have been a train station, an airport, the dock of the *Queen Mary*. There was no mirror over the sink but I saw my reflection all the same and my reflection saw me. We were an unshaven fugitive in a gas station men's room and insane men were after us with guns and King James Bibles. We had left Harper alone to take a bus to New York and there would be no one to water the peperomia back home. We had walked away living from the burning house and if Mother could have seen us now, in borrowed clothes and refugee eyes, she'd have wept bitter tears, so we hung up the sorry life of an outlaw, my reflection and I, and we smiled and we frowned and we smiled.

4

The north side of downtown St. Paul in the early seventies was a white and Indian ghetto, an area of no more than a dozen square blocks, boundaried between Seventh Street and the freeway and by Market Street and the cathedral, with North Wabasha cutting through the heart of it like a gray, sick river. There were numerous bars, run-down apartment houses with laundry hanging in the windows, abandoned warehouses too far from the Mississippi, competitive porno shops, cathouses called rap parlors—"tell a woman what's on a man's mind"—and more vacant stairways, hallways, empty rooms, broken windows, chipped paint, faulty wiring, and rusted plumbing than the city housing authority could ever inventory, fund, and repair. The city council had come to the same conclusion. They had decided to tear it all down.

I lived there with two or three hundred others, in this city within a city. Indians from disintegrated tribes ran the show on the north side. There were Oglala Sioux, Santee Sioux, Mandan, Chippewa, Cree, and all manner of half- or quarter-breeds, but they all made up one tribe and it was a drunken tribe if not always a mean one. They ate at Shanty's or Mickey's or wherever they could rest their bones and most made their living as beggars in the day and thieves at night. Some of them had homes, but many others slept wherever they could find a place, underneath a stairway or in the black darkness of a doorway, huddled in newspapers and each other's arms. In the mornings, bad sleep leading to bad awakening, they hunted the change slots of phone booths, the gutters, the sidewalks, the generosity of pedestrians, and whatever they came up with would decide the day for them. Sleeping drunken on the ground, their ears pressed to the ce-

234

ment, they heard nothing from underground. The passing of cars in the night. The shifting of the hollow earth.

I had fallen so low only for a short time. Some guardian angel, wings beating furiously, had kept me afloat with a job and a bed, but I was living in the heartland, in a run-down apartment building on Ninth off Wabasha, where Rags, the landlord, housed the fringe of the poor, the lost and found with money. Early on, I noticed a man there who was always coming in and out the alley door. He slept in the back of the building, on a stretch of dirty cement just above the boiler room, one of the warmer of the abandoned corners, and he always carried nearly everything he owned with him. He wore several layers of clothes, various sweaters, T-shirts, a spring-weight nylon jacket, two pairs of long pants, and two Salvation Army gray coats. According to Marian Embrace All Things, he made his scant living much as she did, collecting odds and ends and turning them over to the Salvation Army or recycling agencies. His specialty was newspapers, which he would keep piled up in his hall corner, the *Pioneer Press* or the Minneapolis *Tribune*, any wind-blown copies he could dig off the street or from the downtown garbage bins. His newspapers made a mattress for each cold night and whenever the stack reached the ceiling he would borrow a hand trolley from the porno shop and wheel his collection to the city paper-recycling plant and come home with all of five dollars. He was the type of man whose age cannot be guessed, who had a perpetual four days' growth of dirty beard, bad teeth, and muttered to himself in passing. I ignored him as best I could, stepping gingerly over his outstretched body when I had to pass him in the hallway. One evening as I was coming home from dinner at Mickey's, he greeted me near the alley door. His eyes were blown red and he was excited about something and bade me follow him back to his corner. I was still new to the territory and in a constant state of fear and suspicion so even as I followed him I was planning on where I would kick him if he tried anything funny. I'd thought all such men were thieves or rapists. He led me down the half-darkness of the yellow hallway to his home, the six-by-six hole covered in newsprint. Reaching into his two coats, he extracted an envelope. ''I found this,'' he told me. I opened the envelope and inside was a holy card, like those my mother had given me when I was too young to stop going to church. It was a drawing of St. Theresa the Little Flower, but on the back was printed the prayer of St. Francis, "Lord, give me the strength to change. . . ." Two months later, when I found this same man, named Sliver, in the snow outside, although he had been beaten and robbed of whatever little he had, he still was clutching half of the holy card in his hand, as though someone, thinking it to be money by the tenacity with which he defended it, had torn it away from him. For weeks afterward, he carried a headless Theresa in his breast pocket and I often saw him take it out and look at it the way other men look at centerfolds.

I had thought he was a thief. I had thought they all were thieves when I'd arrived in late November on the Greyhound bus. Tired of hiding out in Sioux City, I had sold the car and bought a ticket for Minneapolis, but the first stop had been Luverne where I'd left the bus just long enough to buy some food and a bottle of Southern Comfort. Change your whiskey, change your luck. The bottle was empty from grief and from thirst by the time we reached Mankato and I slept the deep and neutral sleep of the dead, my head bouncing like a ball against the Plexiglas window. When the bus stopped at the Minneapolis terminal and nearly everyone got out, I was unable to rouse myself. Thinking I would sleep until someone came along to kick me off, I was surprised to hear the engines rumble anew, then the bus made its last leg, a ten-mile run across the Mississippi River to the poor side of the Twin Cities, St. Paul. It was unquestionably the end of the line and when I staggered from the bus station into the street the first place I saw was a converted car from an old train, Mickey's Diner, and I had my fill of hamburgers and french fries until the winter sun set like a stomachache over the smoky brick of downtown St. Paul.

It was November 30. A *Field and Stream* calendar, with each of the preceding days neatly X'd over, told me so. I had about seven hundred dollars, some old clothes that needed washing, and an abandoned sister unmoving in her rocker. Ordering another coffee, I took stock and would have wept with despair just then had not the aged black man at my side suddenly addressed me. Throughout my dinner he had been reading a newspaper, following the words with his index finger, but suddenly he had folded his paper and tossed it to the side. Turning to me, he said, "You know the difference between flotsam and jetsam?"

I said I didn't.

"I looked it up. I looked it up in the library. *You*'s flotsam. That mean you been lost in a shipwreck like some old box and you just be floatin on the high sea. Me, I'm jetsam, cause I was *throwed* offa the boat."

We shared a long silence during which his eyes narrowed. "You listening?" he asked.

I assured him I was.

"You a mess cause your boat sunk. That's all."

I wanted to ask him if it showed that much but he turned and unfolded his newspaper and continued to read, his index finger pointing the way.

My money, if not my time on earth, ran out. When I was down to fifty-five dollars I began to look for ways to save. Shoplifting helped. I got a new shirt from J. C. Penney's, thinking that if I cleaned myself up a little I might have more luck with my job hunting. The floor security man in my favorite supermarket began to follow me around the counters, so I changed neighborhoods, palming tins of sardines, dried beef, or crackers from any of three different places on the east edge of downtown. Then I would hike all the way back to my hotel to devour whatever I had taken. Thievery took the last rough edges off whatever pride I had once felt in myself. It simply wasn't my branch of crime. During two of the coldest days in mid-December, I took refuge in a movie theater and saw the same film at least five times. I ate popcorn, chewing it slowly to make it last, and I sipped warm Coca-Cola from a straw. One time I fell asleep and in my dream warm shadows moved around me and voices came to me as though from a far room. I heard squealing tires and gunshots, the wail of an unfed child. I dreamed of Rose but her voice was not the same, it was the voice of the actress in the movie and whatever she was saying Rose was saying too. I awoke to the white lights and the closing of the curtain, instantly aware that the dream and the movie were inseparable, my own life on celluloid seen five times in one day. When I finally left the theater, I found myself walking just like the man in the movie who'd walked out on his loving wife.

* * *

In my hotel room, I read and reread the letters that Harper had written to me, all of those that Marvin had received and saved for me. Hiding out in various Sioux City hotels, I'd at first used imaginary return addresses. Any letters Harper had written would remain undelivered, molding in an unmarked bin, or be returned to her, unopened. Later, I'd written to her to send any mail to Marvin and I called him and told him to hang on to the letters until I knew where I'd be.

"Sounds grim out there, Jesse."

"It's damn cold, Marvin."

"Watch your ass, man. Bolt's still making noise about you."

"Any word from Dusken?"

"Nada."

"I'll be in touch."

"I'll be holding my breath."

Harper was in love with New York despite the tautness of her first few letters, despite how she had missed me and felt alien and lonesome there. There were a hundred photographers in her class and she felt like an amateur in comparison with most of them because she didn't know half the technique that they did and they could chatter about this filter and that lens with the same ease with which mothers discuss diapers or Pablum. She had been to the Empire State Building, to Rockefeller Center, all around Central Park and Greenwich Village, but she hadn't made a single picture, nothing she could get through the lens, that had pleased her. "The faces here are unforgettable. Every one of them has something sad or sinister or misplaced or street-wise in it. I take my best pictures without my camera but it doesn't do my techniques class any good." In her later letters, she had been more relaxed, had found the groove, so to speak, and wrote less about missing me. She had received my letters but wondered why I hadn't answered hers. "I keep getting your letters but I get the feeling you aren't getting mine," and there was a space of three weeks when she hadn't written at all, fol-lowed by a letter telling me she was seeing a man from one of her classes but I wasn't to make anything of it and anyway what was I doing so far away, please forgive me I miss you I'm just afraid of staying alone all the time. Her next letter had been a love letter, written late at night when she couldn't sleep. She

reminded me of our visit to her father's farm, what it had been
for her to make love under the open sky, how she had not believed then that I would let her go alone to New York. "You
might have come with me anyway but you are obsessed with
your singularity, you insist on denying that I love you, you insist
on staying away." She added, "What you don't seem to understand, Jesse, is that all children run away from their parents.
Some of us just do it more slowly than others and that's a luxury
you were denied." Rereading that letter for the tenth time, I
abruptly packed my things and checked out of the hotel. Bent
forward against the falling snow, I walked six blocks to the bus
station and went straight to the ticket counter.

"How much for a bus to New York?"

"Fifty-six dollars one way. Hundred dollars round trip."

I raked the last dry bills from my pockets and began to count.
I was more than twelve dollars short.

"How close will forty dollars get me?"

"It depends. Pittsburgh or Cleveland. Anywhere around
there."

Later I would wonder why I'd changed my mind. I would lie
in the same bed in the Christopher Hotel and gaze upon the
pattern of rusty water marks across the ancient ceiling, feeling
farther than ever from Harper, farther than the twelve dollars I
needed to get there. I could have hitched a ride from Cleveland
or I could have stolen the money from any dozing old lady in
the neighborhood. At the time, it was enough to know that I
didn't know what I was doing with myself. Living my life as I
did had its merits. I fed on the four walls, loving the fact that
my life was uncluttered with people or things. Everything, anyway, would have to have been carried on my back, like the
souvenirs Rose had always kept with her, her past in that shoe
box that was upended and lost in the snowdrift. I didn't go to
Harper because I wasn't sure I believed in her. Houses burn
down and a souvenir is only trash that hasn't yet realized its
potential. Love inhales and loss exhales. I was expecting, any
time, a kiss-off letter telling me she'd met a man, maybe that
other student, who was well, very good to her and she thought
that maybe she'd be moving in with him.

I was driftwood. I was newspaper in a windblown alley. I felt
mean and cold and spiritless and I felt in my veins the powerful

and undeniable blood of my father. When the rest of my money was gone and the Christopher Hotel refused to extend me credit, I saw firsthand what before I'd only seen in passing. The life. I found a stairway one night, an empty cellar the next. Stealing grew more difficult because I had the look of a man without funds. The trick of it all is in looking like a buyer. Buyers shop and vagrants steal. I learned as well that a bum, a down-and-out as I had so quickly become, is invisible to all but his own kind. The eyes of shoppers, businessmen, delivery boys, bus drivers, and cashiers looked everywhere but at me; I was only seen when my back was turned, no one looked at my face. I felt my own self-worth diminish to that same point of invisibility and didn't want to look at myself either. I had to learn the ropes, I had to condition myself to hold out my hand, palm upward, and say the words. I had to learn to watch the sidewalks for random treasures and I found that the worst that can happen is to find yourself hurrying after what you think is loose change on some freezing sidewalk. Whether it is in fact money or a gum wrapper makes no difference later on. You lie awake running that scene like a piece of film backward and forward, unable to recognize with any certainty that you are that man bent with hope that it is indeed a quarter he has chased and not broken glass.

Cruising a secondhand bookshop, I stole a copy of *The Spy Who Came In from the Cold*, fascinated as I was with the title. I wanted desperately to know how he had done it, how he had come in from the cold, and so, crouching at the bottom of the back stairway of the Radisson Hotel—ears tuned for the sounds of approaching busboys; the wine cellar was five feet away—I feverishly read the story of a spy who, at the bitter end, found himself straddling the thorny summit of the Berlin Wall. To the west were his associates, Allied spies encouraging him to jump to safety. To the east was the only lover he had ever known, trapped below, while East German guards, rapidly approaching, cocked their rifles into place. If he jumped to the west, he might live forever, but with the weight of guilt and his abandonment. If he jumped to the east, he might have the slightest chance of saving his lover. I turned the page with a trembling forefinger and he leaped to the east, where he was immediately machine-gunned. I did not think I would follow his example.

* * *

One freezing night, having no luck in finding a warm place to sleep, I took an Indian's advice—these men knew the ropes—and crossed the Wabasha Bridge to the other side of the Mississippi River. For an hour or so I wandered through West St. Paul before coming to a small Catholic church that hadn't been locked for the night. Swallowing the last of my brandy to warm my heart and lungs, I stretched my tired legs across a pew and made a pillow with my arm. Sleep came like a swift river but I came shivering awake from time to time throughout the night, a stuttering slumber. Near dawn, I awoke to the sounds of Latin and it took me a long moment to realize that what I was hearing were the intonations of an old priest saying the Mass. It was the old-fashioned Mass, in Latin rather than the trendy English version, and from where I lay I could tell that there were no altar boys because the priest was reciting both his own parts and the responses. I remembered being twelve years old and getting up every Sunday at four thirty in the morning. I would dress myself in the cold darkness of my bedroom and make my way through knee-high snow to the Church of St. Jude. I was an altar boy for the old monsignor who could never manage to genuflect and there were usually only three or four old women at the Mass, their heads bowed under cheap black scarves, reading rosaries with their fingers or saying *very loud* Acts of Contrition.

Stretching the cold from my legs, I sat up and watched the Mass unfold. The old priest was conducting his own High Mass, without the usual choir and organ to accompany him. He sang aloud the Latin, then intoned the responses in the way an altar boy might have, his voice altered ever so slightly, higher and gentler and more reserved. There was no one else there but me and I was surprised at how much of the Mass I could remember, and instinctively I recited aloud the *Kyrie eleison* and the *mea culpas* and I tried without luck to remember when I should begin to reconstruct the *Lavabo te. Amen* I knew by heart.

The Mass rolled on without a homily from the priest and after he had blessed and consecrated the host, I felt it only natural to rise and approach the altar. If the old priest was surprised, he gave no sign; perhaps there were numberless days of no one attending his Masses followed by days in which bums like Jesse Dark wandered in to get out of the cold. Dropping to my knees,

I closed my eyes and tilted my head backward, my mouth open and my tongue extended. The priest blessed the host and placed it on my tongue and I swallowed it immediately. Then, the taste of that host driving home my hunger—or perhaps reminding me of the day I breakfasted on Dusken's stolen hosts—I called out to the priest, who had already turned back toward the altar, "Can I have one more?"

The sacrilege was evident. It was written in stained glass and in scripture: one to a customer. But the old priest turned slowly, on fragile legs, and faced me with eyes that were neither red with rage nor rimmed with sorrow. Approaching me again, he stood over me with a chalice in his hands and I imagined I saw him smiling, though it may only have been a dawn shadow through the stained glass windows. Tipping the chalice toward my upturned face, he let me see that there were at least a dozen hosts inside of it, all that he had consecrated in the hope that more communicants, by some miracle, would be on hand. Lifting a host from the chalice, he waved it crosslike in the air and laid it on my tongue. I swallowed it without chewing and opened my mouth for another and he again laid a host upon my tongue. Then another, another, ten or eleven in all, and though I was still hungry, I was less hungry, that was what mattered to me at the time, and when a single host remained, the priest broke it into two and held one half in his fingers, leaving me the other. I swallowed with eyes closed, then opened my eyes and watched him as he blessed his half of host, crossing himself as well as the bread, and he swallowed it with a smile I will never forget.

Newly baptized, I spent New Year's Eve and the following day at the bottom of the Radisson stairwell, curled miserably around a diminishing bottle of Southern Comfort I had managed to swipe on St. Peter Avenue. My need for whiskey had nothing to do with my heritage; the St. Paul winter was merciless and I warmed myself with alcohol, nothing more. How else to fall asleep on a block of cold cement?

Listening to the sound of nothing, my ear pressed to nothing, stone has so little to say.

One freezing morning, I stopped into a porno shop just to warm myself indoors. I moved from magazine racks to display racks to the peep show booths but I didn't have a quarter to spare for three minutes of shake and shiver, so I loitered in the shadows, waiting for my fingers to go from blue to pink, and I could hear an old man, obviously the manager, shouting at his assistant, a tall pimply kid about two years older than myself. The manager had caught his assistant with his hands in the till. He had rung up $.27 for a $4.27 sale and put four singles into his own pocket. We all know this story, it is the story of the world. The assistant was pleading his case rather badly, insisting that if he'd *really* wanted to rip the place off he'd have done it in a much more spectacular fashion. "I don't need to nickel and dime my way up," he was saying. "I got more class than that."

The manager told him to put his class where the moon don't shine. "Anyways, you're fired."

The pimply assistant broke the front door in leaving and as I stood in the midst of a phantasmagoria of nude sex whip screw magazines which seemed to vibrate on their shelves, Rags came storming out of the back office. Rags was the manager. Kicking open the broken door, he screamed bloody murder, shouting for the cops, the mayor, the SS, and the FBI. Getting only a drunken white man asking for a quarter, he stood in the middle of the snowy sidewalk for a few long minutes, his arms upraised as if to catch snowflakes, then he finally came to his senses and strode back into the porno shop. He was in his early sixties and had worked in the place for six years, weathering Jesus freaks, righteous Christians, the city council, and any number of women's organizations. His white hair had begun to fall out but he combed what thin strands were left into small waves, each covering a pink patch of scalp and although he dressed himself in odds and ends, he was always impeccably shaved and he was fond of shiny black shoes. I learned all these things later on. That first morning, I had no idea what I was seeing. Standing to the inside of his broken front door, he shivered and cursed, lifted and jiggled, measuring the damage that had been done to the hinge. The glass of the door was intact but the frame was slightly bent and had been torn completely from the top hinge.

"Ah, Christ!"

Turning round, he noticed me for the first time. I was the only customer in the place.

"You know anything about doors?" he asked sharply.

"Only how to open and close them."

"I can't lift this thing myself," he said. "I'll give you five dollars if you help me put it back on its hinge and hold it up while I change the screws."

It took us a quarter of an hour to lay the door level, hammer the hinge back into place, and replace the five heavy bolts that had come unthreaded in the assistant's wake. When we were finished, Rags offered me seven dollars' worth of merchandise in place of five dollars cash but I told him I couldn't eat porno and anyway I wasn't really a buyer. "I just came in to warm up."

"Everybody says that," he answered. "Everybody's waiting for a bus or just looking for somebody or they need change for a dollar."

"In my case it's the truth."

"I didn't say it wasn't." He examined the hinges on the door, satisfied that they would hold. "I suppose you need a job," he said.

I admitted I did.

"How old are you?"

I said I was twenty-one.

"Can you prove it? You gotta be twenty-one to work in a porno joint. That's the law whether you believe in it or not."

My expired driver's license showed him I would be twenty-one in another month. He pretended not to notice. Moving behind the counter, he rummaged around in a rat's nest of papers and handed me a wrinkled form.

"This is an application. I don't care personally if you fill it out or not, but I gotta know some things if I'm going to hire you."

"I don't have an address."

"That don't matter. Just write down whatever you can and pretend to forget your birth date. We'll fill that in when you're old enough."

It was the usual form, asking about my family (deceased) my education (2 yrs. Univ. of So. Dak.) my military record (None) my criminal record (*None*) marital status color of eyes hair height weight previous employers and personal references (Harper Adams, photographer, NYC).

"This is your big break," Rags told me, adding the first smile I had seen on his face. "Now you're in the publishing business."

I was to be paid fifty dollars a week plus a room above the shop, twelve feet by ten feet, and the bathroom was down the hall. My room faced the alley, its only window looking out into brick and cement walls. The bed was soft and saggy and I didn't trust the lone sheet that came with it, shaded and streaked as it was with the ghosts of other slumbers. The room was barely large enough for the bed, a collapsed dresser with two unbroken drawers, and a wooden chair. It was made smaller by the wallpaper, which was old and faded, a weird pattern of enormous graying orchids on a field of lavender and black. In the night, in the darkness, I could see those orchids clearly and they seemed to throb and to grow. I had a small sink in the corner and early on I bought a mirror to hang above it and despite everything in that sad apartment the water was hot, a luxury I would appreciate throughout the coldest winter I ever lived through.

I knew my neighbors in a very short time. Whenever I would go in or out of my apartment, I would see the woman from the apartment to the right of my own standing in her doorway. Sometimes she asked me for a cigarette, other times if I knew the time. She wore a shapeless black skirt and a frilly red blouse and her black hair was all over the place. Judging by the fact that she was always there, standing in her open doorway, I began to believe that she never slept, never went to work, never had a visitor or a phone call. Seeing her there to greet me when I came home at night only made me feel more lonesome.

My other neighbors were less tranquil. Through the walls I could hear every waking moment of their conjugal lives, this man and woman who seemed to spend each minute of the day or night screaming at each other or having sex. Or both at the same time. Lying in my own bed, I would listen to them in the prelude of their lovemaking, growling and sniping at each other, tossing curses like so many little love taps until the more bitter accusations opened like poison flowers between them. Insults flew like stones and always had to do with money or jealousy, you slept with her I didn't where's my billfold I'll screw her when I want you never leave me anything I told you I wanted slap slap you're hurting me I've only begun to hurt you. And when the tide would crest I invariably heard the rustle of bedsprings like a mad chorus of city crickets, *you bastard* become a coo of pleasure, always followed by what I assumed to be the

headboard, wham wham, against our common wall. I could
listen to them for hours, my attention drifting from the book
before me to the opera going on next door, and the sound of
them, whether it was angry or sexual, was always soothing to
me because at least they were the sounds of human life. I had
no radio at the time, no television, no stereo, and the silence
was more disturbing than the noise. Yet there were times when
I wished that I could shut them off like a radio, when their
lovemaking and not their fighting pierced my loneliness and
filled me with a new sense of bleakness. The woman held nothing back, rasping directions, singing to and encouraging her
lover, and I heard every word or sigh or hiss of pleasure, sometimes even I was awakened by it, and afterward there would be
only a silence from the next room while my blood was noisy
within my veins.

Sliver haunted the building, carrying his Little Flower wherever he went. Rags, who also served as landlord, allowed Sliver
his back hallway corner in return for little favors. Sliver, he told
me, was a man who'd been through every side street in hell and
you could see that the light, the neon, had long since left his
eyes. He had been called Drugstore when he was twenty and
had lived up to the name through a decade-long rutted road from
cough medicine to opium, mescaline to filtered Sterno, high
road and low road. At thirty-three, shaking free of welfare, he'd
found a job as a barback, lugging crates of ice, beer, and whiskey, sweeping cigarette butts, and cleaning the john. He'd married a woman named Jocelyn who happened to be Rags's cousin,
but two months later Jocelyn had found him on a storeroom floor
tangled in a web of female legs, heels kicking at his ass to
encourage him, and she'd broken a bottle over his head. His
coma had lasted a week, the hospital stay much longer. Ten
more years had passed and at forty-five, the fog never lifting,
Sliver looked sixty. The line separating saints from morons is
paper thin, so I will simply say that Sliver was a bit of both. He
looked after the Rainbow as though in its entirety it were his
parish; he swept the hallways and fed the stray cats, prowled the
halls like a watchdog, and kept track of burned-out light bulbs,
broken windows, and blown fuses.

But he was even more valuable, particularly during that winter and the following spring, because he was a listener at city

hall and the information he brought to all of us, in advance of the newspaper reports or official announcements, gave many of us enough warning to get out before the walls collapsed around our upturned faces. What few of us knew—and what in any event didn't matter—was that Sliver was a police informant. Someone on the force, whether from kindness or stupidity, was giving ten dollars a week for whatever bits of information the old derelict could report. Though he knew the territory, though he knew every hooker and dealer by name, I would be surprised if he gave much away to the police. There was a single arrest I can trace to Sliver and it happened within a week after I'd found him in the snow, robbed and beaten, and I can only assume this was his private mode of revenge. Otherwise, saint and moron, he lived the quietest of lives.

It was through his police contacts that he heard all about urban renewal and he brought us the news in the week after New Year's Day. We were to be torn down. Twelve square blocks, the simmering heart of the north side, were to be razed sometime in the spring. For months the city had been acquiring the property from private interests, and the MacAdams brothers, who owned nearly a quarter of the target buildings, had already settled. The Rainbow and GIRLS FILMS HARD PORNO were owned by a man named Alexander who lived in Chicago and whose income was primarily from a chain of porno shops and theaters from Akron to Omaha. He was holding out. Rags, who made a few hurried phone calls, found that the Rainbow was on the edge of the targeted zone and that Alexander saw the chance to have a porno shop in the heart of a new shopping center rather than on the vagrant fringe. But the warehouse district, where Marian Embrace All Things and a hundred other lost souls lived, would be demolished once the spring thaw allowed the wreckers to complete the job.

"There will be an exodus," Rags told me. "I've seen it happen before. They'll come in and take apart two or three buildings and everyone will huddle up elsewhere. The bars will close and reopen somewhere else. They'll blow up everything and knock over what's left, right down to the last building, and when that last building goes there will be a hundred people sleeping under the Robert Street Bridge."

"And then what?"

A shrug. "We all move on. Back to Minneapolis, or to Omaha, Des Moines, Chicago. Someplace without urban renewal. It's when cities get careless and things are left to rot that these people have a home. They live, and you live, in whatever anyone abandons. We make our homes in the shadow of neglect. Figure it out."

He told me the history of the Rainbow.

Years back, before the decline of the city, the Rainbow had been a class hotel. Built during the twenties, it had been the St. Paul House, a rival to the Radisson down the street, with one hundred rooms, a restaurant, a coffee shop, a barbershop, and the largest lobby of any hotel in Minnesota. In the late forties, half of the rooms were sold as office space and ten years later the hotel closed altogether. It had sat empty for fifteen years, then Alexander had bought what was left of it. Where the lobby had been, and later a café, he built the GIRLS FILMS HARD PORNO business, installing the peep show booths where once had been a five-chef cuisine. Of the fifty rooms remaining to the building, forty were turned into single-room apartments, some with bathrooms and some without, and the remaining ten were walled up. Signs of the old hotel were everywhere. There was still a dumbwaiter at the corner of the back stairway and some of the furnishings had little tags sewn into them, identifying them as the property of the St. Paul House. On the door of my room was a list of house rules: No parties, No noise after midnight, No cooking in the room, No illicit enterprise, No pets, and checkout time was twelve noon sharp unless otherwise arranged with the management. Some time after Alexander had bought the place, he had been given a court order to rehabilitate it or lose his rental license, so he gave Rags a truckload of leftover paint cans from other construction jobs. There was half a gallon of eggshell blue, two pints of lime green, a full gallon of cherry red, three gallons of white, and various measures of myriad other colors. Since there wasn't enough of any one color to fill an entire hallway, Rags had started painting with whatever color was available and whenever he ran out he simply opened another can, so that each hallway was a spectrum of blue red green yellow violet and white, and the nickname of Rainbow was obvious to everyone.

I had only arrived and already the mad jungle I lived in was to be destroyed. In and around the Rainbow I saw these old men spitting and puking and scratching old sores, petting stray cats, caressing green pint bottles with their yellow fingers, kicking each other, begging money, coughing. I saw in them my father, snoring on the couch, his breathing like some dissonant symphony, tragic noises, all the same bad odors of my youth, our living room, that burned-down house. It was lonesome and sad as hell, but all the same I grew used to it and felt less and less threatened. I was young and I regarded my present state of affairs as just that, an elongated comma, a loose thread in the abstract embroidery of my life. The news of the urban renewal had a strange effect on me. In place of my disgust I began to feel compassion for those around me, a compassion unsullied by pity. I had taken the job with Rags intending to do as my predecessor had done and hit that cash register with all the force I could muster. I was with them and I was like them, poor and deviant, drowning in my own blood, but I had found myself with one hand on a pile of twenties and my other hand on my heart to still the beating. Rags may have seen me or he may have looked the other way. I had put the money back and shut the drawer. There were worse things than desperation. I could steal only from those I would never know. They were going to tear us down and I couldn't leave until they'd done so.

It was so very sad and funny, all at once, to watch Marian Embrace All Things cross Wabasha Avenue, downtown St. Paul, in a January raging snowstorm. She crossed against the light, she was color blind and in a hurry, and was nearly crippled by a rumbling 12A bus bound for the Capitol building and urban wastelands beyond. Her clothes were the latest the Salvation Army had to offer, ratty sweaters one over the other, green on plaid on blue, and her gait was hilarious, jerky, and oddly sweet for a seventy-year-old Lacotah citified Sioux. She carried an overflowing shopping bag in each hand, the harvest of a hard day around the town where she found things lost by others— combs, magazines, lone shoes, hairbrushes, coins, broken toys, empty pens, eraserless pencils, Coke bottles, coverless paperbacks, dime-store jewels—and stashed everything in wide plastic bags as she walked with one eye on the pavement and the other eye in the gutter where lost things are ofttimes found. She was my friend, Marian Embrace All Things, living up to her name, and I watched her through the frosted double-glass door of the GIRLS FILMS HARD PORNO shop where I worked as a stockboy and cashier. Among other things, Marian read palms. Holding mine before her gray little eyes, she had stared upon them for a long time before telling me in her unique form of Indian English that I didn't really have any future.

"You mean I'm going to die pretty soon?"

"No sir. A long life you will live but no future is there in it."

Staring down a cabdriver who'd tried to inch his way over her body, she made it to the curb and laid down the bags so she could catch her breath. I watched her from the distance, less than twelve feet, warm in my sex shop and happy to see her get where she was going, the proverbial other side. Taking deep gulps of the January air, she shook the ache from her arms and bent to retrieve the shopping bags, then she waddled strutted shivered rocked down Wabasha, toward Ninth, Tenth, left to St. Peter, home. I thought of calling out to her, asking her in to GIRLS FILMS HARD PORNO to warm herself up, but I knew I'd see her later that evening below the stairway where the rummies liked to meet. The drunken, the criminal, and the unemployed; the dirty, the dishonest, and the homeless. My associates. I was becoming and I had become.

Turning away from the door, I went back to my work. There were bundles of unsold magazines to be shipped and bundles of new arrivals to unpack and sort into the racks. The porno business was brisk if not booming and we—Rags and I—were usually busiest toward the end of the afternoon and early evening, when the men in suits were off work and free for a casual purchase of magazines, books, film, a ten-minute shot at the peep show, gadgets, creams, you name it. Rags—Richard Ragland, my boss—was at lunch and had left instructions that before he got back I should have finished the packing and unpacking and gotten started cleaning the peep show booths, which were worse even than cleaning the johns.

In a closet, in a cave, man spies on woman. A peep show is the loneliest entertainment on earth.

We had ten booths spaced in a semicircle around a main floor. The customer could pay a quarter for a three-minute gaze through a five-by-five-inch window. Standing alone in his dark and private booth, he could put his money into the slot and up would lift the shutter over his window, through which he could see Candy Lisa JoJo Angel Lucy or Denise sitting naked on a rotating, fake-fur-covered stool. Candy Lisa JoJo Angel Lucy or Denise would twist this way or turn that way, showing off a thigh ass tits vulva whatever in a bored and unhappy manner and for three minutes at a time the customer could do with himself whatever he wanted. The girls changed every hour, regularly if not quite like clockwork, and some of our customers stayed nearly as long, which is twenty quarters, five dollars, and a lot of bad breath blown onto that five-by-five window. Once a week or so, or as often as Rags thought to tell me, I had to clean those booths, whichever were unoccupied at the time. I hauled around a pail of soapy water, a big sponge, and a roll of paper towels, and I learned how to clean with my eyes closed, to remove the stains, the skid marks, the halitosis, but I could never remove the loneliness on those five-by-five windows no matter how much window cleaner I sprayed. Early on, I had looked through those windows myself, seeing Candy Lisa JoJo et al. from every possible angle, lustless and annoyed on their rotating stool. They were part-time hookers and full-time strippers and once, when Candy gave me the come-on, I could only think of her on that twirling stool with her ankles in her hands.

"Hey kid, whattya say? Ten bucks for an act of congress?"

Funny, funny. "No thanks, Candy."

One night, shortly after Sliver told us the news, I was awakened by what I thought was a child crying and I lay awake for a long time, smoking cigarettes in the darkness. From time to time I heard a sob from above me but little else. There were always the sounds of the Rainbow with its sixty-year-old plumbing and warped floorboards which gave me the impression that I was not in an apartment building but aboard a small ship. Still unable to sleep, I switched on a light and began to read when I heard my neighbors—Romeo and Juliet—arrive home. It was 3 A.M. and they were arguing about money. Putting down my book, I sat back to listen but suddenly they were no longer arguing. The woman was shouting and the man was hitting her, I could clearly hear the sound of his palms across her face, a sound I knew from childhood, and in an instant I was up and pulling on my jeans. The woman shrieked and I heard furniture overturning, the crash of glass, more screaming. Their door was unlocked and when I pushed it open I saw the woman huddled in a corner, her hands held above her downturned head, and the man was hitting her with the back of his ringed hand. Hearing the crash of the door, he stopped suddenly and turned toward me. We exchanged ice for rage. Taking her hands from her face, the woman looked at me through a tangle of hair. A trickle of blood ran from her nose to her lips. "Who the fuck're you?" she said.

I didn't remember who I was. I was a man standing in a doorway. "Are you all right?" I asked her. It was as though I'd interrupted them in bed. The woman cursed me and rose from her corner. The man reached into his pocket and flashed a blade as if by magic. Together they drove me from their bed of paradise.

This was how I got acquainted with Candy and her pimp, Carl. I went back to my own room and lay troubled in a cold bed. I heard nothing more from my neighbors that night, but this time I could hear clearly, from the room above my own, the piano sounds of a young boy crying. It was worse, somehow, than all the howling I'd ever heard next door and I wondered why, until that moment, I had felt so little fear, in all those times I had found myself in the street, covered with my newspaper, shivering and unable to sleep, my ear to the cold cement through which I heard the most terrifying silence. I had not been afraid then and too seldom in my life had I ever been afraid. Longing suddenly for Harper, I turned in my bed, ear to the pillow, eyes upon the wall, discerning in the dark that awful pattern of orchids, the sorrowful wallpaper from years past, and when the little boy above me wept anew, I wept with him, and the orchids, in the obscurity of that lonesome night, bloomed.

5

When I awoke the next morning, I knew immediately that I would be late for work. It didn't matter. I knew Rags would crackle and complain but my waking that morning was peaceful and I was happy simply to lie in bed where I felt, curiously, at home. In the gray morning light the orchids were again lifeless on my walls and from my bed I could see through the window a small wedge of colorless sky, meaning snow would fall before the day was done. I was thinking of how all of it, the warehouses and alleyways and noisy bars, pawnshops, porno shops, liquor stores, all would be replaced with supermarkets, cinemas, dress shops, and parking lots with spiraling ramps, vast emptinesses which would be less weird in sunlight, less threatening, than the rows of staggering Indians and white men who populated the ruins. The day before, feeling as cruel as the weather, I had asked Sliver what his life was like. "In your head, I mean, what is your life to you?" I was prodding his idiocy, I suppose, heckling him in an offhand manner, and he must have misunderstood me, saint and moron that he was, thinking I had said *in your bed* instead of *in your head* and, his tongue curling round his remaining teeth, he'd answered, "Like where I slept last night." It wasn't until that morning, while I lay tranquil and warm in my bed, that I reconstructed our conversation, the misunderstanding between head and bed. It was the moron who couldn't answer me but the saint who had said that in his head his life was like where he slept last night. A more perfect truth than I would ever utter in my own lifetime from the chapped lips of a homeless man.

I had finally risen from bed and splashed water on my face and was about to light the day's first dusty cigarette when I heard a knocking on my door. It was the first time such a thing had happened and I stood in the middle of the room, naked and perplexed, before finally calling out, "Just a minute." Pulling on a pair of jeans, I went bare-chested to the door and opened it. It was Candy. Dressed in red stretch slacks and a glittery blouse, she held a pot of coffee and dangled two porcelain cups on her index finger. Very fancy.

"I'm really shitty at apologizing," she said, "so I brought along some coffee. If you invite me in you can have some."

When I didn't answer right away, still stupid from sleep and the surprise of a human voice, she thought I was being proud or something so she added, "All right, I'm a bitch and I'm sorry. That's the most you'll get out of me."

Shaking my head a little, I stepped backward to let her in and said I really could use some coffee, thank you, come in.

I stuffed my arms into a shirt and smoothed the covers over the bed so she could sit down. Balancing the cups on the mattress, she poured the coffee and we drank it in silence for a few moments.

"Candy's not my real name," she said by way of introduction. "But I'm not about to tell you what it is."

I told her I'd seen her around.

"Yeah? Where?"

She hadn't noticed me, apparently, helping out at the porno shop. "In the peek-a-booth."

She swallowed badly and choked on her coffee. "You go in for that shit?"

"I just clean the place," I explained. "I work for Rags."

She understood. "Yeah. I forgot they fired Ricky."

"Was he the tall pimply guy?"

"Right. A real asshole too. He used to try to cut in on everybody's business. Wanted to be a pimp, I think, 'cept that nobody'd work for him. Carl had to get rough with him a few times."

"Carl?"

"That's the man I live with. We all met last night, remember?"

I said I hadn't forgotten.

Candy didn't blush but she nodded her head in just such a way as to suggest embarrassment. "I wasn't too nice last night,

I know. You were just trying to help me out, right? Lady in distress and all that.''

I finally lit my cigarette and my throat, laced with warm coffee, took the smoke deep. A good cigarette. "I don't know what I was trying to do," I admitted. "I just heard the noise. It wasn't the first time."

"No, I guess it wasn't. You got one of those for me?"

I handed her a cigarette and was about to light it for her but she pulled a book of matches from her purse and lit it herself. Seeing the lighter in my hand, she smiled. "I get it. You're a gentleman. That's okay. I forget how to be around guys like you. Didn't I try to score you once?"

I said I couldn't remember, though in truth she had.

"Not that I'm trying to score you now. I never work mornings and anyway we're neighbors. You're the kind of trick Carl would never let me get away with, no matter how much money you might have."

I told her I didn't have a dime.

"Don't worry about it, honey. Let's just be friends. I like talking to you already."

"What will Carl say about that?"

She poured herself more coffee. "Don't worry about Carl. He's not all that bad. Sometimes he just, you know, loses his cool. Last night was one of his bad times."

"Does he knock you around like that all the time?"

She shook her head. "Only when I make him do it. Sometimes I know just how to get to him, just what to say or do that will drive him crazy. Last night I hit a nerve. I was asking for it."

"Why stay with him?"

She shrugged. "He pays the bills. He protects me. I'm used to him."

"That's enough for you? Sounds kind of sad to me."

"How old are you?"

"Twenty-one."

"And how old do you think I am?"

I looked at her closely, carefully, for the first time. She had one of those shadowy faces, either lovely or homely depending upon the angle at which you saw her or the fall of light and shadow across her eyes. The kind of girl who, in high school, has no trouble attracting boys of my nature—characters on the fringe, neither friendly nor friendless. Whether her nose was too big or her eyes too close together or her chin foreshortened, one couldn't quite measure. A single unidentifiable flaw kept her from being beautiful, that same flaw which she almost certainly, in the privacy of her own mirror, searched with knitted brows. She wasn't quite fat but had a roundness, in her red nylon stretch pants, that could either blossom into obesity or, with a little fasting, be sculpted down to an agonizing sensuality. I was thinking of her bottom and thighs and for the first time I was aware that I was face to face with a prostitute and that despite our early banter I could have her for twenty dollars. At the time I didn't miss Harper; she was a myth, a sorceress come and gone, and Candy would only cost me the three bills that lay wrinkled in my jeans pocket. The glittery blouse, a shiny spun nylon, was pulled apart at the neck into a wide V and she was wearing one of those cheating hooker brassieres that push everything up into a swell of flesh, hinting abundance. Could I guess her age? No; no more than I could estimate the number of men like me who had folded their bills into her outstretched hand and then followed her up some weary staircase for a half hour's bump and grind.

"Come on," she said. "How old am I?"

"Twenty-five," I said.

"I'm twenty-one, like you. I didn't even finish high school back where I come from and I came straight to St. Paul cause that's where Carl was. We're both from Eau Claire [she said it like You Clair] and he sent me the money to come. I didn't know why until I got here. I was only sixteen and my first gig was blowing this sixty-year-old guy. What were you doing when you were sixteen?"

"Running away."

Her eyes brightened. "Yeah? You too? No, hey, let me guess. You're a writer or something like that. Some kind of wise guy trying to get a close look at what the world is like. Underneath I mean. We get all kinds of college nuts for customers. Extramentalists and all."

"I'm just a stock boy in a porno shop."

"Where's your family?"

"Dead and buried."

She was unfazed. "Maybe you got it good and don't know it. I wish some of my family were dead."

"You don't know what you're saying."

"Take it easy, whatever your name is. I just mean my family is nothing to write home to."

"Neither was mine," I told her. "My father was a drunk and my mother put up with him. He beat her, mocked her, cheated on her, and stole her money. He even kicked her in the goddamn throat and she could never talk again but she saved his ass when the cops came."

"That's a funny kind of love."

I told her I had always thought so.

Not missing a beat, Candy said, "I got this friend, she's a working girl like me, named Lila, but I don't think that's really her name. I think she made it up, like me. Anyway, Lila has this pimp who makes Carl look like some kind of prince. Beats up his girls for breakfast, makes them all hustle all night even in the worst shitty freezing weather, tells them they can't come home without at least a hundred bills in their bras. You know. Well, Pierce—that's her pimp—he's this white guy that likes to talk black, you know the type, dresses all flashy like a spade and wears shades day and night and he talks with this real jazzy voice like there's some Afro record always playing in his head. Well, early on, Lila had this rule about her work: no spades. She'd take on rummies, drunks, redskins, Chinese armies, and donkeys, but she wasn't gonna let a black man even touch her, not ever. Pierce got sick of that shit real fast and one night he invited bunch of his spade friends around to the house and he told Lila that if she didn't light them up like chandeliers he was gonna kick her ass out in the snow. Now she *loved* this guy and the idea of leaving him was worse to her than getting gang-banged by a team of niggers, so she went to work on them like they were the last sweet men on earth. She kept her eyes closed at first, she said, but Pierce got wise and told her to *look*, so she did, and she had to watch all these drug dealer types crawling all over her and she began to kind of dig it. You know what she said to me afterward? She said that night she really knew Pierce loved her because only a man who loved her like that could bear to give her to a black man."

I didn't get it.

"Just *think*," Candy said, taking another cigarette from my pack and lighting it. "He could have left her alone. He could have let her keep her rules and her pride or whatever, but he wanted her to be a part of him and all his weird black stuff. He took her into him and she was his."

I said I thought she'd gotten things turned around, like she was seeing everything in a mirror. "What if Carl did the same thing to you?"

She bit her lower lip, forming words. "Carl wouldn't. That's not his gig. Now he only wants to mess around with coke and he's so fuzzy all the time, always up and down. 'What's the weather?' You know what that means? Is there any coke in the house? That's the weather. Good coke, I gotta say the sun is shining. No coke, it's a cloudy day. I'm on the street selling t and a while he's lining himself up for another toot. I been with him a long time though, about five years now. He's been my man all the way down the line and every time I get busted he's there to spring me. Hey, you know I'm sitting here smoking your cigarettes and telling you all these things and I don't even know your name."

"Jesse."

"Nice name. Is it real or did you change it like me?"

I said I'd always been Jesse.

"Well, little Jesse, whatever I've got with Carl isn't love. I'm a born slave. And now I gotta go home and get some sleep. I got all dressed up just to come and apologize to you and I need some rest before I go to work."

Before going out the door, she turned and asked for one more cigarette, then said, "You know, for a while there I was thinking of putting the move on you and I wasn't thinking about money. You know what I mean? Anyway, we're gonna be friends, little Jesse, and if Carl doesn't like it he can get stuffed. All right?"

"Right. Carl can get stuffed."

She yawned. "Well, good night, um, good morning I mean. See you around."

I was an hour late for work and Rags started out by giving me the silent treatment. There were few customers, only the morning riffraff, and Rags kept a close eye on them. Many of our customers were too poor to buy and only came in to get out of the cold or to sniff around. We had two entire walls of magazines, one section of which were the soft magazines, safe enough in those days for anyone to buy and read at home; but the rest were more specialized, bondage, s & m, waterworks, bestiality, homosexuality, lesbianism. There were two six-foot racks of books, the titles defining the angles, teacher-student, father-daughter, white wife with black lover, girl on boy, boy on boy, girl on girl. Rags sat behind a glass counter which contained the paraphernalia, the vibrators and dildos and magic erection creams, playing cards with spread-eagled queens, rubber suits, chains, satin whips, penis extenders, films, the kinds of merchandise that made me uneasy whenever I rang up a sale.

One evening a man had come in about six o'clock and had gone straight to the counter, where I was checking an inventory list. He wore a bankerish three-piece suit and an expensive topcoat and his cigar left a smell of Havana in its wake. He seemed to be in a hurry.

"I want a couple of vibrators," he told me. "What do you suggest?"

Leading him over to the display, I told him to take his pick.

"These are batterized, I hope."

I assured him they were.

"Great. I'll take that purple one there, that plastic one. And, uh, yeah, that one there, the one that looks like a bazooka."

This was my first vibrator sale and I felt slightly uncomfortable. "They come without batteries," I felt obliged to inform him.

"Throw in half a dozen. It could be a long night," he added with a wink.

"Right."

I rang up the sale and tossed the machines into one of our standard brown bags.

"Is there any kind of guarantee?" the man asked me when I handed him his things.

"Only on the vibrators," I told him.

"Only on the vibrators? Hah! That's a good one. Only on the vibrators!" Still laughing, he went out the door.

I was adjusting all too slowly and could not get used to the meanness of the magazine covers, the sneering redheads and satanic blondes, the bondage magazines with pictures of women bent and bound, horribly gagged, with red ridges left from ropes or chains across their flesh, photographed under klieg lights leaving them white and stark and shadowless. I once said to Rags that all in all it was pretty miserable stuff, pornography, and he just told me not to be such a hayseed. He had been in the business for years and years and was beyond feeling for it. He sold parts, things, merchandise (which he pronounced merchand-eyes) and he didn't give a damn about who bought it or why. "Don't be so sensitive," he told me. 'It's just anatomy. Wee-wees and wa-was. Dirty pictures that don't cost all that much."

Just after New Year's, an old guy, his upper lip sweating, came quietly in the door. He was very well dressed and seemed bothered by the bright lights of the shop. He immediately came upon Rags, whom he asked, sotto voce, whether or not the establishment had a book in stock called *The Pearl*.

Rags, a model of discretion, nearly shouted: "What? *The Pearl*? Sorry, we only got fuck books here. None a that stuff about jewelry."

The poor old gent repeated his request, adding, "It's a collection of English erotica. Quite well known."

"English, you say? Naw, we got a whole shitload of French stuff, though. Up that aisle there's a stack of books, all French, you know? Blow jobs and the like."

All this time the old guy was glancing around, afraid of being seen let alone heard, and Rags was making enough noise to let his wife, his grandchildren, and the city council in on the story.

Finally I put down the paper I was reading and went to his assistance. Taking him by the arm, I steered him toward the door, telling him that no, we didn't have *The Pearl* in stock, but that if he cared to he could come back in a week and I'd have it for him. His relief was obvious and he shook my hand in parting, thanking me a dozen times, then in fright he went out the door and vanished into the snow.

I found his book in a respectable bookshop where he could have bought it himself if he'd had more nerve. He returned a week later and insisted on paying three times the list price, then he whispered to me that he'd be grateful if I could order other things for him.

"Just give me the list," I told him. Taking a leather-bound

note pad from his breast pocket, he wrote the titles he was searching for.

"I'll make it worth your trouble," he assured me.

I said I'd do what I could.

This was how I became an erotica dealer for a man whose position in church and public could not be betrayed. We met once a week at Gallivan's bar and after sharing a drink—beer for me, gin & tonic for him—I would slip him a brown parcel and he would pass me a white envelope. I was vaguely reminded of my drug dealer days, all the semielaborate precautions, the poker-faced conversations, the stealth. But this time I was doing nothing illegal. The books I supplied the man were all available in any number of bookstores where he would have been equally anonymous. He wasn't after books like *Chain Gang Sally* or any of the crudely printed stuff that went in and out of Rag's shop like so much garbage; he wanted legitimate trade paperbacks, what everyone called soft porn, a sweeter if no less boring kind of book. He trusted in me, he said, because I worked in a porno shop and therefore had the right contacts. He made no effort to explain his position except to say that, to a large degree, he lived two lives.

"Most of us have trouble living one," I answered.

He stared at me for a moment, blinked once, then said, "Yes. Yes, I suppose that must be so."

I returned home early one evening, too broke to go out for dinner, and sat for a long time thinking of what to do. Again I heard the little boy crying but I'd already come to the conclusion that it was my imagination, maybe what I was hearing was the past. There was someone knocking on my door and when I opened I found my neighbor the ratty-looking lady who stood sentry in the hallway. She was in her usual state, looking not drunk but as though she had been not long before. Her lipstick was smeared like a bruise across her lips and her sweat had dragged lines of face powder so that her face was mosaic'd into segments of chin, cheek, and nose. She wore, of all things, a fur coat, and held a sixty-second camera in her trembly hands.

"I gotta favor task you. You gotta minute?"

"What do you want?"

She held out her camera. "Some pitchers. I need for you to take some pitchers a me. I'll give you five dollars."

Her voice seemed derailed from her mind but she looked at me evenly, intent upon making some deal.

I said I didn't need the money.

"We gotta go to my place," she said, and she turned her back on me, meaning I should follow.

Her room might have been the same size as my own but with so much junk scattered around, it was hard to tell. The dresser was piled high with newspapers and magazines, broken dolls, laundry, and empty cigarette packs. Between the bed and the window were more of the same as well as what looked like a winter's horde of assorted garbage, Coke bottles, potato chip bags, a half-eaten package pie, and an overturned ashtray. On the unmade bed, though, were stacks of new clothes, evening dresses and coats, skirts, blouses, and a dozen pairs of shoes. She took off the fur and underneath she was wearing a blue evening gown, the neck swooping downward in a classy V and showing off a stunning set of pearls around her neck.

"This one first," she said, and after pointing out where the button on the camera was, she stood before the bed, amid a pile of trash, and struck a pose straight from *Vogue*. Lifting the camera, I looked through the lens, incredulous. Her windblown hair was sticky and black and her eyes were glassy but in that dress she was transformed, camouflaged in satin. I clicked and she hurried over to take the camera from my hands, impatient to see the picture develop. As the image emerged, she nodded rapidly. "Okay," she said. "Okay. Okay. Now I gotta change. You turn around now."

With my back to her, I could hear her struggling with the zipper, the sliding of cloth. She tripped once and steadied herself on the bed, then I could hear another zipper, the fastening of buttons. "I'm ready," she said.

This time she wore a long white dress with a wide gold belt and the same pearl necklace.

"Stand back there," she directed, pointing to the door. "You gotta catch the whole works."

I moved backward until I was touching the door and she struck another pose. I was about to shoot the picture when she said, "Wait." Reaching behind her, she chose a silver fur stole which she wrapped around her shoulders, then she threw her head backward and said, "Okay. Now."

We went through at least half a dozen changes and two rolls of film. Sometimes the flashbulb failed and other times she wanted a retake. The final picture was of her in a negligee, black and semitransparent, sheer enough to show the bruises and blotches and folds on her belly and thighs, the incredible age of her body. We took four copies of the same pose and when we were finished she started fishing in her purse for the money.

"Don't worry about it," I told her. "It was my pleasure."

But she didn't seem to hear me. She never seemed to hear anything but the winds that blew across her mind. This was a woman from a planet I didn't know. She pressed the money into my pocket and the nearness of her, the smell, was unsettling. Then she said she had to change and I should go home.

Later that night, again unable to sleep, I heard footsteps in the hallway, three or four men coming up the wooden stairs. They stopped just outside my door and I sat up, expecting sudden company, but then I heard a knocking on the weird lady's door. "Alice," a voice whispered. "Alice, open up."

I could hear the groan of bedsprings next door and Alice went to the door. I heard the men enter her room, one of them saying what a dump it was. I realized they had come for the clothes, probably stolen. Alice must have been the warehouse, the custodian, her apartment just a drop box for things that would never be hers.

When the men were finished they apparently paid her and Alice said, "When you coming again?" but no one answered her. When the footsteps faded on the stairway, I heard Alice's door close gently, then the jangle of her bedsprings, then the beating of my own heart, then silence.

"Take a good pitcher," she had told me while she'd worn a green velvet pantsuit and already I could imagine her thumbing through her glossy prints, watching herself transformed—a slug dressed as a butterfly—or folding them into envelopes to send to God-knows-whom with a note on the back, "This is me, Alice."

> *"You do know what the consumer society is,
> don't you,"* the Pope said, as many nuns held
> up cassette recorders to tape his speech.
> —UPI, November 2, 1982

6

If I stood to the right side of my only window, and if I leaned my head against the wall just so, looking down across the window diagonally, I could see the alley below and all manner of strange goings on. Dope deals were made in those wet darknesses, women sold themselves in the shadows, drunks—from somewhere going some or nowhere—passed bottles to and from each other like gifts. The alley led from Wabasha to St. Peter and was barely wide enough for the garbage trucks to get through, but it might as well have been the Khyber Pass for all the traffic that passed through there. One morning I had noticed an old car was parked there and anyone who passed had to slither round it. It was a Chevy, some early sixties model, and rust had formed along its ridges like a dirty halo. The next morning I looked out my window and saw that the tires were gone and the hulk sat bent and leaning on the slushy asphalt. A day later the hood was open and the engine mount was bare. After another day, the steering wheel, rearview mirror, and hood ornament were gone and I saw two Indians climbing out of the backseat, stretching their arms to the late morning blank winter sky, happy from a good sleep. Dogs pissed on the bumpers, hookers handled their clients in the parentheses of the soggy backseat. A random stone from an unseen hand left a magnificent spiraling mosaic where once had been a windshield. Never was a car more useful, more beautiful, more accommodating.

That same winter, the city paid an abstract sculptor fifty thousand dollars to build a monument to the St. Paul pioneers. Piling old steel girders in rough tepee fashion, he covered the entire pyramid in lime and carbon and washed it all in salt to bring out the rust. Then he cashed his check and went back to Berlin to spend it. The sculpture sat like a heap of waste in the middle

264

of Mounds Park, just above an ancient Indian burial ground, and the first time I saw it I knew the city fathers had been stolen blind. Our monument—the north end rummies'—was that shelled-out, stripped-down Chevy, glorying in rust and shadow. And we had it, as we had everything else, dirt cheap.

Showing kindness, I learned, can be worse than hard labor. With a mixture of sympathy and disgust, I found myself entwined in the broken lives around my own, the constellation of the poor and the derelict. Candy came by at least once a day to borrow money—which she sometimes repaid—or to ask me to pick up her shoes at the repair shop—"you know, those blue spike heels that I broke last week"—or to leave money with me because Carl would search her whenever she got home and take her last cent. On the night I found Sliver in the alley next to the Chevy, one of his three coats was torn at the sleeve and he'd lost two teeth as well as getting two ribs broken by whoever had robbed him. This was the night his St. Theresa had been torn from his hand, leaving only her torso on the front and the last lines of St. Francis's prayer on the back. At the hospital, a doctor X-rayed him and said the ribs were only cracked and while he wrapped the old derelict's chest with a tight gauze he told me he was tired of ministering to drunks who fall down the stairs.

"He's not a drunk," I corrected him.

"Like fun."

Sliver was more concerned about his St. Theresa than his ribs or the missing teeth. I told him I'd find another one for him, any Catholic church had to have loads of holy cards, but he just kept shaking his head like some little boy whose dog has been run over. "Not like this one. I *found* it." That was the catch. Sliver was a man who valued what he found, not what he was given. Checking out the urban missionary who made a weekly tour of our neck of the woods, I asked him if he could get his hands on a few holy cards for me.

"Aren't you the boy who works at the porno shop?"

I said I was.

"God will not be mocked."

If you walk away from a building, someone will tear it down. If you walk away from a car, someone will steal the hubcaps. If you walk away from God, you'll forever after have to do everything for yourself. I found the holy cards in a religious supplies shop on Robert Street. There were three varieties of St. Theresa, including a 3D number that showed her raising and lowering her hands as if encouraging us all to fly away, but none of these was the same as Sliver's original. I bought four of each anyway, then went around the Rainbow, dropping them in obvious places where Sliver, making his rounds of the hallways with his broom, would be sure to find at least one. But a week later, going back to the corner where he lived, I found him lying on a mattress of newspapers and gazing at his headless Little Flower. He'd either been too stupid or too absorbed in grief to find what I'd left him.

When I told this story to Rags, he recounted to me the time he'd worked in a religious supplies shop. "That was a long, long time ago," he said. "But I was older than you already and I had a better nose for con men." The owner had been a man in his fifties, a perfect hybrid of evangelism and capitalism, his hair graying just so at the temples, his suits immaculate, and his pitch well honed. He'd dealt in all the usual paraphernalia, guardian angel nite-lites, holy cards, Bibles, prayer books, plastic St. Christophers with magnetic bases, posters, calendars, and rosaries of wood, plastic, or mother-of-pearl. But he had specialized in semimiraculous goods for the true believer, all of whom had the money for his magnificent discoveries. Rags had seen the man filling jars with ordinary tap water then tagging them as Lourdes water. He had made a deal for twelve hundred dollars for a sandal that had once been worn by Pope Clement IV. A dying woman had purchased a sliver of St. Peter's cross. "They crucified him *upside down* to deny him the consolation of having died like Our Lord Jesus." Rags had finally spoken up when his boss had offered a remnant of St. Christopher's cloak to a pair of weary-looking spinsters.

"Everybody knows St. Christopher never lived," he told the ladies. "He's a myth, like that piece of rag there. I saw this old fart cut it from a horse blanket in the back room."

"And do you know what he said, the old bastard, when the spinsters took off? He held his arm high in the air like some cranky old prophet and his eyes burned down at me with all this biblical wrath, and he shouted 'You're excommunicated!' I figured that meant fired. After that I got into selling porno. Though even here I had a guy who asked me if I could get hold of a used pair of Elizabeth Taylor's panties.''

Marian Embrace All Things, priestess of St. Paul, seventy years old, had been arrested for soliciting an off-duty cop. Sliver found out that the man who busted her was a rookie patrolman, twenty-one years old, from up north somewhere. Veteran cops, old hands around the north end, derided his eagerness and had given him the tip that there was an old Indian woman living in a warehouse off Ninth Street, that he shouldn't be fooled by the rags she wore because she was really a central figure in all that went on around there, the drugs, the thievery, and especially the prostitution. What the cop didn't know, among other things, was that Marian Embrace All things was the neighborhood mystic as well as a sharp-eyed junk collector. She found things in the street and traded them for food; she spoke Lacotah aloud to herself and broken English to anyone else, though I had once heard her speaking what sounded like French to a barman at Shanty's. She dealt in relics and destinies and would ask a man to break his empty wine bottle against an alley wall so she might read the pattern of broken glass and tell him who he might be. At times, her answers were long and elaborate, stories of wandering ancestors, ruptures with the natural world, family wars, all leading to the birth of that sad-looking rummy with the broken glass at his feet. Other times, she had very little to say, single words at a time: Lost. Found. More. Less. Heads. Tails. Once I'd seen a man break three different bottles when she'd told him to and she spent nearly an hour pawing through the splinters while a small crowd gathered round, stamping in the cold. The man for whom she'd read was a bouncer at the Nite Lite Dance Hall, the worst joint in the Twin Cities, a man who'd broken innumerable arms and bruised the family jewels of myriad tough guys, red and white. He'd stood over her while she read, watching her lift and examine jagged glass edges then replace them one by one. Finally she'd stood and told him simply, ''She never loved you,'' and the man burst into astonished tears. When I met her, she had reached an opaque brown hand to my forehead, then, sniffing her fingers, had told me that I came from no tribe she had ever known of. She was a charlatan, a ratty old woman so sincere that she even believed herself. When the cop, off duty, came upon her in front of Mickey's

Diner, he had recognized her immediately. Engaging her in conversation, he had found her answers unintelligible (looped and burdened as they were by Thunderbird wine) and he had finally admitted to her that what he wanted was information. Nodding, she'd led him to an alley and asked him from which source she might best tell him what he needed to know. He had no idea that Marian Embrace All Things could also read erections, that a man's whole destiny, his passions and weaknesses and wants and dreams, could be charted in the course and tapestry of his red and blue veins, in the length and shape of bulb and foreskin, in the rhythm of his throbbing. So when the cop said he wanted to know about sex, she'd told him to drop his pants. He'd done so with great embarrassment and when she'd extracted him from his shorts and with tender fingers had begun to explore him, he'd figured that was it. Flashing his badge, he'd zipped himself up and taken her in. She'd spent a single, joyous night in the warmth of the county jail and been released without a fine on her own recognizance. Chastened and humiliated, the young cop had bought her breakfast at the Holiday Inn, where she'd stolen her knife and fork, a heavy glass ashtray, and the patrolman's unused coffee cup.

The hard labor of kindness. Breaking rocks to make a bed of sand.

Candy's problems multiplied. She lived a complicated life. One of her regular johns, an alcoholic car salesman from Minnetonka, had gotten rough with her and when she'd bitten him he's split her lip and taken back his money as well as some of her own. Carl, thinking she was lying about the money, had kicked her into the snow and she'd come whimpering to my room, begging to sleep on the couch.

"Look around, Candy. I don't have a couch."

She showed me her lip and the bruise Carl had left on her shoulder. "Then give me the money for a hotel."

I reminded her she already owed me twenty dollars.

Setting her ass on my bed, she said it certainly was big enough for two.

"And when Carl asks you where you spent the night?"

"I'll say I was with Lila."

St. Jesse slept on the floor that night, even though Candy, from the warmth of the bed, kept telling me how silly I was, how straightlaced. "I mean we don't have to *do* anything, do we? Besides, I hate to sleep alone."

Sometime in the night, chattering from the cold, I pushed her to one side and slid under the covers. The cold was unbearable but I soon felt a hand resting on my thigh. I turned my back to her and pretended to be already asleep. Her hand followed me, neither caressing nor inviting, only touching. Then I felt her body move behind my own and we lay for a while like spoons, breathing in unison.

"Jesse?" She had the voice of a twelve-year-old.

I told her I was asleep.

"You got a cigarette?"

Kicking away the blankets, I rose and took a pack from the dresser. Returning to bed, I lit one for each of us.

"I knew you weren't asleep," she said. "I can always tell. My daddy used to pretend a lot, in the morning, when I'd come to wake him up. I could tell by the way he was breathing, you know, and anyway, when he was really asleep he would snore."

I reminded her I had a long day of work ahead of me, starting in a few hours.

"So okay. You don't have to listen. I just feel like talking."

"Where's the ashtray?"

"Over here."

She leaned out of the bed toward the night table and for the first time outside of the peek-a-booth I saw her body, her breasts swinging, in the blue darkness. I shivered.

Lighting another cigarette with her first, she went on talking, telling me about her family in Eau Claire, the first boyfriend she ever had—Donnie? Ronnie?—how she hated the town and the family but she was the best-looking number in her high school. How Carl was older than she was but had always had his eye on her, how she had plans but no ideas, how she had been gaining weight and had decided to start a diet, how, you know, it's nice to talk to someone even if they're pretending to be asleep, and on, and on. Finally she said what was really on her mind.

"I'm knocked up."

"Pregnant?"

"Yeah. Same thing."

I sat up and lit my cigarette with hers. "You're sure?"

She nodded in the darkness.

"Who's the father?"

"You got a phone book?"

"Sorry. I forget things."

"Never mind." In the darkness, she was a smoking statue, still as a grown woman. Only in her voice was she ever a child.

"But listen," she said, "Carl doesn't know, so keep it cool."

"Aren't you going to tell him?"

"No way. He'd make me get an abortion."

"And you don't want one? You want to keep the baby?"

"*Have* the baby. I want to *have* it."

"And then what?"

She hesitated. "I got . . . plans."

For a moment I believed that the woman in her had overcome the slut, but then she added, "This is my chance for some real money, a way out of this town and away from Carl."

I didn't know what she meant and somehow knew that she wasn't going to tell me. She had said what she wanted to. By the time I'd crushed out my cigarette, she was fast asleep. Leaning my head toward hers, I listened carefully to her breathing to be sure she wasn't pretending.

Each day I rose at dawn, just before the coming of the light; not because I was needed at work—I never started until past ten—but because I was anxious for the daylight. I fretted in the predawn dark of my cozy little hovel, smoking the day's first cigarette, heating water for coffee, treading naked from bed to window, and listening to my newly purchased secondhand radio, the news and the weather, now five below zero and the high may reach two.

I lived my life in imitation of what others thought my life to be and only in retrospect have I asked myself if I was then a success or a failure, a hero or a villain. Living my life among storytellers, I have often thought to myself that no life is uninteresting, only some are badly told. It is never enough to say merely what we have seen—what I saw outside my lone window: the brick wall, the abandoned car, an electric line, a broken wedge of sky which told me how long until the sunrise, how soon until night. I have told you nothing. I lived my life in imitation of what I had become.

Each day I had heard the boy crying and it was a sound I

could never entirely ignore. It awakened me in the morning and it kept me awake at night; it was the sound of a bad dream. And finally, one morning early in February, a day of false spring, sudden sunshine, and ice melting madly and sliding in sheets and arrows from the rooftop to the alley, I heard the weeping again, this time just outside my door. Pouring my coffee, I forgot about the sound for a moment, then suddenly heard it again, almost a wail. I went to the door and jerked it open. Standing in the hallway, being gloomily watched by Alice, was a little boy about five years old dressed in blue jeans, his feet and chest bare. Seeing me, he stopped crying instantly. I exchanged glances with Alice. She wanted to know if I could lend her a quarter.

"Later. Where's he live?"

He was a beauty of a boy, with shimmering blue eyes and long blond hair. We blinked at each other in a kind of surprise. He held two fingers toward his mouth as though to suck them but his hand was frozen in midair.

"I never seen him before," Alice told me. Alice who's seen everything.

I stood inside my doorway, still naked, where Alice couldn't see me. Crouching low, I reached out a hand toward the boy, meaning something I would never know. Had I meant to touch him, to claim him, to invite him in? But when my hand was nearly to his shoulder, he turned, and with his small legs churning, fled. I froze for a moment, peeking out the doorway to watch him cross to the stairway and I half followed, out of curiosity or surprise, forgetting my nakedness and Alice, and—though I must have seen at once, though I could not have missed seeing—it wasn't until he had reached the stairway that I saw clearly the hideous ribbon of welts and bruises across his shoulder blades and spine. Drums sounded in the distance. War drums, the drums of madness. Forgetting my nakedness, I chased after him, but by the time I reached the stairway he had already arrived at the top. Taking the stairs three at a time, I came to the third floor just in time to see him scamper into a doorway and push the door shut. I stood stupidly at the top of the stairway, suddenly aware that I was naked. A winter breeze as from a broken window filled the hallway, chilling me to the testicles. The hall was empty. It was just past dawn and the yellow hall light was still burning, a layer of dust on the bulb making it even dimmer than usual. I went back downstairs. Alice, the owl, looked through me, caring less for my body than I for hers. Slipping on my clothes, I went back upstairs. The door before me was white on the top half and blue on the bottom. Taking a deep breath, I knocked twice. There was no sound. That is, there was the sound of the garbage collectors below, the traffic on Wabasha Avenue, webs of machine sounds, the city rising from a broken slumber. I knocked again, harder. For a moment I thought I heard footsteps on the other side of the door, heavy steps, a man, but there was no answer. Then I was certain that the little boy was just on the other side of the door, listening to the sounds of the crazy man in the hallway. I tried the knob but the door was locked.

The fucking door is always locked.

In my own room, behind my blue door, I washed and shaved and dressed for work. Standing before my mirror, I didn't like my face. I thought at first that the mirror was cracked or simply dusty but when I wiped a cloth over it I found I was wrong. My face was my face and I would have to live with it.

"Candy, who's the little boy upstairs?"

"What little boy?"

"A five-year-old. Blond hair, blue eyes."

"There ain't no little boy upstairs."

Rags, sorting through an outdated stack of tits and ass magazines, said that the apartment was rented by a man named Pinder, a piano player. "He used to have a wife but I ain't seen her in a long time."

"Did they have any children?"

"Not that I know of. I can check the form." Sorting through his files, he produced the application form for the lease of the apartment. It was nearly six years old, listing names for John Pinder and his wife, Elaine. No pets, no children. The lease had never been renewed. "This is a pretty informal place," Rags explained.

I told him about the little boy I'd seen and the condition of his back, the mosaic of welts and scars. "Like someone had been hitting him with a stick."

"My own father used to beat me with his belt. So what?"

"This was worse. I want to call the police."

Rags laid a hairy hand over the phone. "Try that and you're out on your ear. The last thing I need is to give an excuse to a lot of detectives to poke around in the rooms upstairs."

Marian Embrace All Things said she knew who John Pinder was but that she hadn't seen much of him lately. "His wife was run away it was long time ago."

"Did they have any children? A little boy?"

"I am hardly knowing. John Pinder plays on the piano at a bar."

"What bar?"

"I don't remember."

I was about to walk away when she said no wait, she did remember.

"The name of the bar?"

"No, the wife. She was big once with a baby. It was a long time ago. I read for her a destiny." She told me how, lifting Elaine's blouse, she had placed her ear to her belly and heard what had sounded to her like waves on a beach. "Which is funny because I have been to the sea never."

I grew impatient. "Was it a boy, Marian?"

She shrugged. "Could be. Though I have never seen him born."

Sliver, carrying his mourning over the torn holy card to incredible extremes, had nothing to say about a little blond boy.

"It could grow back," he said, referring to St. Theresa's head. "It could grow back and be all right again."

In search of Sliver's brain cells.

The next afternoon I was alone in the shop. It was Rags's day off and he'd gone to Duluth to go ice fishing on Lake Superior. Business was slow and I was sitting behind the counter reading the newspaper when a well-dressed man came into the shop. He was in his fifties, balding, and nervous looking. Though he stood for a long moment in front of the magazines, it was obvious he wasn't looking at the covers. The only customer, an out-of-work Indian I knew fairly well, counted his change and decided he didn't have it to spare, so he left. I was alone with the well-dressed man. Without hesitating any further, he approached the counter.

"I'm looking for a woman named Candy Evans. I believe she's a dancer here."

A dancer?

"She's not working today. I think JoJo's in the booth."

There was something in his eyes that told me he wasn't looking to peek or to boo. He was there for something else. "Do you know where I might find her at this time of day?"

"You can try her apartment. It's through the door on the side of the street, third floor. She's behind the silver door."

"I've tried there already. Her friend said she wasn't in." He placed slight accent on the word *friend*.

"Then you might try the bars. Mickey's, the Blue Fin, Shanty's, Sawbucks."

He nodded gratefully. "Yes, I know the places." For some reason I believed him. "At any rate, if you see her, would you tell her I was here. My name is Charles."

"Charles was here to see Candy."

"But there's no need to tell anyone else." He pressed a five-dollar bill into my hand in parting.

Candy came in at five o'clock for her hour shift in the peek-a-booth and I passed on the message that a man named Charles had come looking for her.

She was surprised. "Did anyone else see him?"

"No. We were alone."

She seemed flustered. "What time is it?"

"Five after five. You better get moving. Denise usually takes a stopwatch in with her and just walks out when her time is up. I had to pass out a dozen quarters to the watchers last week."

"I got time," she said. "Listen, did he leave anything for me?"

"Just the message." It must have been the way I was looking at her; maybe I was smiling or maybe I wasn't. At any rate, she was suspicious.

"How much do you know?"

"Besides everything?" The old game: I knew nothing.

"Damn. You haven't told Carl have you?"

"We're not on speaking terms."

She lit a cigarette. "Christ, I don't feel like working tonight. You must think I'm awful."

I only shrugged.

"Jesse, I wouldn't sell this baby to just anyone. You see how Charles is. He's like a gentleman. We can trust him. He found a nice family, too. He showed me a picture of them. And she can't have babies, that's all. I can. I'm like a rabbit. My ovaries are just her good luck."

I must have shivered. "You're *selling* the baby?"

"YOU SAID YOU KNEW!"

"I said I didn't."

"Jesus Horatio Christ!" Her eyes narrowed. It was the whore who glared at me and not the friend. Then she began to tremble. "I suppose you're going to want my money, like everyone else. Just to keep your mouth shut."

Denise, a great big naked mattress of a woman, came storming out of the back room. "Jesse, goddamn it, if you don't tell Rags to turn up the heat in the peek-a-booth, I'm quitting. How can I look sexy when my tits are turning blue?" Seeing Candy, she said, "You're late."

"Go on back in, Denise. I'll be there in just a minute."

"Like fun. I'm going home."

When she was gone I had to refund quarters to four of the men who had been watching when she'd taken off. One of them, a regular, asked Candy if she was working tonight.

"In a little while. Hold your horses."

"Jesse, I'm gonna need some more quarters." He handed me three dollars and I gave him twelve quarters, enough to last him nearly an hour. "See you later," he said to Candy, throwing her a wink.

"Yeah, sure," she told him, but once he was out of earshot she added, "creep." Turning to me, she said, "I don't want to have another abortion. I've had two already and they were awful. You hurt inside and all over. That last time I kept throwing up just cause I felt so bad, you know, in my heart."

I told her that what she did was her own business.

"But listen, Jesse, you could fuck it up for me real good. One word to Carl and it's over. And if Charles gets spooked, this family'll go somewhere else."

"I don't want money, Candy."

"Like hell you don't. Just say how much and I'll give it to you."

"One dollar."

She didn't hear me. "And anyway, I can go on working for a little while, right up to the end of the fourth month, then they'll send me to a clinic in Chicago. It's really private, like a hotel, but there's a nurse and a doctor living there. Charles has it all arranged. He knows what he's doing. After I have the baby I won't even get to see it. And the parents will be there the next day to take it away. I'll be able to start all over again with what they're paying me. I can get away from Carl and the peek-a-booth, hooking, everything."

"How much are they paying you?"

She bit her lip. "Five thousand dollars."

"What if the baby is black?"

"It won't be."

"You're sure?"

"Yeah. I kind of planned it so I quit taking on blacks around the beginning of December. That's why I'm not pulling it in the way I used to. Carl thinks I've lost my stuff."

"Tell me about Charles."

"I'm not saying another goddamn word. You already got me in a corner as it is."

"Hey, Candy, you coming?" It was the customer with a pocketful of quarters.

"I'll be right there." To me she said, "Just name your price and Charles will pay you out of what he's gonna owe me."

I started to tell her again that I didn't want her money but she had already turned and hustled through the stage door into the peek-a-booth. Fully dressed.

There were no mailboxes at the Rainbow and that night I found a letter from Harper under my door. It was the first in two weeks. Tearing it from its envelope, I read it in the lamplight. She was no longer seeing the man from her Intro to Photo Tech class, she wrote. He had begun to insist on sex and although she couldn't blame him she couldn't give in to him either. "I'm being faithful to you without knowing why. He was a nice man and I was always happen to be with him. He couldn't help it that he wasn't you." Her own photography was going better, she said. From time to time, she was able to finish a small collection that drew praise from her professors but she hadn't sold anything except reprints from the Jesse collection. "I'm beginning to understand the term 'starving artist.' The scholarship money ran out about a month ago so I've taken a job in a department store selling scarves and handbags. If I keep it up much longer I'll have varicose veins from standing behind the counter. It doesn't pay very well but it fills up my Saturdays. The only day I feel lonesome is Sunday. You may notice that I write most of my letters to you on Sundays." She mentioned that she would have two weeks off at Easter and was trying to save enough money for a trip home. "I would have come at Christmas but I didn't know where to find you. Could you put up with me for two weeks? In your letters you write about coming to New York but you never seem to get here. Maybe the mountain will have to come to Muhammad. The sad part is that I'm getting used to not seeing you. Absence makes the heart grow mute. I won't sign this letter Love. You'll have to guess."

I had begun a reply, writing "Dear Harper, Convince me . . ." when I heard a loud rap on the door. It was nine o'clock so it couldn't have been Candy. I opened the door expecting to see Alice but before me was the well-dressed man, Charles, in a three-piece pin-striped suit, his fur hat in hand. "I think we need to talk," he said.

Shanty's Irish Pub, according to a dusty plaque over the bar, had been founded in 1908. By the look of it, it had been going downhill ever since. There was no music, no television, and nothing to eat except pickled sausages, salted peanuts, and potato chips, but I went there often because the beer was cheap and the clientele, half Indian and half descendants of northern Europeans—Swedes, Danes, Germans—left me in peace. I sat in a back booth with Charles, who looked as out of place as a nun. Ill at ease, he had insisted on taking the side of the booth with a blank wall to his back.

"Wild Bill Hickok did the same thing," I told him.

"Who?"

"Wild Bill Hickok. Don't you know your westerns? He lived in Deadwood in South Dakota about the time of the gold rush. He was a gambler mostly and always sat with his back to the wall. That's the legend. Only once he forgot and sat with his back to the door."

"What happened?"

"A man walked into the saloon and emptied a six-gun into the back of his head."

"I don't play cards," Charles said.

I opened my coat. "And I'm unarmed."

Charles nodded toward the bar, the other clients. "But are they?"

We each ordered a beer and I drank mine quickly. Charles sipped at his as though it were a crème de menthe.

"Candy tells me," he began, "Candy says you've let yourself in on our little business affair."

"The baby? Yes, she told me. She must be in her third month by now."

"I would prefer that we leave the subject unspoken."

"I agree. This is none of my business."

Charles was surprised.

"I don't care what Candy told you," I went on. "She's not what you'd call believable anyway."

For the first time I saw Charles smile.

"But if she says the baby won't be black," I added, "I think you can believe her."

Charles reached into his breast pocket and extracted a billfold. He was about to take out a few bills when I told him to put it away. "Unless you want to be followed home tonight." I nodded toward the bar. "They aren't with the Vienna Boys Choir."

Charles placed the wallet in his lap. "I can offer you five hundred dollars for your silence. I am not prepared to bargain. There are people who could be hurt, good people, if you were to talk about what you know."

I ordered another beer and waited for it to come before answering. "I knew you'd offer me something," I said, "so I thought at first I'd squeeze you a little. I've never been an extortionist and it seemed like a good game." Charles only nodded. "But I don't want your money, or Candy's either."

"Then what *do* you want?"

"Candy's a whore. Sometimes we play as if we're friends but when it all comes down to it, we can't be. I don't buy her sex,

I don't want it. I don't care what she does with herself. If she wants to make a living with her ovaries, that's her business. Abortions, like she says, are messy anyway.''

''I don't understand. You—''

''I only want to survive the winter and get out, go home, see my sister who loved me. Shall we get drunk, Charles? I'll tell you about love and the past and all. I need a bus ticket to New York, and worse.''

Charles was by now thoroughly confused. ''You want a bus ticket? Is that it?''

I laughed softly. ''No. Hell, no. Let Candy take the bus ride. I'm just curious is all.''

''About what?''

''Your business. The kind of man who buys and sells babies.'' I smiled. ''You must have interesting inventory problems.''

Charles was too sober to follow me. ''You can judge me if you like. It won't make any difference. I'm merely an agent. I only help people get what they want. Other times, I find a home for babies who otherwise wouldn't have one.''

''Such as?''

''Black babies. The kind no one wants to buy.''

I nodded as though I understood.

''What very few people realize,'' Charles continued, ''is that in America there are no more white orphans. At least not the way there were once. Times have changed and between the pill and abortion, the white orphans have disappeared. The babies, I mean. Hardly anyone wants to adopt an orphan of five or six years old and the only babies available to childless families— without a three-to-five-year wait—are black babies, Indians, or Hispanics.'' He stopped and took a long drink from his glass. ''Candy's baby will be white and if she follows my instructions and doesn't drink too much or take any drugs, he will be healthy as well.''

''Which makes him worth five thousand dollars.''

Charles nodded. ''To some people, more.''

''But it's illegal.'' I wasn't smiling.

Again Charles nodded. ''Which is why I'm going to trust in your silence.''

''Who buys the babies?''

''The white babies? Nearly always families without children.

People with physical disorders or who have already lost a child at birth.''

"The rich?"

"Not always. But we refuse to provide children to the hopelessly poor."

"We?"

"There are several of us, though I am the only one in St. Paul. We find women who are early in their pregnancies, who are seeking abortions, and convince them that it might be better to have the baby than to destroy it. We pay for medical care, provide a clinic, and the day the baby is born it is given to a new mother, one who will give it love and attention."

"What about birth certificates?"

"A piece of paper only. We manage."

"You said you buy black babies."

"I do. It doesn't help much, but I have contacts, black or white families who will agree to take someone in. I buy from mothers who can't care for already born children, babies I find just by chance. I find them everywhere."

I drank another beer and began to feel drunk, that peculiar light-headedness. "What's in it for you?" I asked Charles.

He shrugged. "The satisfaction of giving children a home."

"Salvation?"

"I'm not a Christian."

"Me neither but I pretend a lot. Another beer?"

We drank for another few hours while a surprising midwinter rain fell outside. Satisfied that I was not going to turn him in, Charles relaxed with me and I with him. He told me how he'd come upon Candy.

"I know an abortionist, a retired doctor who lives in the area. He's a horrible old man but at least his methods are sound. Whenever a woman comes to him, he gives her a bottle of sugar pills and tells her to come back in three days. Then he gets in touch with me. If the woman is white and can certify that the baby won't be colored, I make her an offer. So that she doesn't associate me with the doctor, I make a point of meeting her away from his office. Sometimes the woman will pretend to be shocked, sometimes she really will be. Candy didn't even pretend. She said yes before I could even say how much."

"She planned on finding you."

He nodded. "I had that impression because afterward she tried to bargain. I had to tell her that I never made deals except in cases in which the baby has already been born. Sometimes a woman with a one-year-old child will ask for twice as much and if I have the impression she's abusing the child I have no choice but to pay her. I can usually imagine what life will be like for that baby otherwise. It's the buying price for the new parents that varies, though I should mention that we don't think of it as the baby being bought and sold but our intervention they're paying for. If we find a family that cannot pay five thousand dollars, we charge less. Others more. There are a lot of extra considerations."

I wanted another beer and maybe a chaser this time, but I was already feeling pretty loose. Charles talked on about his business, telling stories of abused children he'd helped find new homes, families with ten children and no money, and women who had come to him a second or a third time with babies for sale. "Now I have to make it clear to each woman that I will only deal with them once. What's the point if they turn it into a business?" He shook his head sadly. "What's the damn point?"

I had started out believing he was a criminal, but now that I was face to face with him I could see that the clothes he wore were old and threadbare, the cuffs frayed, his tie shiny from wear. I sensed that if I looked under the table I would find holes in his shoes. He simply had a dignity I had misunderstood. I had been living so many weeks among the rummies that my eye was jaded.

"Just one more question," I said. "What you do could be done legally, couldn't it? I mean, women have babies all the time and give them up immediately for adoption. Why would anyone go to the bother of paying?"

"That's the magic and the curse," Charles answered. "Because they don't want to wait the five or six years that it takes on a waiting list or because they want the world to identify the baby as theirs, genetically as well as legally. Some don't want people to know they're adopting so they tell their friends that the wife is pregnant, then four months or so before the birth they go off somewhere, as though on an extended vacation. When they return, the woman has a baby in her arms and no one's the wiser. We go to great lengths sometimes to certify the color of eyes, hair, skin tone, everything. We don't want children questioning their own identities.''

When we left Shanty's, Charles was as drunk as I was but he only betrayed it by weaving slightly on the icy street. North Wabasha at midnight was ghostly with vague darknesses. Street lamps shone on the glassy pavement and the sound of dance music filtered up the street from the Nite Lite.

Alone in my room, I contemplated the orchids while Carl and Candy argued next door. I had seldom felt so tired and so unhappy. I had tried to finish a letter to Harper but had been too drunk to hold the pen steady. Listening to Candy bitching about money, I wondered again why I didn't just get on the bus to New York and be done with it. Harper's letter was an invitation that I couldn't ignore and there was nothing in St. Paul to keep me. Slipping into bed, I thought again of Candy and her baby. Soon she would be starting to swell around the middle, her breasts would be heavier and firmer. Everyone was paying for their children in one way or another and I shouldn't have been surprised to learn that for some the price is calculable.

I slept and I awoke. Carl banged Candy against our common wall. Rising, I took up again my letter to Harper, writing more fluidly now, my drunkenness thinned into moodiness. I wrote a love letter without using the word love, telling her the truth of what my life had become, the porno shop and the hustlers, Alice in her looking glass, Marian Embrace All Things, and my belief that when the winter passed I would make my way to New York. As a letter it was poetry, sincere and laced with longing, and I folded it into its envelope and sealed it without knowing how time with its masterly strokes would eventually transform it into one of the better lies I have ever put to paper.

"What is winter but for cold?
I warm my feet with stray cats.
Bad news they cannot tell me."
—MARIAN EMBRACE ALL THINGS

7

In mid-march, the winter disguised itself in rain and the dirty snows were washed away in three days. Then the cold returned, more bitter because of the respite. For a week, the temperature hovered around zero and I shivered in my room, wearing my clothes—jeans, socks, and a sweater—to bed. Even the hot water I had always counted on was slow in coming. I read in the newspaper that three frozen bodies had been found in the basement of an abandoned warehouse on the other side of the highway. Dressed in old coats, three men had huddled together during the cold snap and had died with their arms around one another like a trio of lovers. A water main had burst on the south side of town, flooding basements with icy water. A family of tourists from New York, on their way home from skiing in Colorado, had run out of gas on a back highway. The father, wandering off with a gas can, had frozen to death five miles from the car and the family had been rescued by a trucker on his way to church.

Rags climbed the stairway to give me my notice. Alexander had settled with the city fathers for an amount three times the value of his property. The shop would close its doors for good on the first of May and during the first week in June, the whole works, including the porno shop, would be demolished. In its place would be a center for the fine arts, a decision, Rags said, that was based upon the public taste. "Who says porno isn't art?" he asked. He was disguising his disappointment. "Not that I got anything to worry about. Alexander's got me lined up for a manager's job at one of his theaters in Omaha. I won't starve."

Sliver told us that as soon as the weather cleared up, the bulldozers would get started on the far north edge, between

Eleventh and Twelfth streets. The Nite Lite was closing down in ten days and some of the Indians living in the abandoned hotel next door were already scouting around for new digs. Marian Embrace All Things, loaded with half a dozen shopping bags, had already found a place near the river, an unused granary that was a good mile from the targeted area. "The Mississippi I can see from my window. I made it myself, the window, and the river smells of shit."

According to law, the tenants of the Rainbow were entitled to three months' notice, but to speed things up the city council had offered a two-hundred-dollar payoff to every tenant. Rags handed me an envelope full of preprinted checks and told me to go around to all the tenants, get them to sign a release, and pay them their money. "You can start with your own." I signed the form, pocketed my carbon copy and the check, then went back into the Rainbow. It was already midmorning, but for the tenants of the Rainbow it might as well have been predawn. No one ever rose before noon and my first half-dozen visits went unanswered. Carl came to the door in a silk robe and was about to pitch me down the stairs when I flashed the check under his nose. He couldn't sign fast enough. It took half an hour to convince Alice that no matter what she did she was going to have to move.

"I got friends here," she told me, though I had never seen any. "And this is where my mail comes." I had already learned that what Alice meant by mail were the drops of hot property for her temporary keeping.

"No more post office, Alice. You can leave a forwarding address."

She signed with a snail's handwriting and I handed her the check.

"What's this for?" She looked at me suspiciously, as though I had given her a bribe of some sort.

"Money. You can take it to the bank."

"Don't have a bank."

I went to the next door and knocked.

"Gone," Alice told me. "He's got an early shift at the plant."

The house biographer. The historian of otherwise forgotten lifetimes.

When I came to the white and blue door on the fourth floor,

I was surprised to find it ajar. I had raised my hand to knock but thought better of it. In the past month, I had heard the little boy from time to time but had only folded my arms in despair. Now the door was open. I pushed it forward.

The room was larger than my own, with a private connecting bathroom. An unmade double bed was pushed against one wall and opposite was a threadbare sofa. A film of sunlight shone through lace curtains and illuminated the dust in the air. It was an apartment which simply smelled sad.

The little boy sat alone on the sofa and had two of his fingers in his mouth. He was wearing what looked like diapers though he had to be at least five years old. Seeing me in the doorway, he recoiled with fear, so I stood very still, simply nodding my head hello. When I smiled he seemed to relax. Looking round the room, I saw no evidence of the family, no toys, no magazines piled in a corner, nothing resembling a kitchen. On the wall above the sofa was an impressionist poster curling at the edges. The room smelled of dirty laundry as though the windows had been shut all winter long.

I took a few steps forward and was in the middle of the room. The boy watched me warily, taking his fingers from his mouth.

I asked him his name. When he didn't answer, I told him I was Jesse.

"Grzewl," he answered.

"What?"

"Gaza," he said. "Dadagazl."

My own speech left me at the moment I realized he had none. We blinked at each other in the sunlight and I found I was holding my breath. Grief was no wilting flower; grief was a hothouse orchid. In two movements, I had him in my arms and though he kicked and scratched I turned him face down and examined his back. Old wounds had scarred over but new ones had bloomed in their place. Feeling his neck, I found nothing. Perhaps I expected him to be as my mother had been, strangled if not stupid, but it was clear that his lack of speech was emotional, not physical. He no longer struggled and I realized he was bracing himself, his eyes closed, for a blow. When I touched his shoulder, he flinched. I told him I wasn't going to hurt him but I might as well have spoken Russian. Holding him against me, I felt a trickle of warm against my leg. He had pissed his pants. Lying him prone, I stripped off his diaper and found that there were sores across his crotch and legs, a splash of redness that he had scratched with his own fingers. It was as though he had not been changed in weeks and, left unattended, had scratched himself bloody. He lay silently on the sofa, watching me as though I were some miracle, an unknown angel of unknowable intent. In the bathroom was a small tub which I filled with warm water. Lifting the boy, I carried him naked to the water and though he struggled he didn't make a sound until he felt the water around him. Then he began to whimper and when I rinsed his bottom and thighs, tears rolled down his cheeks but he didn't sob nor did he take his eyes from me. When I left the bathroom briefly to search the dresser for clean clothes, I returned to find him standing in the tub, his head bent as though to see around the doorway to where I'd gone. I let him soak for a long while, changing the water from time to time so he'd be warm. Sitting atop the toilet, I watched him and he watched me. He was no longer crying but the water seemed to trouble him. He held his hands near his chest as though not to get them wet and though I coaxed him to play a little, to splash or make waves, he would have none of it. With a worn bar of soap I lathered his chest and rinsed him; then, taking a washcloth from the sink, I covered his face with it, taking away what seemed to be weeks of grime with one sweep. For a brief moment he resisted me, then he relaxed, "Where is your father?" I asked him, and when he didn't answer I said, "Daddy. Where is your daddy?" The word seemed to pierce him and he was instantly as still as stone. Then slowly he raised his arms to me and I thought he wanted out of the tub. When I reached to lift him, he clung to me, wet and anxious, holding his arms tightly around my neck and pressing his face to my own. I lifted him and carried him back to the bedroom. A towel was draped over a chair and I dried him with it, careful with his legs and back, the wounds that had gone pink and white from the hot water. The sun had moved behind the alley wall and new shadows filled the room. Taking clean clothes from where I'd left them, I dressed the boy in a new diaper, worn jeans, and a sweater. I found a pair of shoes and socks in the corner near the sofa and though he helped me when I put the socks over his feet, he pulled away from me when I tried to slide on the shoes. When I insisted, he rose from the sofa as though to get away from me. "Okay," I told him. "No shoes."

Rags would be waiting for me and I didn't know what else to do. Searching through the cupboards, I found enough to make a sandwich and gave it to the boy along with a glass of water. Holding the sandwich in his hands, he lifted the bread and took out the slice of ham underneath. Dropping the bread to the floor, he chewed the ham happily and I waited until he had finished before turning to go. I was halfway out the door and was turning for a last look at him when I heard—as though from a distant land—"Goodbye." Though I hadn't seen him say it, though when I turned and looked upon him he was busily recovering the bits of bread he'd dropped to the floor, I knew that he had said the word. Standing in the doorway, I said aloud, "Goodbye." Looking up from his bread, he answered, more like a parrot than a child, "Goodbye." We said goodbye a dozen more times, back and forth as in a game, then I closed the door and hurried down the hall, the stairs, back to the porno shop where Rags was handling a lunch-hour rush.

I went to visit Marian Embrace All Things in her new home. The granary had been closed for about two years and vandals had broken the doors and windows, torn the railing away from the staircase, and spray-painted their names and poetries along the inner warehouse walls. Already Marian had forsaken her room with a view for a warmer spot near the center of the building, a small room that had once served as an office and was not open to the riverside breezes. She had made a bed of newspaper and a torn tarpaulin in one corner of the room and in the other she had piled her riches, the hundred-odd treasures that the gutters and alleys had offered up to her. We sat on the floor, cushioning ourselves atop newspaper and rags, and drank from her bottle of Thunderbird wine. With a smile, she asked me if I wanted anything to eat. Since her false arrest, she explained, she'd been eating better. The young cop was always bringing her something, a bag of fruit, a loaf of bread, or even canned food. "Which I could not eat until on Wabasha was this." And she showed me a rusty can opener she had found a few days before.

"They're going to tear down the Rainbow," I announced. "We all have to move."

She said she already knew. "Sliver talks to me." She drank from the bottle, letting a little of the wine run down her chin. "You don't drink?" She handed me the bottle and I drank from it.

It was a Sunday, my only day off. As on so many Sundays, the streets were deserted. All the bars were closed and most of the cafés, so most of the derelicts stayed home. Throughout the winter I had barely left my neighborhood, but with improved weather urging me outward I had begun to walk around the city, each step adding restlessness to my restlessness. This Sunday, my walk had led through the length of downtown St. Paul, past the banks and department stores and garages, down a steep hill that flanked the north bank of the Mississippi, to the old port and Marian Embrace All Things's granary. Birds flew among the warehouse walls as though caged and Marian said that at night she could hear the bats playing tag in the great indoor darkness.

"Maybe you will come here," she said. "When the Rainbow is gone."

I said I didn't think so.

"I knew," she said. "I ask you to hear you say no."

She once had told me that I could have been an Indian. In my past, she asked, were there no Lacotah Sioux? "White men have no patience. All of them have plans. You have patience and no plans. We could make a tribe."

I had imagined myself living with the old woman, carrying a shopping bag from street to street, searching the gutters, the empty doorways, the floors of phone booths and bus stations for my living. Would we have lain together at night, alone atop our newspaper and our rags? Marian Embrace All Things in my young and tired arms might have been as loving as any woman I would ever find.

We drank until the sun had set on the other side of the river and Marian talked about her childhood, in Alberta, Canada, where her father had taken her when she was very young. "He said the reservation was too unhappy. His father was Chippewa, a failed warrior whom they called Good Heart. He had never killed. In the forest we lived, above Edmonton. We all were

Indians—Mandan, Chippewa, some Blackfoot, a few Oglala—
and my grandfather, Good Heart, gave me his English which
you hear and you smile to.'' Opening a second bottle of wine,
she talked on about her life, her four husbands, the two daughters she'd had before the war who had looked white and had
moved to Quebec and changed their names and forgotten about
being Lacotah or Chippewa or anything Indian. In her long life
she had lived in all the toilet towns of midwest America and
central Canada and the more she talked the more I could hear
the broken glass in her words, suggestions of ancient torment
that had been whittled into wisdom. She explained to me that
the word Lacotah came from *koda*, meaning friend, but that
Chippewa, in the same language, meant snake or enemy. ''I live
torn.''

She recounted a time in her life when, at nineteen, she had
drifted away from a husband in Minot, North Dakota, because
he'd always been drunk and hadn't even been able to buy her a
new pair of shoes for the winter. Wearing cardboard on her
feet, she hitchhiked south, ending up in White, South Dakota,
an old farming center with far more men than women and almost
no children at all. She stayed because there was work, though
mostly she spent her time cleaning other people's homes and
peeling the hands of husbands from her breasts and behind.
During one long month she'd gone without any work at all and
then, in February, she agreed to accompany half a dozen of the
farmers to an abandoned farmhouse where they liked to go for
their card games. The game began in the early evening and near
midnight a snowstorm came up, blanketing the house in high
drifts which covered the doors and windows. Too drunk to dig
their way out, the farmers lit their lamps and decided to sit out
the storm. There was no phone, very little food, and not much
to do except play cards, drink corn whiskey or beer, and screw
Marian Embrace All Things in the back bedroom. A stone oven
warmed the room where they played and when the coal ran out
they took planks from the walls and kindled them with back
issues of *Collier's*. It was the great blizzard of 1922 and the men
were trapped for over three days, driven nearly insane by the
frantic howling winds and a cabin fever that was only made
worse by the endless flow of whiskey. Marian Embrace All
Things sustained them; she was a food that they could taste but

not swallow; she was the loser's consolation and during three days each of them lost many times. They installed her in her bedroom with nothing but a mattress on the floor and a few old blankets, and after she had dressed and undressed a dozen times, she gave it up, leaving her clothes in heap at the foot of the bed. The men warmed her. Their unshaven faces and hot breathing took the chill from her legs and shoulders and she invited them to cover her as they wished, anything to stop the cold. Lying on the mattress, she could hear the shuffling of the cards, the fretful conversations, the arguments, the betting and calls, and while one of the farmers heaved and hoed her, she imagined she could see the cards in front of her. One man held a pair of nines and another had three jacks. When they passed the deck, the man gave away his jacks and took a three, a six, and a king so that he could lose. She knew his face. He was the German immigrant with a heart as calloused as a whore's butt and he would be along in a minute or two so she hurried the man atop her, touching him with her hand just so. He sprang within her and collapsed, warm. Toward the end of the third day, everyone had grown too weak for her. Rising from the bed, she enticed whomever she could back to the worn mattress, wanting all of them at once, a half-dozen men to cover her, stroke her, enter her, warm her. But when the weather cleared, they heaved against the door, pushing away the pyramid of snow that entrapped them, and they all went home. Marian Embrace All Things felt a loss unlike any she had ever known and had grieved for days, "with my hips all painted bruised and come like old milk on my legs." Ever since, even in the arms of a man she loved, she had never felt entirely unalone.

In her granary home, fifty years later, she poured herself more wine and as she grew drunk—and I grew drunk along with her—she went backward with her stories, to a time when she was five years old, having climbed a tree, a dying elm with great fissures in its trunk. She had climbed very high, up to where the limbs were brittle and weak and the wind had begun to make her sway. Then abruptly the sky had darkened and the wind had grown strong and cold. Terrified, she'd hung onto the branch, not daring to climb back down. When the rain had begun to fall, her branch had grown slippery. She'd thought she heard Good Heart calling to her but she couldn't see him in the gathering darkness. All the same, the sound of his voice calmed her. She was not in danger. Suddenly she wanted only to stay where she was, amid the thunder and the lightning that split the sky around her upturned face. The universe was destroyed and recreated above and below and her branch swayed as if in ritual, hey yoh hey yah. Then suddenly a great surge of wind bent the tree low, cracking the trunk, and she was tossed in the black sky like a wingless doll and soared for a long moment before falling. She landed, catlike, on both feet, incredibly unharmed, and ran home elated to tell her grandfather what had happened. For weeks afterward she had believed herself to be immortal and had begged Good Heart to let her change her name from Embrace All Things to Lives Forever but he would have none of such blasphemy.

She told me many other stories while I nodded from the wine. I didn't realize I had fallen asleep until she awakened me with her foot. "You go home."

I rose on unsteady legs, more drunk than I'd been in a long time. As a parting gift, Marian had me break my wine bottle against the wall, then she tried to read in the shards the story of my past, but after a few minutes of weaving from fragment to fragment, she turned her withered face to mine and said, "Nothing here but broken glass. More I cannot see."

8

One word. He says only one word. He says goodbye. He would say goodbye to anyone. He says goodbye to me.

Among her stories, Marian Embrace All Things had remembered, suddenly, the name of the place where John Pinder worked. "The Soft Shoe, a nightclub where one time a dancer I knew."

The next day, hearing the heavy footfalls of a hangover in my head, I suffered through work and then refused Rags's offer to go down to Shanty's for a beer. I had found the address of the Soft Shoe in the telephone directory and was determined to go there before my courage, artificially buoyed by the hangover, failed me. The nightclub, decked in red vinyl booths and a chrome bar, was the kind of place which attracts the divorced, the never married, and the transient unfaithful. The kind of place in which there are never more than two or three couples dancing no matter what the band leader says to encourage everyone, where a perpetual woman, looking not unlike my neighbor Alice, stands at the bar with her hip thrust forward and waits for whichever man will take her home at 2 A.M. The kind of place where my father took his girl friend, Dorell; the Hideaway, the worst of bad memories.

John Pinder was already playing the piano when I arrived and I bolted down two short Scotches while waiting for his first break. When he arrived at the bar, one of the barmaids whispered to him that he had a visitor and when he sat next to me, leaning his weight against his elbows, I was surprised at how young he was, as though I'd expected all fathers to be so much older than I was. He wore a frayed blue evening jacket with satin lapels and the white shirt underneath was wrinkled. He was no more than twenty-seven and his hair was already thinning at the temples. He must have thought I was someone else because he asked me whether I wanted one bag or two.

"I didn't come to buy grass."

He shrugged. "My mistake."

The Scotch had not performed the hoped-for miracle. I was not Jesse the Terrible, I was Jesse, trembling. "It's about your son."

The look of boredom left his face. His eyes filled with something like a sunrise. It was as though I had slapped him.

"Martin?" he said, his voice missing a blade or two. "What about him?"

"I saw him today." It was all I could say. It might have been enough. I have seen your son and what you have done to him.

John Pinder lit a cigarette and I noticed that he had bitten all of his nails down to the nub, a bad practice for a piano player. "So you've seen him, so what?"

"His back, all those bruises and scars."

He was gazing into his glass of beer as though into a micro-scope. "He fell down."

"Fell down?"

"Yeah. He landed on the radiator and got burned."

"I don't believe you."

He looked deeper into his beer glass, seeking an alibi. "Look, I gotta play. I only get five minutes at a time."

"I'll wait."

He went back to his piano and played cocktail music for nearly an hour. People called out to him now and then to tone it down or jazz it up or to play a special song. He played grimly, as though the piano were a machine to be operated and not an instrument, and between songs he looked at his watch or toward the bar to see if I was still there. I was. I drank another Scotch, then switched to beer. I was half looped by the time he stood up and came back to the bar.

"Look, whoever-you-are . . ."

"My name is Jesse. I'm your landlord." Stretching the truth of it.

"Right. Jesse. Well, listen, Jesse, I'm in no mood for you tonight. I got a job to do. You follow?"

"You're not working just this minute. Let's talk."

"About Martin? He's none of your business. And even if he were, what do you know about me? About us? I drink too much, I know that. Try working in a place like this and not drink. Every night there's some music lover pushing a whiskey or two my way. Usually it's some sentimental slut trying to make me think she's romantic. That's my audience. That's who I play for."

I wanted to ask what the hell it had to do with his son, but now I was mute. I still didn't know exactly why I'd come, to threaten or to listen?

"I come home at night after eight hours of pounding the keys and I'm not always sober but that don't mean I'm a drunk. You know what I mean?"

Curiously, I did.

"Then, there's Martin. No Elaine, just Martin. He needs everything and he's whining all the time. He still pees his pants and I gotta clean up after him. Imagine that. Five years old and he still pees his pants. I think he's retarded. He can't even talk."

"There's no one to talk to."

"Huh?"

"But he knows how to say goodbye."

"Yeah," John Pinder admitted. "He's got two whole words. Mommy and goodbye."

"Where *is* his mother?"

John Pinder took a long drink of bourbon, swallowing a cube of ice which made him choke. "Gone. She took off, psst, like that, about two years ago. Left me with the kid and then tried to make out like I tossed her out."

Behind us, a jukebox was playing "Sentimental Journey" and a fat blonde—one of Pinder's sentimental sluts?—was putting moves on the bartender. "You don't know," she was telling him, "you don't know what a really real woman is. You just think. You just think you do."

"Go home," the bartender advised her. "Jesus Christ, it's only eight o'clock and I gotta cut you off. Go home."

The fat blonde was shaking her head as though the bartender hadn't understood a word, not one word, of what she'd said. "You. Don't. Know." she repeated. "What I could show you."

Turning to John Pinder, the bartender winked. "Hey, John-John, you wanna lay some pipe in her pants?"

We both ignored him.

"She'll be back," Pinder said. It took me a moment to realize he was talking about his wife. "Not for me, I know better than that. She'll come back for the kid. She didn't love me, but she sure as hell loved that kid. She used to sit up all night just looking at him, you know? Like he made the sun rise in the morning and set at night. I wasn't there much. She said I upset the kid."

"How's that?"

"I lost my temper a few times. No big deal, it happens to everybody. Elaine went overboard. Women do that, you know. Once she even took off with him, tried to leave the state. I had to go after her and drag her back. She didn't believe me when I told her things would be different, but they were. I got a better job, came home earlier, spent more time around the house. I did all right. You never been married, I take it?"

"No."

"Take your time. It's no bed a roses."

For a moment he studied his glass, his frayed cuffs, his own fingers. It took me a moment to realize he was trembling. All that had been guilt left his face and was replaced with a mounting sorrow. I was amazed to see tears in his eyes. "No bed a roses," he said again.

The bartender leaned in our direction. "Everything okay, John?"

"S'alright, Henry. Maybe I need another bourbon."

"Better you just tickle the keys a while," Henry advised him, giving me a warning with his eyes, a sidelong glare meaning, Clear out.

I sat through another hour of John Pinder's music, refusing to drink anything stronger than ginger ale. The fat blonde tried out her charms up and down the bar. Getting no takers, she weaved out the door and into the rainy night, muttering "Fags, fairies . . . wimps."

For the third time, John Pinder sat before me but we had little to say. I was uncomfortable in my role of accuser.

Then I thought of Charles.

"Why don't you give Martin up?" I suggested. "I know a man . . ."

"No goddamn way I'm giving him up. No way in hell. The old lady comes back and he's not there, she won't be staying."

"I could go to the police."

"Don't."

"They would take him away from you and give him to someone who'd care."

"I care. Who says otherwise?"

I was tired. The music and the Scotch had gotten me down and suddenly the place was full of creeps. John Pinder was only the piano player. I rose to leave. "Just lay off him," I said in parting. "If you don't, I'll know."

John Pinder sat unmoving on his bar stool, his eyes upon his drink and whatever miracle was occurring amid the ice and alcohol. "You're just a boy," he said. "I don't believe you."

I carried his disbelief home with me and I listened to my ceiling the way saints listen to the heavens. I listened, not for an answer, but for silence. The next night, around three in the morning, I heard footsteps that could only have been Pinder's. Then I heard weeping and, unmistakably, the sound of a belt across flesh. Leaping to my feet, I hurried down the stairs to the pay phone at the corner where I dialed the police emergency number. ''The Rainbow. Eighth and Wabasha. Fourth floor. Hurry.''

When the cop arrived, I was out front to meet him. ''It isn't the first time,'' I told him as we climbed the stairs. Already I was breathless. ''I hear it all the time. I had to call.''

By the time we knocked on Pinder's door, all was quiet. A single lamp was lit and you would almost have believed that John Pinder had been awakened from his sleep. Martin was on the couch, tucked under blankets.

''Neighbor says you're beating your kid,'' the patrolman said.

John Pinder smiled. ''Yeah? Take a look.'' Stepping backward, he gestured toward Martin.

The patrolman entered the apartment, hesitating just past the doorway. ''You okay, little boy?''

It was so very like the night my father had kicked my mother in the throat and the police had come. Rose and I in front of the television, petrified in white-gray light.

''Zzzla,'' Martin answered.

John Pinder was composed while I was outraged. Stepping from the hallway shadows, I looked into the room as though for evidence.

''I don't know who called you,'' Pinder said, ignoring me. ''I knocked over some things a little bit ago. Maybe that's the noise they heard. I play piano at the Soft Shoe and never get home till late. You know how—''

I stepped into the room. ''Look at the kid's back,'' I told the cop. ''It's all black and blue and scarred up.''

The patrolman hesitated. He was the kind of man who is in the wrong profession; he didn't want any trouble. He wanted to get back to his paperback.

''Martin fell down,'' John Pinder insisted. ''This guy saw a few bruises and got it into his head that I'm beating my kid.''

''I live right downstairs,'' I explained. ''I hear things.''

The cop made up his mind. ''You hear things? Me too. I hear false alarms, three of em a night. I gotta wade through a dozen guys like you to get my job done. You want to find yourself on my list, just keep it up.'' And without another word, he turned his broad back on me and went down the stairs. I was alone with John Pinder.

"They believe the fathers," he said.

Our fathers who art, or who were, in heaven, and he closed the door in my face.

Marian gave me the name of a social worker she knew and I took a long lunch hour to visit her. She was an attorney's assistant, a city employee assigned to battered child cases, and her desk was piled high with files. "Not all of these are child abuse cases," she explained. "We're understaffed and I sometimes have to fill in on other things."

I told her about Martin Pinder and his piano-playing father, ending with the story of my call to the police. She listened as though she had heard the story a hundred times. She had, she admitted.

"There are only two of us here, myself and another legal assistant. Neither of us are full-time, we're just paying our way through law school. We get more than fifteen new cases every month and each one requires a dozen different forms. Each form has to be supported with evidence, testimony from neighbors, photographs, anything that might point to parental misconduct. In two years, we've taken only four cases to trial. Two ended in acquittal." She stopped to light a cigarette with the butt end of another. "Am I being pessimistic enough?"

"Black as night."

"Do you have any evidence other than what you've seen?"

I said I had heard the same sounds nearly every night for weeks.

She shook her head. "Not good enough. Are the other neighbors aware of what's going on?"

"No one else seems to even know he's there. Where I live is hard to describe."

Ashes fell between her fingers to the file in front of her and she swept them away. "Eighth and Wabasha. Isn't that the Rainbow? I think we had a case there a few years ago. I'd have to check the card file."

She rose and flipped through a circular card file, referenced by city zone. Copying down the file number, she went to a steel cabinet and yanked out a yellow folder.

"Right. It was a divorce case, a custody battle. The mother ran away with her baby but was located by the Des Moines police. She sued for a divorce on the grounds of cruel and inhuman treatment, claiming that her husband had abused both her and her child. The husband counterclaimed that because of her criminal record—she'd been a prostitute—she was unfit to be a mother. She got her divorce but he won custody."

"What was her name?"

The woman closed the file. "I'm sorry. I'm not free to tell you."

"Elaine Pinder?"

"Like I said . . ."

"Where is she now?"

"Elaine Pinder? After the divorce, she disappeared."

"Nothing in your files?"

The woman shook her head. "I'm sorry to discourage you so much," she said. "It's good of you to come. We get so little help and it's hard to get used to the kind of work we do."

"Can we open a case against John Pinder? Can you at least start a file? Locate a family that could take the boy in? I need something to show the police besides the scars on his back."

"I can start a file but it's only paper. I don't think we'd have much of a chance."

That matter was beyond me. I was looking at my hands as though for the lines that Marian Embrace All Things might read to tell me what to do. "Any suggestions?"

The woman sat motionless for a moment and smiled just a little, "Kidnap him?" It wasn't until I was back on the street that I realized she wasn't entirely kidding.

I asked Candy if she knew where I could get in touch with Charles.

"I don't call him, he calls me."

"What if it's important?"

"What do you want, more money?"

"Candy, I—"

"Hold your water, his number's in my purse."

Charles agreed to meet me at Shanty's and we sat at the same booth as the first time. A heavy spring rain was falling outside and we both arrived soaked to the skin. Charles ordered coffee but the bartender just laughed.

"No coffee till after ten."

I said we'd have two beers.

"I suppose," Charles said, "this has something to do with Candy."

"Not this time," I answered, and without hesitation I told him all I knew about Martin Pinder. He listened with interest and wrote little notes in a small book, asking me to spell the last name and to give the exact address. Then he tore out the sheet of paper. "After I've memorized this, I'll throw it away."

"Then you think you can help me?"

"You understand that he's a bit old already. I mean, it's hard to find someone to take in a boy past infancy. And anyway, there's the father. How much does he want to give him up?"

"That's just it. He wants to keep him."

"Then it's out of the question." He tore his notes into little pieces. "What you're suggesting is kidnap. That's not my line of work."

"This is a special case."

He gave me a weary look, the look of a man speaking to an idiot. "They're all special cases, Jesse. Unemployed single mothers. Rape victims. Drug addicts. Prostitutes. We do what we can but we don't steal children just because we don't think much of their home life."

"Then I could take care of him. He needs—"

"You're still a boy. You make fifty dollars a week in a porno shop."

"He can't talk, Charles. He's five years old and he doesn't say a word. Just gibbers and jabbers and wets his pants."

Charles rose from the table. "I'm sorry, Jesse. There's just no way."

I sat alone in Shanty's bar and finished my beer. The rain was still falling so I ordered another. For the first time that day I thought of Rose, as though she might have an idea for me. When I finished the beer, I looked out the front window to see if there was rain. It fell in silver sheets, washing the garbage from the Wabasha sidewalk. When the bartender asked me if I wanted another, I didn't say no.

* * *

The next morning, Charles took a file from his shelf and copied down an address he'd been holding for nearly two years. He kept spare documentation in case of arrest. Paper would incriminate anyone he'd ever dealt with, so he contented himself with initials and random addresses and dates, none of them seeming to correspond to each other. The connections were all in his memory.

He'd lost his wife three years ago because she hadn't liked his business. Tell me how many friends you have?

He had none. His life was papered with too many secrets. Hard to be the friend of a man who is a shadow.

Driving north, he took the Roseville exit and turned down a street that bordered the highway. No. 1627 was a white tract house badly in need of paint, with more weeds than grass and not a single flower or shrub in the front yard. He parked along the side of the street and walked slowly to the front door. He did not know exactly what he would say. Too much of his work was charged with emotion, his clients driven not by greed or ambition but by instinct. The hope he offered was too often mislaid. Where do babies come from? From under a cabbage leaf; the gift of a stork. From the man in the three-piece suit, the walking shadow.

It was seven thirty in the morning but he knew she would be awake. She answered only seconds after he knocked. She didn't recognize him.

"Elaine Pinder?"

"Yes."

"It's about your son. I think I've found a way to get him back."

On the Thursday before Easter, six buildings along Twelfth Street were imploded and a fleet of trucks moved in to haul away the debris. According to the *Pioneer Press*, all of the buildings had long since been uninhabited, but the writer had never bothered to ask around the neighborhood to see if that was the case.

That night, just to see if Rags had told the truth, I went down to the Robert Street bridge and there I found a few dozen men and women huddled around the pilons. They had built a small fire in a rusty drum and were roasting potatoes, each of them trying to decide where to go next.

One of them, a tall Indian named Third Crow, said he wasn't going to stick around. "The reservation ain't much but at least nobody blows up the buildings."

An old woman I'd often seen in Mickey's Diner said there were lots of places on the other side of the river but she didn't think she'd have the strength to cross the bridge every day. One man said he had friends in Des Moines but he didn't feel much like going that way. "Too many cops."

All agreed that they had lost their paradise. The exodus was under way.

That night I was half asleep when I thought I heard someone singing. At first I thought it was my radio, then I realized that the sound was coming from the hallway.

" 'You been gone such a long time, Lady/Whatcha got to show for all the things you done?' "

I might have recognized the voice, despite the country western tinges, but I was barely awake and a truck was just that moment rumbling down Wabasha.

" 'Empty days and a stolen halo . . .' "

It was the country sound that threw me off. I was used to hearing him ranting and raving. I opened the door. He was dressed in a blue silk cowboy shirt embroidered with scarlet thread, hat in hand, wearing rain in his hair and an electric keyboard slung over his shoulder. He looked just like an album cover.

" 'A stolen halo,' " he sang.

There was no mistaking Dusken.

He had brought along a new bag of Colombian and I rolled my first joint since Vermillion. It was sweet and rich. I couldn't help but think of Vermillion.

"That's why I came," Dusken told me. "You can't go back there."

I was holding a deep lungful and it took me a long moment to exhale it. "Why not? It's been almost a year now. I must be old news."

Dusken was shaking his head. "That's what I figured. I got sick of hiding out last fall, so I went down to Florida for a winter tour with a cowboy band. That's why I'm dressed like this if you were wondering. It's not so bad. Less wear and tear than rock, if you know what I mean.''

"One step away from a cocktail lounge piano,'' I said, thinking of John Pinder.

"You got anything to drink around here?''

Rising from my chair, I opened the window and pulled in a six of beer I'd left on the ledge to cool. The spring had come too suddenly; the beer was warm as bath water.

"No matter,'' Dusken said, popping a top. "I had a hell of a time finding you. Harper still writes to Lisbeth and we had to get her address to get yours. I found the building in no time but nobody around here has their name on the door. Your wacked-out neighbor told me this was your room.''

"Her name's Alice.''

"Right. A real natty dresser, too.''

I imagined the rock star coming across Alice in the hallway, her hair pointing to the four winds, her lumpy body swathed in satin. The pot was having its effect. Everything—Alice, the death of the Rainbow, Dusken in cowboy duds—seemed suddenly kind of funny. Then I remembered what Dusken had said.

"Why can't I go back to Vermillion?''

"Myths, rumors, gossip. You're more than you think you are.'' He explained that he'd seen it building before he'd gone to Florida. "After you took off, word got around about your escape, jumping out that window and all. That really turned everybody on. People were driving past the house like it was a goddamn monument, taking pictures, measuring the length of your fall . . .''

"How far was it?''

"How the hell should I know? I don't believe in heroes. Anyway, all of a sudden you were hot stuff to all the hippies in Vermillion. Everyone was talking about how they'd bought from you and what a big deal you were when you lived there. Willie was really burned. At least *he* knew you were only a small-time pot dealer. Anyway, the bigger your name got to be, the more important Bolt became. Instead of looking like some kind of jerk-off, he was the man who almost captured *the* Jesse Dark. The city board funded him for a deputy cop, gave him a new squad car, the works. When I got back from Florida, he wasn't even interested in me anymore. He's got a new obsession, you.

I saw him on Main Street and all he said was it's a good thing I got a haircut.''

"You sound disappointed."

But he was not. "Life is easier for me now. The band broke up and I'm no one's priest anymore. People leave me alone and Veronica's almost home again. I'm just another singer with a sore throat."

Finishing the joint, I rolled another. "Hard to believe," I said.

"It's the kids, not Bolt. People who never knew you still talk about you. Stories get made up and passed around until they're gospel truth."

"What kind of stories?"

"The usual. You once had a farm of your own in Colombia and you had three boats that would bring the stuff across to Texas. You went away every summer to Bermuda and lived in a sixteen-room house. You kept a hundred grand buried under a dead tree by the Vermillion River. Bolt had three cops with him when he came to bust you. You fell a hundred feet instead of thirty or whatever it was. You were so stoned that you flew instead of fell. You know, elaborations."

I shrugged. "So Vermillion's out. I didn't really plan on going back anyway."

"You're going to stay here?" Dusken looked around the room as though it were unsafe.

I told him I was thinking about going to New York.

"A good move," Dusken said. "Harper? Still?"

"Harper," I replied. "Somehow."

We finished the beer, all six lukewarm cans, taking time out every half hour or so to wander to the end of the hall to relieve ourselves. Sometime before dawn, we heard the thieves climb the stairs to Alice's room, the whispered exchange of money for clothes. Dusken was impressed.

"You always find such cool places to live. How long have you been here?"

"Since winter," I said. "I hid out in Sioux City for a while before ending up here. But they're tearing this place down in about three weeks. That's when I'm going to New York."

"What do you do for money?"

"I sell pornography and sex gadgets."

Again he was impressed. "No shit? That place downstairs?"

"Right. And I better get some sleep. I start again in another few hours."

Though I offered half the bed, Dusken was the type of man who is uneasy sleeping with another man, so he stretched out on the floor. I threw him a pillow and closed my eyes. When I opened them again, it was noon and Rags was pounding on my door like a maniac.

"Get up, you shit! It's rush hour and I got every jack-off in the Twin Cities downstairs."

Climbing from the bed, I shook myself awake and pulled on my clothes. My first customer was the timid man who always wanted me to buy his books for him. It was his first visit in several weeks. With a shy bow, he handed me his shopping list, then stole out the side door. I rang up half a dozen sales in the next minutes, everything from bondage books to Fether-Lite condoms. Then Charles, looking like a seedy lawyer in his usual green suit, came in the door. Waiting for Rags to go into the stockroom, he moved toward the counter, pretending to examine vibrators through the glass case. "Do you have a key to the boy's apartment?" he asked without looking at me.

"I have every key in the building."

"Fine. I'll leave an address in this magazine." He returned a bondage book to the counter. "Try to be there by eleven o'clock next Friday night. If you're late, we'll wait till midnight, but not later."

"We?"

"His mother and I."

"His mother?"

Rags called from the back room, asking where I'd stocked last week's magazine returns.

"Third shelf from the left, above the dildos!" Lowering my voice, I turned to Charles. "You're really going to help me do this?"

"I'm not involved. Just help the boy find his way to her."

"Jesse! I can't find a goddamn thing in here!"

"Coming, Rags!"

"Can you do it?" Charles asked.

I was only worried about one thing. "His mother, what's she like?"

"An unhappy woman who misses her son."

"I'd rather meet her first."

"Mothers are my job. Getting that baby across the river is yours."

I had a week. The address he'd left like a pressed flower between the pages of the bondage magazine was across the river, on the south bank. My first problem was transport. Or could I carry a five-year-old two miles in the dark? Remembering how outlaws are supposed to cover their tracks, I searched for traces of my own. Digging through the papers in my room, I threw out everything that had my name on it, including two dozen letters from Harper. While Rags was at lunch, I went through his desk and gathered delivery receipts, notes, stock lists that might or might not refer to Dark, Jesse, tenant and porno vendor. Rags had always paid me in cash so I didn't have to worry about canceled checks or bank accounts. I wrote a brief letter to Harper, asking her not to write to me anymore, neglecting to tell her that I didn't want to be traced back to New York. I tried to remember if I'd ever spoken of Harper to anyone in the Rainbow. I might have mentioned her in passing, or simply said that I had a friend in New York, but who would remember? Alice? And I have never, since the fire, spoken of my family to anyone but Harper. I realized that for a long time I'd been living my life invisibly, my tracks erasing themselves in my wake. All but the enormous footprint, in the shape of a broken window, back in Vermillion.

Harper answered my boozy, rainy-night letter with news that she had found a place for us to live. "It's on the Upper West Side, maybe a little too upper. Do you speak Puerto Rican? We can move in on June 1. I've already found all the pots and pans and domestica, but I can't find a bed. Maybe I'll wait for you to get here and we can choose it together. One with a schizophrenic mattress: soft on my side and hard on yours. I still don't believe you're finally coming. Write another letter and convince me."

Though I thought that he would stay a day or two before blowing town, Dusken stuck around. "Slumming suits me." He shrugged. "You of all people should know that by now."

"Why me of all people?"

"Let's say I'm doing penance."

Although I'd made a point of taking him to see Marian Embrace All Things, I found that her charm held nothing for him. Not the granary, nor her language, nor her mystical habits. He told me she reminded him of an old girl friend in South Dakota whom he'd drifted to after Laura's suicide. "She was always all fucked up between her Tarot and her palmistry and her astrology and her Zen Buddhism. The whole goddamn salad. Your Marian Touch All Things—"

"*Embrace* All Things."

"Yeah, anyway. She drinks too much and I can't get interested."

But he was really taken with Sliver. The old derelict, like Marian Embrace All things, spoke a different English from the rest of the world. His words were sometimes as scrambled as his thought patterns. While I was busy ringing up sales for obscene literature, Dusken had risen from the floor on his first St. Paul morning and wandered down the hall to take a leak when he'd come upon Sliver pushing his broom up and down the hall. "I passed by him on the way to the can and he was sweeping away like there was no tomorrow. Then when I came out, he was just standing there with his broom in his hands, staring into space. At least at first that's what I thought. I said howdy as I went past him and he grabbed my arm and pointed to the trash he'd swept into a big ball. There were cigarette butts, candy wrappers, lint, all kinds of shit, but what he was looking at, it turned out, was a big cigar butt in the middle of it all. 'Somewhere,' he says, 'someone had a cigar.' " Dusken laughed. "Well, I wasn't about to argue with him, so I just said, 'Yeah, and somewhere someone was smoking it.' Then he got all excited, as if I'd understood him, and he said, 'Hey, oranges were on special today and everyone was eating them.' " Dusken shook his head. "I don't know where he gets his news. He's just plugged into someplace else."

I recounted the story of the headless St. Theresa.

"Sounds like some kind of modern opera," Dusken said. He looked at his hands. "Maybe I'll have to compose it one of these days."

They hung around together in the afternoon while I worked

in the shop and it wasn't until later that I learned what they were up to. One night in Shanty's, Dusken gave me a clue.

"You know, Jesse, after a winter of singing broken-heart or shit-kicking cowboy songs, it's a thrill to be around this guy. Every time he opens his mouth, I get another idea. The trick is getting him to talk. He's kind of used to shutting up and some-times he needs a little stimulation."

I should have been more aware of what kind of stimulation Dusken meant, but at the time my mind was on a child snatch, a mercy mission, an outlaw act. Kidnap. I was wondering first of all how to pull it off and second of all how I would feel to be wanted in two cities. How long, I wondered, would I be chasing my father and my father chasing me? They believe the fathers, John Pinder had said. I awaken in the night even now, years gone by, legs aching from running in my sleep. In my night-mare, I am chasing a daughter who flees me. I sprint, I gasp, I am faster than the wind. My daughter outruns me as I outrun my father. She fades like a slow fuse all the way to dawn.

9

Sliver's newspapers, his currency for hard times, had been piling up ever since the weather had improved. When the snow melts, all manner of things lost during the winter are found, usually by the Slivers of the world. His April haul had been numerous coins, Coke bottles, occasional jewelry, pens, rusty pocket-knives, a harmonica, countless shoes—though he always won-dered how there was always only one shoe, never the twin—and a soggy wallet with the unmentionable sum of twenty-six dollars folded inside. Sliver had been puzzled for a while because the bills didn't look right to him. Rags had helped him out. "They're Canadian, lame brain. You gotta change them at the bank."

Sliver hated banks more than ever when he emerged with twenty-three dollars American plus change.

"I gave you twenty-six dollars," he told the clerk. "Twenty-six."

No one explains exchange rates to Sliver. On his way out of the bank, he loaded up on loan brochures just to get his money's worth.

Despite his windfall, he went on collecting newspapers. It was easier in the spring. The papers were dry and simpler to carry. They lined his back hallway home from wall to wall and his sleeping mattress grew as thick as three weeks of *Pioneer Press* editions, not counting Sunday supplements. With the money the springtime had brought to him, he hadn't needed to turn in the newspapers. Having all of it at home was like money in the bank. Better even, when one considered that in a bank your twenty-six dollars came back twenty-three.

The night Dusken showed up, asking if he could spend the night, there was more than enough newspaper to make a second bed. Taking stacks from against the wall, he laid out a rectangle five inches thick and crowned it with a six-inch pillow. The top layer was composed entirely of the Sunday funnies. "Colored ink don't rub off so easy," Sliver explained. Though sometimes in summer, sleeping bare-chested, he had awakened tattooed with Little Orphan Annie.

"It's just for tonight," Dusken told him. "Jesse's got something on and said he'd feel better if I wasn't around."

"You're not friends anymore?"

Dusken smiled. "Sure we are. Of course." But he admitted that times had changed. "He used to tell me everything. Now he's full of secrets."

As they had done every evening for the past ten, they smoked Dusken's pot. At first Sliver had been terrified, certain that in no time he'd fall into his old habits. "I can smoke," he'd told Dusken, "but don't give me nothing to drink but water. I'm on the wagon."

"Since how long?"

"Twelve years."

Dusken whistled. "That's a long wagon."

"And a lotta water."

When they smoked, Sliver relaxed. He told stories about his

past, St. Paul, the tenants of the Rainbow. Dusken liked to listen because Sliver had such an odd point of view. He saw the world through broken lenses and reconstructed it all with inarguable observations.

"The walls hold up the ceiling, don't they? I'm glad of that."

"It can't be day and night at the same time."

"That car, the blue one parked over there. It's not mine."

When they had finished the first joint, Dusken rolled another. Already a blue-gray cloud hung in the air around them. "Looks like a smoggy LA afternoon in here," Dusken said.

"What's smoggy mean?"

Dusken stared at him for a moment. "Dirty. Like bad air."

Sliver nodded. "Like the air in the men's room at the bus station. That's *real* smoggy."

"You got it, Sliver."

Toward the end of the second joint, Dusken began to cough. "Harsh," he said. "It's getting too hot to smoke. You got anything to drink?"

Sliver offered a Coke bottle he'd filled with tap water.

"Anything but water."

"There's a place down the street. I can get you something there."

"Like alcohol," Dusken said.

"Sure." Sliver finished the joint and rose to leave.

"Good man." Dusken saluted him. "I'll pay you back."

But the place down the street was a drugstore where the neighborhood went during hard-up times to buy wood alcohol and, following Dusken's instructions, that's what Sliver brought home.

"I can't drink this," Dusken told him. "I'd never sing again."

"You said to get you alcohol."

"A figure of speech." Taking the cap off the top, he took a sniff. "Straight firewater. I'm just not up to it." And he set it to the floor, leaving the cap off.

"More pot," Sliver said.

"Coming right up." Dusken searched his pockets for rolling papers but he'd used them all up. "Do you mind if we smoke from a pipe?"

Sliver said it was all the same to him. "Smoke is smoke."

"I left it up in Jesse's room. Hold the phone."
When he left, Sliver tried to read the funnies on his mattress.

I had just finished stuffing all of my money into my shoes
when Dusken started banging on the door. It was ten thirty and
to stick to my timetable, I had to pick up Martin within the next
ten minutes. I had no car and I had known it would be stupid to
hire a taxi, insane to take a bus. So I planned to carry him across
downtown St. Paul to the river, get him across a bridge, then
make it through the remaining residential streets to find his
mother. Thinking it over, I was afraid of only two things: whether
or not I would have the strength to carry him all that way and
how I could manage to get him through nine blocks crawling
with derelicts without being noticed. Crossing the bridge
wouldn't be so bad. It was too rickety and had been closed to
all traffic except pedestrian. I was dressed in jeans, a T-shirt, a
cowboy shirt courtesy of Dusken, and a heavy sweater, all I
planned to take with me to New York besides my money-lined
feet. Once Martin was safe with Charles and the mother, I
planned to get back downtown to the bus station. The last bus
was out at 12:17. I didn't care where it was going, just so I would
be out of St. Paul. I could get to New York from anywhere.

"Jesse? You in there? I forgot to take my key."
The door was already unlocked and I was slipping on my
shoes when he realized it and opened up.

"What's up?" I asked as an errant ten fell to the floor.

"I forgot my pipe." His eyes followed the fallen bill.

I gestured toward the dresser. "Over there."

He stuffed it into his back pocket and headed toward the door.
He stopped before going out. "What's wrong, Jess?"

"I told you. I've got some business."

"That's why you're stuffing your shoes with cash?"

I nodded. "But you didn't see anything, right?"

"Listen, friend, if you need any help, just say . . ."

"Say goodbye."

"What?"

"Go. Fly. Don't come back to the Rainbow."

We regarded each other from a short distance, close enough
to shake hands, too far to embrace.

"You don't live a simple life," Dusken said.

"I'd like to."

"Sliver says it can't be both day and night at the same time."

"Sliver's wrong."

Reaching into his bag, Dusken took a pinch of grain and pressed it into the bowl, then tamped it lightly with his crippled index finger. His lighter sparked but the flame was weak and continually went out when he pressed it to the bowl. "Lighters," he told Sliver, "should never have sentimental value. That's why I keep this one, out of sentiment, and it never works so I spend most of my time looking for matches. You got any?"

"Nope. Just newspapers."

Dusken brightened. "There's an idea." The floor was littered with scraps of paper but by chance he picked the headless St. Theresa from its place next to Sliver's bed. In the midst of the smoke and the headiness of the high, neither of them noticed what it was. "All we need is a torch." With the feeble flame from his lighter, he lit a corner of the holy card and held the stronger flame to his pipe.

Sliver, sitting cross-legged on his bed, watched impatiently. Suddenly the blood drained from his face. "THE LITTLE FLOWER!"

He swatted the card from Dusken's hand and it flew across the way to a pile of stacked newspaper, lighting a *Pioneer Press* and a Sunday supplement at once. Reaching for the holy card, Sliver tamped out the flame with his palms and burst into tears.

"She's burned! She's burned all to hell!"

"Jesus God, Sliver! We're on fire!" Dusken leaped from his mattress and began to clap at the flames with his bare hands. Sliver took a long time to come back to life. Taking his eyes from the headless—and now charred—St. Theresa, he realized that the fire was spreading. Dusken began to pull stacks of newspaper away from the flames which had already spread through several days' worth of Minneapolis *Star*s and some random magazines. "Sliver, goddamnit, give me a hand!" The heartbroken janitor held his ground. He was paralyzed with grief. Then he saw the bottle on the floor. There were two bottles: a Coke bottle filled with tap water and a plastic bottle of wood alcohol. To Sliver there was only one bottle. He reached for the wood alcohol and threw it on the flames.

* * *

I stood in the hallway in front of my own door, grateful that
for once Alice wasn't standing sentry. There were very few tenants left in the Rainbow. Most had taken their government checks
and gone elsewhere. All that remained were Rags, Alice, Candy
and Carl, the Johnsons of the fourth floor, old Henderson the
retired accountant on the second floor, John and Martin Pinder,
and Sliver. Getting Martin out of the building would be easy. I
had only to take him in my arms.

As I climbed the front stairway I heard a noise from the
ground floor. I stopped. The front door of the building opened
and closed and through the dusty window on the landing I could
see Dusken and Sliver crossing the street. Dusken was clutching
his hands to his chest in pain and Sliver passed him by. From
the other side of Wabasha, they kept on going and disappeared
down Eighth Street. What now? Already it was ten thirty and I
didn't have time to worry about them.

When I unlocked the blue and white door on the fourth floor,
it was as though Martin was expecting me. He was dressed in
jeans and a sweatshirt and his shoes and socks were on the floor
nearby. His eyes brightened at the sight of me. ''Goodbye,'' he
said.

I glanced around the apartment for signs of John Pinder,
knowing full well he would be at the Soft Shoe until at least
2 A.M. An unfinished sandwich was on the table as well as a
glass of water. I asked Martin if he'd had anything to eat. He
only said goodbye.

Helping him put on his shoes, I tied the laces tight, then took
him in my arms. I had already decided it would be foolish to try
to take any of his things along. It would be enough just to carry
Martin. I would leave it to his mother to buy him whatever he
needed. As I reached the doorknob I was thinking to myself that
it was an odd kidnap. The only ransom I wanted was peace of
mind and the little boy who clung to my neck was, if anything,
the prisoner of my memory. I was taking him away as I had
taken Rose and myself away to an abandoned farmhouse. Only
the piano player, home from his hell, would notice he was gone.

When I opened the door I was stunned by a blast of heat and
was driven backward into the room. Martin nearly fell from my
arms. The hallway was filled with smoke and I could barely see

the door on the other side. Squeezing Martin to my chest, I pushed forward, looking left to the back stairway. An orange and yellow glow filled the back stairwell, so I went right, toward the front of the building. Stumbling downward, I reached the first-floor landing before coming upon the flames. Martin was screaming into my ear and I could hear sirens from the street below. Somewhere down the hall a door collapsed, blowing flames and cinder in both directions. Martin struggled in my arms and I saw a curl of flame on top of his head where his hair had caught fire and I patted it out with my free hand. Setting him to the floor, I made him hang onto my leg, then I swiftly took off my sweater and covered his face with it. Then I lifted him again into my arms, holding his head to my neck. There was only one way out, through the flame that circled the stairway and the front door. I leaped down the remaining stairs and found that the doorway was free. Two firemen who had already entered the ground floor each lifted one of us and carried us out into the street. Taking a breathful of air, I began to cough and vomit at once. I felt a hand on my arm, someone asking me if I was all right. I nodded and retched again. Lifting my head, I shouted for Martin.

"He's all right. He's over here." It was Rags. He was standing over a stretcher which held Martin. He was being cared for by a medic.

"His hair caught on fire," I told him.

"It's okay," the man said. "He's unhurt." I recognized him. He was the same man who had bandaged Sliver's ribs after he'd been robbed. The one who was tired of tending to old drunks.

Rags handed me a pint bottle of bourbon. "Drink it. It'll keep you from puking."

I took a long pull from the bottle and my head cleared. "Is everybody out?"

We looked around. There were three fire trucks and half a dozen police cars. Candy, in only her underwear, huddled next to Carl, who stood gazing at the fire as though it were a magnificent hallucination. Old Henderson leaned against a cop car, cursing it, the ground, the cops, and the hotel. The Johnsons stood frozen at his side.

"Where's Sliver?" Rags shouted.

"He's out," I said. "I saw him."

That left only Alice.

There was slight danger of the fire spreading. All the buildings around the Rainbow had already been demolished and there was very little wind. The firemen were only trying to contain the flames. Beaten back by the heat, they regrouped, forming a line of pumps that shot liquid upward through the windows leaping with flame. I ran over to them to tell them there was still someone inside but at that moment she appeared in the smoky doorway like a queen come upward from the past. Dressed in a blue evening gown, her throat laced with rhinestones, a fox stole draped over her forearms, Alice stepped clumsily over the ashen threshold, catching her hem on a fallen plank. ''Shit!'' Yanking at the material, she freed herself and clacked on heels too high for her heavy body over to where we awaited her.

The rummies of the kingdom, attracted by the light, had come out to watch the burning of the Rainbow. They gathered in small clusters across the street and passed bottles of Thunderbird wine back and forth to dry their throats. Marian Embrace All Things was among them. Seated on the curb, she watched the fire as though it were the coming of the Great Spirit, her small eyes grown large in its orange light. The flames climbed to the fourth floor and the firemen trained their hoses upward. I heard the captain shouting to shift a unit to the back of the hotel. ''This place is earmarked for demolition anyway. Keep the fire under control but let it burn to the ground if you can.''

Alice's borrowed clothes, the robes and sashes and stoles and satin slippers, all ash. Dusken's keyboard, Candy's lace brassiere, half-slip, lipsticks and lotions. Carl's cocaine and his velvet shirts, alligator shoes, switchblades, and .38, lifetimes and volumes of tits & ass magazines, sizzling vibrators and smoking dildos, women in bondage in flames in the porno shop, the peek-a-booth in its last scorching act shivering and crumbling inward, St. Theresa finally cremated with the rubbers and inflatable dolls, a cash register melting numbers across the glass counter, and the orchids, my orchids, growing gold, then brown, peeling once and forever from that ancient wall, nothing blooms forever, let it burn to the ground why not we were going to tear it down anyway.

I was reaching for Marian's bottle of wine when I saw John Pinder burst through the crowd past a knot of cops, shouting for

Martin. One of the cops tried to restrain him but the pianist slipped past him and headed for the door. By the way he ran, I guessed that he was drunk. He lost a shoe but kept on running. The firemen in front of him had their eyes on the fire. I tore after him, catching his arm at the doorway. I have always assumed he thought I was trying to harm him. I have no way of knowing. A look of hate worse than the flames flashed in his eyes and his fist rocketed across my face. I saw stars in his wake as he leaped through a halo of flame just as it was collapsing like the picture of a television just turned off, a circling of blackness closing in with a jetlike rush. Two helmeted men jumped in after him. Rags lifted me to my feet and I was dragged backward to safety. We watched the doorway, frozen in silence. More sirens were sounding in the distance, other fires, other crimes. Seconds later, the firemen emerged with the body of John Pinder. His limbs were smoking and alive with embers. Where once his face had been there was only a coalish black hole.

If I pray, I cannot pray to any god in particular. When I pray I may only be talking to myself. The gods and saints are always so hard for me to distinguish, between the virgins and the martyrs, the popes and the paupers, sacred and blessed and holy. Fathers on earth or fathers in heaven. I was always confused between Ingersoll and Bill, and now John Pinder, too, had died drunk in a fire; dead, I was thinking, of desperation. Or as a prayer would say it, of faithlessness. They laid him on the sidewalk and covered him with a blanket. Rags, of all people, crossed himself.

Passing the pint bottle back and forth, Rags and I sat on the curb and watched the Rainbow burn. It took longer than I'd thought it would, considering its age, but Rags said he wasn't surprised. ''Hell, half that structure is cheap cement, the other half is good hard wood. You notice the floors aren't caving in?''

He was right. The Rainbow burned but it didn't fall apart. Flames poured from two dozen windows but the walls held up. The Rainbow burned like an enormous oven, heating the city, but it wouldn't burn to the ground. On the other side of the police cordon, a group of Jesus people were singing and cheering the flames upward. A sign, it was a sign. ''It should have burned down years ago. All that filth!''

"I think I'm gonna like Omaha," Rags was saying.

It was past dawn when the last of the fire was out. I had seen an ambulance come for Martin and he'd been loaded into the back of it, even though the medic had told me it was only so he could be examined at the hospital. A woman I had never seen climbed into the ambulance with him. She was about thirty and her eyes never left him. In the ambulance, she touched his face, then she took his hand in hers and held it tightly.

The daylight was disappointing, breaking up the party the way it did. The rummies scattered to their shadows and the fire trucks drove away. Rags and the others rode in a police car to a shelter house that had been arranged for them, but I went to Marian Embrace All Thing's granary and slept most of the day. When I awoke she had made a sandwich for me and I washed it down with a bottle of Thunderbird wine.

"Sliver was here and your friend who sings. His hands was burned. Not bad but not pretty to look at. Sliver put wood alcohol on the fire to put it out."

"Where did they go?"

"Sliver took a train to Chicago. My money bought his ticket. Your friend goes to Luverne where is a doctor he knows."

"You should have wakened me."

Marian Embrace All Things said she never wakes sleeping people. "They might be dreaming. Dreaming is prayer only better."

I noticed with a start that my shoes weren't on my feet. "Where are they?" I asked.

"Under my mattress. *With* the money. Though some of it I took to buy us food. Are we a tribe now?"

The police asked me if I'd seen Sliver but I had nothing to tell them. I was commended for having saved Martin and was tempted to tell them the rest of the story but didn't see much sense in it. "Is there anything else? I was planning on leaving town."

I was told I should stop by the city finance office first.

"What for?"

"Your envelope."

In my envelope was a check for three hundred dollars from the city's disaster relief fund. "It's for relocation and reimbursement," the clerk told me. "Just sign here." This was the gold at the end of the Rainbow. I gave half of it to Marian, even though we weren't yet a tribe.

John Pinder was buried in the municipal cemetery, but I didn't go to the funeral service. A column in the *Pioneer Press* recounted the tragic story of the pianist who died saving his son from the fire. Greater love hath no man. The last I saw of Alice was the night of the fire. She was being escorted to a patrol car by a cop who was curious about where she'd bought her clothes. Candy, I heard, was already working a new neighborhood.

"Well?" Marian Embrace All Things asked me a few nights after the fire. "Do you say or do you go?"

I told her I didn't see why I should stay.

"Going is a bad habitude," she answered. "Where you go you take yourself with you."

One last time she read my palm, her old brown eyes scanning the various wrinkles. After a long while she said she saw a baby boy.

"Martin Pinder," I told her.

"No," she answered. "Not Martin. This baby is an infant, born today."

I put it down as so much gibberish. She had already finished a bottle of wine and was well on her way through a second.

The next afternoon I was having lunch in Mickey's Diner when someone told me that Rags had been looking for me. By the time I arrived at the shelter home he had already gone.

"He had a suitcase with him. I think he was headed for the bus station."

I hurried that way, uncertain whether it was to say goodbye to the old man or to get the fifty dollars he still owed me. But by the time I arrived the bus for Omaha had already pulled out. To get my fifty dollars I would have to go to Omaha and visit Rags at the Egyptian Deluxe Triple X. I kissed my last porno money, and Rags, goodbye.

I had already stepped out of the bus station into the sunlight when I suddenly asked myself what for. I had no job and only Marian Embrace All Things for company. Harper was waiting for me on the Upper West Side of Manhattan, practicing her Puerto Rican and plumping up the pillows. I pictured her already humming a soft samba while opening a bottle of wine.

Jesse, it's been so long.

Going back into the station, I headed for the men's room. Sitting on a toilet, I took off my shoes and counted two hundred eighty-three dollars. This time there was no reason to wait. I paid for my ticket and sat as still as a saint, waiting for that three o'clock bus, certain that if I moved something else might happen to me, more pinball, and I would never get to New York. The time was heavy on my hands. It was measured by the beating of my heart, the sound of small stones hitting the water. One. After. Another.

At 3:05, a bus left St. Paul bound for Chicago, Pittsburgh, Harrisburg, and New York. The east, where the sun rises. At least, I believe that the bus was on time. One can never know such things. I was on a different bus, my feet propped up on the empty seat next to my own, lazily smoking a cigarette and hoping I would be able to sleep to relieve the boredom. I was headed west, toward Yankton.

West, where the sun goes down.

West, where the outlaws live.

I had to say goodbye to Rose.

The Nameless Legend

1

Crippled Horse said he didn't want a lawyer from the reservation.

"I've never met an Indian who knew how to save another Indian's hide. Something about our skin, two positives make a negative or something. One of your average white men'll do just fine." When we were alone in the cell block, he added, "Anyhow, I don't plan on being here for the trial. You hear me, Jesse?"

My own lawyer, Simon Larsen Butt, came to the jail just after noon with the notarized affidavit, signed by me in duplicate, in which I promised to leave a child and his adopting parents alone forever.

"I suppose you've heard the news from Vermillion," I said.

Simon Larsen Butt adjusted his tie. "Formal charges haven't yet been filed. That will be for the arresting officer, Lieutenant J. E. Bolt of Vermillion Special Forces. But on the face of it, it appears you've been quite the drug pusher."

"Innocent until proven guilty," I reminded him.

"I know the phrase, Mr. Dark. But why is it I already feel your case is hopeless?"

"Because you know how to defend criminals but not outlaws."

Bolt arrived just before lunchtime. He looked at me as though we'd known each other a long time but I had the impression he was trying to fix me in his memory. My Yankton arrest report had escaped his notice, he said, but his deputy had recognized the name. "It's a name people have come to know," he added. "Ever since you jumped through that window. Sometime soon I'd like to hear more about that."

Then he read the charges against me, the same I had heard the day before: possession of a controlled substance; intent to sell said controlled substance; suspicion of sale of controlled substance to minors; assaulting an officer of the law; resistance of a lawful arrest; interstate flight; damage to private property.

"To tell you the truth, I didn't think you'd ever come back to South Dakota. I'd have had a hell of a time getting you extradited from any other state. Most states don't think men like you are dangerous. I have a daughter in the ground who tells me otherwise. What brought you back here?"

I knew better than to say Home. Outlaws usually shrug in the presence of the law, but I couldn't do that either. "Tourism," I answered.

"Tourism?"

"I wanted one more look at the hands of Dusken Lowe."

He went white, he went red. He went away.

I spent half an hour talking it over with S. L. Butt and he just kept shaking his head as though the situation were long past hopeless and was quickly sliding toward the ridiculous.

"Listen," I told him. "I sold pot and nothing more. I never sold to minors, that wasn't my nature. There were a dozen of us in the same business; some sold pills and some sold anything the drugstore had to offer."

"You're being modest. What about the assault charge?"

"It's fictitious. I bumped him on my way out the window, that's all."

"And interstate flight?"

"Ten steps in either of two directions from Vermillion and the least jackrabbit finds himself in Nebraska or Iowa or Minnesota."

Butt just kept shaking his head. "You're whistling in the dark, Jesse. Unless something new comes up, I see you headed for ten years in Sioux Falls."

Ten years.

"That's parole after three, maybe four years. It depends on who's governor. Give that some thought."

I shared lunch with Crippled Horse, who was up for murder one. Lunch was a tray with leveled compartments, like a TV dinner, and if you held it on your trembling knees the peas rolled into the compartment for the mashed potatoes and the juice of the roast beef spilled onto your pants.

"Quit shaking, white man. You're making *me* nervous."

"Let's hear your plan, Crippled Horse."

"For getting out of here?"

"Yes."

I listened all through lunch. It was the worst plan I could have imagined, straight from a Zane Grey western paperback, full of shootemup and improbable moments of idiocy on the part of our night watchman.

"How in hell is he going to believe we *both* have appendicitis at the same time?"

"Food poisoning, then. Hey, don't be so negative. We'll iron out the fine points. What's important is once we get out."

That part of the scheme was for real. Crippled Horse had friends he could count on. I had only S. L. Butt, Attorney at Law.

"If we can get to Pearl Street and the railroad tracks they'll be waiting for us. Then all we gotta do is wait for the train to Meckling. I've taken it before and it always slows down around Pearl Street."

"When I'm out," I told him, "I'm headed for the river. Just think of a better way to get me out the front door."

"You're the white man. You figure it out. Just so I'm along for the ride."

2

A legend is an inscription, as on a coin, an engraving to be deciphered. Or a legend is a myth, a saga, a romantic fable that may or may not have something to do with history. Or a legend is the key to a map or chart, a method of interpretation by which we may understand place and distance, locate ourselves *here* and know that for every inch from *here* there are so many miles to *there*.

Wherever I had gone, I had remembered my mother's hands and Rose's words. My mother was my past and Rose was my memory. I had remembered my father as well, but every memory of him was as incomplete as Sliver's headless Theresa. I remembered more of what had never been than of what had been, more of what I had missed than of what I had seen. Harper asked me from time to time if I had forgiven him, but forgiveness was seldom a part of our interminable card game. I could recite to myself his numerous crimes but I could never fathom what led him to commit them. He had no dreams, no visions, beyond the blue-black screen of delirium tremens, nothing he could impart to me as his own to be handed down. Nothing except his name.

Getting off the bus, I began on Pearl Street where the ruin of the Dark house lay glowering beneath the regrown branches of scalded elms. It was a pointless visit because there was nothing to recognize. The house had burned to its foundation and in three years even the ash had been blown away or had dissipated beneath heavy snows. All the same, the earth seemed to hold a shadow of blackness, as though the ash had mingled with the soil and made it dark and unnaturally loamy. Was I only imagining that the weeds were more lush, more profuse, than I had remembered them? The foundation still shimmered in the sunlight, its brandy-bottle mortar as indestructible as that of a temple. Somewhere would be my father's name chiseled into stone and the date of completion, sometime after my birth. Bits of glass were embedded in the weedy grass and even a few scattered dandelions were growing amid the foundation. I was pleased that no one had bought the land, that no house had been built over the ruins, that the foundation was covered in weeds and dandelions, and that it shimmered, as always, even in partial sunlight. These were my only thoughts. Otherwise, I was as indifferent as some tourist, hopelessly trying to imagine who had lived there and what on earth had happened to them.

Bloodlines are bloodstains. No man alive ever walks the earth without reciting to himself, at least once, his genealogy. And it is not a tree, it is not a network of roots, of aunts, uncles, cousins, sisters, the biblical begetting, it is not a red-checked tablecloth and a basket of bread, it is not the great and threatening arm of God, or His breath blowing breath into you at birth. It is getting from the floor to your knees and then to your bare feet, feeling the carpet below and the great weight of your child head upon your shoulders, seeing that carpet below and in some great distance there are a pair of muscular arms, there, beyond that shadow, those heavy arms with the enormous hands. It is taking a step and falling into those arms. Or it is the feeling when those arms fail to catch you on your long and terrifying fall to the floor.

I lived the legend of falling to the floor. I survived to live other legends. He owes me nothing and we're even.

Though I could have taken a local bus, I chose to walk out to the mental hospital. It was beyond the north edge of town, on the same route I'd taken to the farmhouse I'd shared with Rose, three or four miles from the ruin on Pearl Street. The money in my shoes grew damp with my perspiration and I developed a blister from all the rubbing back and forth. From the time I was little, I had kept my money in my shoes. It was a habit that I picked up from my father, who now and then would pull his empty pockets inside out as if to say, What, you're asking *me* for a handout?

That was a good trick, Dad.

What trick?

Showing him your pockets like that.

What do you mean?

You got fifteen bucks in your right shoe and ten in your left.

How'd you know that?

I been watching you.

Good kid, just keep quiet about it. Here's two bucks. Go get your mother a pack of cigarettes and keep the change for yourself.

A legend is a vocabulary, a lexicon, a translation. I followed First Street to Highway 81 and remembered which way was north. A spring breeze pushed me that way and in half an hour I had crossed the city limits and was only a mile from the hospital. I limped from the blister but I left my money where it was.

Hey, Jesse, you got a few bucks?

Sorry, Dad. Look at these pockets.

Jesus, I'm really feeling it and there's nothing in the house but ginger ale. You sure you don't have a dollar or two?

In the bathroom I had drained a shoe of its bills, one two and three. Then I had put back the third.

Is two enough?

Where'd that come from?

From a distance, the hospital looked more weather-worn than I remembered it to be, more tragic in sunlight than in the shadows of winter. It had been nearly a year since I'd last visited Rose and I was grateful for the green of the trees, the sunlight, the plethora of squirrels in the great yard. The massive security door of the Angel Ward opened with a horrid clang, its iron bolt like a piston: bang, open; bang, shut.

"I'm here to see Rose Dark."

"You should have called ahead."

The head nurse led me down the familiar blue hallway to the room. Rose was in her chair before the window, unchanged. Her eyes looked outward and when she blinked I tried to remember if she'd done that before. Maybe it was a sign of progress.

"Does she always blink?" I asked the nurse.

"Every day," she told me. "It doesn't mean a thing."

I examined her as though to measure her well-being. Her hair was clean, her nails trimmed, her teeth as sound as ever. She seemed to have gained a bit of weight and I thought she looked pale but I presumed she had spent the winter shut indoors. I said her name aloud but I might as well have whispered it.

"She's feeling much, much better," the nurse told me.

"Better than what?" I asked. "Has she been sick?"

"Sick? What do you mean?" She clapped a hand to her mouth. "You don't know?"

"Know what?"

"My God, I thought you knew!"

"Knew what? What are you talking about?"

The nurse fled the room and I followed her down the blue hall to the nurse's station. She dialed a number and asked for the ward supervisor.

"Mr. Dark is here," she said. "Yes, Mr. *Dark*, Rose Dark's brother. Yes, he's here in front of me. I'll tell him." Setting down the phone, she said, "The ward supervisor will be here in a minute. You can wait in the lobby."

The ward supervisor was a tall Swede in her fifties with an officious air that put me instantly on edge. She was at least a head taller than me and I had the feeling that she liked looking *down* into my eyes. We touched hands but I can't say that we shook them.

"I'm surprised you've come," she said.

"I've been out of town," I said. "I couldn't come before."

"You should have written to us. You had a responsibility. I've been trying to contact you for nearly five months. The only address I had was in Vermillion. . . ."

"What about Rose?"

"Your sister has had a difficult few months."

"What kind of difficult?"

The woman hesitated between two ways of putting it and finally said nothing. Drawing a breath, she said, "I think it's best if you come with me."

We crossed the long blue hallway and turned left, still on the Angel Ward. Having never ventured beyond Rose's room, I was surprised at how many inmates there were, the depressives, the regressives, and the catatonics. In full afternoon there were many of them about, wandering the halls without maps, or maps that were indecipherable. At the end of the hall, the ward supervisor took out her keychain and unlocked a door. Inside was a freshly painted room with only a white dresser, a small table covered with a blanket, and a bassinet. A nurse leaned over and adjusted a blanket.

"We have no idea how it happened," the ward supervisor was saying. "Your sister was six months pregnant before anyone even guessed it. We keep all kinds of records but in the case of catatonics, I admit, we're often lax when it comes to menstrual cycles. So many of them cease to menstruate altogether and there's never been any need, until now, to keep such records up to date." She waved the nurse out of the room. "We considered a drug-induced abortion but it was inadvisable considering your sister's condition. Such an abortion requires the guidance of the patient's response and we couldn't risk a stillbirth for the same reasons."

I was slow, painfully slow, in understanding her.

"It's a boy. We haven't named him, you understand. After all, such a thing has never happened here. We can't imagine how on earth she got pregnant. It's as though she willed it, except that catatonics have no willpower. Through the last months of pregnancy she never responded. Because we had no way of detecting labor pains, the baby was born by cesarean section."

I approached the crib and peeked over the edge.

"We tried to contact you once we knew she was pregnant. We needed a signature in the case of abortion, then later for the certificate of birth. It's still unsigned, you see. We didn't know what to do."

"A boy?"

"I understand your surprise, Mr. Dark, and I assure you—"

"A boy. My sweet god in heaven."

He lay in his crib, his tiny fists circling in the air around his head. He was three days old and had not yet dared to open his eyes to the world.

"I suppose," the woman added, "that it's divine providence that you've finally shown up. The adopting parents would be relieved to have a release with an authorizing signature."

Her words came to me as from a distance. My eyes were on the child and I was barely listening to her.

"You need my signature? What for?"

"For the release. He's been adopted."

The words, their weight, landed like stones all around me.

"That is, unless you intend to make some claim on the child."

"Of course I do. He's my family."

The woman seemed to stand a full inch taller. "Are you married, Mr. Dark?"

"No, but I—"

"Then I suggest that you'd best leave this child to the adopting parents. They are fully prepared to—"

"No. They can't have him. He's ours." Mine and Rose's.

"I'm afraid the right is on their side. You have come too late with too little. As it is, the adoption papers have already been drawn up and the release may go through with or without your signature. All you can do is make things unnecessarily unpleasant."

I was breathless. "He stays with me," I said through my teeth.

"I'm afraid that you've come too late, Mr. Dark. And I should add that I am aware of your legal situation. In trying to contact you in Vermillion, I came across certain information regarding your activities there. Don't misunderstand me. I don't care one bit about your criminal record. But if you persist in pressing a claim to this child, I will tell what I know. Is that clear?"

Her gaze was as level as a Dakota prairie. We measured each other, two shadows over a squirming, nameless child. For some reason, Marian Embrace All Things came to mind.

"What is your tribe?" I asked.

"Go home, Mr. Dark. I'm sorry. Just please go home."

I had no luggage and the night manager at the Hotel Charles insisted that I pay in advance. "How many nights will you be staying with us?"

"I don't know. Two or three. Or maybe only tonight." When I added that I was in town on business, he rolled his eyes.

"Why don't you just pay a day at a time. That might be the simplest."

Unashamed, I removed my right shoe and counted out the price of a room.

"There's no restaurant in the hotel but if you go down the street and turn right—"

"I know. Star's Diner."

"I meant to say the Town and Country Restaurant."

I went for a stroll through the small downtown, stopping in at various bars, the Junction, the Hideaway, Swede's, where I recognized faces to which I could apply no names. The man who, the woman from, when I was. All of my memories of them were unfulfilled. I drank a beer in each of the bars I came across, thinking I would get pasty-faced and cause a scene or two, but I couldn't manage to get into an ugly enough mood. My thoughts were spiraling around Rose and the miracle of her baby boy. Leaning over the bar at Swede's, a shot of Wild Turkey and a glass of beer before me, I tried to imagine her during the pregnancy, as her belly had swelled and the baby had kicked through the waters of amnion. I wondered if she had felt him there, if she had secretly smiled to herself, and I imagined her alone at night in her bed, her eyes upon the ceiling, blinking to the shadows. Throwing down the shot and chasing it with beer, I felt myself blurring over. The bartender watched me without interest, as though he had already seen a hundred versions of me and I was nothing new to him. I ordered another shot and drained it, my father's son, then I was wandering through the Yankton streets again, kicking through the few fallen leaves, in no mood to go back to the hotel just yet. Unable to race through the burning house to collect keepsakes, valuables, photos, anything that might identify me to myself, I fixed the baby in my mind as recompense. His birth had altered everything, even the past, and I had forgotten about Harper and the easy road into her arms. Walking the streets of Yankton, I drunkenly decided on a different road, one that led backward, not to Harper's arms but to a hundred possible dead ends, each of them marked Jesse was here.

I rented a car with a passenger seat that folded down flat, making enough space for my needs, then I began my shopping tour in a department store where, on instinct, I bought a small basket, pillows, blankets, disposable diapers, towels, and an assortment of baby clothes. Cruising a supermarket, I stocked up on canned milk, baby formula, cotton, and a few baby bottles. There were no bottle warmers in the supermarket so I drove back to the department store and bought a batterized one as well as a dozen batteries. I bought two books on baby care and began reading them even while driving back to the hotel. From my room, I called the bus station in Omaha, more than a hundred miles away, then copied down the schedule of buses headed toward New York. Then first was at seven in the morning, so I adjusted my schedule so that I would arrive at the station no sooner than six and no later than six thirty. Taking the back roads rather than the highway, I figured I'd need three to three and a half hours to get from Yankton to Omaha.

In the Hotel Charles I studied the baby care books, concentrating on what I would have to do for a newborn, and I copied out a list of things I would need to remember: feeding every three hours, change after feeding, keep him warm but not smothered, don't cover him with a loose blanket, keep his nose and mouth clean, keep him away from drafts. At the bottom of the list I added, Give him a name.

Just after dark I went out to the car and prepared it. I packed all but three cans of milk, one bottle, the bottle warmer, and three diapers into the backseat, which also held a folding crib. I installed the basket in the front seat, lining it with blankets which I pinned back against the rails. Wedging the basket between the door and the gear shift, I jiggled it to make sure it was secure. Then I covered everything with another blanket so that it couldn't be seen from the street.

I wished I could sleep but I knew it was out of the question. Sitting in my room, I reread the baby care books just to kill time. My idea was to ditch the car in Omaha and take the bus from there. A bus ride is anonymous; no such thing as a passenger list. But I wouldn't go directly to New York. I would have to stay somewhere else for a day or two in case anyone thought of Harper and remembered how she knew me. The hours, on this last night, were surprisingly short. I had finished reading the second book by the time it was two in the morning. Time to go.

As I was going out the door of the hotel, the night manager called after me to take a front door key. "I sometimes fall asleep and would rather not be awakened."

I threw the key in the gutter and started the car.

"You never keep anything," Rose once told me. "No keepsakes, no souvenirs."

"Why should I?"

"Because memories are so damn weak, you need something to *see* to remind you."

"Remind me of what?"

"Anything, anyone. Imagine what it would be like to be eighty and not remember anything about when you were twenty."

"The past," Dusken told me, "is like a big sack of rocks that gets heavier by the weight of one rock per day. Why drag all that around with you?"

"Imagine," Rose said, "if we ever were to forget each other."

The driver drives from memory. The runner runs from instinct. Approaching the hospital, I remembered someone once telling me that without the uniforms you couldn't tell the employees from the inmates. "They'll hire anybody as a night watchman, all kinds of drifters and drunks. I have to count the silverware twice each shift and I know it's not the crazies collecting spoons."

I leaped toward the flaming doorway and Ingersoll took my place.

I leaped from a window and a gun sounded at my back.

Parking the car along the ditch beyond the front gate, I followed that ditch to where the wall bordered a thin grove of elms. Climbing the nearest elm, I slithered across a low branch until I was hanging over the hospital yard. Overfed squirrels scattered as I dropped to the ground.

The yard was vaguely illumined by two yellow street lamps, but no guards were in the area. There was little to guard in the night and anyway they were guarding the people within and I was coming from the other direction.

The Angel Ward was fifty yards to my left and I had only to move along the shadows of the wall until its great gray brick loomed above me. Not counting the ancient fire escapes, there was only one door, so I took off the sweater I was wearing and replaced it with a white busboy's shirt I'd swiped at a truck stop, praying that it wouldn't be far different from what the kitchen crew wore. When I was certain I hadn't been seen, I stepped into the light and climbed the steps to the Angel Ward. The twine I was carrying made a noticeable lump in my right pocket, so I walked with a slight limp, bending to my right ever so slightly to keep it hidden. There was no one at the front door and I climbed the stairs to the second floor. Reaching into my pocket, I removed the twine. I had never bound anyone in my life and I was wondering just then how I would do it, what kinds of knots I should use, and whether or not I should use a gag as well.

The nurse's station was abandoned.

Slipping behind the desk, I took three keys from their slots. With the first, I tripped the electric door and the bolts snapped open. I hesitated for a moment behind the desk, listening for the sound of footsteps, guards, crazies, or the nurse come back from the ladies' room. In the silence there was silence, night full of night, and outlaw that I was I hadn't the instinct to fear a job that was somehow too easy.

I went first to Rose's room and found her sleeping like a saint in a halo of lamplight. Standing over her bed, I kept my hands to myself, though I was tempted to touch her, to give her animation, to spark her into recognition of me, the last of the tribe. "I've come for him, Rose."

I have no souvenirs. I never need them to remember Rose Dark. I was certain I would never see her again so I looked upon her as though for all time. I was still holding the twine in my hands and I left it on the floor near her bed. There was no one for me to bind but myself.

The hallway was an empty blue channel through which I tiptoed to the end. Turning right, I saw the way was clear and I hurried to Nameless's room and pushed the key into the lock. His room was dark and I was afraid to turn on the light, so I treaded darkness with my hands before me until I felt the bassinet brush my fingertips. The darkness was made terrifying by the life beneath me and I reached down with both hands, identifying him with my fingers, his face, his arms, his kicking legs. Folding the blanket around him, I lifted him to my chest and hugged him there as he struggled against me. We were surrounded by darkness. Even the window seemed to give no light, not a single star or moonbeam. I thought he would cry when I lifted him but he was silent, though wide awake. His hands and legs pushed against me as though to measure the man who bore him and I only hugged him closer, afraid of dropping him or of losing him in the darkness of that room. I moved slowly toward the doorway, listening for footsteps, but I heard nothing. The door seemed to open by itself and I sensed the nearness of our

deliverance, already imagining the open road, the rising sun at
the bus station, the life we would lead, my nephew and Harper
and I, when I realized that the door was not opening by itself
but was being pushed open by the woman I had seen the day
before, the tall Swede with the ice-blue eyes. She switched on a
light and it blinded me, coursing through my veins like an electric shock. She stood in the doorway like an avenging angel,
flanked by three night watchmen with billy clubs.

"What did I tell you?" she said to them. "Didn't I say he'd
be here?"

They seemed to bow to her, though perhaps they were only
nodding. Then one of them stepped forward to take the baby
from my aching arms.

That's when Jesse made a run for it.

That's how Jesse met Crippled Horse.

3

We could hear them arguing all the way down the corridor, from
the middle jail cell where we shared our lunch.

"Roast beef, my ass," Crippled Horse complained. "Tastes
more like dog to me and I know what I'm talking about."

"Quiet down, I can't hear."

Bolt had come just before noon with a deputy I didn't recognize and for the past hour he had been arguing with Sgt.
Juneau, my Yankton protector. I had only heard bits of what
they were saying but it was obvious they were arguing over me.
Bolt wanted custody and insisted that the arrest was his. The
kidnap charges had been dropped once my affidavit had been
notarized and I was no longer wanted in Yankton County but in
Clay County, where a warrant had long since been filed. Juneau
argued that I was a prisoner of the state and as such I could not

be transferred without a court order from Pierre, the state capital.

"You gonna drink your orange juice or not?"

"Drink it and shut up!"

Bolt had said something about his friends in Pierre but I hadn't caught it all.

"You know, white man, I don't much like the way you're talking to me."

It was too late. I heard the front door open and close and could only assume that Bolt had driven away.

"Take it easy, Crippled Horse. It's nothing personal."

Simon Larsen Butt came with a briefcase full of news and advice. Sgt. Juneau had filled him in on Bolt's intentions and the case seemed even more hopeless to him than before.

"Word has gotten around Vermillion of your *capture*. That's what they're calling the arrest, as if you were some kind of hero. Lieutenant Bolt wants you transferred because of the notoriety. He's getting all the mileage out of you that he can. Newsmen from Sioux Falls, Rapid City, and Pierre have already been asking Juneau questions and there was a small demonstration at the university in Vermillion." He took a flyer from his briefcase.

At the top of the flyer, in bold black letters, was printed: FREE JESSE DARK. But the text had nothing at all to do with me; instead was written a series of criticisms against the war, ROTC, segregated dormitories, curriculum requirements, and the cost of seats at football games. The flyer had been circulated by the law students and was signed by a committee of five. I read the names and they were all strangers to me. All but one: D. Lowe.

"I can't be certain," Butt was saying, "but I'd guess Bolt wants to transfer you for his own personal gain. He's gotten a lot of mileage out of you in your absence and your arrest is the big payoff. As your lawyer, I'm advising that we fight the transfer. The less notoriety, the better. These kinds of cases come up all the time and we find that the anonymity of the accused is usually in his favor. We don't want you to be made out to be anyone special. Judges hate to be pressured by public opinion."

I admitted that I wasn't in any hurry to go to Vermillion.

"Fine, then we're agreed. I can't guarantee that you'll still be here tomorrow and in the case of a transfer you'd also have a new lawyer appointed by the court. All the same, let's go through it again.''

"Where do we start?''

"From the time you left the party at the farm. You were with Dusken Lowe, in his MG. He was driving and—"

"I was driving.''

"Right, my mistake. You drove along the Missouri River on the South Dakota side and you stopped twice. What for?''

"Once to piss and once to throw up.''

"I'll have to reword that in your deposition.''

"Sure. Go ahead.''

"It was about midnight. You were among the first to leave. Who saw you leave the farmhouse?''

"Rachel. And I think Two Trees was there.''

"Rachel who? What's her last name?''

"I don't know.''

"And Two Trees?''

"His first name is Harry.''

"Could either of their testimony do you any good?''

I shook my head. "Rachel used to do a lot of drugs. She's kind of . . . windy. And Harry Two Trees barely knew me. He stuttered and played pool. You know.''

"No, I don't.'' Butt made a few notes, asking me to continue.

They want you to remember when you're trying to forget. They want you to put your feet on the ground when you feel yourself walking the ceiling. You are going down the stairs and they say, "One or two steps at a time?'' We retraced the night in exhausting detail and Butt noted everything down, including, word for word, the bedtime prayer I was reciting when Bolt had burst in the door. He told me he would draft a deposition for me to sign if I didn't feel like writing one myself. I agreed and he left in time for me to have dinner with Crippled Horse.

"Just my luck to get locked up with a famous white man,'' he said. He was pretty steamed.

"What are you talking about?''

"I been listening to the radio. A bunch of students in Vermillion are organizing a rally for tomorrow. They gonna come to Yankton to demonstrate in front of the jail. You know what that means?''

I shook my head.

"Cops, man. And guards from here to high stinkin heaven. No way I'm gonna bust outta here with *you* sittin in the kitchen."

That night I lay in my bunk and listened to the bottles breaking against the Icehouse wall. I had been too young, when I'd lived in Yankton, to buy beer on my own, but my friends and I had often gone down to the riverside just below the Icehouse to coax older kids to buy it for us. The Icehouse was on Capitol Street, not far from where the boats had landed by the hundreds during the Black Hills gold rush a century before. There was still a landing there, though it had been abandoned by all but fishermen with small outboards or river rafts. When I was fifteen and sixteen, about the time when Rose started going downhill, I had hung out there during the spring and summer, drinking beer that was more expensive because of the big boys' commissions that we'd had to pay. There was a long pier that had long since collapsed in the middle of the river, leaving a wooden ramp that arched upward toward the sky rather than downward into the water. We would sit on that ramp and drink beer from endless cans and watch the river flow slowly past us. Invariably, one or all of us wanted to go look for girls or get into a fight, so as the night grew late our numbers would diminish from eight or nine down to one or two, and sometimes I would find myself happily lonesome in the blue moonlight at the end of the pier.

But a pier is not a bridge. It takes you to the middle but never to the other side.

One steaming August night, when I was alone on the broken ramp, I drunkenly decided I was going to swim to the other shore, to Nebraska and back. Stashing my clothes beneath a loose plank, I stood at the foot of the pier and got a running start. My momentum carried me up the ramp, then I leaped into the open night sky, feeling miles above the water, then I came down fast and hard, splashing into the water feet first. But the Missouri is neither the Mississippi nor the Nile. Its depth varies from five inches to five feet and I landed hard on my right ankle, spraining it in the mud below. The current carried me downriver and I struggled to the shore, then followed the treeline back to the pier. I was still a little numb from the beer I had drunk but my ankle hurt like hell. I walked home with one shoe on and one shoe off.

The sound of breaking bottles reminded me of that night and I fell asleep thinking of my nights at the water's edge, drinking and dreaming with friends I had barely seen since, while we'd sat on the edge of that broken ramp which lifted us upward by the ass and forced us in our drunkenness and surprise to face the sky and its immeasurable swoon of stars.

Though the demonstration had been announced to start at 3 P.M., the organizers had feared that Bolt would cross them up and transfer me beforehand, so they arrived before noon and set up camp in front of the jailhouse steps. Crippled Horse saw them coming from his corner window.

"They're here, white man. Your whole goddamn fan club."

Bolt and his deputy arrived half an hour later and immediately the old lieutenant started in on Sgt. Juneau. "Where's my cover? You said you'd have this place cordoned off!"

"We weren't expecting those kids till three o'clock. What the hell am I supposed to do?"

It was a peaceful demonstration, more like a party that was slow in getting under way. It was as though no one seemed to know exactly what they were expected to do. By twelve forty-five there were nearly two hundred people crowded around the steps and sidewalk, taking in the sun. Joints were being passed like petitions. Someone was playing a guitar. A girl in a head-band circled under my window and passed a dandelion through the bars.

"Wow, thanks."

I tried to toss the dandelion down to Crippled Horse but it landed in the middle of the corridor. Sgt. Juneau, coming to get me, crushed it under his shoe. As I stepped out of my cell he held his palms outward as if to say none of this—the arrest, the demonstration, Bolt—was his idea. My eyes forgave him his uniform.

I stood in the patrolmen's office while Bolt signed for my release and transfer. He presented a written order from the state attorney general and asked for a photocopy of my arrest report.

"Do you think it's wise," Juneau asked him, "to take him out just now? Why don't you wait until two thirty? I'll have a dozen men to keep that crowd in order."

Bolt just shook his head. "Don't let a bunch of dumb-ass

students get your goat," he advised. "I've been dealing with kids like them for twenty years. They won't try anything."

His deputy led me into the sunlight and from the doorway I could see them. They were standing, sitting, or reclining along the steps and sidewalk, and some of them were in the street, huddled around Bolt's car. Someone shouted, "It's him!" and their eyes turned to me from all directions. I imagined the popping of flashbulbs and the oblivion of confetti. A chant started softly, like a badly memorized prayer, and then in unison, "Free Jesse Jesse free Jesse free free Jesse Jesse free Jesse, Jesse Free, Free Jesse, Free Jesse, FREE JESSE, FREE JESSE . . ." and though I wanted to laugh I could only smile to the deputy who held my arm with a hand that would have been more comfortable wrapped around a football. His lips pursed, he led me down the steps. "Free Jesse," I said into his ear and he told me to shut the fuck up.

Bolt had been delayed at the doorway by Sgt. Juneau but now he came thundering down the steps after us, pushing the students aside and cursing them. The crowd gathered around us, edging against the car. It was Bolt's personal car. He had meant to keep the hour of transfer a secret and had left his squad car in Vermillion, forsaking his radio and protective backseat screen for anonymity.

The Free Jesse crowd moved in. I recognized none of them. As Marian Embrace All Things would have said, they were not from any tribe I knew of. Then one face emerged from the sea of others: Dusken. He was wearing a buckskin shirt and sported a cowboy hat. He waved toward me with a bandaged hand.

The deputy opened the front door and just then Bolt started screaming at him. The crowd was still chanting and I couldn't hear it all. I could only pick out the word *cuffs* as Bolt beat his wrists together. Cuffs. They hadn't handcuffed me. I held my palms in front of me in disbelief. There were no handcuffs in the car, so Bolt sent the deputy back into the jail to get a pair from Juneau. All the while the crowd was getting noisier. Nothing like a foul-up to inspire a bored group of students. Bolt held me with one hammy hand and with the other he pushed people away from us. Then a bottle flew from the crowd and crashed against the windshield of the car, leaving a web of cracked glass. Enraged, Bolt wheeled round to see where the bottle had come from and in doing so he let go of me for the barest moment. Then I felt another pair of hands pulling me backward into the car. I found myself in the driver's seat and Dusken, on the other side of the front door, shoved it closed. "Happy trails," he said with a Dusken smile.

The key was in the ignition. I turned it and the engine flared. Had the car been a stallion it might have reared and neighed.

A group of demonstrators stood before the car and Dusken pushed them toward the sidewalk to let me pass. I inched forward and just as they were clear of the car I gunned the engine. Bolt managed to open the back door and as I pulled away he leaped inside. I sped up First Street away from the jail and felt Bolt's hand on my shoulder. Yanking the wheel to the right then to the left, I made the car swing wildly around and Bolt fell backward. Pushing his weight forward, he grabbed for me again but I continued to steer the car in zigzag fashion to keep him off balance. It was like a dance. Each time he touched me I swayed crazily to one side and he would fall backward like a doll. I pushed the pedal to the floor and then rapped on the brake. He fell to the floor of the backseat and held his head in his hands.

At the end of First Street I turned right onto Capitol. In the rearview mirror I could see Bolt struggling to get his gun out of his holster so I jerked the wheel to the right once more and he flew against the door, banging his head on the window. We sped past Yankton Auto Parts and Elizabeth Bad Hand's apartment where I'd lost my silver bullet, then we passed the Icehouse on the right. A dozen bikers scattered as I approached and again I felt Bolt's hand pulling my arms away from the wheel. I might have turned right to skirt the river's edge or left toward the farmers' granary, but with Bolt holding my arms it was enough for me to hold the wheel straight. We crashed through a thin fence at the end of Capitol Street and rumbled down a short stretch of sand to the pier, the broken-down pier with the ramp at the end. Bolt's hands left my arms and circled my neck. He squeezed and I saw blue, the blue of the sky above the brown river. Gripping the wheel, I pushed my foot to the floor and we sped along the ancient pier to the ramp and we flew, my captor and I, his hands a steel halo round my throat, into the Dakota sky toward the endlessly wide, surprisingly shallow brown river.

4

Marian Embrace All Things was wrong. She had read my palm and had seen an endless highway. Reading the shards of my shattered wine bottle, she had seen only broken glass. She had not seen Harper at the end of that highway, in a city by the sea, nor had she seen my sons in their cradles, nor my safety, nor my peace, nor my happiness. She had not seen me anywhere but in the modern ghetto of north downtown St. Paul and could not have recognized in me what I hadn't recognized in myself. In the night, in a darkened bedroom, facing the aquarium glow of the ceiling as taxis pass in the darkness, I hold Harper in my arms and I remember Dusken and Rose and I remember Nameless, all of them legends, memories in the light of which I can read my own palms, my own broken glass.

That car flew as though winged into the open air and when it landed in the Missouri mud I banged my head against the ceiling, then the river water began filling the car. It rose to my chest and stopped there. We were no longer sinking in the mud and when I looked into the backseat I saw Bolt passed out, his head resting above the water, tipped against the window. I rolled down my window and struggled out of the car. The water reached to my waist and the spring current was strong. Except for a swollen skull, I was unhurt. A group of bikers from the Icehouse had hurried to the shore and some of them had come out on the pier. One of them called to me to ask if I was hurt. I didn't answer. Turning to the other shore, I faced Nebraska, which for the moment was only a line of trees, a rolling hillside with fields in the distance.

A legend is an inscription, a saga, a myth. Waist deep in water, my shoes sinking hopelessly into the mud, the current bearing me elsewhere, I looked upon that other shore with both eyes searching. Home is my legend. Stepping out of my shoes, I finally headed that way.

About the Author

MICHAEL DOANE was born in Sioux Falls, South Dakota, and now lives in Paris. He is the author of THE SURPRISE OF BURNING and SIX MILES TO ROADSIDE BUSINESS.